Her attacker was back.

Flashlight in hand, she ran to the attic steps, taking the offensive. She wouldn't be a victim again.

"Don't move," she shouted.

But it wasn't her attacker coming up the steps. Chief Winters came toward her. She should take a step back but she couldn't move. Something about him had her heart fluttering. He lifted her chin with his finger.

She wanted to tell him what a romantic cliché his action was, but then she'd be admitting her attraction. And she couldn't admit that. She'd never risk her heart again.

"What are you doing up here again?" he asked her.

She couldn't tell anyone what she'd done, especially not him. "Chief..."

"Jewel, don't you think it's about time you call me Colin?"

His voice was so gentle, she could almost forget he was here on official business. But that would be a mistake.

"Colin, I—"

But she never got a chance to speak. A scream tore through the attic.

MOUNTAIN SECRETS

ELIZABETH GODDARD

&

USA TODAY Bestselling Author

SHARON DUNN

Previously published as *Deception*
and *Hidden Away*

LOVE INSPIRED
INSPIRATIONAL ROMANCE

If you purchased this book without a cover you should be aware that this book is stolen property. It was reported as "unsold and destroyed" to the publisher, and neither the author nor the publisher has received any payment for this "stripped book."

LOVE INSPIRED®
INSPIRATIONAL ROMANCE

Recycling programs for this product may not exist in your area.

ISBN-13: 978-1-335-91233-6

Mountain Secrets

Copyright © 2021 by Harlequin Books S.A.

Deception
First published in 2016. This edition published in 2021.
Copyright © 2016 by Elizabeth Goddard

Hidden Away
First published in 2018. This edition published in 2021.
Copyright © 2018 by Sharon Dunn

All rights reserved. No part of this book may be used or reproduced in any manner whatsoever without written permission except in the case of brief quotations embodied in critical articles and reviews.

This is a work of fiction. Names, characters, places and incidents are either the product of the author's imagination or are used fictitiously. Any resemblance to actual persons, living or dead, businesses, companies, events or locales is entirely coincidental.

This edition published by arrangement with Harlequin Books S.A.

For questions and comments about the quality of this book, please contact us at CustomerService@Harlequin.com.

Love Inspired
22 Adelaide St. West, 40th Floor
Toronto, Ontario M5H 4E3, Canada
www.Harlequin.com

Printed in U.S.A.

CONTENTS

Elizabeth Goddard is the award-winning author of more than thirty novels and novellas. A 2011 Carol Award winner, she was a double finalist in the 2016 Daphne du Maurier Award for Excellence in Mystery/Suspense, and a 2016 Carol Award finalist. Elizabeth graduated with a computer science degree and worked in high-level software sales before retiring to write full-time.

Books by Elizabeth Goddard

Love Inspired Suspense

Mount Shasta Secrets

Deadly Evidence
Covert Cover-Up

Coldwater Bay Intrigue

Thread of Revenge
Stormy Haven
Distress Signal
Running Target

Texas Ranger Holidays

Texas Christmas Defender

Wilderness, Inc.

Targeted for Murder
Undercover Protector
False Security
Wilderness Reunion

Visit the Author Profile page
at Harlequin.com for more titles.

DECEPTION

Elizabeth Goddard

As far as the east is from the west,
so far hath he removed our transgressions from us.
—*Psalms* 103:12

Dedicated to my Lord and Savior, Jesus Christ,
who paid my ransom.

Acknowledgments

My heartfelt thanks and gratitude go out to all
those who support my writing endeavors. First
I thank my family, of course—my husband and
boys, who put up with my frequent forays into
other worlds without them. We've been eating a lot
of pizza and fast food lately, I know, but hey, don't
you love it when Mom gets that book money? I also
want to thank my dear writing buddies, you know
who you are, and my new writing friends—
I couldn't do this without your encouragement and
support. And as always, thanks to my amazing
editor, Elizabeth Mazer, for her insights into making
my manuscripts the best they can be. Last and
never least, I appreciate the encouragement from
my agent, Steve Laube. Signing me as a client
(has it already been over five years?) was a
huge validation to me as a writer. Thanks, Steve!

ONE

Dead Man Falls
Mountain Cove, Alaska

Edging closer to the precipice that overlooked the plunging waterfall, Jewel Caraway risked a glance down. Vertigo hit. Dizziness mingled with worry.

Meral and Buck should have beaten Jewel to the falls where they had planned to meet up.

"Meral!" she yelled.

The roar of the water that cascaded hundreds of feet below drowned out her calls, sucking them down with the rushing water. A foaming whirlpool twisted where the frothing, tumbling force pounded the pool at its base. Misty spray drifted up and enveloped Jewel in a sheen of moisture. The sound of her voice could never compete with the rumbling growl of the cataract.

She tugged out her cell phone before she remembered she would get no cell signal here. The only signal she ever had was in Mountain Cove proper. She put the cell away, her gaze drawn back to the waterfall.

Powerful and dangerous.
Beautiful and terrifying.

Dead Man Falls was a force to be reckoned with. That was if one were to take the plunge and get sucked into the swirling torrent at the base.

Kayakers had attempted to navigate the drop and failed.

Part of a rainbow, transparent and fading into the mist, caught her attention. Mesmerized, Jewel stood at the edge of the rocky, moss-covered ledge that was flanked by spruce and hemlock, firs and cedars in the lush, temperate rainforest. She watched the churning at the bottom of an endless vortex that would trap anyone or anything unfortunate enough to fall. She wondered what secrets it held in its depths—then flinched at the memory of how she had buried a secret of her own and never thought about it again. That was until Meral, the sister she hadn't seen since Jewel had eloped twenty years ago, had arrived on her doorstep with her new husband.

And now they were both missing.

"Meral!" she called again. "Buck!"

Uncertainty roiled inside, tumultuous like the falls.

Those two had gotten lost somehow, which seemed impossible. They'd been hiking together when Jewel realized she'd forgotten her water and had needed to go back. They had gone on ahead of her on the well-defined trail, and the plan had been they would stop at the falls and wait until Jewel could catch up. Where could they have gone?

A twig snapped. Before she could turn, a blunt object smashed into her back. Pain erupted along with her scream as the force of the blow propelled her forward.

Airborne, Jewel plummeted through the clouds and

mist, feeling as if her stomach had been left behind on the cliff's edge.

Terror was catching up with her.

The spray of the waterfall engulfed her. At the last possible moment, she dragged in a breath and fell into the jaws of the beast she'd admired with a healthy fear only moments before. The wrath of the whirlpool plunged her deeper, twisting and tossing, bashing her against sunken boulders.

Dizziness and nausea held her captive within the vortex. The pounding water pushed her deeper, then turned her over again in the same way a crocodile rolled its meal to make it tender.

I'm not ready to die!

Lungs burning, Jewel shoved down the fear. The most important thing she'd learned from self-defense classes with local police chief Colin Winters was not to panic. The violent water was nothing more than an assailant bent on harming her. She could only escape by slipping out of its grip. On the fringe of consciousness, Jewel did a flutter kick, swimming with all her might, and forced her body down and deep below the backwash.

Then she felt it.

The smooth water.

She'd escaped!

Disoriented, unable to tell which way she should go, she allowed the current to sweep her downstream and away from the falls. Jewel opened her eyes and fought through her exhaustion to try to swim toward the surface.

I can do this.

But fear and doubt clawed at her, threatening to drag

her down and keep her under. Her lungs burned and screamed as she fought her way to the surface. And in that moment, the instance before she breached, she saw rocks and trees blurred at the top of the ledge from which she'd fallen…along with a figure. A *human* figure.

She'd thought, she'd hoped, that a branch had fallen from a tree and somehow shoved her in the back, sending her over to plummet into the river.

The way the figure stood there, the wide, deliberate stance, she knew…she *knew* that he or she had pushed Jewel. Intentionally shoved her into Dead Man Falls to what should have been her death. And she hadn't made it to safety yet. She could still die today in this river.

Why? Why had she been pushed?

The figure disappeared in the thick canopy even as the current dragged Jewel away.

Finally breaching the surface, she pulled in a breath and braced herself for a new battle to survive the river with its multiple tiered rapids and falls.

Jewel couldn't be sure how long the river had taken her captive. How long she'd allowed herself to be carried away, floating on her back in order to save her energy for that moment, that one moment, when she might have a chance to escape. Except her reserves were almost depleted.

That moment hadn't come.

How much longer could she keep her head above the rushing torrent?

Her limbs grew tired and numb, even with her effort to conserve energy. She searched the bank for calmer waters to swim toward. A branch to grab. Anything.

She needed out of the water before she hit the rapids and another set of falls.

God, help me!

Just ahead she spotted the trunk of a dead tree, branches sprawling and reaching. This was her chance and likely her last one before the rapids. Before she drowned.

Jewel reached, but the current, ripping and swirling as the rapids approached, twisted her away. She had no control over her own body. Her own life. She wouldn't be able to grab the trunk.

Jewel was going to die. Despair engulfed her.

Excruciating pain stabbed across her shoulder and back. Her body suddenly jerked and her forward momentum stopped. Something had caught her. Wrenched her from the river's grasp.

Stunned, recoiling in pain, Jewel twisted around. A branch from the fallen trunk had snagged and cut her deeply, but had saved her life even as it had wounded her. She held on with everything in her.

This was the chance she'd been hoping for. She wouldn't lose it. After coughing up more water, she dragged in air and allowed a measure of relief to set in. Now to pass the next test.

This was no time to rest. She had to get out of the river.

She gripped the slick trunk and pulled herself up, higher out of the water until only her legs were beneath the surface. Slowly, she inched toward the bank.

Her left hand slipped, and she let out a cry as she slid deeper into the water. But she reached again, grappling with another branch to keep from slipping completely back into the river's grasp. If only she weren't already so weak from her injuries and exhaustion.

Finally, she reached the rocky outcropping of boulders hugging the bank and pulled herself out of the river completely. Laying flat across a slick boulder, Jewel rested her gaze on the swift river and its endless push toward the deeper waters of the channel.

I made it out. Thank You, Lord.

Jewel rallied and pushed to her knees to climb over more boulders. Every ache, every bruise, every scratch and sprain screamed in agony as the numbing power of cold water that had served as an anesthetic now seeped away.

Free of the rocky edge, Jewel crawled until the river was no longer a threat and fell face forward into the mossy loam. She clung to the dirt, breathed in the earth. She'd made it this far, and she would be grateful for small things.

She wouldn't think about getting out of the wilderness. Maybe by now Meral and Buck would have reported her missing.

How long would they wait until they called for help? How long would it take that help to find her?

Terror snaked over and around her like a living, deadly vine and squeezed. It would crush the life out of her if she let it. She shoved her growing fear down and focused on surviving. She'd escaped the river and would draw confidence from that.

But it wasn't just nature she had to contend with. Another danger loomed out there somewhere. Someone had pushed her into the falls. They could still be out there.

Had they watched the river carry her away? Were

they tracking her now, on the verge of approaching to finish her off?

The pain in her back throbbed in rhythm with her innumerable other injuries. If the person who'd tried to kill her found her here now, nearly incapacitated after fighting and surviving Dead Man Falls and the river, Jewel wasn't sure her self-defense classes would do her a bit of good.

But she held on to the hope they believed she had drowned in the falls as per their intent.

Since Tracy—her friend and previous employee at Jewel's Bed and Breakfast—had dealt with a vicious stalker about two years ago, a visceral fear had taken over Jewel, a dread that followed her everywhere with the awareness of just how easily danger could get close. It had taken them all far too long to realize that the stalker, who had hidden his appearance from Tracy, had actually been staying as a guest at the B and B.

Jewel had taken the self-defense classes, hoping to instill confidence in her ability to protect herself and to push away fear. Yet now that fear twisted deeper, hooking her full and well.

If help didn't arrive soon, Jewel would have to spend the night here and rest before she could find her own way out. She crawled forward and into the brush to hide, hoping it would be enough camouflage if the person who'd tried to kill her came looking.

All Chief Colin Winters wanted to do was take the week off. The month. Or maybe even the whole year. What would it feel like not to answer a phone? Not to have an endless list of problems vying for his attention?

But when his cell rang and he spotted the fire chief's number, he answered.

"Winters." Something in David Warren's voice had Colin on edge.

"What is it?"

"It's Jewel Caraway."

Colin's heart seized up. He couldn't speak.

"She went into the river at Dead Falls Canyon."

As police chief, Colin was trained to push down the panic and act. But at this news he couldn't move, couldn't think. He pressed his hand against the wall for support. "Is she…"

"Someone called the state troopers, and we have an incident number. North Face Mountain Search and Rescue is on the scene, and I'm calling you. I knew you'd want to know immediately."

Colin heard the meaning behind David's words. David was aware that Colin thought Jewel was a special woman. They all did.

They hadn't found a body, but his relief was short-lived. Dead Man Falls deserved the name.

Colin had already exited his office and was making his way to the back door to get into his Jeep.

"We're meeting at the trailhead by the mouth of the river."

Sherry, the dispatcher, called after him. "Chief! Chief!" He ignored her.

"I'm on my way," he spoke into the phone.

When he plowed through the back door, a truck screeched to a stop in the parking lot.

"I figured you would be." David leaned out the open window.

Colin shoved his cell in his pocket and climbed in.

He'd let the new fire chief drive. Though he was anxious to get to the river and be part of the search, his hands trembled. He wouldn't be any good at the wheel. Nor did he want David to see how he was struggling with this news. It hit him much too personally when he had no right.

David swerved out of the parking lot and onto Main Street, going over the speed limit, but Colin wasn't about to stop him. This was an emergency.

"You doing okay?" David glanced his way intermittently.

Colin barely nodded. "What happened? Do you know?"

"According to Tracy, she went hiking with her sister and brother-in-law. I don't know what happened or how she fell in."

"She's a skilled hiker. Knows what she's doing." So how did this happen? He couldn't reconcile this with what he knew about her.

"I hope she's a better swimmer," David said.

Colin thought he would be sick. *God, please let her survive.*

But it seemed impossible.

Twenty aching minutes later, David parked his truck at the boat dock. Colin hopped onto the Warren family boat. Others from the North Face Mountain Search and Rescue team had already left for the scene. But David, who was on the team, too, had stayed behind, knowing Colin would want to be there.

"Thanks, David."

David started up the boat. "For what?"

"For waiting. For taking me there."

"Of course. You've saved my skin countless times.

You were the one to figure out who had put Tracy in danger."

All part of the job. "Still, I appreciate it."

"I knew you'd want to help find Jewel."

The wind whipped over his face as the boat sped away from Mountain Cove. Colin stared ahead, going through all the possible scenarios in his mind, except the worst-case scenario. He couldn't think about finding Jewel's body.

The boat ride took far too long, and he was glad others had gotten to the trailhead and started the search before he and David arrived. Kayaks and other boats rested along the shore, all empty, all except one. Cade Warren—David's brother—stood on the deck hovering over maps. Colin followed David over to the boat and climbed aboard to speak to Cade, who was in charge of the search at the ICC, or Incident Command Center.

"Anything?"

"Nothing yet."

"Tracy's here with Solomon," Cade said. "You knew that, right?"

David straightened. Grinned at his brother. "I wouldn't have it any other way. Jewel means the world to Tracy. Solomon'll find her."

Colin wasn't surprised to hear the news. David's wife, Tracy, was trained at search and rescue, as was her dog, Solomon. Plus, she used to work for Jewel at the B and B until the twins came along, and had a close relationship with her employer. It made sense that she'd rush out to help as soon as she learned what had happened.

"Where are they?" Colin asked.

Cade pointed at the map. "Sent them off here to search the riverbank. Later, we'll be looking…"

When Cade glanced up at Colin, he let his sentence trail off. He was glad Cade decided not to finish. He didn't want to think about dredging the river or this channel for a body. He was glad he wasn't in charge of the search.

Hopping off the boat and onto the small deck, he left David and Cade behind.

"Winters! Where are you going?"

"What do you think? I'm going to look for Jewel." He marched up the trail.

He didn't have time for pleasant conversation.

"Hold up." David left Cade behind to follow and jogged up to him.

Colin didn't wait for him, hiking up a few yards, then veering off into the forest to the left toward the river. That raging, deadly river.

David gripped his arm. "We'll find her, Winters. Though I have to say," he added with a frown, "I didn't realize you were in this deep."

"What are you talking about?"

Tracy rushed up to her husband. Breathless, she pointed. "I think Solomon's found something."

Colin and David followed Tracy through the woods, around trees and fallen trunks, over rocks and boulders to Solomon's bark and whine. Colin tensed at the dog's signals. He knew Solomon had finally gotten certified as a cadaver dog.

He braced himself, unsure what they would find—a living, breathing Jewel or her body.

TWO

Something wet slid across her nose, eyes and mouth. Jewel stirred and tried to turn over to defend herself, but a bone-piercing throb coursed through her wrist.

A dog's whimper and continued licking steadied her breathing. Calmed her fear. She recognized the animal.

"Solomon." Her voice didn't sound like her own.

Footsteps, twigs snapping and breaking, resounded through the undergrowth on the river's edge.

"Jewel," Tracy said. "Are you all right?"

Relief swelled inside. "Depends on your definition."

Tracy spoke to someone nearby and then radioed others that Jewel had been found.

"Shouldn't you be home with your babies? Your twins?" Jewel managed.

"Grandma Katy needs her time with them. Besides, you had to know I would come looking for you. Solomon and I."

"Jewel!" A familiar, masculine voice joined Tracy's.

Jewel heard the immeasurable relief in his tone. That ignited her heart. She was alive. She had survived.

"Chief Winters," she croaked. *Colin.* She had always called him by his official title to keep personal feelings out of it. To keep her distance. Otherwise, the man could undo her resolve to protect her heart.

Her bruises throbbed with any movement or effort on her part. She squeezed her eyes shut, unwilling to look at him.

"We're here now, Jewel. You're going to be okay. You just rest now."

As other SAR members arrived and focused in on Jewel, they crowded him out and away.

"No! No... Chief Winters." She reached for him.

He stepped forward, closer again.

"I'm here, Jewel. I never left." His electric blue eyes pierced hers, concern and relief spilling from them. "What is it? What do you need?"

"Someone pushed me into those falls."

Anger rose in his gaze and maybe a little disbelief. "Can you describe him?"

"No... I..."

Chief Winters grabbed her hand. "Whoever it was, we'll find him, Jewel. Don't you worry. You're in good hands now. I have to go and make sure nobody else gets hurt."

Then he slipped out of the way of her search and rescue friends. Jewel endured the poking and prodding and assessing and finally the hefting and assisting her back to civilization.

On the helicopter ride back to Mountain Cove, Jewel closed her eyes, wanting to forget what had happened, wanting to pretend it had simply been a bad dream. Wanting to wake up with a body free of pain and evidence of the nightmare. But she couldn't let go of the blurred image of the person she'd seen standing at the top of the falls.

There hadn't been room for Chief Winters on the helicopter, and maybe she was glad about that so she would have time to think about what she'd seen exactly before having to answer his questions. But he was probably searching for who could have done this. Making sure others were warned a crazy person was out there.

At the small Mountain Cove hospital clinic, Doc Harland attended to all her bruises and scrapes. He didn't like the look of the deep gash along her shoulder and back from the fallen tree trunk's branches, but she knew that though painful, that injury had saved her life.

That particular gash needed stitches. Her sprained wrist was already wrapped. Doc assured her it would heal within a few days.

"Hold still, dear." Doc Harland had anesthetized the gash so she couldn't feel the needle pricks as he stitched her up. "You aren't afraid of needles now, are you?"

"I can't stop shaking. My body has a mind of its own. I'm sorry."

"No need to apologize. You've had a scare. We'll give you something to calm you if you like."

"No, thank you." Jewel needed to stay alert. Figure this out. "Are Tracy, Meral and Buck still out there in the waiting room?"

"Far as I know. You want me to send someone to check?"

"No."

"I've treated a lot of folks in my life, but never anyone who has gone into those falls and survived. What happened out there?"

"If it's all the same to you, Doc, I'd like to forget about it." Jewel stared at the sterile wall. She might want to forget, but she knew she couldn't.

"I want to run a few tests. Draw some blood. But not today—you've already been through enough. I want to see you back in a week to look at those stitches and your wrist. We'll get the blood then."

Was Doc wondering if she had some sort of medical condition that had caused her to fall?

"There. All done." Doc Harland flipped down her gown.

"Jewel?" Meral peeked through the door. "I brought you some dry clothes."

"Come on in," Doc Harland said. "I'll leave you to change."

Doc Harland nodded and left to give her privacy.

Meral set the clothes—a pair of jeans, teal T-shirt, light jacket, shoes, socks and undergarments—next to Jewel. "I'm so sorry, Jewel. If we'd just stuck together this would never have happened." She wiped at the remnants of tears on her cheeks.

She started to hug Jewel, but then acted as though she'd thought better of it. Jewel must look terribly beat up and bruised. Admittedly, a hug would hurt right now.

Meral, short for Emerald, was in her thirties and ten years younger than Jewel. She'd been a teenager when Jewel had run away to marry Silas. Beautiful as she was, she looked fragile and pale at the moment.

"Are you okay?" Jewel found herself asking.

"I'm feeling nauseous. Buck insists on taking me back now. Are you almost ready?"

"Sure, I just need to change."

"You need help with that?"

"No, you go on now. I'll be out in a minute."

Meral nodded and left Jewel. Poor thing. She probably didn't know how to take what had happened. Jewel wasn't sure she did either. It was hard to comprehend.

Jewel took far too long to get into her clothes. Every movement, every twist and bend of her body hurt. She risked a glimpse in the mirror over the sink.

Big mistake.

She didn't even recognize herself.

Someone knocked softly on the door. Meral had timed it just right. They were both ready to get home. But how could Jewel let her guests at the B and B see her like this?

"Come in."

The door opened and in stepped Chief Winters, standing tall and intimidating in his official tan police uniform.

Her pulse jumped.

Whether from being startled at seeing someone other than Meral, or if it was her reaction to Chief Winters himself, she wasn't sure.

Seeing him here, clearly concerned about her, brought her more pleasure than it should.

She reminded herself he wasn't here for personal reasons but to question her officially. But she wasn't sure she was ready. Everything that had happened was starting to blur together.

What had she really seen? Had she simply imagined the figure on the ledge?

Chief Winters stepped completely in and closed the door behind him. His electric blue eyes always saw everything, and now they flashed with a powerful emotion. Before she could define it, the emotion was shuttered away.

What was the man thinking?

Jewel averted her gaze. She didn't see the chief of police often outside the self-defense class. And in the class she tried not to think about how tall and rugged he was, or the confident air he had about him. He was in his late forties, the same age as her husband, Silas, would have been if he hadn't died a decade ago. Silas and Chief Winters had been friends, not close, but friendly enough that they were on a first-name basis. And he'd always been warm and friendly to her, as well, and somewhat protective after Silas had died. All the more reason to keep her distance.

Jewel hung her head for a moment, instinctively, hating for him to see her like this, but then she quickly lifted her chin and faced him. She couldn't let him see how he affected her. She was surprised to see that today something new burned behind his gaze, and it wasn't warm or friendly. It was downright terrifying.

"What are you doing here?" she asked.

"Checking up on you. You had to know I'd come. How are you, Jewel?"

"Did you find them? The person who pushed me?"

He shook his head. "Not yet. I know you're tired and hurt, and this isn't the best time, but I'm going to need you to think about what happened and tell me everything. Start from the beginning. Who pushed you into the falls?"

"I don't know."

Jewel wanted to scream. She wanted to cry, but she wouldn't do that in front of Chief Winters. She missed Silas—wished she had someone here to hold her. She wanted to feel strong arms around her. Someone to tell her everything was going to be all right. That someone hadn't just tried to kill her, and she was only imagining things. And in a moment of weakness like this, Colin Winters was the only man who could fulfill those needs.

But she couldn't let him in that deep.

She'd lived in Alaska long enough that she was well aware of how to take care of herself. She'd run her B and B near the edge of the wilderness for more years than she wanted to admit. She wouldn't give in to that weakness.

I know how to survive.

I can do this.

Chief Winters stared at her, waiting patiently. She'd always liked that about him. But how did she answer his question? What could she tell him that would make any sense?

Jewel moved to sit in the chair against the wall. Colin didn't rush her, giving her a moment to think on the details of what had happened.

Some days Colin hated his job, and today was one of those days. He hated having to pry answers out of people—especially people he cared about personally.

"Accidents happen, Jewel. People fall where they shouldn't all the time, including in the shower, where some die every year." He hated himself for this, but he had to ask her. He had to be certain. "Are you sure someone pushed you?"

She stared at the floor. Was she thinking it through?

Seeing Jewel like this undid him. Unraveled him from the inside out.

Jewel Caraway was a beautiful woman. One of the most beautiful he'd ever seen, and that included on the inside, where it mattered most. She was beautiful like Katelyn—a woman he'd loved—had been. Had a quiet elegance and grace about her, and the most captivating hazel-green, gold-flecked eyes. Colin shouldn't be thinking about her in that way, but he couldn't stop himself. Had never been able to stop himself for as long as he'd known her.

Except today, circles darkened Jewel's eyes, and her usually shiny, ash-blond hair was askew. Her face was bruised in a way that turned his stomach into knots.

He was the police chief, but he was a man, too, and Jewel had caught his attention the first time he'd met her. She reflected light like a precious gem. Her parents must have known she would when they had named her. She carried herself with the confidence of experience, but she'd never looked a day over thirty to him, though she was in her mid to late forties just like Colin.

Then he remembered himself.

In a professional capacity he'd come to make sure she was all right. But his true interest in her went deeper, even though he'd never let himself act on it. Her husband had been a friend, and Colin had never let his mind or heart stray before. Nor would that happen now, even though she was a widow.

In his eyes, she'd aged ten years in the past few hours. Colin thought maybe he'd aged that much, too. Maybe more.

She could have died out there.

She pressed her face into her palms, her shoulders shaking. He'd never seen her undone like this, but it was understandable. Colin lost it then, too. He pressed his hand against her head, felt the softness of her hair. His heart thudded against his ribs.

"Please, Jewel. Talk to me."

She drew her face up, and her haggardness caught him afresh, sending a new pang through his chest.

"Meral, Buck and I had gone kayaking. They just got married and arrived two days ago. Were excited to be here and wanted to see southeast Alaska. She's my sister, and I haven't seen her in twenty years."

Jewel seemed to regret her last words, which came out rushed. An outburst to cover some deeper emotion hidden away? He'd let her tell him that story another time. Yet maybe there was something here that played a role in what had happened today.

"Go on," Colin said, nodding.

"We secured the kayaks in the bay and decided to hike up to the falls. We planned to be out for a few hours. A day at the most. I forgot my water and went back to get it. Buck and Meral went on ahead. I said I'd catch up to them. Meet them at the falls where the trail stopped. From there you could choose between two other trails, and I didn't want them to go farther without me. It shouldn't have been so complicated."

"And were they at the falls when you got there?"

"No. I stopped to watch the waterfall. Silas liked to explore waterfalls. Maybe you remember that we used to travel around to see the falls in the region, even as far south as Ketchikan. He liked to study them. Kayak over them, if possible."

"And what about you? Did you enjoy that, too?"

She shook her head. "I'm not into thrills."

No. He hadn't thought so. She was adventurous, yes, but was more the kind to enjoy the beauty rather than the challenge of nature.

"So did you call for Meral and... What is his full name again?" She'd only given her brother-in-law's first name when she'd mentioned him earlier. Colin didn't want to be too invasive. Let her tell the story. He hadn't met Buck yet. Apparently he'd just missed the man and Jewel's sister when he'd got to the clinic.

"Buck Cambridge. Yes, I called out for them when I made the falls, and they were not there. I heard a twig snap behind me. Before I turned, something slammed into my back."

Colin hated thinking about the bruises that covered the rest of her, if her face was any indication. "I'm just glad you survived. It seems…"

"Impossible. I know."

For a moment, Colin let himself visualize her battle, experience it with her. If he let himself think about it too long, he'd be visibly shaking, trembling like she was.

"Tell me the rest."

"After my initial panic, I swam beneath the back-wash and let the current pull me away from the churning falls. I swam toward the surface to get air and happened to glance to the top of the falls."

"And what did you see?"

"Someone. Just a figure. My vision was blurred by water, but I saw someone for a split second before the water pulled me away."

"You sure it wasn't Meral you saw, arriving after you'd fallen in? She was the one to call this in. Her quick thinking got the search for you going."

Jewel closed her eyes. After a moment, she shook her head. "I don't think so. No, I'm sure it wasn't Meral. The jacket she's wearing is too bright—even though I couldn't make out the face of the person I saw, that color would have caught my eye. It was the person who pushed me in. They were standing exactly where I'd been before being pushed."

Colin hated that her story could be picked apart, especially since she appeared so frazzled. And after his experience in Texas, he resolved to look at the facts and only the facts. He couldn't go on gut feelings alone.

Jewel's experience and what she'd seen could be based entirely on her emotional state. But this was Jewel Caraway. Writing her off wasn't something he was willing to do. Colin would take her seriously. If someone truly had tried to kill her, then he would do everything he could to make sure she was safe.

He frowned. "Was the person you saw male or female?"

"I couldn't tell." She looked up at him again. "You do believe me, don't you?"

"Of course." He believed she wasn't deliberately lying, but could her memory be faulty? Eyewitness stories almost always conflicted. Everyone had his or her own perspective. Had Jewel really seen someone? And had that person pushed her?

"Did you see anyone else on the trail during your hike?"

"No."

"I'll need to question your sister and her husband." He wouldn't divvy this out to his officers. No. This investigation belonged to Colin.

"Of course. They're waiting out there. I'm surprised you didn't already meet and question them. They *are* still out there, aren't they?"

Colin let out a slow breath. Would she be disappointed if he told her they had already gone? A fact he found strange. What was more important to them than Jewel's well-being?

"Oh, wait. Meral wasn't feeling well." Disappointment edged her voice. "Maybe Buck wanted to get her home. Maybe they decided not to wait for me to get dressed."

Colin's throat tightened. Nice guy. "I'll take you home, Jewel. Don't worry. Now can you think of any reason why someone would try to kill you?" Maybe this wasn't a random act, though he couldn't think of a single enemy she would have made. She was kind and generous, and her guests always raved about their experience at the B and B. But if he'd learned anything as a twenty-five-year police veteran, it was that everyone had dry bones buried in the backyard. As hard as it was to believe, Jewel would be no exception.

"I almost wish I did. Then it would be easy to find out who pushed me."

Colin agreed. "In that case, I don't want you to be alone until we figure this out. Do you understand?"

"That should be easy enough to comply with. After all, my sister is here now for a short visit."

Colin didn't bring up that she was supposed to be with her sister when someone had tried to kill her—Meral hadn't been any protection for her then. At any rate, maybe her sister and husband would stay until this investigation was closed. "Come on. I'll give you that ride home now. Doc give you some scripts?"

"Yeah, painkillers and an antibiotic, I think."

"Fine. I'll get you home first, then I'll run those over to the pharmacy for you."

Jewel stood, ready to leave, her confusion over the day's events evident, mingling with exhaustion from the strain on her beaten body. Colin was glad to be the one to see her safely home. If it was actually even safe. He'd determine that when he arrived.

He pursed his lips, envisioning what he wanted to do to her attacker or attackers once he got his hands on them, and before he put them in a jail cell. But that was all it was—a vain imagining.

He opened the door and assisted her out to the waiting room, where they found Tracy with David. Tracy said she had encouraged Meral to go back to the B and B, seeing that she wasn't feeling well, reassuring them that she and David would get Jewel home. Colin could see the relief in Jewel's eyes that she hadn't been abandoned, but all Colin could think was Tracy and David were behaving more like family to her than Meral and Buck. While Jewel thanked Tracy for finding her, Colin talked to David about going back to the falls to look around.

Then he ushered Jewel through the exit where his Jeep waited and assisted her into the passenger seat, taking care he didn't hurt her. On the drive back, he took the bumps and the potholes slowly and carefully.

Anger boiled beneath the surface at the thought of her injuries. At the thought of someone actually trying to hurt her. At the image of someone pushing her into those falls.

He would have to prevent them from trying again.

But he knew firsthand how difficult it could be to stop a killer. He'd attempted and failed before, and as a result, Katelyn, the woman he'd planned to propose to, had been murdered.

And he'd known all along who had wanted to kill her,

and still Colin hadn't been able to prevent her murder. With no idea where to even look for Jewel's attacker, how was he going to be able to keep her alive?

THREE

The next morning, Colin walked the trail with one of his officers, Terry Stratford, along with Cade and David Warren, who were friends and had been part of the search and rescue for Jewel.

He almost wished Dead Falls Canyon, both the river and several waterfalls, were far from town, where they'd be less of a danger to the people under his jurisdiction, which included the city and borough of Mountain Cove and encompassed two thousand square miles, most of that wilderness in the Tongass National Forest.

But the majestic scenery and unparalleled adventures of the region were all part of the package. The splendor, the pristine nature and magnificent views brought tourists. One of the many reasons people chose to live here.

But beauty had turned deadly more than once.

After his officers and forest rangers had searched the area yesterday and came up empty-handed, he'd decided that Jewel's attacker was long gone, and there wasn't reason enough to close off the whole region to nature enthusiasts.

Today's revisiting of the crime scene hadn't turned up any evidence or clues either, so far. Jewel's party hadn't been the only one to hike the trails or view the falls, so there was no way to try to trace anyone's tracks.

Colin maintained a keen sense of his surroundings in case someone was watching him. He had that sensation as they hiked the trail, but it could simply be curious hikers wondering what had brought the police out on the trails today.

They'd walked the five-mile circular trail that led to the top where Jewel claimed to have stood and looked down. This was some of the most beautiful scenery in the world, and now it would likely be ruined for Jewel unless she could somehow put those events out of her mind.

He was asking for the impossible. Colin had moved to Mountain Cove to escape his own devastating experience in Texas. He hoped Jewel wouldn't have to take such drastic measures.

Under normal circumstances, he'd have his officers roam the woods now, searching again for evidence, rather than coming out here himself. He had enough paperwork stacked on his desk and phone calls to answer to last a lifetime, and the tourist season was only beginning.

But this wasn't normal. This was Jewel Caraway. The thought of losing her, that moment when he'd thought she could have been dead, had forced him to look deep, even though he knew he couldn't make it too personal and had to tread carefully.

As police chief, loving someone would only cloud his judgment and get someone killed one day—he'd already paid that price. He would never let that happen again. He found it easy to care about someone from a distance, but better not to care at all.

David and Cade stood next to him, staring down at the crushing force of rushing water. Listened to the roar. Felt the moisture cloud envelop them. No wonder she hadn't heard someone approach from behind until the instant before impact. And she certainly hadn't known to be wary of someone who would push her over.

"I'm still wondering how nature could push a body under and keep it there, and that body still survive," Cade said.

"Maybe it's more the nature of God that she survived." It was easy to believe that Jewel had a special place in God's heart like she had in Colin's.

"Why would someone try to kill her?" David asked. "Was it just a random act of violence?"

He voiced the question they were all wondering, but had no answer for yet. David had endured a fight to protect the woman he loved not long ago and understood better than most there had to be a reason. A secret not shared.

Finding the person responsible for the attacks against Tracy had taken far too long. Colin could still hear the questions from the city council echoing in his ears, and they mingled with the new questions. The same questions.

What are you going to do about it? How are you going to stop it before it happens again?

Two women approached the falls from the trail, pulling Colin from his thoughts. He nodded to David, Cade and Terry. They'd seen enough for now. They moved away from the falls and headed back down the trail.

"What do you know about her sister and brother-in-law?" Colin asked.

"Not much," David said. "They're newlyweds, I hear. I imagine it means a lot to Jewel that they've come to see her, since she's been estranged from her family for a long time. Once when Silas and I were out fighting wildfires in the interior, he shared a little about Jewel. What a rare find she was."

Colin wouldn't argue with him there. Her name said it all.

"She comes from a wealthy family, and they didn't think Silas was good enough for her. When her parents made it clear they disapproved of him, he almost walked away. He loved her too much to tear her away, but in the end, he'd been selfish, after all. He couldn't let her go. They were young and impulsive."

"And that's why she hasn't been in touch with her family all these years?" Colin asked.

"They didn't give her much choice—her family disinherited her when she chose to marry him."

"What kind of parents did that? Disowned or disinherited their child?" Cade asked.

"That's just weird," Terry spoke as he led them down the trail.

Colin couldn't say much. Guilt and shame over how he'd treated his own family had followed him here to Alaska. He'd left his parents behind in Texas and, as they aged, his sister was forced to take sole responsibility for their care. Colin hadn't been much of a son or a brother, but after what happened, he saw himself as a burden to his family—one they would be better off without. They must see what he wanted to forget every time they looked at him.

"She left it all behind—her family and the wealth—

to follow Silas to Alaska." David kicked a rock down the path.

"I can see why he would think she was special," Colin said. "She must have loved the man deeply. It's not easy to live here or to give up your family. To give up wealth on top of that."

"You know, she could love deeply again, right?" David studied Colin.

Cade and Terry walked together up a ways. Colin was glad they hadn't heard David's question. He was just prying into Colin's personal thoughts. Either that or nudging him toward a place he had no business going.

They'd almost made the trailhead where they would kayak back to Mountain Cove, following the path Jewel's group had taken in their search. Colin eyed his friend. Understood the meaning behind his words.

"Jewel deserves someone far better than me." And if she had a wealthy family, she was more like Katelyn than he'd realized. That wealth had come between them more than once. Her wealthy family had questioned his investigation, blamed him for her murder as if he hadn't already been weighed down by it.

"So what do you think? Who do you believe is a suspect?"

"Hard to say at this point. The fact she has a wealthy family could be motivation for murder."

"But how if she's been disinherited?" David asked. "There has to be more to the story."

"There always is."

Meral had gone down to the kitchen to get Jewel a cup of green tea. Jewel was glad to have a minute of relative privacy. She was glad that she had people who cared about her enough to want to help her, but the hovering was already starting to feel overwhelming.

She definitely didn't like being confined to her room, even though her body was sore and she needed to recover from her injuries. Not to mention she had guests to attend to, but neither could she let any of them see her like this. She'd give it a day or two, leaving running the B and B to her staff, and hope it didn't take a week for her bruised body to heal. Jewel would give anything to forget about the fall and her injuries and to go back to life as usual. She needed normalcy. To get that, she would have to stop taking the painkillers. They made her groggy, and she couldn't think straight.

When she sat up, dizziness swept over her. She made the mistake of glancing in the mirror over the dresser, and her mouth dried up.

Chief Winters saw me like this?

She shoved thoughts of what he must think of her out of her mind. His opinion shouldn't count. She couldn't care about that. After Silas's death, she almost hadn't survived the heartache. She'd given up her life and family to be with him, and now all she had left of that life were memories and heartache. The price of loving someone was too high.

She couldn't survive that pain again.

So for now she had to focus on other things until the unwelcome feelings in her heart went away.

One question nagged her. Why would someone want to kill her? Had it simply been random? Or had she been targeted? Jewel had no enemies that she knew about. No reason for someone to push her over.

Unless…

My secret.

Jewel pressed her hands over her heart. *God, please no.* She needed the secret to remain dead and buried. She wasn't the same young woman who had made that mistake. Besides, no one knew about it, so no. That couldn't be it.

She was back to her question. And she didn't know why someone would try to kill her. When she was a child, her parents had taught her to be on her guard, not to trust easily, because there were too many people in the world who might try to hurt her or kidnap her because of their money. But it had been years since that had been an issue for her. No one in Alaska had even known she'd once been wealthy. Until Meral and Buck arrived a few days ago.

Now suddenly her life had been threatened.

Could the two incidents be related?

And what of Meral's new husband, Buck? What did Meral really know about the man?

Jewel should be ecstatic that she had a second chance with the family she'd given up to come to Alaska. She thought she'd gotten over that hurt, too, until Meral. She wanted to be happy to see her sister, who had only been fifteen when Jewel had left. In fact, she had not known how much she'd missed her family.

But something was wrong. Very wrong. She should thank Buck Cambridge for bringing Meral—a wedding gift, he'd said. He'd found Meral's long-lost sister. But Jewel wasn't sure she really wanted to be found.

Something about Buck disturbed her. He didn't look at Meral the way Jewel's husband had looked at her when they'd fallen in love.

But who was Jewel to judge? How could she bring up her misgivings about Buck with Meral, a sister she barely knew? They were only just reconnecting. Getting to know each other again. It wasn't her place. She wouldn't do anything to destroy this chance at having her family again. If Jewel questioned her sister about Buck, then she would sound just like their parents had sounded when Jewel had fallen in love.

Those memories came rushing back, crushing the breath from her.

Jewel shoved from the bed. She wouldn't do that to Meral. She'd give her sister—a grown woman in her thirties, an experienced woman who had already been married before—the benefit of a doubt.

Jewel would let Chief Winters investigate and see what came of it without mentioning her suspicions about Buck.

She could trust Colin Winters. He was a good man and a good chief of police and had served Mountain Cove well. Maybe there were some in town who blamed him for the rise in the crime rate in recent years, accusing him of not being hard enough on suspects and criminals. Then others blamed him and his officers for using too much force. So much pressure from the community pushing him in different directions had to be brutal on him.

Jewel had never blamed him. People wanted to remove God from the equation of life and expect law and order to reign in His place. Without God ruling people's lives, there was only chaos.

The words snagged at her heart, bringing to mind her own shortcomings. Her own hidden secret. She needed to check on it—see if it was still safe. Jewel peeked out the door into the hallway. All clear.

Jewel's bedroom was on the second floor. She tiptoed up another flight of stairs. Though unintelligible, Meral's voice could be heard, along with Katy Warren's, drifting up from the kitchen.

Katy was here? The grandmother and matriarch of the Warren clan was a dear friend, and Jewel wanted to go down and greet her, but now that she had a moment alone—something she might not get for a while—she needed to take a good long look at her past.

The one she'd buried, tucked away forever, safe and sound.

Creeping to the end of the hallway, she gently pulled down the stepladder to the attic. She climbed up into the hot and stuffy room. She flicked on a light to add to the sunlight spilling through a dirty dormer window at the far end.

A raccoon had tried to nest up here, and Jewel had come up to chase it away on more than one occasion, but other than that, she hadn't been up here for months.

Dust motes and cobwebs had taken over the space. Jewel brushed away the webs as she moved. When Silas had bought the B and B, he had believed it would keep her occupied so she wouldn't worry about him traveling to fight wildfires. They'd hoped to turn the attic into an office or another room for a guest. Instead, it ended up serving as storage for old furniture and collectibles that Jewel planned to use to refresh the B and B decor, switching things out for seasons or special occasions.

And when he'd been away, she'd stored her more valuable collectible—if you could call it that—not just *in* the house but *with* the house.

If the house burned to the ground, her valuable would survive.

Jewel headed for the far corner, dreading what she was about to do. Acid churned in her stomach.

She moved a trunk, feeling an ache through her back and across her legs and arms. Maybe this wasn't such a good idea. She might accidentally tear the stitches and open up that nasty gash.

Plus, moving the trunk had made too much noise. She had to be quiet, or Katy and Meral would hear her movements.

Creak.

She froze. Her pulse jumped.

The sound had come from the attic. The rafters settling beneath the simple plywood flooring? Or something—someone—else?

At the falls she'd heard the snap of a twig right behind her. Shuddering, she slowly turned to look. See if someone was there, fearing what would happen if they were. She couldn't see the steps down into the hallway for the boxes and furniture stacked in her way.

Ever since Tracy's attacker had stayed in the B and B, Jewel had known she needed more protection than the rifles stored in a gun closet or a 9-millimeter semi-automatic pistol tucked away in her nightstand. She had needed to train in self-defense in case a day ever came when she would have to protect herself without the use of a firearm.

Granted, none of that had come in handy at the falls, except maybe to give her confidence to swim her way to freedom. Would she find herself using that training now? When she heard nothing more, she looked at the wall where the item was hidden behind a plank and reconsidered. Maybe she wasn't in the right frame of mind to revisit the past.

But there was only one reason Jewel could imagine someone would want her dead. She hadn't wanted to think about it, but as the walls of the attic closed in around her, she had to face the truth.

Another creak had her stiffening. Preparing for the worst.

"Who's there?"

How could anyone have come up here with her? She would have heard them, right? "Meral, is that you?"

Her knees shook. She was far weaker than she wanted to be. Too weak to deal with her secret right now. Jewel would come back another day. Maybe when Chief Winters returned from his look at the falls she would tell him everything.

Except he would be disappointed in her, and she didn't think she could bear that. She made her way through the maze of junk, heading for the steps out of the attic.

The sense of a presence and the rush of wind were all the warning she received. Someone grabbed her from behind, wrapping an arm around her neck.

There was no doubt as to his intention—to choke her to death.

Her pulse skyrocketed. Heart pounded.

But Chief Winters's words penetrated the fear that gripped her mind and body.

First, don't panic. Take slow, deep breaths to relax. Then assess what is happening. But do it quickly. A quick reaction can save you.

Breathe. She had to breathe. *Hard to do. When. He's. Choking. Me.*

Second, grab his arms. Drop your weight.

She let herself drop, but his grip didn't waver.

Stomp on his foot.

Jewel jabbed her heel into his foot. Then she tried to move. That was the whole point. Move and slam her fist into his groin. But he kept her pinned tightly.

She couldn't budge. Her stomp made no noticeable difference. Again. She tried again.

Next she raised her arm, preparing to turn into her attacker and strike him with her elbow. She'd practiced this and had been successful in class demonstrations. But her attacker seemed to expect her every move and squeezed her tighter, holding her in a vice.

Breathe.

She couldn't breathe.

Darkness edged her vision. Bright pinpoints of light sparked across her eyes.

She struggled and twisted. Had to try something else.

If you can't get away, try to head butt. Grab his ears, nose, anything to gain an escape.

Jewel threw her head forward and then back against her attacker's face. His grip loosened enough for Jewel to break free. She pushed forward and away. Took off running as she gasped for oxygen. No time to stop or even scream.

Had to put distance between them. Escape. She had to get away.

She ran for the only exit.

But he slammed into her back. Toppled her. Jewel fell forward, her body slamming hard against the floor. Pain sliced through her, exacerbating her previous injuries. His body weight pressed heavily against her. His breath was hot across her neck.

God, please, no!

Lungs still burning, Jewel screamed, releasing what little air she'd grabbed.

She couldn't catch her breath, but there were two things she needed to know. "Who are…you? What do you want?"

Voices resounded from below.

Katy and Meral had heard the ruckus.

Jewel tried to scream again to let them know where she was. "Help—"

Boxes toppled, slamming down on her bruised body. Crashing into her head.

Darkness engulfed her.

FOUR

It was late afternoon by the time Colin steered his Jeep up to the B and B. Terry headed back to the police station to finish paperwork, and Cade headed home to his son, little Scotty, and wife, Leah, who was pregnant with their second child. But David had ridden along with Colin and would pick up his truck and Katy, his grandmother. Colin stepped from his Jeep and studied the house. Picturesque and peaceful. A bald eagle soared above the property. Trees rustled in a cooler-than-usual August breeze.

David climbed from the Jeep and walked around, waiting on Colin. "Quiet on the outside. I just hope there's nothing wrong on the inside."

"That makes two of us."

Colin noted David's truck and Jewel's Durango parked to the side. He didn't see Meral and Buck's rental, which caused him concern. Meral had promised to stay with Jewel, but maybe her husband had the car and was running errands in town. Colin had met Meral earlier—as beautiful as her sister but several years younger—but he had yet to meet Buck Cambridge.

He wanted to know more about the husband. Meet

the man and get a sense of him. See his interactions
with his wife and sister-in-law.

Colin had watched Meral with Jewel and could easily
see she loved her sister. In his mind, in his gut, Meral
wasn't a suspect, though she'd been conveniently missing, as had her husband, when Jewel had gone into the
falls. Regardless, Colin refused to depend on his gut
feeling. He'd get the facts.

He and David headed to the porch.

"What are you going to tell her?" David asked.

Jewel would be disappointed they still knew next
to nothing. He didn't like to heap more pain on her injuries.

"I'll reassure her we'll do our best to find whoever
did this." Colin opened the front door and stepped into
the foyer.

Cell in hand and eyes wide, Meral rushed forward.
"Oh, I'm so glad you're here! It's Jewel…" Meral fum-
bled and dropped her phone, but didn't bend to pick it
up. Instead, she ran away.

Colin glanced at David, his heart plunging to his
knees, and took off after Meral. "What's happened?"
he called after her.

She ran up the stairs and called back to him without
pausing. "She's hurt."

And then another flight of stairs.

"But what happened? Does she need medical attention?"

"Maybe. Boxes fell on her. I don't know what happened. We just heard her scream and found her in the
attic. I came downstairs to grab my phone and was calling 911 when you came in."

Colin shoved past Meral and climbed the short steps

up to the attic, where he found Katy hovered over Jewel. With unshed tears in her eyes, Katy looked at Colin. "She's alive."

Katy moved away and Colin took her place. He shoved the boxes away from Jewel to make more space. None of them were crushingly heavy, but they'd done damage nonetheless. Carefully, he examined her injuries, then realized his mistake.

What am I doing?

He moved out of David's way.

David was a paramedic firefighter, and Colin let him determine if Jewel could be safely moved. David examined her, then started to lift her to carry her from the attic.

"Let me do it." Colin carefully slipped his arms under her neck and knees. Holding Jewel close and tight, Colin stood, kicked junk out of his way and headed for the steps out of the attic.

In the hallway, he glanced at Meral. "Where's her room?"

Meral led him down another set of stairs to the second floor and then into a warm, cozy room decorated with quilts and nautical decor. He gently laid her on a rumpled bed.

"Jewel, wake up." *God, please let her wake up. Please let her be okay.*

"Did you call for help?" he asked. He remembered Meral dropped her cell phone when she'd seen him.

"Well… I was about to. I thought… You're here."

"She needs to see a doctor."

"We could take her in. Would be faster than waiting." David began assessing her injuries, focusing on her head. He had the credentials and experience, after all. Much more than Colin.

Yet Colin didn't want to relinquish Jewel's well-being into anyone else's hands.

"Right here, feels like she has a fresh knot on her head." David moved aside. "She likely has a concussion."

Colin ran his hand over where David indicated, his fingers weaving into her soft hair, searching. "See if you can get Doc Harland out here. I don't think Jewel wants to go back to the hospital."

Katy and David shared a look that he didn't like. He wasn't giving Jewel special treatment. Was he?

"I'll call Doc. See what he wants us to do." David snagged his cell from his pocket and went into the hallway.

While David turned his attention to the call, and Meral and Katy spoke in hushed tones, Colin focused on Jewel. *Lord, please let her be okay.* He didn't think his heart could take any more loss. If he'd thought he'd toughened up enough over the past twenty years since coming to Alaska to flee his bad experience in Texas, he'd been wrong.

Why had this happened on top of yesterday?

"Ladies, please tell me what happened."

Katy pursed her lips. "Well, I don't exactly know. We were in the kitchen."

"I'd come down to get Jewel some tea." Meral frowned.

"I thought we agreed she wasn't to be left alone." He eyed them both.

"But how could I have known that meant I couldn't get her tea? That I couldn't leave her room? Or that *she* couldn't leave her room? I just went to get tea. It shouldn't have been so hard." Meral pressed her face into her hands.

"No need to blame yourself." Guilt hit Colin for being too tough on her. "I'm just trying to protect Jewel and get to the bottom of all this."

"To be fair, dear—" Katy sent a regretful glance Meral's way "—we'd gotten caught up in chatting. Maybe I kept you too long."

"Chief Winters, I'm so sorry this happened," Meral said. "We heard noises coming from above us. I thought I heard someone cry out, so we came first to Jewel's bedroom and that's when we discovered she was gone."

"Then we heard the awful crash." Katy sat on the edge of the bed. "We ran up to the third floor and found the attic door hanging down."

"And so we climbed the steps and found Jewel covered in boxes." Meral fidgeted. Glanced out the bedroom door. Was she waiting on Buck? Wondering where he was? Colin certainly was. This was the second time the man seemed to be missing when Jewel was hurt.

"She could have been crushed." Katy rubbed Jewel's leg as if coaxing her to wake up.

"The boxes weren't heavy enough to crush her." But there she was in the bed, unconscious, regardless. Colin didn't want to think about what could have happened. "I don't know why she'd go to the attic, but she's not in any condition to move around an obstacle course."

A moan escaped Jewel's lips.

He turned his attention back to her. Pressed his hand against her face. Felt her soft skin. "Jewel, can you hear me?"

Her eyelashes fluttered.

"Jewel, wake up. It's me, Colin…er… Chief Winters." His heart was getting the best of him. "Doc Harland is on his way."

He hoped.

"He is," David confirmed from behind.

When her lids finally opened, he could see the pain in her eyes. "I know, hon. I know it hurts."

"Again?" Her question came out in a groan.

"Looks like it, yes. But you're going to be all right. You hear me?"

"No, no, I'm not."

"Don't say that. You're just fine. You have a concussion probably, and a few new bruises, but nothing worse than that. Doc will fix you up right as rain." Colin sounded as if he was grasping for hope.

"Doc can't fix what's wrong with me." Jewel frowned, clearly in pain. "Someone is trying to kill me."

When had Jewel decided she was the specific target?

Colin eased onto the edge of the bed, sitting closer. It should feel wrong, him sitting here like this when Jewel had her sister and Katy Warren to comfort her. What was Colin doing? Hadn't he decided he shouldn't do this? But one close call too many had the protector in him coming out and rearing its big head. The comforter in him that he hadn't realized resided inside was taking over.

"I'll find him. Don't you worry. We went to the waterfall today. We'll find out who did this." He hadn't wanted to bring that up yet since he didn't have any real leads to share, but it was all he could think to do to reassure her. His words portrayed more confidence than he'd felt, though. "In the meantime, you need to rest and recover before you start exploring on your own."

Jewel opened her intense hazel-green eyes and turned them on Colin. His heart jolted in his chest. He couldn't remember a time when his heart jumped into his throat this high, this forcefully. Jewel grabbed his hand on her face. "Don't coddle me, Chief Winters. Forget about the waterfall. He was in my attic."

Surprise mingled with disbelief in the police chief's eyes. That hurt Jewel more than she wanted to admit.

"You've been injured, Jewel." He reclaimed his hand, leaving a cold spot where warmth had been. "You've had a knock on the head. Think about what you're saying."

She wanted to tell him that his words upset her. But then she'd be admitting out loud that his opinion was important. Meral watched her, sympathy carved into her beautiful features. Did she think Jewel had imagined it, too?

"But we were all here. How could someone have been in the house without us knowing about it?" Meral asked.

"How could he have hidden in the attic all this time?" Katy joined the doubters. "We would have heard the noise."

"You *did* hear noise," David said.

"Yes, but only for a minute or so before we heard the crash."

"I thought I heard you scream." Meral pressed her hand over her mouth, eyes wide. "You think…you believe…he was here?"

Jewel grabbed her forehead and slowly sat up, ignoring Chief Winters's protests, along with those of Katy and Meral.

"I don't think. I don't believe. I *know* what I'm saying. I *know* what I saw. I know that I fought an attacker. I know what I experienced before I was knocked out. This time, he tried to strangle me. I got free for a second, only he tackled me before I could reach the door. But I think Meral and Katy scared him off when they responded to my scream and the noise. Maybe he thought he'd killed me. He could have done just that. I should be dead right now."

She turned her eyes to her sister and Katy. "Thank you," she whispered.

Chief Winters lifted her chin, his touch light and gentle. He looked at her neck and his frowned deepened. Then his eyes shot back up to hers, the scolding in them well and alive. "You walked right into that attic without being suspicious or careful. You were told not to go anywhere alone."

She knew he was right, but she couldn't help defending herself. "I'm not accustomed to sitting around and doing nothing. I don't like others waiting on me. I have work to do. Besides, it's the middle of the day and this is my home. I wasn't expecting to find an intruder in the attic."

"You weren't expecting someone to push you into the falls either." He crossed his arms, leveling his gaze.

She turned away, but avoided that stupid mirror. "At least my guests are still out and about. This didn't happen with any of them here."

"And maybe that's the exact reason he thought he could attack you in the middle of the day here in the B and B. That could be the reason he thought he wouldn't get caught. But at least you got a look at him this time. Do you know who did this?"

"He attacked from behind. The attic was dimly lit,

and the small window doesn't give much light. I fought him, but he was strong and finally I had to head butt him to get free. I didn't have time to look back—I just ran, but he toppled me."

She eyed the nightstand drawer, wanting to pull out her Glock and hold it, keep it close, but she didn't want to scare the others. Jewel shook her head and stared at the floor, remembering how it felt to fight for her life. Her breath caught. What good was self-defense if she couldn't win that fight? She fully expected Chief Winters to give her some lecture on the correct moves, what she had and hadn't done right.

Instead, his voice was gentle. "You did well, Jewel, using what you've learned to escape. You can't expect the real experience to be like what we practice in class, though we can try. So take comfort in the fact you're likely alive at this moment because you were able to fight back."

She nodded. It gave her a measure of relief, though not much.

"You called your attacker a he," Chief Winters said. "So you know it's a male this time."

"Yes. Of that I have no doubt."

"Height, weight?"

"Taller than me by half a head or more. Strong, but not muscle-bound. Heavier than me."

Chief Winters resisted the urge to hang his head. Her description wouldn't do them much good, but it was more than they'd had before.

"Just one more question, Jewel."

She rubbed her arms. Doc Harland appeared in the doorway, his brows furrowed.

"What's that?" Jewel directed her question to Chief

Winters but stared at that good doctor, wishing he would come in and save her from an interrogation.

"Why did you go to the attic?"

Why indeed.

She must have blanched, because Doc came all the way into the room, looking concerned. "Any more questions can wait until later. If everyone wants to give us some space, and Jewel some privacy, that would be appreciated."

Everyone left except Chief Winters.

Doc gave him a stern nod. "And you, Chief. Can I see my patient alone?"

Chief Winters complied with a frown, but the look he gave Jewel told her she wasn't off the hook. He expected an answer to the question. Jewel didn't have one she felt comfortable delivering.

When he left the room she sighed with relief. Doc Harland paused, stethoscope midair, and looked at her. "It can't be that bad, Jewel. You just relax. This has been too much stress on you. Falling into the river and now taking a tumble in the attic."

How much did Doc Harland actually know?

Jewel nodded as he rambled.

"Tell me where you hurt the most."

How could she possibly explain? More than physical pain, the emotional pain of being assaulted in her own home overwhelmed her. There were no words.

And now she could only think of one reason someone had attacked her. Jewel wished she had a confidante. Someone she could trust enough to share her secret. If she'd trusted Silas enough those twenty years ago, then maybe this wouldn't be happening to her now. Maybe someone wouldn't be trying to kill her.

FIVE

Frustration roiled inside as Colin crept up to the attic with a flashlight. He'd have to wait for answers from Jewel, so he'd use the time to see if the attacker had left behind any evidence.

What had Jewel been doing up here? What had been so pressing to drag her out of bed when she'd been through so much already?

Downstairs, Meral had gone to see Katy out. A nurturer, Katy had wanted to stay and help Jewel, but David insisted on taking his grandmother home. Evidently, she was already booked as a babysitter, thanks to Heidi and Isaiah Callahan.

Mountain Cove had some good people, and that encouraged Colin, kept him going when so much else seemed to be deteriorating into chaos and crime. Katy Warren and her entire family were pillars in the community and they had proven themselves to be his friends. He could always count on them.

Katy had that glow about her—loving the great-grandmother years now that they had finally arrived. For too long she hadn't been sure any of her grandchildren would marry. But they were all happily settled now, growing their families with healthy, happy babies for her to spoil. Little wonder she was a spry one for her age.

He only hoped he could be as active when that time came. But if love and family were what kept someone young, then his prospects looked bleak.

He'd never fallen in love and gotten married after losing Katelyn, and he had no legacy. No children. He hadn't allowed himself to think on those things. How did Jewel feel about children? She and her husband had never had them. Had they agreed not to, or was there some other reason? Or had Silas's life been taken from him too soon? That seemed the most probable explanation. As if it was any of Colin's business.

He shoved away the errant thoughts and focused on his investigation and protecting Jewel. He couldn't think of anything that was more important to him at this moment.

In the attic, he flipped on the soft lighting, then added to it as he shined the flashlight beam around where Jewel had fallen. Where the attacker had possibly stood to strangle her. The dusty floor was too disturbed in the scuffle to get any footprints.

Colin wished he had gotten an answer to his question. Why had Jewel come to the attic? Had she heard a noise and come up to investigate? He couldn't believe she would have done that alone after what had happened. Unless she thought it was that raccoon that kept nesting.

That had to be it. She hadn't been thinking about a possible intruder, only about protecting her investment. She needed to start thinking about her safety now. The

B and B was secondary. Or was it tertiary now that her sister was back in her life?

Meral held a special place in Jewel's heart, and from a family who had hurt her, too. Disinheriting, disowning someone had to have cut Jewel in a way Colin couldn't fathom. And now the sister and husband had suddenly shown up. Why now, after twenty years? And why was Jewel's life in danger right after they arrived?

He didn't want to rely on instinct, but neither did he believe in coincidence.

Why would the attacker have come to the attic? To hide? Or was there some other reason? Making assumptions was never a good idea. Colin walked around shining the light on boxes and old luggage, trunks, furniture, toys, knickknacks—some of which he'd seen decorating the B and B over the years. She could have come up here to think on moving some things down. One fact he had—he wouldn't solve this until Jewel answered some very pointed questions. He wished he had a crime-scene division to gather fingerprints. But Mountain Cove had no budget for that. Investigating this would take good, old-fashioned police work. And anyway, gathering prints didn't always give an answer or paint the correct picture.

Colin made his way back downstairs to look around the rest of the house for clues. He was torn between hoping that Doc Harland would give him the free and clear to question Jewel further and hoping he'd be told to leave her alone for a while longer. Every time he looked at her, asked her a question, he felt as though he was beating her up. She needed to recover fully, and Colin wasn't helping.

But she would keep getting hurt until he found the

person attacking her. And to track down the culprit, he needed answers.

He heard voices downstairs. A male voice that didn't belong to David. Maybe one of the guests had returned? Or had Meral's husband, Buck, finally shown up?

Colin made his way to the first floor and found Meral in the kitchen in the arms of a man nearing fifty, a good ten if not fifteen years older than Meral, around the same age as Jewel and Colin. They both tensed when they saw him. Meral stepped out of the man's arms.

"Hello, Chief Winters," she said. "This is my husband, Buck Cambridge."

Stepping forward, Colin held out his hand to shake Buck's. The man had a strong grip in return. Well-groomed, graying chestnut-brown hair and a beard framed his mostly square, tanned face. About the same height as Colin—five foot eleven. Stocky but solid. Brown eyes stared back at him, measuring. Gauging.

A strange sensation raked over Colin.

Blocking the wariness creeping in, Colin nodded at the sacks on the floor. "Did some shopping?"

Buck laughed, the sound so jarringly familiar that Colin had to take a steadying step back as he listened. He couldn't put his finger on the associations he had with that laugh, but he knew they weren't good.

"We thought we'd hike the Bledsoe Glacier as soon as Jewel is ready. Maybe we can hire a guide and see one of the ice caves." He hugged Meral closer. "We're here in Alaska to see Jewel for the most part. The scenery is just gravy. Had to get the proper clothing and gear to walk on a glacier. Isn't that right?"

"I suppose. Just a tip, you can always rent the gear you need, too."

Displeasure flickered in Buck's eyes. Colin read that to mean the man didn't like being given tips.

Colin tucked that away for later. Good to note.

Doc Harland entered the kitchen and gave as good of a report on Jewel as he could. He introduced himself to Buck, and Colin studied the man further. He used Doc's distraction to gather his composure. He shouldn't have lost it to begin with.

But something was painfully clear. Somehow Colin knew this man. He couldn't remember from where, but every instinct in him told Colin to be on his guard, that this man couldn't be trusted.

He needed to get Jewel alone to find out what she knew about her sister's husband. And he'd need to tread carefully. Jewel hadn't said so, but he could tell her relationship with Meral was fragile as well as vital. He'd seen a light in Jewel's eyes he hadn't seen in years.

That was her sister's doing.

But Meral's husband was giving off nefarious vibes, and the fact that he'd entered this circle near to Colin's heart—Jewel and her B and B—right before trouble had started set off additional warning sirens in Colin's head.

During his conversation with Doc Harland, Buck held Meral close like a possession, not like someone he cherished. He glanced at Colin, and behind the man's gaze, Colin could swear he saw a smirk.

The man recognized Colin, as well. That had to be it.

Colin's gut tensed. He mentally drew the weapon holstered at his hip.

Doc Harland swung his gaze to Colin. "Now, now, Chief Winters. Jewel is going to be all right."

The man had mistaken Colin's expression for concern over Jewel, which meant he wasn't hiding his emotions. At all. He forced a smile and gave the Doc his due, but stayed fully aware of Buck Cambridge standing to his left.

Colin shook the doctor's hand. "You're a good man, Doc, to come out here to check on Jewel. I know you have other patients and responsibilities."

"I make house calls when it's called for. But Chief Winters—" Doc's expression turned sober "—you find who did this. You take care of our Jewel of the Mountain, and I don't mean the B and B."

"I hear you, Doc." Colin watched the man nod to Meral and Buck and head out of the kitchen. He heard the front door to the B and B open and close.

Attuned to every sound, it was as if they all had been waiting for the doctor to leave. When Colin turned his focus completely on Buck, the man appeared prepared. As if he was expecting to be interrogated. But that wasn't an unusual response.

Now to the more serious question. "Buck, have we met before?"

The man laughed. That familiar, unnerving laugh that Colin couldn't place. "I think I'd remember if we had. I've never been to Alaska before meeting Meral."

The man wasn't lying about Alaska. Colin would trust his instincts on that. But Colin hadn't missed the careful way he'd phrased his answer. No, Colin hadn't met Buck in Alaska. But he hadn't lived in Alaska all his life. Suspicions aside, he needed the facts.

How could he leave Jewel alone in the house with Buck? Her attacker had proved to be much closer than any of them knew. Colin had a feeling he hadn't gone very far. And this time Colin needed to listen to his instincts.

* * *

Jewel rested, both to follow Doc Harland's instructions and because she was well and truly exhausted. She'd heal quicker if she'd give her body the chance to recover. But even though she lay still, she couldn't turn off her mind. Too much had happened, and thoughts constantly bombarded her mind. Who was trying to kill her? Was she safe right now? Would others be hurt because of her? Had the man who wanted to kill her followed her into the attic, or had he already been there either hiding or searching?

One of Katy's framed cross-stitched Bible quotations hung on the wall. Jewel had made the right decision in hanging them. She had hoped to plant seeds in the lives of her guests. Give them peace when they had none. And now she was grateful because she was the one who needed that calming reassurance that could only come from the Lord. She read the words from Psalm 23, letting them wrap around her heart.

The Lord is my shepherd, I lack nothing. He makes me lie down in green pastures, he leads me beside quiet waters, he refreshes my soul.

She knew the scripture already, but seeing it on the wall, created with care and love, reminded her there were good people in the world. Loving people. And that God also loved her. Then, finally, she closed her eyes and felt herself drifting to sleep. But a soft knock came at the door. Jewel inwardly groaned. Her lids were heavy, and she kept her eyes closed as if already asleep. Stirring to answer the door would wake her fully.

She heard the door open.

She heard Meral's whisper and Chief Winters's soft reply.

He'd wanted to ask her about why she'd gone up to the attic. But he'd have to wait for another time, for which Jewel was grateful. She could feel the weight of her past pressing in on her from two floors above behind the plank in the wall.

There hadn't been a raccoon up there.

She hadn't heard a noise.

But had her attacker been in the attic for the same reason as Jewel? Her heart told her yes. But her head still wasn't sure.

To Jewel's surprise, Meral crept all the way into the room and set something next to the bed. The aroma of soup teased Jewel's nose. Chief Winters was there in the room, too, oddly enough. She heard his soft steps, the rustle of his clothes. Felt his presence. His musky scent mingled with the scent of cowboy soup.

She felt his gaze on her face, and her heart cringed at what he must see, but somehow she knew he looked beyond all the damage to the inside. Part of her longed for him to press his hand against her face as he'd done earlier when he'd coaxed her awake.

She couldn't care about him that way. Could not afford to go there with anyone. She was resolved never to give herself away as she had once done. But that didn't make the pain go away. Her determination didn't make it easier.

Meral and Chief Winters left her alone, and Jewel let herself fall the rest of the way to sleep.

Days later things had quieted down, and her bruises were healing. The stiffness and soreness decreased. Though Doc had told her two weeks on the sutures, that was now only days away. She could almost forget what had happened. Almost pretend she was safe now. Except she wouldn't forget. Not until this was over.

Chief Winters had questioned everyone staying at the B and B, including Meral and Buck, about their whereabouts during the attacks. Jewel had successfully evaded his question about the attic.

Patience had ridden the waves of emotion in his eyes. He very likely could wait her out. But Jewel wasn't sure she would ever be ready to tell him what she wanted to forget. Not unless she was sure her past had anything to do with her attacks. If it didn't, then her secret could remain buried.

There was always a police officer sitting in his vehicle outside, and twice a day he did a walk through the B and B per Chief Winters's orders. A rash of burglaries in Mountain Cove had drawn away the chief's personal attention. She could tell he was frustrated he couldn't be by her side every minute, but why he felt so personally invested in her safety, she refused to examine. It was best she wasn't with him too much.

A plainclothes officer always checked the house after the day's departing guests had left in the morning, and just after they arrived and settled in for the evening for additional security. But never to disturb or cause anyone concern. She found the gesture both frustrating and endearing. It somehow felt like overkill, but also reminded Jewel that her attacker was still out there and could try again.

Tracy and Katy had volunteered to come in to help Jewel's regular employees, Jan and Frances. She thought they secretly wanted to keep an eye on her. So the chores had been done early, and dinner was already simmering in the slow cookers without any effort from

Jewel. She should be grateful, but instead, she felt almost smothered. She couldn't stay cooped up like this forever. Like the B and B had been turned into some sort of safe house. It made her wonder if Chief Winters was trying to repair his reputation. Restore the citizens' perception of Mountain Cove as a safe town.

But she made a decision.

This was absolutely the last day she would stay in her room resting, reading books or watching television.

Meral and Buck had gone out snorkeling with Sylvie and Will Pierson this morning. They had returned earlier than Jewel would have expected from the excursion. Funny to think of calling Billy Pierson *Will* now, but that was what Sylvie, his new bride, called him, and the rest of the town had caught on. She'd moved here after they'd got engaged and they'd married quickly. Even before the wedding, Will and Sylvie had added a scuba diving tour business to his bush piloting. It made Jewel happy to think two opposites like that could be together. Reminded her that obstacles could be overcome when two people knew how to love each other. She'd had that once.

And a freak lightning strike had taken it from her.

She thought back to Chief Winters's words to her in the hospital right after the fall.

"Accidents happen, Jewel. People fall where they shouldn't all the time, including in the shower, where some die every year."

He'd been attempting to reassure Jewel. Convince her she had no blame in what he'd thought then had been merely an accident. Jewel had said similar words to Tracy when she'd needed reassurance that her attacker would be caught and she would be safe. Those words, that conversation, came back to haunt Jewel now.

"We'll get him before he takes someone else down."

"You can't promise that, Jewel."

"No, I can't. But there are no promises in life. People die every day, people who don't have a killer after them. I lost my husband a few years back. He was a firefighter—he mentored David Warren, in fact. But he didn't die fighting a fire. No. He had to get struck by lightning while he was hiking in the mountains. A lightning strike killed my husband."

There were no guarantees in life, but Jewel knew she could count on lightning striking again in the form of her attacker. The question was—would he succeed in killing her the next time?

A car door slammed outside, and she glanced out the window to see Buck driving away.

There was no time to lose. Jewel went down into the kitchen. She had things to do. Questions to ask.

As soon as they spotted her, Tracy, Katy and Meral suddenly stopped talking, and each tried to hide a guilt-ridden expression, as though they'd been talking about Jewel.

Tracy stepped forward, concern in her gaze. "Jewel, how are you doing?"

Jewel waved away her concerns. "I'm sick of sitting around. Resting is overrated."

She smiled, trying to persuade them she was much improved. Given that her purple bruises had turned to a sickly green, she wasn't surprised that her appearance didn't convince them.

"Where's Buck?" she asked as casually as she could, grabbing an apple, but out of nowhere it sounded strange. She'd seen him leave and wanted to make sure he wouldn't be back for some time.

Meral's eyes widened. "I don't know. He went exploring, looking for a creek to fish in, I think."

If Buck wasn't here, then now was a good time to ask the questions burning inside. "Meral, I can't tell you how happy it's made me that you've come here to see me, to find me. I hate all the years that have been wasted."

Meral slid into the chair at the kitchen table. "We don't have to think about that. We have each other now."

With so much riding on the answers to her questions, Jewel could only offer a tenuous smile. "Meral... I... I need to know."

Her sister reached over and grabbed Jewel's hand. "What do you need, Jewel? Anything. I'll tell you anything."

Jewel's throat grew tight, her mouth suddenly dry. Her sister loved her, and the suspicions running through Jewel filled her with shame.

"Why, after all these years, did you decide to find me? To come and see me? Why now?"

Her sister's mouth dropped open. Then, "I don't understand what you're asking."

Jewel could see that she had approached her need to find answers in the wrong way. She was messing this up. Her fear was seeping through, affecting how she came across. She sat in a chair across from Meral, trying to dial down the tension.

"What's this all about?" Katy squeezed Meral's shoulder and gave Jewel a gentle but questioning look.

Honestly, Jewel wished she could have some privacy with her sister, but she never found herself alone with

Meral after the attacks. And if the other women were gone, Buck was around and wouldn't let Meral out of his sight. Jewel had no choice but to forge ahead.

"Did you ever think about coming to see me over the years? Ever think about finding me? A phone call? An email or a letter?" Jewel regretted the accusing tone.

Meral pursed her lips, wounded surprise in her gaze. "I could ask you the same."

"Of course I did. But I was hurt, so hurt. I don't think I even realized it until you showed up at my door, and you weren't even to blame. I got caught up in living life in Alaska and loving my husband and—" Jewel hung her head, regret clinging to her heart "—and trying to forget I even had a family."

Jewel lifted her gaze to meet her sister's beautiful eyes. "I'm so sorry now, for everything."

"I thought we decided to put the past away, Jewel, and move forward. You need to quit beating yourself up. I forgive you, and I hope you forgive me for not trying harder to stay in touch. But when I was young, I idolized you. Looked up to you. Then you decided to leave us all behind for Silas. I thought you didn't love me or care about me. It's taken me years to get over that, but like you, I got busy with college and then fell in love and got married the first time. I tried not to think about the sister I'd loved and lost. The sister who had hurt me."

"Was it your idea, Meral?" Jewel finally asked. "Was it your idea to come and see me now?"

Meral put her elbows on the table and pressed her face into her hands. "I don't understand why it matters whose idea it was. Buck knew that I missed you. He knew our family's history. He found you for me. But I wanted to come. Like you, I didn't realize how much

I'd missed you or I couldn't admit it, until Buck surprised me with this trip as a wedding present. I can't think of a better gift. Or a better husband. I hope you're not hurt that I didn't initiate the trip. I hope all that matters is that we've found each other. Let's never let anything come between us again." Meral reached for Jewel's hand.

Or anyone, Jewel wanted to say, but she knew that was impossible.

"I'm not hurt." Jewel hung her head, knowing she'd caused her sister pain. Fearing she might lose her when she'd only just found her if she pressed further. She couldn't bring herself to risk their tentative truce by asking Meral if she'd known what Jewel had taken all those years ago, and if she'd told Buck. Not now, and definitely not with Tracy and Katy looking on.

"I'm going to take a long hot bath." Jewel stood, feeling as though the stiffness and aches had returned with a vengeance. "Just letting you know in case you knock on my door and I don't answer."

Jewel left her friends and her sister and climbed the stairs to her room. Coming here had been Buck's idea. Not the answer she'd wanted to hear. But an answer that could bring her closer to the truth about who had attacked her.

SIX

She ran the bath water, poured in bubble bath and let it rise. Shut off the water and left the bathroom, shutting the door behind her. She would take that bath.

Later.

Now she crept up another flight of stairs and then climbed the ladder into the attic. This time she'd brought a flashlight to chase away the shadows that remained after she turned on the light. At least the dormer window offered a little more illumination. She glanced at every dark corner of the place, positioned a board over the entrance so she'd hear anyone who might try to come inside, though she was certain her attacker couldn't be in the house this time.

Jewel crept all the way back, stepping around boxes and trunks and memories. Once she was on the other side of this trouble—if she came out of it alive, that was—she needed to spend time organizing the attic. Switch out decor downstairs again. Carefully, Jewel stepped so she didn't make too much noise and worry Tracy, Katy and Meral all over again.

She swiped away the dust along the wall looking for that plank. Could it have been so long ago that she couldn't remember exactly where she'd hidden it away? It should be here, yet the plank wouldn't budge.

Propping the flashlight just right, Jewel used both fingers, sliding her fingernails between the boards. She dug her fingertips into the crack as leverage and tried to work the plank loose until she finally felt the slightest shift in the board.

Pain stung her finger. Jewel snatched her hand back. A sliver had caught under the skin. She spotted a nail on the floor and picked it up. Poking it into the crack, she twisted and angled it, working it back and forth until the board shifted enough so she could grab it.

There.

She tugged and twisted the plank that fought back. It didn't seem to want to give up its resting place after twenty-some years. That, she understood. She had been comfortable, too, letting her secret stay hidden. That was until Meral and Buck had shown up. Now she had to look back in order to move forward.

Finally, she removed the cranky old board entirely.

And there inside the hole in the wall rested the box.

Emotion punched her stomach so hard she gasped. She hadn't considered the effect this would have on her. Tears spilled down her cheeks. Long pent-up anguish, regret and pain poured out of her. She had never allowed herself to give up the grief, to cry over her mistake, to truly put it behind her. Until now, she had never regretted her decision. She hadn't allowed herself the luxury.

Now, twenty years later, she realized her mistake. She'd been young and impressionable and reckless when she'd left her wealthy family behind for love. Left her dreams and career pursuits behind.

But she'd met Silas Caraway, and it seemed as though

all the plans she'd made were nothing compared to loving him. She'd known that Silas wasn't the kind of man her family expected her to marry. Her parents had had big plans for her in terms of carrying on the Simmons family name and legacy in Simmons Diamonds.

Jewel had been warned that once she left, she wouldn't be allowed to come back. She wouldn't see a dime from the estate and wouldn't be assisted if needed. Shocked by the pronouncement, she'd been terrified of the risks her future held, yet she hadn't been able to turn her back on love. So Jewel had stolen a valuable family heirloom when she'd left, keeping it tucked away in hiding as a safety net.

Just in case.

What if things hadn't worked out with Silas in Alaska?

She'd been willing to give up her lavish lifestyle for love. Believed what she had with her husband was strong. But it never hurt to have a backup plan. Except she'd never told her husband that she'd kept anything belonging to her family. After what they'd put her through, it would have seemed to him as though she hadn't trusted him enough. He would have seen her need to have a backup plan as proof that she'd expected their marriage to fail.

How that would have hurt him. She hadn't wanted him to ever know. Therefore she couldn't keep the diamond in a safe-deposit box in the bank of a small town, because he would have found out eventually. She'd found an adequate hiding place in the big old house.

She tugged out the box, her heart pulsing erratically.

After wrapping her fingers around it, she opened the box and stared at the Krizan Diamond, a glisten-

ing yellow stone cut from one of the Golconda diamonds—an ancient mine in India. The diamond had
been handed down through the generations in Jewel's
mother's family.

How it still shimmered a vivid yellow, the color in-
creasing the value of the 20.25-carat stone.

Though only one of many such family diamonds,
how silly of her to take it. Had someone reported it
stolen? Was insurance filed on it? Doubtful she could
have ever sold it without everyone knowing the truth of
her crime unless she dipped her fingers into the black
market somehow and found a collector. Odd the things
people did when they were young.

Today, she never would have done such a thing. But
she was older and wiser.

This had to be why someone wanted to kill her. It
was valuable enough to be a powerful temptation to
someone greedy and ruthless. But who knew she'd taken
it? Who knew she had it? She suspected her mother had
known she took the diamond, but Jewel couldn't see her
mother telling anyone, not when it might get Jewel into
trouble. Jewel had always imagined that when she'd
seen her mother peeking out the window as Jewel had
left with Silas, she'd seen the glimmer of approval in
her eyes; had chosen to believe that her mother would
have wanted her to have this security.

But maybe she had fooled herself. How could she
have been so naive to hope that no one else in the family would realize she'd taken it?

Did her sister know?

Doubts filled her about the man Meral loved and
had married. Had Meral told Buck about the diamond?

Her hands trembled.

But then it hit her afresh. She still possessed the Krizan Diamond—a stone worth millions—and all it represented to her were fear and guilt. The diamond's value, the danger she likely had brought on herself by possessing it, struck her like a bolt from the sky and singed her skin. She dropped it, letting it fall into the box.

She placed the rudimentary container back into its hiding place.

Jewel pushed the plank into place and quietly shoved boxes in front of the wall. If someone were searching in here, it would be easy enough to discover where she had disturbed the dust. She'd need to clean the entire attic to cover her tracks. But what was she thinking?

It was too late. Her attacker had already found her in the attic—already knew that that was where to look to uncover her secrets.

A noise disturbed her thoughts—the board over the entrance to the attic. Panic sent Jewel's pulse racing. She grabbed the flashlight and ran to the entrance. Best to take the offensive move while she had the high ground.

"Don't move," she said.

"Or what?" Chief Winters stared up at her. "You're going to hit me with a flashlight?"

"Chief Winters."

She dropped the flashlight, her only weapon. She should have brought the Glock. Clearly, she wasn't ready for any serious self-defense. He was probably disappointed in his student. She started down, but Chief Winters stepped up and Jewel inched back as he climbed the ladder until he was standing in the attic with her.

"What a surprise that I should find you in the attic again."

She hadn't wanted to answer questions about the first

time she'd come, and she'd managed to evade him—
but there would be no escaping him now. Of course, he
would have to stand much too close.

Jewel's pulse hadn't slowed since she'd heard the
noise. What was he doing standing so near? His proximity made her tremble.

She sucked in a calming breath. She should take a
step back, but she couldn't move. Instead, she hung her
head, feeling like a teenager when she was anything
but. Something about this man sent her heart racing
and tumbling around inside. He lifted her chin with
his finger.

What was he doing?

She wanted to tell him what a romantic cliché his action was, but then she'd be admitting that the moment
felt like something out of a romance novel, because she
was attracted to him. And she couldn't admit that to
him or to herself. She would never risk her heart again.
Even if she were willing, her family heirloom stood between them.

She was a thief.

He was the law.

A beam of sunlight streaked through the dirty window, illuminating the dust motes dancing around them.

"What are you doing up here again? And by yourself?" His sharp blue eyes turned dark.

What should she tell him? She couldn't share what
she'd done with anyone, especially him. Not yet. "Chief
Winters." His name came out in a desperate tone.

His gaze softened. "Jewel, don't you think it's about
time you call me Colin? I can see you calling me by my
title when we're around others, out of respect, but we're
alone now. We've been friends long enough, haven't

we?" He finally dropped his hand. "There's no need to be so official with me all the time."

Her heart rate jumped higher. Jewel had thought he would press her for answers. His suggestion was the last thing she'd expected.

His voice was so gentle, so endearing, Jewel could almost forget he was here on official business. That was *why* he was here, wasn't it? A knot twisted in her throat. Calling him by his official title, thinking about him only as the police chief, helped her to protect herself, to keep her resolve to never fall again. If she could fall for anyone, it would be this man.

But would it be so bad to call him by his name? "Colin… I…"

"There." He grinned. "Was that so hard?"

Her heart tilted. She opened her mouth to speak—

A woman's scream broke through the attic.

Jed Turner, the officer Colin had stationed at the B and B today, was facedown in the woods near the house. Colin knelt by Jed and checked for a pulse, though he already knew what he would find. The man was dead.

Still kneeling by the fallen officer, Colin's gut churned as he searched the woods that grew thicker in the distance. The murderer was long gone.

Colin's heart was a chunk of lead in his chest. Jed was in his late fifties, only a few years away from retiring. He had a wife, Clara, plus two grown kids and three grandchildren. Though Jed's troubles were over, Colin would now have to face his wife and give her the news, a task he didn't relish. The absolute worst part of his job.

What had happened to draw his officer into the

woods after Colin had instructed him, after Colin's own arrival, to leave?

Colin thought about Buck Cambridge. From the moment they'd met, something about Buck had made Colin think of a venomous, wild creature that would bite if pressured.

Had that feral creature—a human in this instance—been pressured to bite? Killing a police officer would only up the stakes and bring on a full-out manhunt. Obviously, Jed must have seen something incriminating, discovered something to identify Jewel's attacker.

Colin glanced behind him at the others who had gathered, waiting at the edge of the woods. Jewel hugged herself, her face twisted in anguish. Next to her Katy and Tracy, Meral and Buck, hovered and comforted each other over this new development.

Colin stood, wanting to search the woods, but he wouldn't leave them alone. He hiked back to his vehicle and called for backup and for the retrieval of Jed's body.

Jewel approached him. "I'm so sorry, Colin."

He couldn't begin to convey in words the anger, grief and guilt roiling inside. Add to that hearing his name on her lips again, and he realized he must have been nuts to ask her to say it. It made him all kinds of crazy, and he knew better.

He *knew* better.

Katelyn's death, her murder, had happened because Colin had been emotionally involved. That should be enough warning for him. He pulled his gaze from Jewel's torn features. If he looked at her any longer, he'd pull her right into his arms. Not to comfort her but to comfort himself, something he didn't deserve in the face of Jed's death.

"For what, Jewel? This wasn't your fault."

"Yes, it is. Someone is trying to kill me. To get to me. And now Jed Turner is dead because he was protecting me."

His radio squawked and Colin answered, detailing the events to Terry Stratford, who was headed this way. There'd been a skirmish in town, but Terry had settled it. Skirmishes were preferred over murder.

Colin glanced at Buck Cambridge, who held a crying Meral against him. The man had checked out when Colin had looked into his background. Was clean. No priors. He was a simple businessman. An import-export consultant. Those were the facts, and Colin could only use those, but his gut told him there was more to the man. Something dangerous, sinister.

He allowed his gaze to fall on Jewel again as she comforted Katy and Tracy. He needed to convince Jewel to leave Mountain Cove for a while, until he could get this taken care of. She wasn't safe here. Her friends and family—namely Meral—had promised to stay close. Everyone wanted to protect her, yet he'd found her alone in the attic. Alone. *Again.*

And now no one was in the house. Colin would have to check every nook and cranny before he let anyone back inside.

What if Colin hadn't been here? Hadn't been up in the attic with Jewel?

He slipped his hand around her arm, drew her away from the others and kept his voice low. "You need to leave, Jewel. You can't stay here anymore." Colin wasn't sure he trusted himself to protect her anymore either. He was failing at his job, after all.

Again...

He didn't want to think about the past, but the images drifted through him like shadows all the same.

"This is my business. My livelihood. I can't leave. There are guests to take care of. And Meral's here. You don't have any idea how much that means to me. I can't just leave."

With Jed's death it was clear there could be collateral damage—that others around Jewel were in harm's way. Didn't she see that? But where could she go that was safe? He'd tried to create a safe house at her B and B.

Her striking hazel-green eyes were usually so transparent, filled with warmth and care and honesty, but that was all shuttered away from him now. He didn't like it. Jewel was purposely hiding something from him. Disappointment in her, in the situation, nearly overshadowed Jed's death.

But in her gaze he saw something else. What he never expected to see. Never wanted to see. Jewel was disillusioned with his abilities. She wanted him to do his job and catch this guy, felt let down that he hadn't done so already. He saw in her eyes the lack of trust and faith that he'd seen in the mayor's eyes, in the city-council members.

Colin released her arm. Pulled the knife from his heart that Jewel hadn't even known she'd stabbed into him and twisted.

He was getting too emotionally involved, more so than would do either of them any good. How did he protect her? Colin wished now that she would call him Chief Winters again, for both their sakes. He needed to ask the hard question, and his emotions stood in the way of that, too, but Jewel would die, others would die—as someone already had—if he didn't ask.

"When I came to you in the hospital, I asked you if you knew who had pushed you into the waterfall. At the time, I thought maybe you were a random victim. Simply at the wrong place at the wrong time. But now I think we both know that's not the case, and I'm going to ask you again, do you have any idea who would want to kill you? And if not who, then *why* someone would want to kill you?"

Jewel hesitated as though considering his questions.

Cruisers pulled into the B and B drive along with the ambulance that would take Jed's body. Given the murder of a police officer, Colin would be calling in the Alaska State Troopers on this investigation. Meral and Buck approached Jewel, apparently wanting to protect family. Either that or interfere with his investigation. Colin was running out of time to get answers.

"Someone died today, Jewel. If you know something that you're not telling me, I need you to tell me now so I can stop this before someone else dies. Before they come for you again. I'll put two officers on the house and on you this time, but we'll be better prepared, better able to face an attack if we know what we're looking for. I need more information if I'm going to catch this guy."

Finding the murderer would be the best way to end this.

"Is everything okay?" Meral put her hand on Jewel's shoulder and squeezed. Buck hovered just behind.

Jewel nodded, pressing a hand over her sister's. To Colin she said, "I don't know who's after me."

He frowned. He'd thought Jewel was about to tell him something before her sister approached. Did she understand she was putting others' lives at risk and prolonging the risk to herself? He gave her a hard look.

"If you think of anything, you know where to reach me."

SEVEN

Jewel watched out the front window, grateful the ambulance and the last police cruiser had finally left. Well, that wasn't entirely true. An unmarked police car was parked outside, two officers dressed in plain clothes now walked the grounds and stayed in the extra rooms in the B and B—the rooms vacated by guests due to the murder.

Other officers still searched the woods near the house, looking for clues to find a killer.

All the police activity was sure to ruin her business, but she cared about Jed's family more than her business. He'd lost his life because of her. Would one of her guests be next? Should she set it all out for them this evening as each of them returned from their outings so they knew the risks?

She pushed down the anxiety swirling inside. How had it come to this?

It would be so much easier if she knew who was trying to kill her instead of just having suspicions that she hoped and prayed weren't true. Suspicions she was holding at bay against all reason. If she knew for certain, then she wouldn't be so torn about telling Colin everything. It felt strange to think of him as Colin now instead of Chief Winters. But it also felt natural, and that particular wall she'd erected as a safety net was already broken down. In fact, when he'd assigned his officers to stay and watch the house, Jewel had been disappointed—she had wanted Colin to stay.

Being near him was dangerous. She should be relieved he'd left, but the relief didn't resolve her disappointment that he'd chosen to assign guard duty to his officers.

Jewel sighed. She was losing her mind.

After Colin had checked the house to ensure her safety, he'd nodded at her just before he'd walked out the door. His demeanor had told her that he was also disappointed in her. Maybe even angry with her. She'd never seen that look in his eyes—he knew she was holding back, purposely hiding information.

A man had been killed because of Jewel, and she wanted to keep her secret?

Despite Colin's frustration with her, he hadn't pressured her to give more than she'd been willing.

Her heart shifted, inched toward him. How could it not?

She wanted to shove aside her fears, confess what she'd done in the past and tell him her suspicions. Tell him what someone could be after. But Meral and Buck had been right there when he'd asked, and then Meral had promised to stay with her at all times.

Behind Jewel, her sister sat on the sofa and chatted on the phone. Jewel had no idea where Buck had sauntered off to now. She hoped he wasn't in the attic searching for the diamond.

She dropped the curtain and plopped on the sofa.

Though absorbed in her phone call to a friend in Baltimore, Meral glanced at Jewel, her brows drawing together. Jewel didn't want to concern Meral with her anguish, so once again she turned her attention to the window.

Guilt chewed at her insides, making her forget about her stitches and bruises. For years she'd been dishing out advice and words of wisdom to friends and even to guests when they confided in her. Jewel had always thought that was her one gift, but now when it came to her own life, wisdom escaped her. Everything was twisted into a ball that she had no idea how to untangle. What right did she have to give advice when she harbored such a secret?

Maybe she was trying too hard to figure it out on her own so she could protect herself. There was only one thread for her to pull. One thing to do, and then let things unravel as they would.

I have to talk to him. Tell him everything.

Jewel made her decision. She stood from the sofa and tried to get Meral's attention, but Meral lifted a finger for Jewel to wait. Instead, Jewel went to her room and changed. She rummaged through her dresser for makeup, which she hardly ever wore except on special occasions like Christmas. This wasn't a special occasion, but her reflection was gaunt and, frankly, terrified her. What was it doing to others? Making them think she was weaker than she was? Vulnerable? Well, Jewel was strong, and she was ready to make a stand.

Ready to end this once and for all.

A knock came at her door. "It's Meral."

"Come in."

Her sister stepped inside. "What are you doing? Where are you going?"

"I need to go to town and talk to Colin… Chief Winters."

Her sister's frown turned into a soft smile. "You like him, don't you?"

Meral's words surprised Jewel. Her sister hadn't been here long enough to know that, had she? "What makes you say that?"

"I have eyes. Besides, he likes you, too, Jewel."

Jewel didn't say anything to Meral's comment. Just worked to cover her haggard appearance with concealer. Spiffed up her bobbed hair that was more difficult to deal with than when it had been long. Funny, she'd cut it to make life simpler. Maybe Meral thought she was trying to look good for the chief of police. Jewel paused. Was she?

Well, Jewel was about to put an end to that once and for all. Once he knew the truth, Colin—Chief Winters—couldn't like her anymore. She would drive a much-needed wedge between them with her words. But she feared she would also drive a wedge between her and Meral, losing two people she cared about deeply in one fell swoop.

"You can't go alone, you know. I'm happy to ride along."

Jewel sighed. She'd never felt more smothered. "I need some air." Some space.

She was going through the motions, hoping she'd get up the nerve to actually go through with telling Colin about her past and her suspicions. She could be way off base and sharing a secret she didn't want anyone to know. Implicating a man who might be innocent. Meral

would be devastated and would leave, then Jewel would
never see her again.

Jewel put her brush in the drawer and eyed her sister
in the mirror. For all Jewel knew, Meral was also after
the diamond. Had their parents threatened to disinherit
her for marrying Buck, cutting her off completely, just
as they had Jewel for marrying Silas? Jewel frowned
and averted her gaze.

"What's wrong, Jewel?" Meral asked.

She shook away her misgivings. "Nothing."

"Let me tell Buck where we're going and that I'm
riding with you."

No! No, don't...

But she couldn't stop Meral. Couldn't tell her the
reasons for her uncertainty.

Nor should Jewel be afraid of her own sister, yet
her hands trembled. She stood tall and tried to project
confidence into her words. "We'll just okay it with the
officers first, but I'm sure it will be fine. I'm heading
into town to the police station to talk to Chief Winters.
How could they object to that?"

Maybe on the way Jewel could somehow bring up
the topic and ask Meral what she knew about the diamond. Yes. This was a good thing, after all. Jewel would
finally be alone with Meral without anyone around to
hear them.

"Let me freshen up and grab my purse," Meral said.
"I'll let Buck know. He's taking a nap. All this excitement has been draining to both of us, as I'm sure it has
been to you."

That was an understatement.

"I'll meet you downstairs," Jewel waited until Meral

was gone, then slipped the Glock out of the drawer in her nightstand and into her bag.

Her efforts at self-defense hadn't worked that well. She couldn't count on those skills. Still, she hoped she wouldn't be forced to use the gun. Silas had taught her about using weapons, and she was a decent marksman. Living on the edge of the wilderness, she needed to know how to use a gun in case a wild animal accosted her or a guest. But Jewel hadn't wanted to use such a deadly weapon to protect herself from another human being, hence the self-defense classes.

At any rate, now she would be doubly armed, if she counted her meager self-defense skills. Wouldn't it be nice to face off with her attacker, Jed's killer, and end this once and for all?

She could almost pray she would see the man again today. Almost.

As it turned out, arming herself didn't matter. Officer Roberts wouldn't let her drive into town without him. She would go crazy if this didn't end soon. Because he was driving Jewel, Meral decided to stay behind after Buck asked her to. Not that Jewel could have had her conversation in the same vehicle with Officer Roberts.

Jewel got into her old Dodge Durango, and Officer Roberts rode in the passenger seat, leaving the unmarked vehicle behind for the officer remaining at the house. As she steered along the bumpy drive on her property to the road back to town, Jewel's palms grew moist. She felt uncomfortable, as though Officer Roberts was watching her every move, scrutinizing her for some mistake. But it had been days since she'd gotten the concussion. She was fine now.

Except that she was nervous under Officer Roberts's gaze as though she were guilty of some crime.

Well...

Maybe the officer was still unhappy that she had insisted on going. When she had first told him that she wanted to drive to the station, he had demanded that she tell him what she wanted to say to Chief Winters, and then he would relay the information.

Jewel had had to stand her ground and remind him that she wasn't a prisoner in her home, and she was going to town with or without him. He was a younger officer. Nice and friendly. But she had given him a choice. He could go along or not, but she would only speak to Colin. Chief Colin Winters was the only person she could trust with her secret, though she knew he would be more than conflicted with the news. If it helped them solve the murder of an officer, to catch the killer before he struck again, then Jewel had to reveal her past.

I can do this.

Have to be strong. Stronger than I've ever been.

It surprised her just how hard this was going to be.

"You seem very tense, Mrs. Caraway, if you don't mind me saying so."

"It's Jewel, please. Everyone calls me Jewel."

"Yeah, even the chief, I noticed."

"We've known each other a long time." Jewel noted that Officer Roberts didn't ask her to call him by his first name, which was Matt. She stifled a chuckle. He'd want to keep himself official, especially when he was working, which she understood.

"Well, Jewel, you seem nervous to me. Are you sure

you don't want me to drive? You can pull over, and I'll drive and you can relax."

"You promised you wouldn't give me a ticket if I messed up." She forced a laugh. "I just need to drive, to feel like I'm free. To do something with my hands."

"I understand." Officer Roberts stiffened next to her. His hand fisted around the handgrip on the door.

She picked up speed as she drove a lonely stretch of road with a great view of the mountains and the glistening blue waters of the channel, as well as the town of Mountain Cove, in the distance. This scenic drive into town was one of the reasons Silas had bought the property. Jewel let herself smile, if only for a moment.

"How's your family doing?" she asked, wanting to keep Office Roberts talking. She knew his parents had moved to Mountain Cove from Juneau when he was in his early teens and now he was a police officer. They had to be proud. Maybe a normal conversation would relax him *and* her.

"Watch out!" Officer Roberts yelled, then grabbed the steering wheel.

At the same moment, Jewel saw the grill of a big-wheeled black Suburban heading straight for them from the woods across the road. She punched the gas pedal to move them out of the way at the same time Officer Roberts yanked the wheel to the right.

The Suburban slammed into them.

Behind her, metal crunched and twisted.

She could have been killed instantly had Officer Roberts not reacted. But it wasn't over yet. The Suburban kept pushing, tires grinding and squealing as the Durango slid dangerously toward the edge of the drop-off.

She couldn't get out, and before Officer Roberts could open his own door, the Durango rolled onto the passenger side. Jewel's body jerked to the right, and she hung there, her seat belt keeping her in place. The vehicle tilted, hesitated.

Jewel screamed.

Officer Roberts yelled, "Hold on!"

The momentum rolled them over again. Now they hung upside down as the Durango tilted and rolled again.

And again.

In slow, wavering revolutions.

Each roll had Jewel squeezing her eyes, gasping for breath as she prayed for their lives.

The cab of the Durango shrank, the ceiling punching in as the weight of the vehicle slammed against hard ground and rock with each turn.

Finally, the Durango stopped with a jolt after crushing against a tree on the passenger side and jarring every bone in her body with the impact. She could only be grateful they had stopped rolling.

Am I still alive?

Her heart beat wildly against her rib cage. Definitely, she was alive, but for how much longer? She felt the ache across her chest from the seat belt for what would surely become another bruise.

She released a half sigh, half cry, then looked at Officer Roberts. "Are you okay? We have to get out of here."

But he didn't respond.

Oh, no. God, please, no. They'd hit a tree, which could have been deadly. She thought of the boy he had been. The parents who had raised him.

Bracing herself, Jewel released her seat belt and

grabbed his arm. He didn't appear to be injured, but it could have been internal. He could simply be unconscious and would wake up with nothing more than a concussion. Jewel wished, hoped and prayed it so.

Pebbles and dirt trickled down from above. The telltale sounds of someone coming, scrambling down, echoed.

Oh, no!

She shook the police officer. "He's coming," she whispered. "We have to get out of here."

But it was no use. Officer Roberts didn't wake up.

She searched for her purse, where she'd stuck the Glock, but it was out of sight and reach, crushed somewhere in the twisted vehicle. Officer Roberts was dressed in regular clothes. She hadn't seen where he kept his weapon. Didn't see it now, or any communication device. She'd search him if she had to, but she'd prefer if he woke up.

She and Officer Roberts both had been fortunate to survive the initial impact and subsequent rolls, but how could they stay that way? If they couldn't get out of this vehicle and away from the man who'd run them off the road, they both would die.

Then he stirred.

"We have to get out of here," she whispered. "He's coming."

Officer Roberts groaned. "Who? Who's coming?"

The man who pushed me into the falls. The man who attacked me in the attic. The man who killed Jed.

"The man driving the Suburban just now. Don't you remember? He pushed us over the edge. He's coming to finish the job! Please, Officer Roberts… Matt…we have to get out."

Finally, he opened his eyes, though he squinted in pain and looked at her. Fear ripped across his features, then he stiffened, coming to himself, projecting himself as an officer of the law. He moved in the seat or tried to. Then his head fell back and he shut his eyes.

"What's wrong? Where are you hurt?"

He glanced down and tried to pull his legs up. "My leg is… I think it's broken…" His words trailed off as pain contorted his voice.

Then he opened his eyes again and peered at her. "Go."

"No. I won't leave you."

He pushed her. "You have to get out of here. I'm not going anywhere. But I can call for help. I have a weapon, so I can protect myself, but I can't protect you. You're in the line of fire, and you need to hide."

"Give me your gun and I'll be the one to protect us both."

He shook his head, his face scrunching with the effort. "No. This could be your only chance to get away. You have to climb out and hide in the woods until help comes. Do as I say before it's too late."

Jewel pressed her foot against the console for leverage and scrambled over the wheel. She tried to shove open the door, but it wouldn't budge. "How do I get out of here? I can't open the door."

"Climb out the dash window." He barely lifted his leg—the good one—and kicked the cracked window out. "Here, you take the Taser. This is a new toy for the department, and I don't much like it anyway."

Jewel wrapped her hands around it. Uncertainty about leaving him behind slowed her exit.

He nodded. "I'll be okay. I'll call for help while you

hide. Do not let yourself be caught, and only use the Taser as a last resort. Now go."

Tears pooled in Jewel's eyes. She hesitated.

"We'll both die for nothing if you don't get out of here," he said.

What did he mean? He wasn't expecting to die, was he? Looking at his face, she realized that that was exactly what he expected. And then Jewel knew she had to draw whoever was coming away from Officer Roberts. She didn't want to leave him, but, if anything, she could save him by drawing the attacker away from him.

Jewel climbed out, careful to avoid glass from the windshield. Clinging to the twisted hood of the now-destroyed Durango that she'd had for years, she listened. Nothing. She heard nothing. But she sensed someone watching. Goose bumps rose on her skin.

Was she in his rifle's sights? Is that how he would kill her now?

Her only chance was to climb down from where the vehicle rested against the tree, practically hanging there as the ground dropped away. She studied the terrain. The road above her twisted and curved around a towering mountain that swept into a thick, old-growth forest with eight-hundred-year-old trees. Just beyond, only a few yards from her vehicle, was a granite cliff that dropped into a misty fjord.

If not for the tree, Jewel and Officer Roberts would have gone over. Is that what the killer had intended? Jewel had to hurry. But she worried if she jumped from the Durango she'd slide the rest of the way over the cliff.

Sensing that she had run out of time, Jewel sent up a quick prayer and leaped for her life.

EIGHT

Heart pounding, Jewel hit the ground. Her feet dug into the mossy earth, but they slid out from under her as her momentum pushed her toward the cliff's edge. Dropping the Taser, she grabbed the thick ferns, fingers stripping away fronds. Still she slid. She sank her fingers into the ground, nails gouging the earthy loam.

"Come on!"

She rolled to her back to see her doom. Pebbles and rock and sticks dug into her back as she watched the approaching cliff. She was slowing down, but not enough to save her.

A huge cedar grew off to the side of her path. It could stop her momentum. Just like the tree that had stopped the Durango. Just like the fallen trunk that had grabbed her from the river.

That was her only hope. Jewel stretched and reached, could feel her stitches tearing apart, ripping skin. A scream tore from her mouth as pain sliced through her, but her arms caught the tree and she dug in, held tight as the bark grated across her arms.

Jewel scrambled her legs up the side of the trunk and under her, craving the protection of the tree that had kept her from falling to her death. If only she could stay there.

Pressing her face into bark, drawing in the scent of cedar, she almost wept. But she knew she had no time to catch her breath or gather her composure. Jewel crouched and watched the area near the Durango, searching for the man after her, but she saw no one. She scrambled forward on her knees until the ground leveled out enough that she could stand and took off running to the south toward town. Away from the cliff and the Durango. She could only hope that her absence from the Durango would draw the attacker after her and away from Officer Roberts, but at the same time she didn't want to be found.

With her injuries, fighting the dense undergrowth was no easy task, but the thick copse of spruce, cedar and hemlock would help her hide.

This was the beauty that had drawn her to Alaska. This was the beauty that would keep her here and safe. She had to live another day to enjoy it. From tree to tree, around ferns and over mossy logs Jewel pressed as hard and as fast as the terrain would allow her.

When she could run no more, she hid behind the trunk of a spruce as wide as a dining table. She leaned against the tree and slid to the base, resting for only a moment. Though she knew the tree could hide her from sight, her desperate pants for oxygen were too loud and would give her away.

God, please don't let him hear me. Please don't let him find me. And please protect Officer Roberts.

Jewel didn't doubt God listened to prayers and answered them, but she wondered if maybe the mistakes she'd made and the secret she carried that had cost a life already and might cost more before this was over, kept Him from listening. Or kept the prayer from reaching Him. She didn't have the answers, but she couldn't lose hope.

Jewel sucked in oxygen, breathed in the earthy scent of the ancient forest until finally her heart rate slowed. She was still alive for the moment.

She listened. Whoever was after her didn't seem to be running—she couldn't hear any footsteps. Had he even followed?

Finally, Jewel stood. Her body hurt, but she had to keep moving. Pressing her hands into her thighs, she bent over her knees, stretching her back.

Was it Buck who had done this? She had suspected he was behind her attacks. But he was back at the house with Meral, wasn't he? This new development messed with her suspicions, and the whole reason she'd been going to town to talk to Chief Winters.

Footfalls crunched on needles.

Jewel turned and pressed her body against the tree, leaned just enough to see beyond the trunk and not expose herself. She saw no one. But still she heard him coming.

She pushed from the trunk and crept deeper into the woods. Fighting the greenery, especially since she tried to move quickly, made too much noise. If only she hadn't dropped her weapon.

How had it all gone so wrong so fast?

She could ask questions later, but first she had to survive. All she had to do was stay alive until help arrived. Had Officer Roberts been able to call for help? Was he still alive?

Her stitches hurt and her body ached afresh as though

she'd come crawling from the river just this morning. She'd already tried using self-defense tactics against her attacker, but she was in pain and the man was much stronger. That didn't lend her much confidence to try again, and instead, terror gripped her.

She dropped next to another tree, catching her breath.

"Who are you? What do you want from me?" Jewel yelled, and her voice cracked with a cry from deep inside she hadn't expected. She sounded desperate and afraid—which she was, and now he knew it. She had revealed too much, proven that he had her just where he wanted her. The sound of her voice echoed through the forest, sounding eerie and like something from some twisted horror movie.

And Jewel was crumbling.

A cry broke from her throat. What was she doing except leading him right to her? Her questions didn't matter. He could hear her movement, could see where she'd been. Could have caught up with her by now if he'd wanted. Why was he torturing her?

Exhaustion and pain ate away at her resolve. She wanted to drop to the ground and wait for him to find her. After all, it was inevitable, wasn't it? Why not wait here and hang on to what energy she had left to fight?

Jewel reached deep down inside.

Get.

Up.

And run.

Hide.

She knew the area—probably better than her attacker did. Knew the woods and could use that to her advantage somehow.

She skirted the rocky outcropping and kept going.

She had to make it back to the road up farther, closer to town, where her chances of running into someone and getting help would be greater. That would mean miles of running and hiking, but Jewel had spent the past two decades hiking in the woods. Participating in many of the outdoor activities her guests enjoyed, sometimes serving as a guide. She could likely outlast her pursuer.

That was if she wasn't already injured.

As she continued on, pain lashed at torn stitches and her chest ached with every deep breath while doubts clawed at her. She came upon a hiking trail, which would make it easier for her. While she had the chance, she had to put as much distance as possible between her and the man after her. Once he found the trail, he could easily catch her.

Jewel found that even on the trail she couldn't move as fast as she'd hoped. She limped along, tried to keep from breathing so hard, but it was impossible. Her heart pounded too fast from exertion. From terror. And it all drained her energy much too quickly.

All her plans to make it to the road, to use her knowledge of the area, wouldn't work if she couldn't move, but her legs felt as if they were stuck in concrete that was quickly drying.

Pulling from what little reserve remained, Jewel limped harder and faster, pushing around the curve in the trail that led deeper into the dark canopy.

She slammed into something.

A body.

A man.

Heart palpitating, Jewel flailed away, fear stabbing through her.

He gripped her arms. Jewel screamed and fought

back. Moments ago, she'd felt as if her energy was gone, but in this moment adrenaline fueled her self-defense techniques. She stunned her attacker. And freed herself from the man's grip.

Surprised, she pushed away from him, but tripped and fell on the trail. She scrambled to her feet to run, fight-or-flight hormones surging through her.

"Jewel!"

Her brain caught up with her body, cleared away the panic and confusion.

Chief Winters.

Colin.

She turned to see his approach. Then she collapsed against him.

His arms held her tight, held her up. His words comforted her, calmed her racing heart. She was safe. How many times had she dreamed of being in his arms? Having them around her to comfort her? And how many times had she scolded herself for those forbidden thoughts? But this wasn't the same thing. She could allow herself this. And for that, she was glad.

Gathering her composure, Jewel leaned away, though he still held her. "It's not safe here. He's coming."

"Who, Jewel? Who is coming?"

"The man who has been trying to kill me. Officer Roberts—"

"Is fine. A crew is pulling him out of the vehicle even now." Pain flashed in his eyes. "I'm glad you were able to escape. I wasn't sure—"

"What are you doing here?"

Colin's broad shoulders straightened. "Looking for you. I thought it would be quicker to head you off at this trail. I figured you would come this way because you know the area."

"But what about…the man after me?" Jewel had almost said Buck, but she had too many doubts about that. Especially now. He was with Meral, and the Suburban wasn't his.

"Two officers are searching the woods, following the direction Officer Roberts thought you'd taken." He pulled her closer. "Jewel."

The way he said her name sent warmth flooding through her being. This wasn't how police officers acted with those they were sworn to help. No. Jewel recognized it for what it was.

That forbidden attraction they'd skirted for years. That Jewel had tried to ignore. With her energy focused on staying alive and solving this, the barriers protecting her heart were quickly crumbling. Her attraction to him—which went far beyond the physical—was taking hold.

Her heart pounded harder, almost making her believe she could take the risk with him. A longing she'd forgotten threatened to pull her over and under. She squeezed her eyes shut, savoring the moment—a moment she'd never dreamed would happen. A moment she couldn't allow to continue.

It was wrong. All wrong.

She stepped from his arms and immediately missed the strength and comfort of his embrace. A chill moved in fast. But she couldn't risk the pain that she knew would follow eventually. Inevitably.

It was a matter of survival.

Colin lifted his hand to cup her cheek, but the warning look in her gaze stopped him. Conflicting emotions filled her eyes—regret and longing—and those emotions nearly did him in.

He cleared his throat and attempted to put his head and heart straight again. Should he apologize for wanting to comfort her? For wanting to be close?

He hadn't expected his own reaction. Hadn't expected to lose control when she'd fallen into his arms, needing safety and comfort. Jewel was strong and self-sufficient and, even in this desperate crisis, he hadn't expected her need to surface like this. Or maybe he had.

Maybe he wanted her to need him.

Enough with pretense, already. He wanted to hold and comfort Jewel Caraway. And so much more. He always had. But he couldn't. From now on he should muster more control. Try harder.

Because right now he hadn't shored up his heart and mind enough. That much was clear. Already his heart was tripping and tumbling inside because she'd been attacked.

"I'm just glad I found you. Are you all right, all things considered?"

"I need to see Doc again, but I'm mostly fine. And I'm glad you found me, too." She covered her eyes for a moment, then dropped her hands. "It's not safe. He could still be out there."

"Did you see him this time?"

She shook her head and searched the woods and trail, as did Colin. "No, I was too busy running, but I heard the footfalls. I even called out to him and asked what he wanted."

Colin held his weapon, prepared to use it and end this once and for all. He almost wished the man would show himself. But with his officers combing the woods from the opposite direction, it was likely the attacker had taken off.

He used his radio to call his men. A vehicle matching the description of the black monster Suburban used in the attack had been stolen yesterday. As soon as Colin had heard the truck's description, he had known it belonged to Jim Humphrey. Good man. Made his living as a commercial fisherman. He also knew that Jim was in the hospital fighting an infection.

So far there was no sign of the truck. Colin's officers had found nothing but tracks. He could work with tracks. There were only two ways on and off this side of the mountain, and neither involved four wheels.

Colin reached for Jewel's hand. "Come on. Let me get you out of here." He paused and studied her. "Are you okay to walk?"

She nodded.

After everything she'd been through, he wasn't so sure. He gently urged her ahead of him as he watched the woods surrounding them. They had no way of knowing if her pursuer was working with someone or working alone. Better to take no chances.

If Jewel had someone like a bodyguard to stick with her all the time, maybe this would already be resolved.

But he couldn't be certain of that since an officer had been killed and another injured while watching over her. A lot of collateral damage considering the target was one smallish middle-aged blonde woman—beautiful and strong though she was.

At the trailhead, Cobie and Adam Warren stood next to the minivan they'd purchased for the arrival of their baby. They looked ready for a hike. Colin smiled to himself. Seemed like they had plans for a bigger family. That thought stabbed him just a little. Reminded him of the big hole in his life.

Adam was wrestling a hiking pack out of the back of the van while Cobie held her baby. Colin tried to remember the baby girl's name but fell short. Was she three months old now? Time flew so fast.

When Cobie saw them, she glanced at the weapon in Colin's hand. A look of alarm flashed across her face. She tugged on Adam's sleeve. He turned and saw Colin and Jewel. For a second he froze, then dropped the pack. "Hey, Chief Winters, Jewel." His gaze jumped from Colin to Jewel. "What's going on? You run across a bear or something?"

Colin didn't want to start a panic. Nor did he want to see others hurt. "Not a bear. Two-legged creatures can be more dangerous at times. These woods aren't safe right now. Jewel was attacked and, though I think he's long gone, her attacker could still be out there."

Cobie gasped. "Oh, Jewel. Are you okay?"

"I'm fine."

But Cobie's expression said she didn't believe Jewel.

Adam's brows drew together as he directed his words to his wife. "Get in the car."

His tone was authoritative, driven by his fear and a man's need to protect his family. Cobie nodded her agreement and got into the backseat with the baby. As Cobie busied herself with putting the baby in the car seat, Adam focused on Jewel.

"Grandma Katy told me you had a scare. Got pushed into the falls. And she told me about Jed. I'm sorry about that. About all of it. I'm sorry this is happening to you, Jewel."

What did one say to that? An image of Jed's wife,

Clara, flashed in Colin's mind. That's where he'd been—talking to Jed's widow—when he'd been told about the accident involving Officer Roberts and Jewel. He'd had to rush out and leave Clara with the news.

"Thank you, I guess." She flashed a weak grin and sagged against Colin.

She was in more pain than he had thought. He wanted to kick himself.

To Colin, Adam said, "I didn't realize that it wouldn't be safe out here. You've got your hands full with this investigation, huh, Chief Winters? Is there anything I can do?"

"Just keep your family safe. All of them."

"Do you know who is behind the attacks?"

"Not with any certainty."

Jewel stiffened against him, then eased back and looked him in the eyes. What was she thinking? Was she any closer to telling him what she knew?

"We'll get out of your way, then. I'll make sure the rest of the clan knows," Adam said.

The baby started crying, and Cobie glanced over her shoulder at her husband, urgent concern carved in her features.

"I wonder if it's safe for Grandma Katy to be helping at the B and B," Cobie said.

Adam shifted as though he regretted his wife's words. They could be taken wrong, sounding accusatory toward Jewel. But on the other hand, Colin wasn't sure anyone was safe anywhere near Jewel until her attacker was caught.

Colin didn't want to have that conversation in front of her, though. He scraped a hand around his jaw. "Can we talk later?"

Jewel pulled away from him and headed to Colin's Jeep, which was also parked at the trailhead.

"Does Jewel need another place to stay?" Adam asked. "I mean to throw this person off her trail? You know Grandma Katy is more than happy to have her stay at the house."

Katy Warren had already brought that up to Colin, and he had shut her down.

"You don't need to talk around me like I'm not even here," Jewel called from the Jeep. "In answer to your question, Adam, thank you, but I don't want anyone else hurt. Staying at Katy's wouldn't be any safer for me and would be more dangerous for her."

Exactly.

Adam's face paled. Did he regret making the offer? Jewel wouldn't be the first person to find a safe haven at Katy's place, but it was somehow different this time. Jewel had been brutally attacked three times now, and an officer murdered near the B and B.

No. Going to Katy's wasn't the answer.

Gunfire resounded in the woods behind them. Inside the minivan, the baby's cries grew loud and piercing. Adam dashed around to the driver's side, but then hesitated. "Are you sure there's nothing I can do to help?"

"You get your family out of here."

Adam nodded and climbed into the vehicle. Seconds later, he backed out, then drove off down the road toward Mountain Cove while Colin joined Jewel at his Jeep. He assisted her into the seat, though she tried to resist. Despite her pride, she was exhausted. His chest hurt thinking of what she'd been through. How could he keep her safe? What could he do to comfort her now?

Frowning, Colin jogged around and climbed into the

driver's side. It was then that his radio squawked. One of his officers had been struck in the head with a thick branch, but he got a shot off in self-defense. He thought he hit her, but she kept running.

"Her?" The radio at his lips, Colin jerked his gaze to Jewel, whose eyes were wide.

"Yes, chief. It was a woman."

"Keep searching." He ended the call, but his eyes never left Jewel's. "I thought you said it was a man who attacked you."

Her beautiful but tired eyes shimmered. "Whoever attacked me in the attic was a man, yes. He was much bigger and stronger than me, if that's an adequate measure. I was pressed against his chest while he was choking me, and he was solid. Nothing feminine about him."

Colin took it all in and then got on the radio again with further instructions for his men. He needed more police in the woods to wrap this up before things escalated. He'd already put a call in to the Alaska State Troopers because of Jed's death, but it would take them time to get involved and up to speed, and things were moving fast. He didn't like any of this.

He turned on the ignition and spun the Jeep out of the trailhead. Idling next to the road, he hung on the steering wheel and looked out at the mountain and the deep greens of an old-growth forest that hid a murdering fugitive.

"I've mentioned this to you before," he said. "But I think you should consider getting out of town, just for a while, until we catch this person. I don't think there's such a thing as a safe house in Mountain Cove. Is there some place *away* from Mountain Cove that you could go? Family, friends you could visit?" Colin felt like a real heel saying the words, given what David had told him about her family. Unless Silas had a cousin or someone Colin didn't know about, the only family she had that she could turn to, lean on when times were hard, was here with her at the B and B. And, of course, her Mountain Cove friends were like family to her. But he couldn't stand the thought of another person he knew and cared about deeply getting hurt.

Especially Jewel. He didn't think she could take much more. One more incident could break her.

"If I thought for one minute that leaving Mountain Cove would end this, I would do it." Her worried gaze searched the dark woods around them.

Colin shifted in the seat and watched the woods, too. A misty fog had begun to creep through the forest, making it look ethereal and turning the woods more dangerous. He was glad he'd found Jewel when he had.

Come on. Come on out and face me, whoever you are. The both of you. At least now they knew there were two involved in the attacks against Jewel. In Jed's murder.

He needed to be out there tracking these people with his men. He hated to send them into a dangerous situation, to the front lines, when he wasn't leading the way, wasn't sharing the danger with them. He'd lost one officer and almost another one to Jewel's attackers. He feared that one by one he might lose them all.

Someone was outsmarting them. Someone was two steps ahead.

"What are you keeping from me, Jewel?"

"Nothing. I thought I knew something that could help, but I don't."

"Why don't you let me decide if it's important? That's part of my job. Help me to do my job better."

He wanted to press, to argue with her, but when she turned her eyes on him, he knew he wouldn't get another word out of her. What she was hiding was a mystery that he would have to discover on his own. What could be so important to her? He had to push down his frustration in order to be patient with the woman next to him.

He brushed her soft, ash-blond hair back, and her eyes slipped closed. What was he doing? Not very professional of him, but he couldn't seem to break away, get free from the undercurrent between them. All these years he'd kept his distance, but now he was being swept away in a river that was all woman with hazel-green eyes and a deep inner beauty he found impossible to resist. The current that was Jewel held on to him, dragging him under. How did he escape without drowning in her?

NINE

Jewel rested in the passenger seat as Colin drove her to the hospital clinic in Mountain Cove to have her injuries checked. Again. For the moment she believed she was safe, but that didn't halt her thoughts of others who had been hurt, and killed, because of her.

She searched the woods around her. Would another vehicle shoot out from the shadows and ram Colin's Jeep? Would he be the injured one this time? Or worse? Would he get killed because of her?

Lord, what do I do? Help me to do the right thing!

Head pounding, it was hard to concentrate on his cell phone conversation. But she did her best.

A woman had been shot. A woman had driven Jim Humphrey's monster Suburban into Jewel's vehicle. A woman had hunted her down when the crash hadn't killed her. Nausea roiled. The police were looking for the woman, expecting her to need medical attention, hoping the bullet had been more serious than a graze.

Jewel didn't know what to make of it. She sank deeper into the seat, letting discouragement engulf her. She'd been suspicious of Buck, but not Meral. A pang shot through her heart. A deep, wrenching ache that overshadowed all other pains.

She struggled to ignore it, to cover it up, so Colin wouldn't see her anguish. He would see right through her, and he probably already saw that she was hiding something. What was wrong with her that she wasn't strong enough, wasn't selfless enough, to tell him about her past? So what if her image, everything she'd worked to build here, would be destroyed with the truth that she was a thief? What did her reputation matter in the light of this new revelation?

Please, God, please don't let Meral be involved.

She didn't believe it, and if there was another woman involved and not Meral, then Jewel's assailant couldn't be Buck. Or could Meral be involved, and Jewel was too naive, too blind, too unwilling to see the truth?

Jewel didn't know if she could handle yet another betrayal. And, yes, she'd felt her family had betrayed her by disowning her all those years ago. But they had believed Jewel was the betrayer, willing to leave them, to leave her inheritance behind for a man—someone without wealth and means. Someone who could never make her happy, they'd claimed.

She'd fallen for Silas because he'd filled a deep need in her that she couldn't explain. That she couldn't make her family understand.

Colin's Jeep hit a pothole and then a speed bump, tugging her from her thoughts. Jewel rallied herself as he turned his Jeep into the clinic parking lot and assisted her out, ushering her quickly into a private room, per his request.

The nurse, Doc Harland's wife, Shana, appeared, her mouth in a flat line. "I know my husband's going to be upset seeing you in here again like this." Her eyes flicked to Colin. "You mind leaving us some privacy, good sir?"

"Fine. I'll be right outside the door." He had that demeanor about him as though he would never leave her side, but she knew he had more responsibilities than watching over her.

"Can you tell us about Officer Roberts, Shana?" she asked, believing Colin wanted to know the answer, too.

Shana's grim expression lifted a little. "He's going to be just fine. His leg is broken. Got a concussion."

Again, Shana stared at Colin. "Doc'll be in soon, Chief. We need that privacy now."

"Right outside the door, Jewel." He pinned Jewel with his gaze that told her he hadn't forgotten she was hiding something, and then he stepped into the hallway, leaving the door open. Across the hall, he leaned against the wall where he could still see Jewel and crossed his arms.

Shana closed the door on him, then turned her attention back to Jewel. "I see you pulled your stitches, hon. Doc's not going to be happy about that, I can tell you right now."

Jewel sat on the examination table and let Shana jabber on while she took Jewel's blood pressure. "Your BP's a little high, too, but that's understandable given the circumstances. You stay right here, and Doc will be in with you in a moment."

She left Jewel alone. Jewel closed her eyes. Quiet. That was all she needed. A moment alone. Jewel thought about Colin's words. Maybe he was right. She would have to leave Mountain Cove. Maybe even Alaska. But for how long? What if she left for good? She could sell the B and B and live off that money. She'd had a few offers over the years. And somehow she had to figure out how to rid herself of the diamond—the very reason someone was trying to kill her. Or was it? With these new developments, she wasn't so sure anymore.

Doc Harland entered the room much too soon. Jewel wasn't up to his friendly conversation. She smiled and nodded the best she could, but she probably reacted more like a zombie to him. She hoped he understood.

When he examined her gash, she winced and let out a soft cry. Then he restitched it in places. "Sorry, if I hurt you. You sure don't need anything more to add to your pain."

When he was done, he went to the small sink and washed his hands.

"Despite your pain and torn sutures, I'd say you're healing up nicely. But it looks like you have some new bruises from the seat belt that likely saved your life."

Jewel could only nod. She had no energy for speech. No words of wisdom for anyone, especially herself.

The good doctor dropped his stethoscope and stared at Jewel until she focused on him. He had her attention now like he wanted. "Seems to me what hurts the most is in here." He pointed at her head. "And here." And then to her heart. "And I'm very sorry, but I don't have a salve for that."

Jewel appreciated that he paid attention and saw through her physical pain to what was going on inside. "Even if you had medicine, it wouldn't work until this is over, if it ever could work." *And if it ever ends.* Especially if Meral was involved.

Jewel was beginning to doubt it would end until she was dead.

His left brow arched. "I'm sure you're right. My only advice to you is to stick close to the Lord. I know you're a praying woman, Jewel. This is a trying time for you, but never doubt God loves you. Easy enough to see that He sent you a protector. So you only need to stay close to that man standing out in the hallway who cares deeply for you. But by the looks of things, he isn't going to give you much choice. The good news is that he'll protect you and maybe offer the healing touch to your heart that you need, as well."

The look in Doc Harland's eyes and the deeper meaning behind his words warmed her cheeks. At that moment, Jewel knew that a fortyish widow could blush as easily as a young twentysomething. But she didn't want anyone to get the wrong idea.

"There's nothing between us." The words rushed out.

Doc nodded, his expression reflecting that he didn't believe her. When he was done, he opened the door. "She's all yours, Chief."

Colin stepped into the room. He hadn't left even to check on Officer Roberts? He squeezed Doc's arm. "Thank you for taking care of my officer, Doc. I can't lose another person to this. And thanks for looking after Jewel, paying her special attention."

"Jewel is a special woman, and don't you forget it." Doc Harland winked at Jewel. "Matt Roberts will be fine. His family's here. They'll get him back to you as good as new."

Colin smiled as the doctor left, then he shut the door behind him before pinning her with those stark blue eyes that didn't miss a detail. That could practically read her mind. She tried her best to shutter away her pain. And her secret.

"I don't want to keep you," she said. "I know you have a job to do."

"You mean protecting Mountain Cove?"

"That's the job, yes."

"I can guarantee you that everyone wants Mountain Cove police to find the person who killed Jed Turner. To stop this person before someone else gets hurt or killed. This case is my priority. Nothing is more important to me."

"And I'm...in the center of that."

"You're the target, yes. You're my priority."

Of course this would be his priority. But there was something else, some anguish winding through his gaze that told her this was personal. She averted her own. She didn't want that from him.

That's a lie...

Jewel had never been good at lying to herself. Okay, so maybe she would admit that she did want that from him, but what difference did it make? Wanting and having were two different things. She'd have to work harder to keep her distance from him. That was all. Yet the pain in his eyes reflected back to her and made her realize that she could hardly stand to hurt him any more than she wanted to risk her own heart.

He had read well enough she was hiding something, and that had hurt him.

Hurt him.

Oh, Colin, if you knew the truth...

She wanted to tell him everything. Her doubts and fears, but she'd already decided that telling him she'd stolen something years ago, even if it was from her family during a crisis, would dim the light she saw in his eyes.

As an officer of the law, he would think less of her. How could he not?

And Jewel couldn't stand the thought of that. Since Buck didn't seem to be her attacker, that meant the attacks had nothing to do with the stolen diamond, so she wasn't hurting anyone by keeping her secret.

She remembered when Colin had found her today. She'd fallen against him in relief. Gone right into his arms, to an emotional place she'd never been before with him. She thought back to years gone by and realized that he'd been there for her so many times—just in the background, just on the edge, but he'd been there watching over her all the same.

"I'm taking you to the B and B now, but you should know, as long as you insist on staying there, I'm going to be there to watch over you myself. I'll switch out with my officers and take the night watch. Nothing is more important than catching these guys and keeping you safe."

"That would be like working two jobs. You can't be my personal bodyguard and run the police department."

"You might be surprised at what I'm capable of."

Meral came rushing into the exam room followed by Buck. "Oh, Jewel, are you okay?"

Surprise and relief whooshed through Jewel as Meral hugged her, careful to avoid her back where the stitches had been repaired. Holding her sister, Jewel tried to determine if Meral had suffered an injury, even a graze from a bullet. The officer hadn't been certain his shot had found a target, so Jewel couldn't be certain about anything either.

Still, Jewel desperately wanted to believe that Meral could not be the woman in the monster Suburban who had rammed her vehicle off the road. Who had hunted for her in the woods to kill her. Behind her, Buck appeared concerned for Jewel's well-being, as well.

In her peripheral vision, Jewel saw Colin stand back and study them. Scrutinize them as though he suspected them. Why? What reason could he have? He didn't know Jewel's secret. Then again, as chief of police, he was probably suspicious of everyone.

Meral released Jewel and brushed away her hair, like any loving sister. Not like a woman who had only appeared in her life to search for a small fortune or to stab her sister in the back. How could Jewel have ever suspected Meral?

Shame threatened to undo her, but she buried it. Fought to rise above all that pulled her down.

"Jewel, listen, Buck has come up with a great idea." Meral looked at Colin. "I'm glad you're here, too, Chief Winters. I think this could solve all your problems."

Colin stiffened. Dropped his arms to his side.

"We're chartering a boat to explore southeast Alaska. The Inside Passage."

Jewel's stomach lurched. "But…you're leaving already? How would that solve any problems? I don't want you to go yet."

A grin slipped on to Meral's lips. "You're coming with us."

"But I have a business to run and can't abandon my guests."

"You can't stay in that house either. It's dangerous for your guests, too. Wouldn't you agree, Chief Winters?" Meral directed her question to Colin.

His lips pursed. "I can't argue with that."

Jewel wasn't sure that leaving would make her any

safer. But it might draw out her attacker and bring things to an end. It would mean she wasn't just waiting around for another attack. That she was being proactive.

She pursed her lips.

"Don't worry, Jewel. You can leave," Meral continued. "I spent this afternoon talking to your employees, Jan and Frances, and to Tracy and Katy. You've thoroughly trained them to pitch in as needed. I think you can take a few days off, a week or even two, for your own vacation. That would get you away from this insanity. Nothing can happen to you on a boat with just your family."

Meral stepped away from Jewel and into Buck's arms. "Besides, we've already chartered the boat. We leave in two days."

Jewel pushed her face into her hands. She couldn't take all the eyes on her. Couldn't take the pressure of having to make such a hasty decision in the face of everything that was happening. But Meral was right. She couldn't keep her B and B open if she stayed there. She couldn't expect the Mountain Cove police officers to continue putting themselves in harm's way to protect her either.

And she had the feeling that Meral would go with or without her. Jewel couldn't let her time with Meral slip away so fast. Colin had suggested she leave, get out of town, and this could be the answer. She could also keep an eye on Buck for Meral's sake. She still had the feeling Buck was using Meral.

As if she could protect Meral, given she'd done such a great job protecting herself.

Why hadn't Meral seen through Buck before she'd married him? But then, maybe that was how Jewel's parents had felt when Jewel had chosen Silas. Except they had been wrong about him.

Could she be wrong about Buck?

She looked up. Everyone was still waiting. "I need to think about it."

"You have a day. We'll need time to get you ready for the trip. But I really don't see you have a choice," Meral said.

Jewel locked eyes with Colin. Why wasn't he saying anything? But he'd already told her to go. Maybe that was enough.

It would mean she couldn't stick close to the man who wanted to protect her, like Doc Harland said. Doc seemed to believe God had put Colin in her life to protect her, but what happened now if she left that protection behind in search of a safe place?

Colin sat in the chair across the antique mahogany desk from Mayor Judy Conroy. A driven woman in her early fifties, she liked to dress the part of a politician. Had a stylish hairdo and ordered her suits from some fancy place out of Seattle. No matter the weather, she would always wear matching pumps. And she liked to control and intimidate.

But she hadn't called him into her office today. No. He'd come here of his own volition, needing to detail his plans and ask permission, something he never liked to do. Especially since he could see in her eyes she had plans of her own—to berate Colin.

She sucked in a breath, opened her mouth and her cell buzzed on her desk. After a glance down she released that breath, then looked back at him. "Sorry, Chief. Gotta take this. It won't be but a second."

"No problem."

She was on the cell before he responded. He released a pent-up sigh and tried to calm himself. The call would give him a few seconds, hopefully minutes, to regain his nerve. He tapped his fingers on her desk while he waited for her to end the phone call.

Where did he start? How did he present his case?

She jabbered on with her niece, Taney Westmore, while Colin tried to ignore the conversation. He got up to pace the room. What he wanted to do was put his fist through the wall. He'd never been so frustrated.

He'd been the one to suggest that Jewel get out of town, and now he was incredibly bothered by the idea that she was taking his advice. He should have considered that if Jewel left town, Buck would be with her because Meral would be with her.

But Colin hadn't thought that through very well. "Idiot," he mumbled under his breath with a quick glance at the mayor. Wouldn't do for her to think he had just called her a name.

No, he needed her in a good mood. Problem was he had been the one to put her in a perpetually bad mood lately. Now add that one of his officers had been murdered and another one injured, and the mayor would likely tear into him before he got a word in edgewise.

The pressure was on and seemed to be measured by the pounding in his head.

Finally, he plopped in the chair again, afraid that if he kept pacing he would, in fact, put a fist through the wall in the mayor's office, and that wouldn't go over well. He noticed a Holy Bible sitting at the corner of her desk and took a minute to seek some guidance. Closing his eyes, he drew in a calming breath.

God, I could use a little help here. I'm in a serious predicament. Help me to do what needs to be done. Help me get Jed's killer before he kills again. Help me keep Jewel safe.

"Sleeping on the job?"

He opened his eyes to see that she had ended her call. "No, just saying a little prayer."

"That bad, huh?" Her brows drew together. "Sorry about the call, but I had to take it."

"No problem." He should ask if everything was all right with Taney, but that would send them down a road he didn't want to go right now.

She pressed her elbows on her desk and rested her chin in her clasped hands. "What can I do for you?"

Colin could see it in her eyes. That was a trick question—she was waiting for him to say something she could criticize. Everything he was about to say went against his personal policy, his resolve to act only on the cold hard facts. He pulled in a breath.

Here goes nothing or everything.

"I have a possible lead on Jed's murder and on who attacked Jewel Caraway."

"Is that so?"

"But I need to follow it up."

The mayor dropped her hands and pushed from the chair. Now she was the one pacing. Building up steam to blast him with, no doubt. "And by follow up you mean what?"

Colin scratched his chin. Explaining this wasn't going to be easy. "This all started when Jewel's sister and husband, Meral and Buck, arrived. I checked on him, but he came back clean. He's some sort of import and export consultant."

"What aren't you telling me, Colin?" Now the mayor had gone personal with his name. Never a good sign.

"I need to leave. Jewel, Meral and Buck are going on a short cruise, a tour of Alaska. A week or two. I need to be there with her to protect her and to find out if Buck is the man who killed Jed."

There. He'd spoken his mind.

"It would mean you wouldn't be here for Jed's funeral."

He nodded, hating the timing. "What's more important? Getting Jed's killer or attending his funeral?"

"What reason have you got to suspect Buck? Give me something, anything, and I'll think about it."

"A feeling."

Her eyes blazed. *Here it comes.*

"Let me get this straight. You want to go off on what amounts to a vacation while we have a murderer out there based on a feeling?"

"No. It's not like that." He knew the man from somewhere, and though he couldn't remember the circumstances, Buck gave him a bad feeling. A very bad feeling.

"Oh, I think it is. You're infatuated with Jewel. Let me make myself perfectly clear, Chief Winters. You think that you're under pressure now? Let me assure you that I am under tremendous pressure as this town's mayor. People want to know why this is happening to our town. And what about Jed's family? How do you think they are going to see your actions? His wife, his kids and the town want to know why someone—a fine and upstanding officer of the law, no less—has been murdered. Not long ago others were murdered. Businesses burned down. People were scared to come out of their houses or even go to the dentist because maybe a bomb would blow up while they were sitting in the chair. You took far too long to solve those cases, and this one is still open, with a killer still free. So, no, I can't let you go on a trip with your precious Jewel based on nothing more than a feeling."

The mayor's face was red. Though he'd been the object of her complaints before, this was the worst dressing-down he'd ever gotten. He supposed he'd given her reason enough.

"You see, here's the thing." He stood to give himself the edge. "The reason I didn't solve those cases quicker is because I refused to listen to my gut. I refused to go on anything but the facts. But the hard truth of it is that solving an investigation takes a good measure of both gut feeling and facts. Not one or the other but both working together. I have to ask myself what kind of police chief doesn't listen to his gut instincts? A poor one. And I'm sorry that I didn't realize that sooner. Now, please, let me follow my instincts on this." He was so tired of second-guessing himself, and for the first time in a long time, he believed he was doing the right thing. Now if only he could convince the mayor.

She took a seat and sighed. "Give me something. You have to give me something solid, Chief. What are people going to say?"

As if he cared anymore. Colin detested politics, but there was no getting around them. "Even if I give you a reason, a solid lead or evidence, they're going to talk. They're going to spin this trip in a negative light."

"True." The mayor sagged in her seat and slowly shook her head. "I'm sorry. I can't let you go. You're going to have to figure out how to solve this case here in Mountain Cove while working in your capacity as chief of police, not gallivanting around the Inside Passage with the woman everyone knows you love."

Love? Colin narrowed his eyes. He was about to open his mouth to speak, but she beat him to it.

"I'm sorry, Colin. I shouldn't have said that. It's none of my business. If you want to protect her, then get this guy, but you'll have to do it while remaining in your jurisdiction and functioning in your full capacity as the Mountain Cove chief of police. If you need a presence there with Jewel, send one of your officers, but I can't let you go yourself."

There was that image of his fist slamming into the wall again. Wasn't she listening? The only way to get the bad guy was to go with Jewel. Nobody else could do this. It had to be Colin. He was the one with the gut feeling. He didn't dare risk another one of his men or send them into danger on instincts alone.

As for gathering evidence against Buck, he'd contacted a friend, the forensic artist from Juneau that Mountain Cove sometimes used, to take some years and pounds off Buck's photo to help Colin figure out why he recognized him. But it wasn't under the official umbrella of police business, so it might not come in time. He couldn't tell her about that—it might be a dead end.

I have no choice.

His next words pained him, weakened his legs, but he had to do it.

"Okay, then, maybe I care about Jewel more than I should, but this isn't about that. It comes down to the fact that I couldn't live with myself if something happened to her, especially when I know how to prevent it."

He'd already experienced losing someone he loved, but he wouldn't tell the mayor about that. He'd already said too much. He didn't need to explain himself, but maybe part of him hoped if he showed a little more of himself, she would be more understanding.

It all flooded back and swirled through his mind in a quick second before he could blink and formulate his next words.

He'd planned to propose, but Katelyn had been murdered and all because she had witnessed a crime. He hadn't been able to arrest the man without her testimony, and afterward the charges brought against the man for her murder had been dismissed because of shoddy DNA and the killer's airtight alibi. Colin had failed Katelyn miserably. That was why from then on he'd made sure he only worked off the facts. He'd made sure he wasn't emotionally involved with a woman he needed to protect.

But that couldn't be helped this time. And he wouldn't fail Jewel. He wouldn't let himself get any more involved with her either. He'd keep it professional. Wouldn't let his heart even dip a toe in the water, but he would protect her if it was the last thing he did.

Another problem drilled through the tension. He hadn't been invited to go with Jewel, but the boat left this afternoon and he had to move quickly. He'd already deliberated far too long about how to handle this. And now it came down to worst-case scenarios. Had he convinced the mayor? Or not?

Her eyes softened, but it wasn't enough. That much he could see. "Colin… I…" She blew out a breath, clearly unsettled by his words. "I'm sorry."

"You'll have my resignation letter on your desk by the end of the day."

TEN

The privately chartered yacht, *The Alabaster Sky*, waited at the dock for the passengers to board. From the outside, Jewel could already see the yacht was modern and luxurious, and she guessed between sixty and seventy feet long. Though it had only been chartered for the trip, it had to have cost a small fortune. A year's salary for some. She'd forgotten what real wealth could buy. When she'd offered to pay for her portion of the trip, Meral had reassured her it was all taken care of.

Next to her, Buck and Meral unloaded the rest of the luggage from the cab.

Jewel's palms slicked. Nausea swelled. Was she making a mistake?

Colin had told her to get out of town so she would be safe. So she could escape her attackers before they succeeded in killing her. But Colin had had no idea that she suspected Buck when he'd said the words. And even though it didn't seem possible that he was involved in the incident that totaled her vehicle and injured an officer, her suspicions had crept back in with a vengeance and she couldn't let go of them.

With the Krizan Diamond burning a hole in the bag

she shouldered much too protectively, she would find out sooner rather than later. She'd managed to sneak up to the attic again and pull the rock from its hiding place. She couldn't bring herself to leave it there to be stolen, if that's why her attacker had been in the attic— to search for the diamond.

She should have put it in a safe-deposit box, but she hadn't been able to break away from Meral and Buck. And to ask them to stop at the bank for her to take care of business would have been futile. They would have marched right in with her. Heard her say she wanted a safe-deposit box. Then the questions would have come. It was a small town, and others would see and talk.

She was trapped.

It was all so awkward.

And if Buck was after the diamond, he would know that Jewel suspected his motives. He might even hope that she would bring it with her to keep it safe or, out of desperation, to lure out her attacker. In that case, he might look for it on the boat.

But was she thinking clearly about this? It was hard to know with the attempts on her life holding her mind hostage and the likely reason weighing heavy in her pack.

She was some kind of crazy to attempt this.

Besides, if Buck really was involved, and he really was after the diamond, then putting it in a safe-deposit box in the bank like any normal person would virtually guarantee Jewel's death. Kill Jewel and the items in her safe-deposit box would go to Meral, who was named in Jewel's will after she'd lost Silas, a fact she'd shared with her sister shortly after her arrival in Mountain Cove. That had been her way to make sure the diamond went back to her family. Maybe that was why her attacker had tried to kill her. He thought it was stored safely away—whoever he was. A man and a woman working together.

Meral and Buck.

Her heart sank.

Jewel hung her head. *I don't know, I just don't know anymore.*

She didn't want to believe it of Meral. Yet doubt suffused her. This trip had been Buck's idea, just like coming to Mountain Cove.

Her pulse raced and jumped. Had agreeing to this been a wise decision?

What did it matter? If there was any chance that Meral was not involved, then Jewel had to be with Meral to spend time with her and protect her, if she could.

Meral set Jewel's bag next to her feet. "You okay?"

The question pulled Jewel back to the present. "Sure."

"You don't look okay." Meral eyed her.

Buck paid the cab driver.

"I'll be fine, Meral." Jewel gave her sister a quick hug.

Buck's dark eyes and fake smile landed on Jewel. "Let's go."

Jewel released her sister to Buck. Two men and a woman appeared on the yacht and came down the gangplank to greet them.

The older of the crew members thrust out his hand and shook Buck's in a hearty greeting, then turned his attention to Meral and Jewel. "Good afternoon, ladies. I'm captain of *The Alabaster Sky.* You can call me Mike or Captain Mike, whatever you prefer. This is Gary, our deckhand, and Stella, your hostess and steward. And Mack's the chef, but he's in the kitchen preparing your meal for this evening."

Private and chartered yachts and cruise ships were a familiar sight in southeast Alaska, and some even stopped in Mountain Cove. But Jewel had never met any of the staff that operated those vessels, so it was strange when a sense of recognition pricked her at Stella's smile. Gary had a familiar face, too, but maybe they each just had one of those faces that everyone thought they knew. Jewel was sure she'd never met either of them.

Buck grinned. He gave the captain's hand a second good, hard shake. "Captain Mike here is one of the best. Decades of experience and he knows all the sweet spots in the channels, full of isolated and undisturbed nature. This is going to be the adventure of a lifetime. I'm going fishing for the catch of my life."

With his last words, Buck's eyes locked with Jewel's.

"Let's get the adventure of a lifetime going," Stella said, smiling sweetly.

Jewel bent to lift her luggage.

"Oh, no, I'll get that," Stella said. "All part of the package."

The crew gathered up their bags and lugged everything up the gangplank. Jewel stared at the luxury cruiser yacht. Arm in arm, Meral and Buck followed the crew.

"Come on, Jewel!" Meral yelled over her shoulder.

Jewel's throat went dry.

What am I doing? Was she getting on this boat with a killer? Jewel felt like the absolute worst kind of traitor to think these awful thoughts. Meral was giddy with excitement and looked much younger than her years. Jewel should be happy for Meral.

Instead, she felt seasick and she hadn't even boarded the yacht. She was leaving her self-proclaimed protector behind. Yet, she wasn't truly alone.

God had been her refuge and would continue to be. And she had let Colin go, what small part of him she had held on to in her heart. She had no right to think about him or hang on to him when she simply wasn't willing to risk that much.

Tears threatened, burning her eyes and throat.

But she focused on the yacht in front of her and this new adventure, praying it wouldn't be deadly. A piece of her hoped this trip would force the truth—good or bad—to come out and she would at last be free from the threats on her life.

Finally, Jewel followed her sister and Buck onto the boat, where Stella, carrying Jewel's luggage, showed Jewel to her quarters. Jewel trailed her, containing her gasp at the spacious room, though she shouldn't have been surprised. Stella set Jewel's luggage next to the king-size bed covered in an elegant seashell spread in shades of teal.

Stella held out her hand. "Can I take your bag?"

Jewel tugged it closer. "Uh, no. I can unpack my things, thank you." She forced a smile and tried to relax.

Stella never lost her bright smile and went around the expansive stateroom explaining all the amenities like a well-practiced tour guide. The woman was in her mid to late twenties, slender and athletic, and a full head taller than Jewel. Her warm brown hair was secured in a ponytail and hidden beneath a white cap.

She stood at another door. "And in here, you'll find a full bath with a large shower."

"Thank you, Stella. I appreciate you showing me around."

She clasped her hands in front of her. "Will there be anything else?"

"No. I'll unpack my things and freshen up for dinner. When do we leave?"

"In half an hour or less, when everyone is settled in."

Once alone, Jewel paced the luxurious room, feeling completely out of place, though she'd grown up in an old-money family and shouldn't have felt uncomfortable. Had she been away from it all so long that she felt out of place here?

But one thing was certain. Meral hadn't been disinherited—at least not yet—if chartering a private yacht for a few days was nothing to her. Or maybe Buck, who could have his own money, had paid for it. Jewel didn't know a thing about him, and maybe that was what disturbed her the most.

But after the life Jewel had lived in Alaska, which consisted of hard work to earn a living and make ends meet, Jewel found this kind of wealth difficult to handle.

It didn't feel right. She didn't belong here. Jewel grabbed her bag. Forget her luggage. Easier to sneak off without it. Loathing herself for her indecision, loathing herself for doing this to Meral, she stepped into the hallway. Quietly, she shut the door behind her.

Then froze.

Buck stood at the other end of the hall in a wide stance.

He didn't smile or speak.

He just stood there and stared at her. She should

move or say something, but she felt the urge to turn and run. The skin on the back of her neck crawled, and she had the keen sense that Buck would react like a rabid dog at the prospect of a chase.

No. She couldn't run.

Meral stepped from a room and leaned against Buck, who hugged her to him, but his eyes were slow to pull from Jewel.

After planting a kiss on his lips, Meral laughed and pulled away, only now noticing Jewel. Her smile dropped. "Jewel, what's the matter? Why don't you get settled in your room?"

Oh, how did Jewel tell her sister there was no way she could stay? Her heart crashed against her ribcage.

Suddenly, Meral's eyes focused beyond Jewel's shoulder. Buck's eyes narrowed.

"I finally made it," a familiar voice spoke from behind. "Thought I was going to miss the boat."

Colin.

Jewel whipped around. Chief Colin Winters confidently strode toward her. Her heart bounced around at the sight of him. At the relief that he was here. He was dressed in a casual polo shirt and jeans and carried a duffel bag and jacket slung over his shoulder. He'd always looked good—authoritative and powerful—in his police attire. But now Colin was not the law. He was just a man and not just any man. A slow hum started in her stomach. She couldn't find the words to greet him.

"What are you doing here?" Buck asked.

Jewel almost opened her mouth to ask the same question, but without missing a beat, Colin answered, "Jewel invited me. Didn't she tell you?"

Buck laughed.

Meral gave him a jab. "Shush. Well, we're delighted to have you, Chief Winters."

"Colin. It's just Colin. I'm not on duty now."

A million questions ran through Jewel's mind. Like how had he swung this? Would Meral and Buck make him pay for the ride? Would that clean out the man's savings? But it didn't matter. Jewel wanted to run into his arms like Meral had done with Buck, but she and Colin weren't in that kind of relationship.

There was a question in his eyes.

Would she play along?

Yes. Yes, she would definitely play along. "I'm sorry, Meral. With everything going on, it must have slipped my mind. But remember, he promised not to leave my side until this was over."

Meral giggled. "Yes, but the whole purpose of the trip was to keep you safe. You don't need a protector here. Uh-huh. I'm on to you two. You can't fool me for a minute."

Jewel opened her mouth to correct Meral, but hesitated. She wasn't sure what to say to Meral's innuendos. Protesting that there was nothing between them would make things even more awkward. She had no idea how to act or respond.

Meral filled the silence with her exuberance. "But this will be so much fun!"

Could Meral be so incredibly clueless?

Stella appeared and showed Colin to his quarters down the hall. Jewel slipped back into her own room and let the bag slide to the floor. She was staying after all.

Now, where could she hide a diamond worth a fortune?

* * *

They traveled from Mountain Cove, heading north a short distance to stop and anchor for the night at an isolated cove off a nearby island. From there, they could watch for whales and sea lions. Maybe do some fishing. Buck claimed he was looking forward to catching halibut with Colin.

At dinner that evening they were served on the deck outside, under the stars. This time of year in southeast Alaska, the sunrise and sunset, as well as the weather, was more like that in the lower forty-eight.

A gorgeous night in a beautiful, secluded cove. Colin had to fight hard against relaxing into this dream vacation. It would be easy to imagine or pretend he was here with Jewel for personal reasons. That could be dangerous on too many levels, and if his hunch was right, cost their lives. That sober reminder kept him focused and on task.

Meral and Buck laughed, and the conversation was stimulating, but never veering too close to personal topics for any in the group, which was just as well. Colin didn't want to answer questions about his life before Mountain Cove. Interesting to think they each had secrets—pasts they weren't willing to share. Yet the conversation never ran out. Buck was intelligent and an eloquent conversationalist, knowledgeable on more subjects than most people Colin had met. Which would make him a great con artist.

Buck grinned at Meral, his gaze flicking to Jewel and back.

A memory flashed. Something at the edge of Colin's mind. Why couldn't he remember? He'd gone through photos of past investigations and had come up empty.

It would come to him, but would it come too late?

Jewel excused herself and left the table, promising to return in a minute or two.

While she was gone, Buck turned his attention on Colin.

"So tell me, Chief…er… Colin. How did you get away from town with a killer on the loose?" Buck asked. "I mean, Jewel's here with us and obviously safe, so why would they let you leave in the middle of an investigation? It's hard to imagine that the police chief would be assigned to bodyguard duty in these circumstances. Unless…oh, I know—" Buck snapped his fingers "—you assigned yourself."

Have a care now how you answer. How much should he reveal?

Meral put her hand on Buck's cheek and forced his face toward hers. "Now you leave him alone," she said, but Buck's gaze never left Colin's. It was clear the man had not been happy to see him. Didn't want him on the boat. Why not?

"The mayor trusts me to follow my instincts," Colin said. That should be answer enough.

And then a slight curve came to Buck's lips—that smirk again. A challenge?

A tingling sensation crawled over Colin. He knew that smirk. What good was he if he couldn't remember?

He'd been right to resign from his job and come, of that he had no doubt. When he'd walked into the hall and caught that feral look in Buck's eyes as the man had looked at Jewel, he'd known.

Maybe on this yacht Jewel would finally tell him what she hadn't been willing to share so far. But he had to keep his heart out of it and use his head at all times.

He thought back to the cell phone call he'd received from the mayor right before boarding the yacht.

"Chief Winters, I don't accept your resignation."

"Excuse me?"

"I know what I said in the heat of the moment, but despite our recent troubles, I don't believe we'll find a better man for the job. So I'm going to give you the time away you need. I'll hold down the fort while you're gone, so to speak. I'm not sure whether to tell the boys you're on a covert mission or that you've taken some time, but just do me one favor."

"What's that?"

"Get this guy, Colin. You return with our murderer, and that'll save me a lot of explaining."

Jewel returned, and they finished the rest of the dinner talking about the Alaska scenery.

Stella approached the table and removed their plates, then Meral and Buck excused themselves to go for a walk on the deck.

Colin was left alone with Jewel at the table. A candle burned in the center. While planning ahead for this adventure, he'd known he would be thrust into a romantic setting, and this certainly fit the bill. He just had to remember that it was set against a murderous backdrop. Still, no matter how he mentally prepared himself, he hadn't fully grasped how much being here with Jewel would impact him. Jewel, with her ash-blond hair and striking, lovely hazel-green eyes that shined with a soft inner light had Colin struggling to breathe.

Being here with her like this without reaching over and grabbing her hand, touching her face, reaching out to hold her, might be the most difficult thing Colin had ever done. Jewel was so beautiful. If they let their hearts have free rein, she could be all he wanted. He never doubted that.

But danger lurked on the yacht with them. Whether that danger had anything to do with Jewel's attacker remained to be seen. But he could feel it, sense it. Now that he let himself feel again and listen to his instincts, that danger reading was off the charts.

Focus, man. Focus.

He cleared his throat and tensed, forcing a harsh expression that felt completely wrong for the moment. "Now that we have a moment alone, I want to thank you for covering for me. I meant to…well… I meant to talk to you first and get myself an actual invitation."

"I guess I should have invited you. I didn't think it was appropriate. Or that you could leave your job."

Oh yeah. That. If she only knew.

"So why *did* you come?" In her eyes, he thought he saw that she was searching, wanting to know a deeper truth. One he couldn't admit.

"The reason you gave them. I'm not leaving your side until this is over."

"But how will you catch my attacker if you're on the boat with me?" An odd look washed over Jewel's face, and the moonlit sparkle in her eyes vanished.

"I thought getting away was the answer, but as soon as you made plans to leave, I realized that your attacker might follow you. I'm going to keep you safe just like I said."

She scoffed a laugh like she didn't believe him. Didn't trust his ability to protect her.

Or was it that she knew he didn't have all the information?

"What haven't you told me, Jewel?"

"I haven't told you thank you." She smiled. "I'm glad you're here."

Jewel stood and moved to the rail to look out over the waters of the Inside Passage. He followed her and leaned against the railing next to her.

The only thing to make the moment more perfect would be to see the aurora borealis.

Yeah. This was definitely the hardest thing he'd ever done. Beautiful woman at his side on an amazing Alaskan cruise, and his senses were heightened to her every breath, her every look, her every smile, her shimmering gaze. But not fifty feet from them stood a dangerous man. Colin didn't want Buck to be her attacker. But he also wanted to catch the person who'd tried to kill Jewel and had succeeded in killing Jed.

He watched Buck with Meral in the shadows at the bow. What a strangely precarious situation he was in now. Here to protect Jewel from a killer while he protected himself from Jewel.

God, You have a way of testing us, putting us through trials to make us stronger. But right now I feel weak. And maybe that's Your plan. But doesn't mean I have to like it.

And he didn't like this familiar feeling. Like he was right back where he had been before, trying and failing to protect a woman he cared deeply about from a man set on killing her.

And this time, they were all together like one happy family on the boat ride of their lives.

ELEVEN

The room was spacious, but Jewel still felt trapped. Jewel sat up in bed against a couple of pillows and held another wrapped in her arms as if it could protect her.

How was she supposed to get any rest on this opulent yacht in this crazy situation, which was both dangerous and awkward? It was as if she had jumped from the proverbial frying pan right into the fire. And not only where her life was concerned. When Colin had showed up just in time to fend off the strange vibes coming from Buck, her heart had been instantly in jeopardy.

More pressing was her physical being—her life. Every creak of the boat, every sound, had her on edge. She couldn't possibly close her eyes, much less sleep.

Colin was down the hall in his room, but he might as well be back in Mountain Cove for all the good his presence would do if she were attacked. She still ached from the previous attempts on her life.

Oh, God, what was I thinking to do this? Is Buck the man who attacked me or not? She couldn't decide. Her imagination was working overtime.

Except. An image projected across her mind.

The way Buck had stood there in the hallway, his

wide stance. Hadn't she seen that stance before—above the water on the ledge?

Jewel climbed from bed. Standing, expanding her lungs would help her catch her breath. But after several tries she realized she was hyperventilating. Breathing too hard and fast and getting too much oxygen. She'd never experienced this before. Her life had never been pushed so close to the edge. Though she didn't have a paper bag to breathe into, she could use her hands. She cupped her palms over her mouth to balance out the oxygen with carbon dioxide.

A sound from the hall drew her attention.

She stood still, listening.

Footfalls?

Her doorknob twisted quietly.

Though her door was locked, the fact someone wanted in still terrified her.

Lord, help me!

Jewel ran to the table next to the bed and grabbed the gun she'd brought on board with her bag. She wrapped her hand around the cool plastic of her 9-millimeter pistol, hoping it would reassure her. But any reassurance was lost with the thought that her attacker stood on the other side of the door.

Trying to get into her room.

But she must face him head-on this time. She hurried to the door that had no peephole. "Who's there?"

She might as well face him and get it over with.

"It's me." Colin's voice was soft.

What is he doing here? She cracked the door. "You scared me to death."

"You look like you're still alive to me."

"What are you doing?"

"I'm sorry to scare you. I was checking your door to make sure it was locked. Now get some sleep."

She swung the door a little wider and stuck out her head to look in the hallway. "I'm having some trouble with that."

"That's understandable after what you've been through. But I told you I was here to protect you, so that's what I'm doing. It's no different than me staying at your B and B, if you want to think of it that way." He cracked a half grin, then his gaze dropped. "I'm glad it's not your policy to shoot first and ask questions later. I'm glad, too, that you brought your own protection."

She lifted the Glock, trusting the feel of it in her hands. "Don't worry. I know how to use it. I can take care of myself." But she wasn't feeling secure. Wasn't feeling it at all. The thought of facing off with another human being and shooting him wasn't appealing in the least, even if it meant putting an end to her attacks.

Jewel opened her door wider. "Come in, so we don't wake the others."

He hesitated, something raw anchored in those starkly blue eyes, then shook his head. He wasn't coming into her room. He either didn't trust himself or he didn't trust her.

Her heart did a somersault. He was rugged and handsome and a protector all wrapped up in one way-too-appealing package. And he'd assigned himself as her personal bodyguard. Something inside told her he wouldn't be here if it wasn't much more than police business. If it wasn't personal to him.

"So what? Are you planning to stand guard outside my room all night, then?"

"If that's what it takes."

The disquiet in his eyes tugged at her heart. She reached out and pressed her hand against his cheek, feeling the stubble there. A current surged up her arm. Mistake. It had been a mistake to reach out, but she couldn't seem to pull her hand back. She was enjoying that slow hum in her belly entirely too much.

"I don't know how you can watch over me 24/7," she said. The hitch in her voice told more than she wanted to reveal. "You have to rest, too."

He stepped back, forcing Jewel to drop her hand. His move had been intentional, and she was grateful. What had she been thinking? She couldn't think at all when next to him anymore.

"No one camped outside my room at the B and B, and I'm safer here than I was there."

"That why you brought the gun? You believe you're safe now?" It was rhetorical. He was making a point. "Good night, Jewel."

"Good night." She closed the door and pressed her back against it.

He hadn't expected Jewel to answer, because he'd seen the truth in her eyes and in her actions. They were both dancing around that truth, because Jewel was unwilling to tell him. But now he had confirmation from her that he'd been right to come. He'd been right to listen to his gut if even Jewel thought she wasn't safe on this yacht with her sister and brother-in-law.

And he knew to be even more vigilant. He kept his door open. Sat in a chair and watched the hallway, his eyes on Jewel's door.

Come on, Buck, make a move. Make a move while I'm here so I can catch you and put you away. So I can

*stop the attack and prevent more. Make a move so we
can all get back to our lives. So I can get back to thinking about something besides Jewel Caraway.*

But nothing happened during the night. Buck made
no move to attack Jewel.

Colin joined the group for breakfast and downed
enough coffee to make an elephant jumpy. He thought
Buck had wanted to fish for halibut, but the yacht
cruised toward a new destination that only Buck
knew—a surprise, he'd said.

Doubts suffused Colin's thoughts. If he was the attacker, the killer, then Buck had successfully stayed two
steps ahead of Colin all this time. Jewel was right. Colin
couldn't maintain this pace. All he could do was bide
his time for Buck to make a mistake or for something
else to come through. Something like his memory finally clicking into gear and telling Colin why the other
man seemed so familiar. He knew the man from somewhere, and suddenly he'd showed up here and Jewel
was attacked, her life threatened. Colin didn't believe
in coincidence.

Jewel's attacker had a partner, a woman. As Colin
watched Meral chat with Jewel, he couldn't reconcile
that fact with what he saw and knew of Jewel's sister.
Meral couldn't be the woman who had rammed Jim
Humphrey's monster Suburban into Jewel's Durango.
So who could the accomplice be?

Stella refilled his coffee mug, poured more orange
juice for Meral and Jewel. The cool breeze picked up
and the tablecloth fluttered. Jewel's hair whipped across
her face. She tugged it back behind her ear, looking as
though she hadn't slept better than Colin, but she kept
up a good front for Meral's sake.

Captain Mike chatted with Buck at the rail, while Gary, the deckhand, manned the helm. Colin had seen Captain Mike come and go from Mountain Cove with his chartered cruises, and the certified Coast Guard Master and his crew were not suspects in Colin's mind.

His phone buzzed in his pocket. They must have been passing through limited cell-tower service. He tugged it out to see he had three texts. Two from David, who was just checking on them. The other from his friend and forensic artist, letting Colin know that he would start working on the sketch of Buck. The text had been sent last night.

Colin had asked him to take off fifteen or so years and remove the beard and wrinkles and extra weight, since most people thickened even in the face as they aged. He hadn't met the man while in Alaska, he didn't think, which meant he had to have run into him while in Texas. Taking those extra years off the sketch might trigger Colin's memory.

He jammed his cell back in his pocket, felt his gun under his jacket, though he made no attempt to hide it. Then realized the yacht had stopped. *The Alabaster Sky* anchored in the waters just off where the Bledsoe Glacier terminus met the water.

A loud crack resounded.

Meral jumped up. "Would you look at that?"

They all rushed to the rail.

"That's called calving," Gary told them. Apparently he was not only a deckhand but an ecologist, and could serve as their tour guide when possible. "When ice breaks from the terminus, the end of a glacier, and falls into the water. That's when it's called an iceberg."

They watched in silent awe as ice broke away and fell into the channel water.

After a few minutes, Buck put his hands on Meral's shoulders. "We've got all day to explore the glacier, ice caves and waterfalls. I hope that won't be too uncomfortable for you, Jewel."

"No, of course not. It's a cruise to explore Alaska. I expected as much."

Colin gauged Jewel's reaction to the news. She didn't appear troubled at thoughts of viewing a waterfall so recently after her fall, but he wondered if maybe she was quaking on the inside. She didn't look at him, avoiding making eye contact. Maybe he had his answer.

Was this all part of Buck's plan?

To lure them out into the wilderness and then act? What kind of policeman, what kind of person, was Colin to let him do it? Except Jewel had the right to make her own decisions, and Colin had no evidence to go on. Nothing he could use to accuse Buck and separate Jewel from her sister. All he could do was try to protect her, watch and wait.

He joined Jewel, Meral and Buck in gearing up to hike on the ice, though they'd wait to don crampons, if necessary, when they met with the official tour guide at the US Forest Service's Bledsoe Glacier Visitor Center.

Taking on his own tour guide role again, Gary explained about the region and the glacier before delivering them. Scratching his chin, he eyed them all, his gaze lingering on Jewel. "Glaciers and ice caves are part of the Alaska tour package, but you need to know up front the dangers. Glaciers are moving sheets of ice. They create the ice caves, and the very nature of that creation also makes them unstable. Translated—they're dangerous. Stay alert and follow the safety guidelines."

Gary prepared to take them to shore. Buck and Meral climbed down the short ladder to the skiff. Jewel positioned herself to follow Meral down.

Colin grabbed her arm, stopping her, and pulled her close. "Jewel, are you sure about this? This will be a strenuous activity. You still have stitches. Bruises. And the waterfall. Are you ready to see another one?"

She pressed her hand over his on her arm. "I'll be fine. Really. If I get tired I can stop and rest. Worst case, I'll whine about it and you can escort me back. But I don't want to let Meral down if I don't have to. I know you don't understand."

"How can I? You haven't told me much."

Jewel frowned and started down again, but Colin didn't let go. "Did you bring your Glock?"

"Why would I? I have you to protect me."

Colin released her to go to the boat and followed after her, his own weapon tucked within reach.

They met Preston Jenkins, the professional tour guide, at the center and geared up to hike across the glacier, wearing helmets, backpacks, crampons and carrying ice axes. Colin had lived in southeast Alaska for fifteen years, and he'd never actually hiked a glacier. His experience in this region usually involved getting in and out quickly in a helicopter when there was a need with search and rescue or recovery.

To his way of thinking, hiking a glacier was like walking on a different planet in a faraway galaxy. And he had absolutely no doubt that without Jenkins's skills, they would never have found the ice cave—there was no path that Colin could see.

But after four hours of the most difficult hiking he'd ever experienced, he knew he wouldn't have agreed to this if he'd realized the exertion required. Uneven steps, some places muddy and slippery, scrambling over rock and ice. Meral and Buck's tirelessness surprised him. He was more worried about Jewel with her injuries.

They approached the edge of the glacier on the far side and climbed down to dirt and boulders and pebbles. Jenkins announced that they'd reached the entrance to the cave and allowed them to catch their breaths. The glacier ice was gray and dirty and folded over into the ground, disappearing into an opening, a swirling hole that called them. Finding the cave had been like searching for hidden treasure, and even from the entrance, Colin could see on the inside it shimmered like a gem.

Jenkins led them on, and they followed single file into a whole new world—stunning and strange with cerulean and blue-green ice that had the appearance of glass-like transparent obsidian blooming above them. Colin stood in awe as he stared up at what looked like waves that billowed and rolled—the underside of a river that had been flash frozen.

He couldn't believe he'd lived near such beauty and had never before taken the time to see it. Rocks protruded from patches of ice where they walked. Colin stumbled but caught himself, which pulled his thoughts from the mesmerizing cave of ice and back to the dangers they faced—both from the environment and from the potential killer in their midst. Water trickled and dripped. The cave formed as the glacier melted. For the moment at least, Colin wasn't worried about Buck's intentions—he, too, stumbled around in the cave, head up, neck twisted, humbled by the sight if his reaction was anything like Colin's.

"Looks like chunks are splitting up there, ready to fall down on us. With all this water dripping, I'm going to be soaking wet." Buck hadn't been talking to anyone in particular, then he glanced at Colin. "Kind of creepy, isn't it?"

Colin nodded, but he wasn't thinking about the ice. The way Buck stared at him, grinning; he had a strange feeling the guy knew as much. What was his game? What was he up to?

"How much farther?" Buck called to Jenkins.

"It's a ways. Nothing you can't handle. We can go back at any time."

"What do you think, Meral?"

She glanced at Jewel, who nodded. "I'm good if you are. I've never seen anything like this. I'm not ready to leave yet."

Jenkins led them deeper into the bowels of the cave. The ice swirled over and around. The group was silent, taking it all in, and Colin admitted it was just a little terrifying. Ice caves had been known to collapse without warning—they were constantly shifting and changing with the glacier, melting off, blocks of ice tumbling.

Despite being enraptured with the natural beauty of their surroundings, Colin never let Jewel out of his sight, albeit peripheral vision at moments. He remained near and stood between her and Buck at all times. Had his weapon ready to use if needed.

Jewel paused to rest on a boulder, and Colin waited with her while the others continued exploring deeper inside the cave.

"How are you doing?" he asked.

Colin was surprised at her agility, especially after her injuries. But she'd spent the past twenty years hiking the wilderness and exploring on a regular basis. He supposed it shouldn't surprise him she would bounce back so easily.

She rubbed her leg while glancing intermittently at Jenkins, Buck and Meral, who had entered another tunnel.

Jenkins hung back. "You guys coming? We need to stay together."

Jewel nodded. "We'll be right there."

He didn't look convinced, but disappeared into the tunnel, his voice echoing with Buck's and Meral's.

"This trip seemed like a good idea," she whispered. "A way for me to be safely away from Mountain Cove, but we're not safe, Colin."

She looked up at him, her hazel eyes looking blustery and taking on the crystal blues of the cave. He thought they'd already agreed on that last night when she'd answered the door holding a Glock.

"When I told you to get away, this wasn't what I meant," he said. "Jewel, I know you want to spend time with Meral, but maybe we should let them continue the cruise without us. You and I will get off right here and now. We'll go back to the visitor center and say our goodbyes." He almost held his breath waiting for her answer, hoping she'd agree.

She hung her head. "It seems ridiculous. We're like two couples on a romantic cruise, but you're my bodyguard. Anyway it doesn't matter. I can't do this anymore. So, yes, let's stop this charade. Me pretending I'm enjoying myself, that I'm not worried about my safety. I don't know about you, but I got next to no sleep last night. I'm sure you didn't either. But… Colin…let me be the one to break it to Meral, okay?"

"Okay." Colin was interested to see how Buck would react. "How are you going to explain it to her?" He'd like to hear that answer from Jewel. He prided himself in his ability to ask the hard questions, but he hadn't yet pushed Jewel for answers the way he should. It was long past time he did. "Why do you believe you're in danger on this venture with your sister and her husband, with me, the police chief, as your bodyguard?"

Footfalls crunched. Jewel watched the tunnel and shook her head. The timing was no good.

Jenkins approached and gave Jewel a concerned look. "We need to get moving. You think you can make it?"

She nodded. "Of course."

He led them down the tunnel to join Buck and Meral and then through a tight space, where they brushed against an ice wall and had to move single file. Colin looked up at the cracks in the ice, the icicles, frozen spears, hanging above. This wasn't safe, but he could almost understand why people risked so much to come here in spite of the dangers. It was a sight one couldn't see anywhere else.

"Meral," Jewel whispered.

Meral slowed and let distance grow between her and Buck.

"Meral, listen, I'm not going to stay on the yacht. I thought I could do this, but I can't."

Buck stopped and turned. "What's that?"

Colin tensed. He would have waited until they were back at the visitor center, had their gear in hand, and could stand on the dock and wave goodbye. He'd assumed she would wait to break the news.

Meral appeared hurt and shocked. She grabbed Jewel's arm.

Colin took a step toward them. Instinct. Reflex to put himself in position to intervene, if necessary.

"What do you mean, Jewel? This trip is for you to keep you safe. To get away. Please, no, you have to stay with us. I'm worried about you."

"Maybe Jewel's injuries are too much for her to enjoy all of this." Buck had joined the conversation now.

Was that all part of his plan? Bring her out here and wear her down? But why? What was he after? This wasn't unfolding the way Colin would have wanted or expected. Was he even any help at all?

"Is that it, Jewel? Is this too much? I'm sorry for pressuring you," Meral said.

"Well, then, let's make it through the cave and we can just rest on the yacht. We have it for ten days, and in that time we don't have to do any more strenuous activities," Buck said.

He sounded like he was a man who cared, but Colin wasn't fully convinced—and Jewel didn't seem to be either. It was clear to Colin that she didn't trust her brother-in-law. What was less clear was *why*.

Maybe it all went back to what she knew and refused to tell Colin. He'd been a fool not to press her until he got answers. He must be in much deeper than he could admit. The mayor's words about Colin's feelings for Jewel—that she could see it so easily—should have been warning enough that his feelings were impacting his judgment.

He tried to shove his emotions aside, but it was too late. He was already there with Jewel.

Jewel opened her mouth to speak, but Colin cut her

off. "That'll work. You guys can do the hard stuff. Jewel and I will just relax on the yacht."

She glanced at him. That wasn't what she'd intended. *Please, just let it be. Read it in my gaze, Jewel.* They could announce their plans to leave the cruise, leave Meral and Buck, once they were back.

"Do you think you can make it through the cave?" Meral asked. "Or should we go back now?"

"Going back or forward makes no difference from this point," Jenkins said. "The distance is about the same since we're going to circle around anyway. Might as well make the most of it instead of backtracking over terrain we've already seen."

Meral and Buck stared at Jewel, waiting for an answer. "Yes, of course, I can make it the rest of the way. I'm sorry I brought it up now. We could have talked about this later."

"Everybody good?" Jenkins tried to hide his scowl and look like a patient tour guide, then marched on.

The ice tunnel opened up into a deep and wide cavern with jagged ice sculptures at the bottom. Jewel and Colin both hung back far from the edge while Meral and Buck boldly moved forward to get the best view. Despite her clear nervousness, Jewel kept inching forward to be close to Meral as though concerned for her. Colin had to maintain his stance between Jewel and Buck just in case the man got any ideas. He wished he had pushed for going back instead of completing the circle.

Jenkins shared his vast knowledge of the ice cave and all things glacier related, and Colin eyed Jewel— so beautiful. He'd often seen that same look of awe on her face. She loved nature. The Alaska wilderness. If he knew anything about her, he knew that. Still, in the midst of her admiration for the beauty around them, she appeared distracted.

Seeing her concern for Meral, Colin ushered her back away from the ledge. "I'll watch out for her," he whispered, and left Jewel resting on a rocky outcropping.

Colin went back to stand next to Meral. Jenkins pointed up at the icicles as one broke off and fell to the bottom, where it shattered like glass. Cut like glass, too. Caught up in the man's voice, Colin looked up at the rest of the glass knives hanging in the cavern.

He felt something at his back. A shove, a push...or a nudge. Reacting, he jerked around.

Then he slipped.

And suddenly the deep cavern loomed ahead. He was falling, sliding on the ice. Desperation and survival skills had him twisting around, reaching for the unforgiving ice, hoping he could stop his fall.

Voices cried out, echoing through the cave. Someone screamed his name.

Heart pounding, he reached for something, anything solid to grab hold of, when a hand grasped his.

Buck held on to Colin, his grip strong and sure. Jenkins dropped prostrate, belly down on the ice, and anchored himself. He grabbed Colin's other hand. "We've got you."

Colin's feet dangled precariously over the cavern, and he couldn't gain any traction against the wall even with crampons. His life depended on these two men.

Pulse racing away and roaring in his ears, Colin stared into Buck's eyes. Familiar eyes. Shadowy, malicious eyes, yet Buck had caught Colin, stopped his fall to certain death. Was even now pulling him back to the ledge. The men heaved and pulled Colin all the way, and they all fell back onto the ledge. Colin crawled away from it completely. Sat with his knees to his chest and tried to catch his breath.

What had just happened?

Jenkins started in on him for slipping to begin with. For getting too close. But that wasn't how it had gone down. He eyed Buck. He thought the man was a killer. Colin had been pushed, enough to cause him to slip, but minor enough so it hadn't been obvious. Who had done it?

Confusion crawled over him. *Had* he been pushed, or had it been his imagination? This must be how Jewel had felt with all the questions. Yet why push him only to save him? Jewel's arms slid over his shoulders and then around him as she plopped onto the iced rocks next to him.

She pressed her face into his shoulder. "That was close, too close."

Who did he think he was, trying to protect her? He hadn't adequately identified the true danger and had nearly died himself. He'd suspected Buck and now the man had saved him.

He watched Buck, who'd taken Meral into his arms, and the man stared back, his eyes cold and hard and… laughing.

One question ran through Colin's mind.

Who are you really, Buck Cambridge?

TWELVE

Jewel thought they would never make it back to the US Forest Service's Bledsoe Glacier Visitor Center. This had to have been the longest hike of her life. She kept replaying the incident in her mind. She'd been watching Meral, listening to the tour guide, when Colin had slipped on that ledge.

She'd thought her heart would drop right into that cavern with him.

Thank You, God. Thank You for saving him.

Her legs had gone weak and hadn't recovered. But they had made it back to the visitor center and now sat at a small round table. Colin and Buck had left to get them all coffee, everyone avoiding the inevitable conversation they must have.

Colin stood with Buck at the counter of the café. They were talking about something. She would never have known by looking at Colin that he'd almost died. He stood tall and confident. She smiled a little to herself, admiring his broad shoulders. How could Colin seem so strong and durable after nearly losing his life? He was like a heavy-duty truck. He was a force to be reckoned with.

As if sensing she was admiring him, he glanced back at Jewel. Watching, always watching. Except for that one moment when he'd let down his guard. Had that been what caused him to slip? Had he been too busy watching out for her and Meral?

She already knew they couldn't continue like this, and Colin's near miss in the ice cave served to confirm she'd made the right decision to leave the travel "fun." Joining Meral and Buck had seemed like the right thing at the time, her only choice. She'd thought she could handle it. But she'd been wrong.

"Jewel, I don't know what I'm going to do if you leave the cruise Buck arranged for us." Meral's words pulled Jewel back to the moment. "He's already talking about going back to Baltimore when it's over."

Jewel looked into Meral's beautiful, sad eyes. "I'm not ready to say goodbye yet either. I just know I can't go back to the boat." How much could she share with Meral? What could she say that wouldn't hurt her more?

Even if she wanted to stay, she couldn't ask that of Colin.

Jewel couldn't shake the sense that all their lives were in danger. That Colin's role in her troubles, his decision to appoint himself her bodyguard, had made him a target, not just collateral damage like Jed.

Nausea welled inside. If she were to share her thoughts with a therapist, she would probably be diagnosed with paranoia.

Except it's not paranoia if they really are after you.

"Meral." Jewel watched a group of glacier hikers leave. She should have had this conversation a long time ago, but dreaded it. Had hoped to avoid it. She might not get another chance, since Buck always turned up at

the worst moments, as if he somehow knew what Jewel
was about to say.

"I'm listening, Jewel. I haven't gone anywhere. Say
what you've wanted to say to me. What you've been
holding back from me. You can be open and honest
with me."

"What do you really know about Buck?"

Meral jerked up her chin as though Jewel had slapped
her. Whatever she was expecting Jewel to say, this
clearly wasn't it. "Why would you ask that? I know all
I need to know, okay? I'm in my thirties, for crying out
loud, and don't need anyone's approval. How dare you
question my judgment."

Jewel frowned. Despite Meral's soft invitation for
Jewel to be open and honest, her reaction was anything
but inviting.

"Coming from money you have to be careful, so
careful."

"You mean like you were with Silas."

"He wasn't after money. I gave it up for him, remember?"

Meral's eyes glistened with unshed tears. "Why are
you doing this, Jewel? I came to see you. Buck found
you so we could reconnect. Why are you trying to make
me question my happiness? Are you…are you jealous
of me because I have someone who loves me? Because
I'm married?"

Jewel could hardly stand to hear the hurt in her sister's voice. Her heart palpitated.

This was why she'd wanted to avoid this conversation. She loved her sister. Didn't want to hurt her. Jewel
had missed her family and hated to do anything that
might jeopardize her newfound connection with her

sister. She reached for Meral's hand, but Meral jerked it out of reach.

In her eyes, Jewel could see the deep hurt turning to anger. A defense mechanism. She'd seen the same thing in her father's eyes when she'd refused to give up Silas. It had hurt him badly to realize that she placed Silas above her family. So in return he'd turned his pain into anger and had used it against her, disinheriting her.

But Jewel wouldn't give up. She had to try again. She snatched Meral's hand and gripped hard. And deep concern turned to determination. Even if Meral didn't want to listen to her, Jewel would still speak her mind. It could save Meral's life. "I love you. I don't want it to be like this. Please understand. But I can't stand by and watch without saying this. You could be in danger, Meral. Buck is a dangerous man."

Meral's eyes widened, and she brushed at the tears. Then fury replaced the hurt, and Meral pushed slowly to her feet.

"How dare you." Her tone was a low growl.

"Did you tell him what I took years ago?" Jewel asked.

Meral had to know that she had the diamond. Her family had to have figured out that Jewel had taken it. She'd been so foolish to pretend otherwise.

Jewel saw the truth in Meral's eyes. And she saw denial. Meral didn't want to believe Jewel, but Meral had doubts about Buck—doubts she'd tried to ignore all along. Jewel saw them there as plain as day. She knew her sister. They were flesh and blood, and even after twenty years she knew her.

"There's no need for you to come aboard the yacht

for your things." Meral had turned cold. "I'll get them packed up and delivered to you here."

"You're just going to leave us stranded."

"You said you couldn't go back. Now you don't have to. You'll find a ride home, I'm sure. After all, you have the chief of police following you around wanting to be a guard dog, but acting more like a puppy in love."

Jewel stood, too, feeling the ice behind Meral's words and the agony of her own so strongly that her pain was physical. "Meral, I would never do anything to hurt you. I love you. I'm trying to protect you. Please, don't do this. Don't end our time together like this."

"You haven't changed one bit, Jewel. I remember how you were so self-righteous when you left with Silas, not even caring that you were hurting Mom and Dad and me the way you did. Just leaving us all for a man you hardly knew. And don't say I'm doing the same thing. This isn't anything like what you did."

Jewel lowered her voice so she could be sure that only Meral heard her. They had already drawn the men's attention. "You're right. It isn't. You're in love with a murderer who is using you to get what he wants."

The Krizan Diamond. But Jewel was afraid to say it out loud.

Meral flinched. "How do you know this? If Buck was guilty, your man would have already arrested him. But he's not. There's nothing you can prove."

Could it be true? Was Jewel blind to the truth or being paranoid? "Please tell me you're not involved in this." She instantly regretted the words. "I'm sorry, Meral, I didn't mean it. I could never doubt you like that."

But the damage had been done. Icy daggers shot

from Meral's eyes. "And yet you doubt my choice of husband. Buck has his own money. He doesn't need mine or yours." Meral stiffened. She glanced across the space to Buck, who held two coffees and was headed their way.

He closed the distance quickly and was at her side, with a curious, mischievous half smile for Jewel.

"Buck, I'm ready to head back to the yacht."

"Yes, my sweet." He kissed Meral's head, but where she couldn't see he had a cruel, mocking expression on his face. Even if he wasn't guilty, he was still a creep.

"We'll pack Colin's and Jewel's things, and the staff can drop them here."

"Are you sure?" Buck set the coffees on the table and turned her to look him in the face. "After all, I went to a lot of trouble to find her and arrange this wedding gift for you. I'd hate for you to regret this decision later. Once we cross this bridge, I'm not sure we'll be turning back."

"I'm sure. Don't worry. It's not your fault that your gift of a jewel turned out to be a fake."

Acrid. Who could have thought the woman could be so acerbic to her sister?

Colin could hardly stand to watch the scene unfolding before his eyes. On the one hand, he would be glad to see Meral and Buck gone and out of Jewel's life. Maybe that would end the attacks. He just wanted to get Jewel somewhere safe. But on the other hand, seeing her hurting about undid him. And he still believed Buck was responsible for the death of one of his officers. He needed to catch Buck when the man made a mistake. Colin needed evidence to make his arrest.

He'd heard the mayor loud and clear.

If he was going to come back, he needed to return with the bad guy. He was on the case of his life and career. It all surrounded a woman he cared deeply about. And he couldn't seem to see a way to get Jewel to safety while still catching the criminal.

As Buck ushered Meral out of the visitor center, Jewel pressed her face into her hands, her shoulders shaking. That had been one very public scene. Colin moved next to her and sat down. He held his hand above her back, her shoulder, hesitating, wanting to comfort her, but fearing his growing emotional attachment to this woman.

This is about her. Not you.

Colin pressed his hand on her shoulder and squeezed. He leaned in close to whisper. But what could he say to her when she was hurting like this?

His heart pricked. Anger tangled up with feelings so deep he couldn't fathom them. He wanted to run after Meral and stop her from going away like this, but he knew there was nothing he could say. If Meral wouldn't listen to Jewel, then she certainly wouldn't listen to him.

"Jewel," he said gently in her ear. People were still staring. He had to get her somewhere private.

This was a woman who had left behind family and wealth to move to a harsh land for the man she loved, and then had learned to run her business on the edge of the wilderness on her own after her husband was gone. Jewel could have gone back home, but she'd chosen to stay. She'd been so strong for so very long.

And now she appeared broken.

Reconnecting with her family had ended in heartache, after all.

Jewel sat up straight and wiped her eyes. Drew in a breath and looked at him. Though the grief he saw there was a punch in his gut, he recognized her determination had returned.

Attagirl.

She stood then and waited for him to join her.

"I have to go back to the yacht."

"What? After all that, you want to go back? You can't be serious."

"Dead serious."

Time for Colin to stop coddling. Time for him to make his own demands. "No."

She stood and attempted to walk by him. He grabbed her arm and swung her around, keeping his grip gentle but implacable, ushering her toward the restaurant at the back. Leaning in as they walked, he spoke in her ear. "Listen to me." He kept his voice low. "You can't go back to the boat."

"You can't stop me."

Finding a booth in the corner, Colin practically forced her in.

"You know I can use those self-defense techniques you taught me on you, right?" she said.

Colin slid in next to her, blocking her exit. "Then why didn't you?"

"Why are you doing this?" Her eyes pleaded. "I have to go before they leave."

Colin needed to keep her here long enough to miss the boat, but her pleas tugged at his heart. "This is life-and-death, Jewel."

Something he couldn't read flashed in her eyes, and she backed against the wall.

"What do you mean?"

"I think you know what I mean." Time to ask those hard questions and get answers. "Your sister's husband is a dangerous man. And I think you know that, too."

THIRTEEN

Trapped.

She was jammed against the wall in the booth. The yacht would leave without her unless she headed to the dock soon. But Colin clearly wouldn't let her go until he'd gotten some answers, and he was right. So right. Right that Buck was dangerous, right that she knew it and right that it was a matter of life-and-death. She shouldn't go back, except she'd left something there. How did she make him understand?

His actions should incense her, but deep down she recognized how much he cared about her. His nearness and her predicament had her heart beating erratically. She'd done well to try to protect it, but the recent threats on her life made her vulnerable. She was too busy trying to stay alive and trying to keep Meral safe, too, and she'd let down her guard.

Protectiveness poured off this man, who had her cornered, and his stark blue eyes took her in as though trying to soak her up. A warm shiver ran over her. Jewel had never thought she could love someone like she had loved Silas. And maybe she couldn't. She was a different person now than she'd been twenty years ago, and that giddy love-conquers-all optimism had worn away. But could she be ready for a new kind of love?

With Colin's sturdy form blocking her way—protecting her—maybe it was more that she was afraid to love again. She had a feeling that Colin could be that man if only she'd let him in.

But she shoved those thoughts away. She had to get to *The Alabaster Sky.*

"You're right. He is dangerous. That's exactly why I have to go back."

"To save Meral? You think she'll listen?" Colin's tone challenged.

No. She'd tried to stop Meral. Make her see the light about Buck, but her sister wanted too badly to believe that she'd found her happily-ever-after. She wouldn't listen to a word against Buck. And anyway, there was more to her need to return to the boat than that. More that Colin didn't know. "You don't understand."

She slid toward Colin, acting as though she expected him to move out of her way. But he didn't budge, and now she sat closer to him.

"Then make me understand, Jewel. Tell me what you haven't been willing to tell me before now. I'm done skirting the real issue, dancing around it."

She hadn't wanted to tell him the whole truth at first because she couldn't bear to see his disappointment in her. And then she had hung on to the slim hope she was wrong about Buck. But now? Colin needed to know it all because she'd been wrong to withhold it. She saw that now.

And telling him, seeing his reaction to the truth, would go a long way in burying anything she might

otherwise have with him. She drew in a breath, forti-
fied herself.

"Have you ever done something that completely went
against everything you are or believed in? Something
that you've regretted for the rest of your life?"

"Yes, Jewel. I think we've all done that."

"Years ago, I took something valuable that didn't
belong to me, and I left it on the boat."

He paled. "Something worth killing for?"

"I believe so, yes."

"Why didn't you tell me about this before?"

"It doesn't matter. I have to get it back."

"Tell me what it is and where you've hidden it, and
I'll get it for you."

"There are things you don't know about me, Colin.
For starters, I come from an old-money, wealthy family back east."

The words didn't seem to faze him. Did he already
know? But he couldn't know the rest, and she had to
tell him quickly. They were running out of time. "I was
in my early twenties when I went on a cruise in Alaska
with some friends and I met Silas. That weekend, as he
showed us the wilderness and nature, I fell in love with
this place. But it didn't end there. Silas and I…we had
a connection. It seemed crazy. I thought I'd never see
him again, but he followed me home and even though
it sounds old-fashioned, he courted me. At the time, my
family thought he was after our money."

Jewel shifted. Dragged in air. She was doing this.
Really doing this. "They did everything they could to
keep us apart, but I was in love and wouldn't listen.
Silas made me feel alive. And I knew he didn't care
about the money, so I planned to elope with him. My

father got wind of it and threatened to disinherit me if I went through with it. I knew he was serious—that once I left with Silas, he wouldn't accept me back into the family, even if I came back a few months later and said it had all been a mistake. Risking everything like that for Silas…it scared me. I guess that I wasn't completely convinced it wasn't all a dream. I figured if the worst happened, then I wanted something to fall back on, some security. I didn't have my own money, not in any significant way, and now I see that was a way they controlled me. But there was something else I could get to—something valuable."

Colin leaned closer, intent on her story. "What did you take?"

"I took the Krizan Diamond. It's a family heirloom from an ancient mine in India. It was handed down to my mother, whose family founded Simmons Diamonds. My father married into the business. They groomed me to be part of that business, too. But diamonds are cold and hard and lifeless and don't give love, so I left it all behind for Silas. Except for…the Krizan Diamond. It's worth a small fortune."

He paled and slid away from her in the booth. His move was subtle, but she'd seen it.

It was just as she'd feared. He thought less of her now for stealing a diamond and harboring it in her home—not to mention keeping the information from him. She didn't blame him. But what would he, an officer of the law, do with her now? She wasn't a jewel thief in the typical sense. And once this was over, though she couldn't see how it would end, she was willing to give the diamond back to her family, to Meral. Jewel no longer needed it. No longer wanted it.

In fact, she had never needed it. But she'd been afraid to trust completely.

With Colin's reaction, she saw that perhaps she had been wrong to trust him with the truth.

"Why did you bring the diamond?"

"All these years I had it hidden away in the attic, but with the attacks I suspected that someone might be after it. I've suspected Buck all along. Learning that a woman had driven the truck that rammed me made me doubt my suspicions because I just couldn't believe that Meral would be involved. I thought to put it in a safe-deposit box, but I couldn't get away. And then if I brought it with me on the boat and the attacks continued or the diamond was stolen, I would know for sure that Buck had been behind the attacks." Maybe. Saying it out loud now, she wasn't sure it made any sense.

"And you didn't trust me enough to tell me?"

"Telling you about it meant implicating Buck. I didn't want to believe it could be him. I wasn't sure. But now I have to go."

"No, Jewel. I can't let you go. Buck won't get away. Don't worry. Now I need you to stay here."

"Where are you going?"

Something shifted behind Colin's gaze. It was cold, hard. Professional. "Now that you've told me the truth, I know what I'm dealing with and I need to make a phone call. Promise me you will wait here until I get back."

Jewel didn't want to give him that promise.

"I'm telling you this as an officer of the law, Jewel."

"Am I...am I under arrest?"

He frowned. "Get serious."

Right. The statute of limitations had expired. But she'd kept pertinent information to herself that could have helped him solve this case. Still, what she'd told him had disturbed him far deeper than she would have expected.

She saw that clearly in his eyes. He'd pulled away from her physically. And emotionally. Though she'd protected her heart from falling for this man, the intense pain shooting through her chest illuminated that she was more than halfway there.

Colin stumbled from the booth. Could he trust Jewel to stay? He had no choice. He needed a moment to regain his composure. His vision tunneled as his past swirled before him.

A jewel thief.

I know where I've seen Buck before.

Brock Ammerman.

Buck Cambridge.

Buck Cambridge *was* Brock Ammerman, the jewel thief who had murdered Katelyn twenty years ago. But he was dead. Colin had killed him.

He staggered. Pressed his hand against the wall for support.

It can't be. How can it be?

His cell buzzed. What now? He pulled it from his pocket absently, going through the motions by rote. He must be losing his mind. He didn't believe in coincidences, but neither did he believe in the impossible.

Colin glanced back at Jewel to make sure she was waiting. Her gaze shifted around the room as if she were looking for an exit, but he was blocking the only one.

The text was from the forensic artist. He'd sent the picture he'd created after taking off the years—Brock Ammerman.

Buck Cambridge *is* Brock Ammerman. The man had changed so much over twenty years, and Colin had thought him dead anyway. Little wonder he hadn't been able to place him.

Colin leaned completely against the wall.

Not possible.

How? How could this be? He'd killed this man in self-defense. The charges against Ammerman hadn't stuck, and Colin had wanted to kill him. He had wanted to exact revenge, but that hadn't been his motivation when he'd followed Brock that day. He'd just wanted to warn him that he would put him behind bars for good one day—let him know that it wasn't over. Then when Brock had tried to kill him in response, knowing that Colin would always be watching, Colin had gotten the upper hand and killed the man in self-defense. One bullet to the chest had taken him out for good.

But it had all looked suspicious, and Colin had been put on leave while the department had investigated. It hadn't helped that Katelyn's family had wanted him to pay for her death. Had that all been part of Brock's plan?

But how Brock had survived, he still didn't know. Had someone working within the department helped Brock fake his own death? Had it all been big conspiracy?

No. Colin wouldn't believe that for a minute. His cell buzzed. *Not now. Not now.* He didn't have time. He glanced at it. David Warren. If he didn't answer, David might send the Coast Guard looking.

"Yeah, David," Colin said. "I can't talk for long. I'm…in the middle of something."

"You okay? Cuz you don't sound okay."

"It's too much to explain right now, but I think it's all coming to a head. And I have to figure it out."

Colin had to pull himself together. He still didn't have enough evidence to make an arrest for murder. His story was a tangled mess, as was Jewel's. It would take more than a phone call to untangle it, and Buck still wouldn't be arrested for Jed's murder and the attacks on Jewel. He might disappear altogether.

But one thing Colin knew. Brock was dead. He'd killed the man himself, so what was going on?

Lord, help me to see the truth here.

"Maybe I can help." A giggle resounded over the phone that didn't belong to David.

"Where are you?" Colin asked.

"I'm off today. Tracy's working at the B and B. I can't wait until this is over so I can get my wife back. I never see her. Right now I've got the boys."

Colin nodded absently, thinking of David and Tracy's twin sons.

"So what's up? Tell me what's going on. Do I need to come and get you and Jewel?"

Twins.

"No, not yet. I've got to go now, but just know this, David, your phone call helped."

He made a quick call to his friend back in Texas to start looking for answers. Did Brock Ammerman have a twin?

Colin paced, calming his heart rate so he could function.

Jewel was sitting back there waiting for him to return. What would he tell her? Think. He had to think.

Why would Buck come all the way to Alaska for the diamond? His wife had access to wealth and jewels via her family. Except…if they were willing to disinherit their oldest daughter for marrying without their approval, then he doubted they would allow Buck into the circle, giving him access to anything of value. But maybe it was more than that. Brock's targets hadn't been high profile. Meral and Jewel's family would definitely be a high-profile family, the theft creating too much noise, and the jewels couldn't be fenced so easily or quickly.

That had to be it.

Buck had convinced Meral to come to Alaska because he'd found out about Jewel's secret. Add that Colin was here as chief of police, and Buck must have seen it as a way to get the prize and revenge all at once. Maybe that was why he killed Jed. To get back at Colin for Brock's death. But he might not be finished with his killing spree.

Colin blew out a breath to erase those morbid images that had sent him running to Alaska to start afresh. Brock had murdered Katelyn—and now Brock, or rather his twin, was here close to… Jewel.

And poor Jewel, carrying the weight of believing she'd stolen the diamond, when he could easily see a loving mother making sure her young daughter had taken something of value by either planting the seed or allowing her access. But what did he know about it? That was all conjecture.

Everything he had right now was conjecture. He needed the facts. No matter how much he listened to his gut, his instincts wouldn't hold up in a court of law. He'd been right to follow his gut this far, sure, but he needed to seal the deal. Find the evidence behind the attacks on Jewel. But he could figure that out. Right now he had to get back to her. He turned to enter the restaurant again.

Jewel was gone.

FOURTEEN

"Your sister's husband is a dangerous man."

She should have waited on him. He'd made it clear when he'd pulled the police card. The chief-of-police card, rather. But she'd also gotten that he wasn't going to let her go back to the yacht, where she needed to be. As soon as his focus had turned from her, she'd fled the booth.

Hearing Colin say that Buck was a dangerous man had infused her with determination. She couldn't let Meral leave with that man, even though he was her husband. But how to get her away? How did Jewel convince her?

After slipping through the window in the restroom, she dropped to the ground. Hemlock, spruce and cedar hid her from view. She'd never done anything like this before. Well, other than taking the diamond. But she had to get to the yacht. She had to save Meral, if she could, and retrieve the diamond while she was at it.

Buck wasn't going to hurt Jewel in broad daylight in front of the crew or Meral. She could try one more time to save her sister, despite Meral's vitriolic words.

Pressing her back against the log wall of the visitor

center, she hoped Colin hadn't discovered her gone yet, but he would soon enough. She had to hurry.

She'd seen him on the phone. Had he been checking on old warrants for her arrest for stealing a diamond? The statute of limitations was only a few years, but that wouldn't make her any less a thief to him. She'd seen the shock in his eyes turn to pure disappointment.

Her words had shaken him as much as his reaction had crushed her. But she was a woman who was destined to lose at love. She was glad she hadn't actually been playing that game with Colin. Only toying with the idea.

More importantly, she had to protect her sister and survive another encounter with the man after her life.

No more time to think about Chief Colin Winters, and, yes, she should think of him in official terms from now on. He'd made that much clear.

She crept to the corner of the building and peeked around. In the distance the yacht was still anchored in the channel. Had Meral and Buck been taken back yet? If she hurried, she could make it before they left.

Jewel sagged against the wall. A cedar branch tickled her arm. Part of her wanted to give up. It would be easier to sink to the ground and cry for all she had lost—a list that now included her sister for a second time.

Meral's life could be in serious danger. She could disappear on the cruise. Be pushed overboard, and Buck would likely gain her money, holdings and benefit from an insurance policy as well as obtain the Krizan Diamond either by finding and stealing it or by killing Jewel.

What am I supposed to do now, God? None of this makes any sense.

Why did You let this happen to me? I was doing okay at the B and B. I had made a life of my own already. I didn't need the past to come roaring back.

"As far as the east is from the west, so far has he removed our transgressions from us." Psalm 103:12

Don't You shove the past, our sins, as far as the east is from the west? I even have one of those cross-stitches Katy makes in one of the rooms. Maybe You did remove my transgression, but I've kept my sin close, hidden in the attic and buried away until now. And I'm sorry for that. So sorry.

Jewel shook off the weight of guilt. She could worry about that later.

A pain pierced her side. The muzzle of a gun. Jewel stiffened and gasped. She turned, but a grip forced her to keeping staring ahead. In the distance, *The Alabaster Sky* began heading out into the channel.

"Looks like your past has caught up to you." The familiar voice whispered in her ear.

"What's going on? Why is the yacht leaving without you? Where is Meral?" *God, please don't let Meral be involved. Please keep her safe.*

"Your sister is safe and sound on the yacht. She won't even know I'm gone."

"Are you saying that you drugged her?"

"Works like a charm. She never even realizes that she's missing time. She doesn't have a clue that you hold her life in your hands."

Jewel gasped.

Colin, come on. Find me. Notice I'm gone!

She'd wanted to escape before Colin found her, and now she wished he would hurry up. He hadn't let her

out of his sight until now. Was he still freaking out over
what she'd told him? Still on his phone?

"Come on." Buck pushed her away from the visitor
center and through the trees, away from the center's
entrance and the channel where *The Alabaster Sky* had
been anchored.

Jewel thought to fight him. She wouldn't go will-
ingly. She tensed, preparing to use a self-defense move,
but he pressed the weapon to the base of her skull. Fear
corded her neck. Could she fight him and live?

"Don't even think about it. Remember, you have to
think of Meral. You fight me and I'll make sure she suf-
fers before I kill her."

"What kind of monster would kill his own wife?"
But she knew. She knew what kind of monster. He was
a con artist. He'd never loved Meral. Jewel had seen
that from the beginning.

Buck had turned desperate and was showing his true
self now. What had happened to change his tactics?

He grabbed her hair, sending shards of pain through
her head, and shoved her deeper into the woods. Then
suddenly he stiffened. He yanked her close and stepped
behind a broad cedar tree. Pulling her against his body,
he wrapped his free arm around her waist and thrust
the gun against the side of her head.

He pressed his lips against her ear and whispered,
making her shudder. "One word and you're dead. Think
of Meral."

He was pure evil in human form. She squeezed her
eyes shut, trying to stop the tears. She'd known, felt it
all along.

What had he heard? Someone following?
Was it Colin?

Please, God!

A minute, maybe two he waited, and with his proximity those seconds felt like an eternity. She was so close she instantly felt when the tension drained from him. His fear of discovery had gone.

He whispered again. "I'm warning you, Jewel, don't try your lame self-defense tactics on me. A firearm is the great equalizer. Even if you were a match for me, I'm the one with the gun. I've been impressed with your resilience; I'll give you that. The way you survived that tumble into Dead Man Falls. That alone should have killed you."

He grabbed her hair and shoved her forward and away from the tree.

Jewel stumbled over a root and fell. He didn't relinquish his hold on her hair, so she cried out, the pain searing. She was sure he would rip her hair out of her scalp. Her eye burned.

"Get up," he snapped.

Using her hands to grab his on her head, she stood up, or more likely she was pulled to her feet. She wanted to do her part to make the slow going even slower, to stall as much as she could. Maybe someone would see them. Maybe Colin would finally discover she was gone and catch up to them. But if she delayed his plans, then the monster would do much worse than rip out her hair before it was over. Kill her and then Meral.

They marched deeper through the undergrowth that ended when it banked against the glacier.

"Why kill me? Why not just take what you want?"

Where was he taking her? Why back toward the glacier?

"Because I couldn't get to it—or thought I couldn't.

Our second day at your B and B, I heard you mention to Meral that you'd willed everything to her years ago after your husband died, your way to connect back to your family. Your death would have meant Meral had access to the diamond. I figured you had it in a safe-deposit box in a bank like most people. One quick shove into Dead Man Falls and it would be mine. But no, you had to survive that. Good thing, too. When I saw you sneak up to the attic I knew why."

"How? How could you know?" She turned to face him.

"The same way I know you brought the diamond with you on this trip. I've made a living reading people who have things to hide." He smacked her across the face. Her eyes watered again. "That's for making me work so hard for it."

Cheek burning, Jewel pressed her palm against her face.

"Keep going."

She stood her ground. "Where are we going? Why don't you just ask me what you want to know? Why drag me out here?"

"All in good time. We have to get away from your knight in shining armor first. He's probably on his way to the yacht to look for you. Good thing I made it more difficult. I underestimated you, Jewel. You know how to hide things. Now I've had to go to extreme measures. Things would have been so much easier if you had just died any of the times when you were supposed to."

He pressed her forward. Jewel shivered, growing tired. Through the forested incline she could see the icy edges of the glacier only a few yards down where it hedged against the mountain on its journey to the channel. Jewel stumbled and fell to her knees again, but this time Buck did not have a hold on her hair.

He grabbed her arm and jerked her up. Jewel cringed from the pain. He ushered her forward and down, then around a crack in the ice and shoved her into an opening—a cold chute into another ice cave, different from the one they'd explored earlier.

"Why are you taking me here?" How did he know about this cave at all?

He forced her ahead of him into the cave without crampons or backpack or gear. Her gloves were stashed in her pack. At least she still wore her jacket. As she climbed over icy boulders and slipped a few times, she was positive this was off the tourist path. Then he shoved her to the ground, where she fell between two boulders and cut her hand on the ice.

"Nobody will find you here."

"So you mean to succeed in killing me this time."

"It's simple, really. If you tell me where the diamond is, you can go back to your police chief and sister. I'll disappear. When she wakes up, you get to tell her I'm gone. Tell her the truth about why or not. It's up to you. But either way I'll disappear with the diamond."

Jewel didn't believe him. Why would he let her go? She could then be a witness against him if he was ever caught. No, once she told him where to find it, he would kill her.

Jewel pushed up to sitting, the best she could. Pain jabbed her from new injuries and echoed from her recent ones—all due to Buck's attacks. If only she could have confronted him from the beginning.

"You can't just sell a diamond like that. It won't work."

He laughed. A strange sound coming from him.

"I'm in the business of imports and exports. What do you think that means? I'm a jewel thief and a fence.

I already have the connections. I already have a buyer. All I need is the diamond."

Jewel squeezed her eyes shut. She never could have imagined this twenty years ago when she'd taken what she'd thought would be a safety net.

"Come on, Jewel. The diamond for Meral's life."

"She's your wife."

"And your sister."

"Answer me this, did you ever really love her?"

"She's a beautiful woman with top-notch society connections. Marrying her had more than a few benefits. But what you're missing here is that Meral married *me* for *my* money. She doesn't really love me, although she's convinced herself that she does. She likes to think of it all as a fairy tale. But the truth is she loves that I can provide a comfortable life for her. Her last husband depleted her funds. Meral was broke."

"But if you have money, why go to such lengths for this diamond? Why marry a woman you don't even love?"

His smirk speared through her. "I'm in business. I must keep generating revenue, and we've had a few hard years."

Jewel hung her head, wanting to get as much truth out of him as she could, if she could trust anything he said. "Does she… Does Meral know the truth about you? Was Meral in on your plans to steal the diamond?"

"No. Meral's habit of turning a blind eye, and not wanting to see the ugly truth of how things really are, is how her first husband got away with draining their accounts. She learned years ago, probably while she was still at home with your family, not to let herself notice things that might upset her and simply look the other way when it suited her. And because she did, you were able to get away with the Krizan Diamond when you stole it and left to marry a poor man. She shared the truth about you and the Krizan Diamond with me, her soul mate, the first night we were together as lovers. That same night I knew I should propose. It's a gift, really. A sixth sense for a big opportunity that has paid off well in business dealings. And Meral accepted. After all, I was charming and had money. Marrying me would benefit her. She dressed it up in more romantic thoughts, but getting married was a mutually beneficial business arrangement."

Jewel nodded, understanding things better now. It fit with the image she had of her sister to learn that Meral wouldn't choose to do something she felt was wrong…but she'd be easily convinced to look the other way when someone else did something wrong—as had Jewel years ago.

"Now time's up," he said. He tugged some plastic straps from his pocket.

"Buck, no. You can't leave me in here, tied up so I can't even move. I'll freeze to death."

He gestured with his head. "You've got your coat. But I stashed a few blankets. You'll be fine. I just need time to verify you've told me the truth. If I find it, then I'll make a call and let someone know where you are. And if I don't, then I'll be back with a piece of Meral."

Right. If he found it, then he would leave her here to die, or come back and kill her himself. Either way she was dead.

Buck shifted toward her, lifted her chin with the muzzle of his gun. "Now, Jewel. Where did you hide the diamond?"

* * *

Colin stood outside the cave listening, getting most of what Buck said, but missing a few words.

He'd come around the building in time to see movement in the woods and had followed his gut. Even though *The Alabaster Sky* was already cruising away from the glacier, and Jewel should have been heading that direction trying to catch the boat before it was out of sight, he had listened to his instincts.

That had paid off.

He hadn't gotten a chance to attack Buck, to free Jewel from his grasp, because the man had had a weapon pointing at her head the whole time. With the trees and brush hindering his view, getting a shot off at Buck would have been too risky.

No. Colin had to wait for the right time, and now that time had come. Buck would be leaving Jewel here. Colin could wait until he left to free her, but if she didn't tell Buck the truth about the diamond, he might kill Meral before he came back for Jewel. There could be another murder on Buck's hands. On Colin's conscience.

Better to arrest the man now after both Colin and Jewel had heard the man's confession. Buck had been the attacker that day at the falls. But he hadn't said a thing about Jed. Colin needed that confession, too. He needed something concrete.

"Winters," the man called from inside the cave. "Come on in."

Heart jumping up his throat, Colin sank away behind the tree. No, no, this wasn't how it was supposed to go down. He'd put in a call for help, but it would take too long for backup to arrive.

"Jewel is waiting for you, Chief Winters. Join the party."

Jewel cried out in pain.

He couldn't leave her in there alone with this murderer. He had no choice and felt as if once again he was becoming entangled in a fight he wasn't smart enough or strong enough to win. If he'd been the first to attack, the one to surprise Buck, then this would all be over.

He hadn't brought his department-issued Glock on this venture, but his personal SIG P224. A compact 9-millimeter pistol he could hide out of sight—which he did, tucking it away carefully under his jacket along with an extra magazine loaded with ammo before he strode into the cave.

Buck pointed his weapon point-blank at Jewel, who sat on the ground. When she glanced up at Colin, sorrow spilled from her gaze, followed by fear and something more.

Determination.

Good girl.

She was doing better than Colin right now. Seeing her helpless, a man aiming a gun on her, nearly drove Colin to his knees. But he kept standing and allowed adrenaline to course through him. Fire up his nerves. Reinforce his muscles.

"Good," Buck said. "I wouldn't expect any less of you. Now, hand over your weapon. The nine millimeter you like to stash out of sight when you're off duty."

A few choice words ran through Colin's head. A few scenarios tortured him. Like pulling out the weapon and firing at Buck. Dropping him then and there. But Jewel. What about Jewel? She could get caught in the cross fire.

He pulled the SIG from his back and set it on the ground. His gaze fell on Jewel, who stared at the ground now. Did she think Colin had failed her? He hadn't given up yet, and if he knew anything about Jewel, she hadn't either. They would get their chance.

"Now kick it over to me and back away." Odd that the man would smile now. "You know, I think I was subconsciously hoping you'd find me here with Jewel. Sure, it would be simpler if this game ends with me getting the diamond and disappearing with no muss and no fuss. But seeing you here makes me happy. You are part of what made it more fun."

"You're demented."

"Oh, you have no idea." He inched away from Jewel, still aiming his weapon at her. Knowing that she was his leverage now.

This was exactly what Colin had hoped to avoid. In the meantime, he needed to keep him talking. Get him talking about himself, buy some time and maybe Colin would get his chance to end this for good.

"You're wondering what I'm still doing alive, aren't you?"

"No. I figured it out. You're Brock's twin brother."

"Took you long enough. You know what you haven't figured out? Brock wasn't the one to steal those jewels or kill anyone—not the woman getting robbed or your witness, the woman you loved."

Anger boiled, frothing red-hot magma ready to erupt as he thought back to that time.

Colin had been a detective in Texas investigating a jewel thief and murderer. The victim arrived home and surprised the thief. Colin had a witness—the woman's neighbor, Katelyn Morrison. Over time as Colin investigated, even though it was against the rules, Katelyn had become the love of his life. He'd hoped she would say yes when he proposed, but he'd always feared he wasn't good enough—her being independently wealthy while he was just a lowly police officer.

Colin had been near wrapping up the case so he and Katelyn could get on with their lives when she had been murdered. The only witness, the only real evidence, gone. No one had known about his relationship with Katelyn, and he went on to investigate her murder, too. Brock Ammerman had been charged and put on trial. The DNA evidence found at the scene pointed to Brock. But he'd had a solid alibi. He'd been emceeing at a conference two hundred miles away during the time the murder had been committed. Hundreds of witnesses proved that. The DNA evidence at the scene of the crime had been shot down as being tampered with in some way.

Colin hadn't seen that coming. He should have bided his time and gathered more evidence. Buck had gotten away with murdering the woman he loved because Colin had acted too quickly, before all the facts were in and he'd had the wrong man all along—Buck's twin brother, Brock.

Keep talking, Buck, and I just might rush you and kill you with my bare hands.

"That was all me. That's why you couldn't get the conviction. Couldn't make your charges stick, Chief. And it was that kind of planning, because we share the same DNA, that made Brock and I a successful duo. Partners in crime."

"How did you keep it a secret? How did others not know you had a twin?"

"Simple. We had no idea either until we were in our late twenties. We had been adopted out, separated at birth. I don't think that's even legal these days. Have you ever read those stories about twins that are separated? How they dress the same, marry women with the same name, maybe even pick the same names for their children?"

Colin nodded, grasping the truth. "You ran into each other in the same career."

"Trying to steal the same gem. Imagine our surprise, but we were smart enough to realize we could use that to our advantage. Together we were able to exponentially increase our potential as jewel thieves. After that we wondered how we had ever worked alone before. And we excelled until you came along and killed my brother. But you killed the wrong brother."

"It was in self-defense." Colin wouldn't beg for his life, though.

"You ruined everything. When I learned of the missing diamond from Meral, I did my research and found Jewel easily enough. Giving the gift of a reunion with her sister seemed the fitting thing to do for a wedding present. But I always research the law entities where I'll be working, too, and that's when I discovered you were chief of police in Mountain Cove."

His smile twisted into the familiar smirk. "What a thrill to go another round with you, especially when you had no idea I even existed. I could get my revenge. A life for a life. I could kill the woman you loved. Again. After all, you killed my twin brother."

That was it.

Colin exploded in fury and rammed into Buck.

Gunfire blasted in his ear.

FIFTEEN

Covering her head, Jewel turned and scrambled behind one of the boulders near where she'd been sitting. From there she peered out and prayed for Colin. Bullets ricocheted off the ice walls from two weapons. Colin had grabbed his own gun, and the two fought each other in a deadly battle.

A massive block of ice crashed down, shattering in an explosive display. Fragments hit dangerously close to where Colin wrestled with Buck for the upper hand.

A truck-sized chunk of ice slid across the ground like a bull charging toward her. Jewel pressed against the frozen wall—deeper, harder—turned her face away. Cold seeped through her bones. Sharp edges pinched into her skin. She squeezed her eyes shut. There was nowhere else to go.

She waited for the impact, though it all happened in a millisecond. The deadly ice slammed against the boulder and broke into smaller pieces that slid to a stop near her feet.

Releasing her pent-up breath, she prayed harder. Cried out to God.

If the gun continued firing and more bullets ricocheted, the whole cave might come crashing down on them.

I'm helpless here.

She was no use to Colin.

God, what can I do? Help us, please!

Jewel searched for a rock. But wait. She could use the chunk of ice next to her foot with its sharp, cutting edges.

Maybe.

Carefully gripping the frozen weapon, she crawled from behind the protective boulder. Both men continued their struggle over just one gun now, and it flailed in all directions. Another shot rang out as a bullet whizzed past her ear. Jewel ducked behind the boulder again.

She would be deaf before this was over, if she even survived. If the ice above them didn't react to the concussive blasts, crack and cave in.

What do I do? What do I do?

What if Colin lost this battle? Then what?

Jewel couldn't let that happen. She picked up the broken ice again, as solid as a rock and just as deadly, and charged out into the open. Colin had Buck against the wall, beating his arm and wrist against jagged ice so he would release his weapon.

Buck cried out, fired the weapon, then released it.

Jewel dropped the rock to pick up the gun instead.

But Buck elbowed Colin in the nose and broke loose before grabbing Jewel from behind. Swinging her around to face Colin, Buck had pulled a knife from his pocket and pressed it to her throat. She gripped the gun and tossed it to Colin. It fell to the ground and slid toward him.

In her ear, Buck laughed. "Both guns are out of ammo now, so the gun is no use to the chief."

Had they fired that many rounds? They were fortunate the ceiling hadn't fallen down on them. With her thoughts, a resounding crack split the air. They stood frozen, waiting to see if the ice cave would collapse on them. Even Buck tensed. But nothing happened.

Then she saw it. Colin had been shot. Blood oozed from his shoulder and his nose. He staggered, almost imperceptibly, but she caught it.

Jewel searched Colin's gaze. She wanted to fight back like Colin had taught her. She positioned her feet in a wide stance. But to her surprise, he sent her a subtle shake of his head.

No.

What? He didn't even want her to try?

"Come on." Buck tugged her back and away from Colin.

She held her ground, refusing to move. "You're not going to kill me. Without me, you'll never find the diamond."

"Don't test your theory." He pressed the cold blade harder against her neck. A sharp sting pricked her skin; warmth slid down. Her legs went weak. "And I wouldn't worry about the chief saving you. He's in no shape to follow."

"No!" she screamed as Buck dragged her away, pressing the knife into her throat. "You can't leave him to die."

"Believe me. This is not how I wanted this to end. I wanted him to suffer more."

He dragged her deeper into the ice cave, where the greens and cerulean blues turned dark and ominous.

And the deeper they went, the farther she was from Colin. Would he survive? Would she ever see him again? Why hadn't he run after Buck again? He must be badly wounded, possibly dying; otherwise he would come for her.

She twisted, but any movement she made other than forward with Buck meant potential death as she felt the sting of the knife, the small trickle of blood already running down her neck.

"Colin!" she called back to him. Jewel sucked in too much air and won herself another cut. "Listen," she said to Buck. "I'll tell you where the diamond is and you can just let me go. Colin needs help. I can't let him die."

"Why not? He failed you, just like he failed the woman he loved in Texas. Why would you want to help him now? He deserves what he gets."

"You're a monster."

"So I've heard."

"It makes me shudder to think you're married to my sister." She tried to jerk away. "Where are you taking me?"

"Plans have changed. I can't be sure others won't show up looking for the chief or for you, so you'll need to come with me. You can show me the diamond yourself. I might like that better. You can put the diamond in my hand and beg for your life. Let's face it, if I kill you, Meral might inherit everything, but that doesn't mean we'll ever find it. You've hidden it well so far. And my business is overextended at the moment. Taking the diamond from you is like a moonlighting weekend, nothing more."

"Then you should pull the knife away because you're

going to accidentally kill me before you have the diamond."

Buck responded. Jewel was free from the knife.

Now that it no longer threatened her within an inch of her life, she pressed her face into her hands, stumbling as she went, thinking of all her regrets.

She'd never really trusted Silas, the man she'd loved, with her life. If she had, she wouldn't have stolen the diamond in the first place, and all of this trouble could have been avoided.

If I had known what the future held, God, I never would have done it! But, God, I want to move past my mistakes. I want to live to see another day. I want a chance at love again.

She wanted a chance to love Colin. What an idiot she'd been not to see that. Not to take a chance at having a complete life again. At loving again.

Maybe…maybe she had loved him all along, but from a distance.

Had she ruined their chance to be together? For all she knew, he could be dying right now. But, no, that wasn't true. Jewel had a feeling, a very strong feeling, that Colin was alive. Or maybe she just refused to believe he would die when he had so much to live for. Together they had so much to live for. And Colin wasn't the sort of man to give up as long as he had breath.

Maybe she hadn't completely trusted Silas, but she would trust Colin to be the hero.

Still, maybe she could give him some help along the way. New determination filled her. Buck squeezed her arm and jerked her forward then back. She glanced at him. He didn't know his way, after all. She didn't point out that he was lost. How could she use this?

She hadn't lived in Alaska without gaining a few skills, and on that point she had an advantage over Buck. Left lost and alone in the cave or even in the wilderness, he would be hard-pressed to survive.

But how did she get away from him, since he had a knife? If she could get her freedom and incapacitate him in some way, she could run back to Colin. Together they could escape.

Buck finally made his decision about which direction to traverse and dragged her down a tunnel to the right. Thankfully blue light filled the tunnel, lighting their path. But he'd made a bad choice. The walls closed in so that they had to slide through pressed against one side. Buck could only hold on to her arm with one hand. The knife was in his other hand.

Now.

Now was her chance. Likely the only good chance she would get. But it meant her plan to run back to Colin wouldn't work. Up ahead, the walls opened up more. Then her chance would be over.

Should she take this? Or wait for another one that she might not get?

Her temples throbbed. Time was running out. She had to make a decision. She had never been more indecisive in her life. But none of her options was good enough. There was no clear path to reach a good outcome.

"Keep moving." Buck's iron grip tightened. "What are you doing?"

Her hesitation had only made him grip harder. Why had she thought she could escape?

She kept moving forward. The wall of ice narrowed even more before it would open wider. Up ahead she spotted a jagged strip of ice protruding like a shard of broken glass. It would be tough to make it by without injury.

And *that*, she could use.

As she neared that sharp edge, Jewel took a few breaths, but failed to calm herself. What did it matter? She needed adrenaline flowing to make this happen.

Here it comes.

She inched forward, Buck gripping her arm.

Wait for it.

She pressed back and away as her body crossed over the ice knife.

Now.

She swallowed and pressed forward and against the wall just as Buck's hand gripping her arm followed. The jagged edge of the ice cut him quick and hard.

Behind her, he cried out.

His grip loosened only a little. It was enough.

Jewel broke free and pushed through the narrow passage until it widened. Then she ran. She didn't know where she was going, but she had to get away. In her mind she pictured Buck breaking free right behind her, but she knew his hand was badly mangled and the pain would slow him down.

From behind he shouted at her, using colorful language that singed her ears. But Jewel didn't look back. The problem was she could only move so fast through the ice cave without risking falling or slipping on icy patches.

With her breath rasping in her ears, she turned a corner. Paused and leaned against a wall. Listening for Buck.

Buck's ragged breaths echoed through the cave along

with his angry rant. She couldn't let him catch her. He would kill her this time, diamond or no.

The cave angled down and deep.

No, no, no. She wanted an escape. But then she saw light ahead and heard a rushing, roaring sound. A familiar sound. A glacier stream forming a waterfall?

Jewel followed the sound and the light, running as fast as she could, knowing that Buck would be on her soon. The cave opened up over a partially frozen waterfall. The bottom churned with icy cold water as it rushed out into the open to connect with the river and then the channel.

The beauty took her breath away. But she had no time to appreciate it.

Buck was going to kill her if he caught up.

Lord, what do I do?

If she jumped she would be free of Buck. Memories quickly seized her of her time fighting the other waterfall and then the rushing river. Surviving. Her body still ached. If she jumped her limbs would likely give up from the too-cold glacier water and she would drown.

Her choices came down to two.

Death by drowning.

Death by Buck.

Jewel wouldn't give him the satisfaction. Besides, she held on to hope that she could survive the icy water. It was more hope than she gave herself with Buck.

She lunged toward the falls.

Strong hands gripped her from behind.

Gun at the ready, Colin crept forward, following the voices.

The hardest thing he'd ever done in his life was to

watch without interfering as Buck had forced Jewel away at knifepoint. Colin had decided it was better to bide his time again. Let the man believe Colin was too incapacitated to follow.

As soon as the two were out of sight and earshot, Colin had grabbed the extra magazine holding twelve bullets that he'd successfully hidden away and stuck it in the Sig, then chambered a round.

He had this one chance to get it right. To get Jewel away from Buck. He'd tried to make another call for help and explain the urgency, but had gotten no cell signal. He hadn't expected one, but had thought it was worth a shot.

And now as he followed the blood drops on the ground, his pulse ramped up. His heart pressed against his rib cage.

God, please don't let Jewel be hurt. Please help her, save her. Please help me to get there before it's too late this time. I can't go through losing someone again. I couldn't live with that. Jewel has to survive.

He heard the roaring of the falls before he turned the corner. Just up ahead, Buck's words were filled with hate and anger. This was the end of the line. One way or another, Buck was going down. Either Colin deserved to be an officer of the law, the chief of police, or he didn't. Regardless, Jewel deserved to live. She deserved his best effort.

Even his life.

Holding his weapon in position, Colin rounded the corner.

At the edge of the falls, Buck pulled Jewel's hair and yelled in her face. He flashed the knife in her face, letting her know what he wanted to do with her. Colin suspected he would follow through if it weren't for the diamond. All this couldn't be for nothing.

Still, Buck could kill Jewel even if Colin called out, threatening to shoot him.

Jewel cried out in pain as Buck twisted her hair around. She opened her eyes and saw Colin. Hope infused her face.

No, Jewel, don't telegraph that I'm here.

Colin's cell suddenly rang. He gripped the gun harder as Buck jerked around to face him. Stupid cell signals came through at the worst times. He ignored the call.

Jewel grabbed Buck's bloodied hand and jabbed her thumb into what Colin could see was a badly bleeding injury.

Buck threw her down, clearly not worried about her escape. She was between the waterfall and Buck. He could snatch her back before she jumped, if that had been her intention.

Colin closed the distance. Buck jerked up and around. Started for Jewel.

"Freeze!"

Buck moved to Jewel, grabbed her hair. Flashed the knife.

Colin fired at his feet. "I killed your brother. Don't think I won't kill you, too."

And Colin wanted to. God help him, he wanted to kill this man.

Buck dropped the knife. Did as he was told.

Colin ignored the voice screaming in his head, telling him to shoot the jerk. He had to do this right. Every decision he made had to be for the right reasons and not to seek vengeance for the past or for Jed's life. Or for Katelyn's.

God, I didn't know how hard it would be!

"Back away from her. Up against the wall."

Buck couldn't seem to lose his smirk, no matter what. Colin wanted to wipe it from his face. He tugged the handcuffs from his jacket pocket, offering a smile himself for thinking to bring them.

"You mean this whole time you carried those things with you?" Buck's eyes were round with shock.

Colin liked to see it. Liked to see he'd knocked the smirk from Buck's face, too. "Guess you could say I was pretty confident this moment would come."

"The charges won't stick. You have nothing on me."

"I have Jewel's testimony."

"It's my word against hers."

"And mine."

"You're just trying to make up for the past. Your testimony won't count."

"Jewel, come over here away from the falls. Hold the weapon on Buck. Shoot him if he moves."

She moved toward Colin, relief shining in her eyes, and something more that made his heart swell. But he had to finish this business. Jewel took the weapon and aimed it at Buck. Her hands trembled as she slipped her finger into the trigger guard.

"Easy now," Colin said. "You don't want to shoot him accidentally."

Jewel nodded. Steadied her hand.

Colin approached Buck. "Hands out." They still had to make their way out of here, so Buck would need his hands out in front.

"The charges will only stick if Jewel is around to give her testimony. You think she'll make it to trial? Don't you have enough experience to know better?"

Colin stared, the whole thing unfolding in his mind, reminiscent of the past. Close, much too close, to what had gone before. Buck and Brock had been working together, throwing the investigation.

"They'll stick because this time you're working alone." Colin cuffed one wrist.

An eerie look came into Buck's eyes. "I never work alone."

Colin cuffed the other. He had him this time. But the confidence he'd expected eluded him. Instead, he was more terrified for Jewel's life now that he knew what she'd face as a witness. Could he walk this path again?

And what had Buck said? He never worked alone?

This wasn't going to end. It was never going to end until Buck was dead, too. Colin hesitated too long. Buck punched Colin in his already injured nose. Pain nearly blinded him. Colin gripped Buck, wrestling for control yet again, even though Buck was restrained in handcuffs.

He hoped Jewel wouldn't try to shoot, though he knew she could hit her target under normal circumstances. Buck slammed his fist into Colin's gunshot wound. Colin twisted Buck's injured hand, the battle roaring in his ears and growing louder.

Buck pushed Colin and he teetered on the lip of the cave, hovering over the ledge and waterfall. Just like before. And as he stared into Buck's cold, hard eyes, Colin knew without a doubt Buck had pushed him before, but had saved him in the end, just to be able to torment him a little longer.

What about now?

Colin flailed and reached out for his nemesis and gripped the short chain linking the cuffs, unsure if he meant to stop his own plunge or to take Buck Cambridge with him into the falls. Regardless of his intentions, a force beyond their control pulled them both down toward the frothing base of an icy waterfall.

Colin fell through empty space. Plunging fast. Buck released him. Time shifted. What took mere seconds seemed like minutes as they fell together. Jewel screamed his name from above, her cries melding with the rumble of the waterfall.

SIXTEEN

"No! Colin, noooooooo!"

The violent water rushed beneath the ice, then burst through halfway down the side of the cliff before churning at the base, drowning out her screams.

She watched the two men plummet, then disappear in mist and foam. Her heart sank beneath the water with them.

Oh, God. No.

How could he survive the drop to the bottom, much less the icy water? Fear wrapped around her very core. The day Silas had died she'd heard thunder, a rare event in this part of the world. She remembered thinking about that, but at that moment, she'd had no idea that the sound had followed the lightning strike that had killed Silas. Her husband.

And if she had been there to see it, what could she have done?

Nothing. Maybe she would have died with him.

But she couldn't stand here and do nothing now.

Jewel looked for a way to make it down from the cave. But it was a straight drop. Distress threatened to force her to her knees. She pushed down the panic and dread, turned and ran back through the cave, hoping she remembered the way out of the icy maze. She followed the drops of blood, easy enough to see on the white ice, then slipped through the thin walls where she'd made her escape. A lot of good that had done.

She was running, pushing herself harder, even though pain stitched her side. Jewel wasn't sure she could find her way back to the watercourse or what she could do to help Colin, but she had to try.

God, help him, help him, help him…

While she ran, she prayed harder than she'd ever prayed. Whatever it meant, the deeper meaning of it, she didn't know or care. She only knew that Colin was everything to her. Finally, she could admit that now. Despite protecting her heart all these years, she was here all the same, losing someone she loved, if it wasn't already too late. But she wouldn't think like that. She couldn't lose him, too.

Finally, Jewel rushed from the cave's exit, then hurried back through the woods and around, taking the same direct path that Buck had forced her to go.

"Help!" she called as she ran. *God, please let there be someone out here to help me.* "Help me! Help us!"

She would have thought Colin would have called for backup once he'd discovered Buck had taken her. But maybe he hadn't had time before he'd come chasing after her. If so, then it was her fault for sneaking away. Maybe her mistake had been the catalyst to a tragic ending. Through the woods she could see the river in the distance. It spilled out from the falls a couple of miles from the visitor center. Out of breath, Jewel made her way to the riverbank, searching for Colin. Hoping she wouldn't see Buck.

"Colin!" she called, searching the water and rapids, remembering her own fight with a river.

Jewel only thought she had been helpless before.

She stumbled over a rock and fell to her knees at the river's edge.

And there.

Colin floated facedown in the water. Dread washed through her. Jewel stepped into the liquid ice and hauled him onto the bank. He was heavy, especially with wet clothing, but Jewel was undeterred. Jewel tugged him up farther away from the bank, then rolled him over to immediately start CPR.

She could only hope and pray he hadn't been in this condition for long—five minutes or less and the freezing glacier water would slow any neurological effects like brain damage.

Colin rolled to the side and coughed. Then he got to all fours, hung his head and expelled the river that had nearly drowned him. Groaning, he fell back on his back. His eyes cut to Jewel, but he said nothing.

What was he thinking? "Your lips are blue," she said, breaking the silence between them. "We have to get you warmed up."

"Jewel." He lifted a hand. She leaned in to let him cup her cheek. "You saved me."

"You're the real hero here, Colin. You saved me first. Protected me, then rescued me from Buck. If you hadn't been there..."

His gaze clouded over, a flicker of emotion shuttered away. What was Colin thinking? Did he hold her responsible? This all had come about because of her mistake. Colin had almost lost his life because of her. And he still might if they didn't get him warmed up.

Shivering, Colin twisted and climbed to his feet. Jewel joined him. He started to pull her into his arms and then hesitated. Because of his disappointment in her?

"For whatever it's worth," she said, "I'm sorry about everything."

"Oh, Jewel." Again, he cupped her cheek. His hand was as cold as ice. "No need to apologize. I just… I don't want to make you any colder."

He shook almost uncontrollably and blood oozed from the bloodshot wound. Not good. Blood loss was dangerous enough on its own—it was worse when he was struggling against hypothermia. Jewel wrapped her arms around him. She could use her body heat to warm him until help arrived. Was help even coming? "Does anyone know where we are?"

"I called for help when I learned he had taken you."

"It's taking them long enough."

He nodded. "There."

Jewel let go of him to see where he pointed. Coughing, he stumbled forward. Jewel couldn't hold him up without following him.

In the distance she spotted two men hiking toward them.

"Looks like someone from the state police and the local PD," Colin said. "We still need to find Buck."

The two men approached. Jewel spoke first. "We need to get him somewhere warm. I pulled him from the river." She explained as best she could everything that happened and that Colin had helped her to escape a kidnapper.

"Thank you, ma'am. We'll take it from here," the state trooper said.

"The kidnapper might still be in the river," Colin said. "We need a search and rescue."

One officer nodded and assisted Colin up and took him away. The other got on his radio to get a SAR mission number initiated.

Jewel followed, worried the hike down would take too long. Colin had called for help, for backup in taking Buck in, but not for medical assistance.

Hiking behind them she listened as Colin explained about Buck. That he could be dead or he could have escaped.

Oh, Meral! How would Jewel tell her sister? She would be devastated. After their argument, Meral could still believe Buck was innocent, and the blame for this would fall on Jewel.

Then she remembered Buck's words. *I never work alone.*

A chill ran over her, adding to the cold that had seeped into her bones. She glanced at the woods around them as they hiked. Was someone out there watching?

This wasn't over yet.

Colin sat in the park ranger's office off the glacier visitor center, wrapped in a blanket and drinking hot coffee. Considering that he had nearly drowned, he thought he was past the worst of it. He'd let the ranger use the GSW kit on his superficial wound until he could get real medical attention.

No time for that yet.

The trooper stepped into the room. "We found a body that matches your description. His hands were cuffed. He seems to have drowned."

Colin hung his head. "He never had a chance."

Jewel entered the small room, her eyes red rimmed. The fierce need to comfort and protect her rose up in him. Why had he ever denied himself loving this woman? The battle with Buck and then the waterfall had opened his eyes. Losing his life until she had revived him, the excuses he'd made before seemed just that. Excuses. But…she was a wealthy woman far out of his league. Colin had been out of his league before with Katelyn, and it hadn't ended well. He would do what was best and walk away from anything more with Jewel. They were not finished with this business, and Colin needed to keep his head in the game.

"We need to tell Meral. How are we going to tell her?" Jewel asked.

The authorities were trying to locate *The Alabaster Sky*, which had pulled anchor and disappeared.

Colin had already given his statement, as had Jewel, but there was one thing he'd forgotten. He stood and let the blanket drop. "Cambridge said he didn't work alone."

Silence filled the small office as the words sank in. The ranger sitting across from him scratched his chin.

"But that doesn't mean it was Meral," Jewel pleaded. "When he first captured me, he said he had drugged her. That she had slept through all the incidents. That she was clueless. She isn't his partner."

No. Just his wife.

"Regardless, we need to tell her what's happened to her husband." Colin eyed Jewel. Telling someone they had lost a loved one was the worst part of being a police officer. "And maybe we can find out the truth, including the identities of Buck's accomplice or accomplices.

But you need to stay vigilant, Jewel. Your life could still be in danger."

And he knew that well enough from his past.

Ryan, the police officer who assisted Colin, rushed back into the office. "We've located *The Alabaster Sky* docked at Alder's Bay." He nodded at Jewel and Colin. "I'll transport you there."

"Wait," Colin said.

"What are you thinking?" Jewel asked.

"The yacht has to be waiting to rendezvous with Buck. I hadn't suspected the crew, but now I don't know if the crew or the captain is involved in his crimes or not. This could be our chance to find out."

"Buck planned to take me back so I could show him where I'd hid the diamond. Other than tearing the boat apart, I don't know how he would have found it."

"What's your plan?" Ryan asked.

"I'll return to the yacht and gather the staff and Meral and tell them what's happened," Colin said. "We'll see how they react. If you wouldn't mind sticking around, maybe you can catch anyone who tries to leave. In the meantime, can you get someone to run a background on the crew of *The Alabaster Sky*? See who might have any connection to Buck Cambridge."

"I'm going, too," Jewel said. "This is my sister. I want to be there for her."

Colin hung his head, wondering if Jewel would ever forgive him for his next words. "I'm not sure that's a good idea, Jewel. Despite what you believe, Meral could still be party to Buck's crimes."

Her eyes blazed. "Look. I know my sister, okay? She isn't capable of this."

He didn't have the heart to remind her that she hadn't

known her sister for at least the past twenty years of her life. "I hope you're right, Jewel. For your sake, I hope you're right. But we can't ignore that possibility, and in that case, you're vulnerable. She could threaten your life to save her own."

His words cut her. He could see it in her eyes, but they had to be said.

With a deep frown in her brow, she rubbed her arms and averted her gaze. But she said nothing in response. She knew it was true.

With his words he'd begun to sever his emotional connection to Jewel. He could see it in her eyes. Nearly losing himself, everything that had happened, had him vulnerable and willing to let himself love. But he'd come to his senses. He couldn't let himself get any closer.

Caring too much for Jewel had kept him from pressing for answers from the start. If he had just pushed harder, found out about the diamond earlier, then maybe Buck would be in jail instead of dead, and Jed would still be alive. Getting emotionally involved just caused problems.

Back in Texas he was too close to the witness in a case, and he'd kept that under wraps because his chief would have taken the case from him. But he'd fallen in love with her and had wanted to be close and keep his hands on the investigation. To make sure things were done right and she was safe, he'd told himself. And all along, he'd had his eyes on the wrong man.

That had cost her her life.

A person could never know where seemingly innocent decisions would lead or what lives would be affected. Knowing was beyond the realm of humanity. Only God knew these things.

What irony that his bringing charges against the wrong man over a decade ago in Texas would end in him facing off with the right man years later. Colin feared his own mistakes—both from the past and more recently—would cost Jewel more than her diamond.

He couldn't trust himself to protect her. He couldn't rely on his own strength. He'd done that before and had failed.

Please, God, help me to keep her safe!

SEVENTEEN

Jewel boarded *The Alabaster Sky* with Colin, her heart torn over what she was about to do. She had successfully negotiated that she would be the one to tell Meral. But Colin wanted the staff there to hear the news at the same time and went to find them all. Jewel didn't like this.

There had to be a better way to find Buck's partner in crime.

She found Meral in the salon, curled up with a blanket around her. Worry lines made her look much older. Jewel rushed to her. Meral immediately jumped up and hugged her sister.

"You're back. I thought you weren't coming." Meral held Jewel at arm's length and then, seeming to remember their earlier argument, dropped her arms. "What's happened? Why are you back?"

Meral's gaze reflected her fear of the worst. She moved away from Jewel and continued. "Tell me what's going on."

Jewel opened her mouth, but she couldn't find the words. Where did she start? But Meral started jabbering instead.

"After everything that happened, I had a headache

and took a nap. Buck's so good to me. He found my pills to help me rest. When I woke up, he was gone. Stella told me he would be back soon, but she didn't say where he'd gone. He isn't answering his phone. For all the good cells do around here. But that doesn't explain why you're here, Jewel." Meral's eyes softened. "Unless you've come to apologize. That's it, isn't it? I hope you know how wrong you were about Buck and you're going to stay now."

The way Meral rambled on, Jewel could see how someone else might suspect her of being guilty of knowing something, but from Jewel's perspective, it was clear she'd been sleeping. Her speech was even slightly slurred. Buck had told the truth on that point. He had drugged her.

"Meral." Colin stepped in.

Behind him stood the other crew members he'd gathered together.

Jewel had intended to break the harsh news, but she lost her nerve. She stepped back, standing next to him, giving him permission, though he needed none. Even though he had taken a bullet and had almost drowned, strength and confidence emanated from him. Jewel tried to soak it in. She was going to need strength to help Meral.

"I'm sorry to have to tell you that your husband is gone."

Meral gasped. "Gone? What do you mean?"

"I'm sorry, but he was found dead."

They had made a mistake by being the ones to do this. Now Meral would want to know how it had happened. How would she react when she learned both

Jewel and Colin were involved? She might blame them. Accuse them.

Glass shattered behind them.

Glancing back, Stella's face contorted. She covered her mouth. She looked at Colin. Must have seen something in his eyes. Recognition? She turned and ran up the steps to the deck.

Colin gave Jewel a glance and took off after her. Jewel should stay with her sister, but she feared for Colin, too. If Stella was Buck's partner, then she must be the one who had forced Jewel's Durango off the road. That meant she was as dangerous as Buck was.

Jewel ran up the steps and onto the deck, but didn't see Colin or Stella.

Where had they gone? Had Stella jumped overboard and Colin followed her? Jewel rushed to the rail and looked over into the water.

Nothing.

Eerie tingles ran over her arm. "Colin," she whispered. "Where are you?"

This wasn't how any of this was supposed to happen. What about Colin's backup near the dock, waiting to corral anyone who tried to escape?

Jewel realized her foolishness. She would go back down with Meral and wait this out. But she felt cold plastic against her head. A Glock? How many times would she go through this?

"You're coming with me," Stella said.

"Why are you doing this?"

"You killed my father."

"Buck is your *father*?"

"Yes. Dad and I worked together. This should have been an easy job, but you just wouldn't give up."

"You mean I just wouldn't die."

"Your words. Not mine. Now tell me where you hid the diamond. I can't leave here without something to show for it. I need something from you to make up for my loss. It's either that or your life."

All this time, Stella must have been searching, even while Buck had kidnapped Jewel, and she still hadn't found the diamond on the yacht. Jewel had to keep her talking until Colin could find them.

"How did you get a job on this yacht? Or is the whole crew involved?"

Stella scoffed, digging the gun deeper. "Because that's how it all played out. I got the job when the other steward conveniently became ill. Dad convinced the other guests who'd already booked the boat to take a later cruise. He paid them for their time. Who could say no to that? Dad's brilliant. He knows how to work things. Or at least he did."

"Where's Colin? What did you do to him?"

"Shh." Stella tugged her back into the shadows. "Say one word and I'll kill him."

Colin jogged around the deck, clearly looking for Stella.

Stella tugged her deeper into the shadows. Pulling Jewel closer, Stella shifted the gun and pressed it into Jewel's side, sending her message loud and clear. Like father like daughter.

Enough of this.

Even with the gun pressed in her side, Jewel knew she could take Stella. She was beyond tired of this, and it would never end until Jewel ended it.

She used the same moved she'd used in the attic on

Buck, slamming her head back. It worked beautifully and left Stella splayed on the deck, gun sliding away.

And then Colin was there, standing slack mouthed and staring at Stella. He looked from her up to Jewel and grinned.

"Finally." Jewel dusted off her hands. "Meet Buck's daughter and partner in crime."

Colin radioed to the other officers, who quickly boarded the yacht and took Stella into custody. Jewel went back into the salon to find Meral curled in a ball, sobbing. It would take her time to accept all that had happened.

Back at the B and B, Meral and Jewel tried to come to grips with everything they'd been through during the past few days. Statements had been given, the Krizan Diamond referred to as a family heirloom. Meral explained it had never been reported missing or stolen, convincing Jewel that it belonged to her as much as anyone in the family. Jewel wasn't sure what to do or how to feel about that.

With everyone questioned, finally the investigation was closed. Stella had been arrested and charged as an accomplice to murder, plus attempted murder and numerous other crimes involving jewel theft throughout the country.

But that didn't mean it was over. Not for Meral, whose life as she knew it was ruined.

"I'm so sorry, honey." Jewel ran her hand over Meral's head, hoping to comfort her, but there could be no comfort for Meral. Only time would bring healing. Jewel was glad Meral would stay with her for the time being.

"How could he do this to me? I thought he loved me. I don't understand." Meral sobbed into another tissue and shook her head. The pain in her eyes broke Jewel's heart. She couldn't help but feel that in a way—a long, roundabout way—she'd done this to her sister.

"How can I ever trust again? How can I ever love again?" Meral asked.

Jewel had thought she would never trust or love again herself after losing Silas, so she understood Meral's misgivings. "First you have to heal and you need to give yourself time. I once thought I could never love again. But now I realize I was just scared. Trusting is a risk, yes. Loving again is a risk. Then I found someone special, and now I'm willing to take that risk."

Meral blinked up at her. "Chief Winters."

"Colin. I'm in love with him. I tried to deny it, to hide it, to keep it from surfacing, but what is life without love?" Jewel regretted her words. This wasn't the time. "I'm sorry, Meral. I shouldn't have…"

"No, it's okay. I think…deep down, I knew something was going on with Buck. That his business wasn't on the up-and-up. I didn't understand it anyway, so I just chose to look the other way. If anything, I should be the one who is sorry. If it wasn't for me, he never would have come after you."

"No. You have nothing to apologize for. Wait here. I have something to show you." While they'd dined on the deck that first night, Jewel had left to quickly refresh herself in her cabin, and she'd taken that chance to transfer the diamond to Meral's luggage, where no one would think to look. Jewel tugged open Meral's luggage now and rummaged around until she found the inner lining. From there she pulled out the Krizan

Diamond and held it out to Meral. "I want you to have this. I don't want it. I don't want to be wealthy. I don't want or need anything except, well maybe…"

"Your police chief."

"Right, except I'm not sure he'll have me now that he knows I stole a diamond. That I'm kind of a jewel thief like the man who killed the woman he loved years ago. To have a chance with him, I think he needs to know I no longer have the diamond. I'm giving it up. He needs to know that I trust him. I didn't trust Silas, not enough, but somehow I have to convince Colin that I trust him enough not to need a backup plan anymore. I have to convince him to forgive me for not telling him everything when it mattered the most. When it could have made a difference."

Meral eyed the precious gem. "I don't want it, Jewel. I can't take it. It will only remind me of Buck's duplicity. You keep it." Meral curled back into a ball.

Jewel held on to it, wanting nothing more than to throw it into the ocean. She hung her head, wishing she could get back the past few days. If she could, she would do everything differently. She would tell Colin everything, maybe even that she loved him.

Someone cleared a throat.

Jewel looked up. Colin. He gestured that he wanted to speak with her. Meral was resting with her eyes closed. Jewel left her sister, who needed privacy, time alone anyway. Meral needed some space to process the pain. It would take years for it to go away completely, but now that she had fully faced the truth, she could start the healing process.

Heart beating unevenly, Jewel approached Colin and

held out the diamond for him to see. "How long have you been standing there?"

Had he heard her confession of love?

He tipped her chin up. "Long enough."

Her gaze widened slightly. He saw uncertainty there as he drank deeply from the pool of her hazel-green eyes. He touched the soft skin of her cheek, twisted his finger in a tendril of her ash-blond hair.

She held the diamond out, and it shimmered in the dim light. He'd been so busy with everything there hadn't been time to see the "family heirloom" that had caused the trouble.

The yellow stone glistened and sparkled and took his breath away. Never had he seen anything like it up close and personal.

Jewel began explaining about cut, color and clarity. "It's just over twenty carats, natural fancy intense and internally flawless."

"If you say so," he said. All the diamond-speak had his head spinning.

"Do you know they have to mine over two hundred and fifty tons of ore just to find a one-carat colored diamond? And the radiant cut means it has seventy-seven facets."

Colin wouldn't tell her he had no idea what she was talking about. How could he when she was clearly in her element? The diamond looked like she'd captured sunshine in the palm of her hand, and that sunshine reflected on her face as she talked about what was near and dear to her heart—her family and the family diamond business. She may have left it all behind twenty years earlier, but she clearly hadn't forgotten a thing.

The fact she talked long and knowledgeable on a subject he knew absolutely nothing about reminded him all too well she was out of his league, really, as he'd always thought.

He pressed a finger on it—cold to the touch—and sucked in a breath.

And then he knew he couldn't do it. He couldn't step away from her. This diamond might be cold, but the jewel before him was anything but.

He wrapped her hand around the diamond and covered it with his own. "This isn't the jewel I want. This belongs to you. Your confession, your past, has no bearing on how I feel about you, Jewel Caraway. How I've always felt but denied."

His throat grew tight. "I thought that you and I would both be better off if I stepped back. Turned away from this force that pulls me to you at every turn, but I'm not strong enough to walk away from you anymore. You're more precious to me than anything in this world. Even my own life. And I've wasted so much time already."

He searched her eyes for understanding. For the love he wanted to see reflected in her gentle hazel gaze, unclouded by fear or uncertainty or doubt. And he was not disappointed.

How many years had he imagined, dreamed about this moment, then shoved aside his longing to do what he had thought was right for them both? But right now he was weak, so very weak. His will bowed to the current running between them, a quaking force that shook him to the bones. Or maybe he was finally strong enough to accept the path that God had wanted for him all along. To stop running in fear from the prospect of getting hurt again.

Colin slowly wrapped his arms around Jewel and pressed his lips against hers. She kissed him back, and he savored her response.

Accepting. Eager.

Ecstasy. He was enraptured at the slightest pressure of her soft lips. Any more and he would lose himself completely. He breathed in deeply the jewel he'd longed for, and realized that somehow his heart had carved the perfect place for her within him.

He could have stayed forever with Jewel in his arms, letting her know how he felt about her, but he had to rein in his emotions. It was dangerous to linger. He inched back. Still, he was close to her, closer than he'd ever been physically and emotionally, even spiritually. There was something about loving a woman who loved God, and he could feel that in her, as well.

He let go of his resolve never to love. God didn't want that for him, and he didn't want it for himself— not when he had the treasure of Jewel's love as recompense. Her heart in exchange for his own.

"I heard you tell Meral that you loved me. I love you, too, Jewel. I think I always have."

Her eyes shimmered with what he hoped were tears of joy along with her beautiful smile. Despite the tragedy and pain around them, she was free of her stalker and her past, as was Colin.

"This experience has taught me something," he said.

"What's that?" Her voice was lyrical, and he loved that about it.

It felt wonderful to be free finally to enjoy everything about Jewel, instead of always pushing thoughts of her away.

"If I didn't know before, I know now how precious

life is and I don't want to waste a single moment. I don't want to waste time regretting the past or fearing the future. I don't need days, weeks or months to get to know you. I've known you for years. I'll court you, ask you on a real date first, if that's what you want, but I feel like in my heart I've been secretly courting you for years. And there's so much more I want to do with you."

She laughed and nodded, wiped at a tear.

"Will you be my wife, Jewel? Will you marry me?"

She shuddered, hung her head back, but the look on her face was pure elation. Then she rolled her head forward and smiled. "How about next week? You can marry me first, and I'll take the courting for a lifetime."

* * * * *

Ever since she found the Nancy Drew books with the pink covers in her country school library, **Sharon Dunn** has loved mystery and suspense. Most of her books take place in Montana, where she lives with three nearly grown children and a hyper border collie. She lost her beloved husband of twenty-seven years to cancer in 2014. When she isn't writing, she loves to hike surrounded by God's beauty.

Books by Sharon Dunn

Love Inspired Suspense

Montana Standoff
Top Secret Identity
Wilderness Target
Cold Case Justice
Mistaken Target
Fatal Vendetta
Big Sky Showdown
Hidden Away
In Too Deep
Wilderness Secrets
Undercover Threat

True Blue K-9 Unit

Courage Under Fire

Texas Ranger Holidays

Thanksgiving Protector

Visit the Author Profile page
at Harlequin.com for more titles.

HIDDEN AWAY

Sharon Dunn

Remember ye not the former things, neither consider the things of old. Behold, I will do a new thing; now it shall spring forth; shall ye not know it?
—*Isaiah* 43:18–19

To my Lord, savior, friend, counselor and king.
Jesus, for more than thirty years,
we have walked this journey together.

ONE

Despite the windows being shut against winter temperatures, a chill skittered across detective Jason Enger's skin. Hidden in the trees that surrounded the property, he stared at the monitor in his surveillance van as a man made his way toward the door of the secluded mansion.

Ten miles from the house and nestled in the Montana mountains was the town of Silver Strike. The booming tourist spot was not only a place for world-class skiing and fly-fishing, but also ground zero for an international smuggling ring. Couriers used empty vacation homes as pickup points for valuable smuggled items that were often of cultural significance to the country they'd been taken from.

As a private detective, Jason had been working with the FBI for months to identify the couriers and the buyers in hopes that one of them would lead to the mastermind behind it all. The Bureau coordinated with US Customs to track when artifacts had been stolen from museums or personal collections.

As Jason watched the man type in security codes on the keypad by the door, look around nervously and step inside, he was pretty sure he'd hit pay dirt. Figur-

ing out how the thief had gotten the security codes was
a piece of the puzzle for the Bureau to discover. Jason's
job was to take photos that would lead to identifying
all the players involved.

Three weeks ago, an eighteen-karat-gold bookmark
that had belonged to Mussolini had been stolen from a
museum in Italy. The Bureau had been watching several empty properties ever since.

Jason took a deep breath. His camera hadn't recorded
a clear picture of the man's face, so he'd wait around
until the perp came back out. That way he'd be sure
of a positive ID. The thief had walked up to the mansion. He must have parked his car in some out-of-the-
way place so it wouldn't be spotted in the driveway of
a house that was supposed to be unoccupied. The falling snow would cover the man's tracks in a matter of
minutes, leaving no trace.

Jason stared at the monitors. A car pulled up, and
a woman stepped out. His heart beat a little faster as
he leaned closer to the screen. She tilted her chin and
squared her shoulders with none of the nervous body
language the man had displayed. Everything about her,
from her posture to the way she dressed, projected confidence and money, very Ivy League. Who was she?

The woman punched in the security codes and disappeared behind the ornate wooden door. Jason's throat
went dry. Was she an innocent homeowner unexpect-
edly walking into a dangerous situation or was she al-
lied with the thief?

If she was not involved, he needed to get her out of
there before she crossed the thief's path. Most of the
men in the crime ring who had been identified had a
history of violence. The thought of harm coming to a

woman made Jason's chest tight. He wrestled with indecision. He couldn't risk blowing this operation either; months of work would go down the tubes if the smuggling ring found out the Feds were onto them. Arresting the couriers would be an act of futility, since only finding the kingpin would end the syndicate.

He reached for a work shirt with the name *Mel* written on the pocket and a clipboard he kept in a tote, part of his go-to kit for his work as a PI. Walking around a neighborhood in a uniform meant most people didn't notice you. He put his zip-front hoodie and coat back on.

His chest muscles squeezed tight. He was taking a huge risk in showing himself, but a woman might get hurt if he didn't.

He pulled the van into the driveway, grabbed his gun from the glove compartment and placed it in his waistband so his winter coat covered it. He prayed he wouldn't have to use the gun. Snow cascaded and twirled from the sky as he hurried toward the door.

Usually it was easy enough for him to get a read on people. If the woman was innocent, he'd find a way to convince her to leave. If guilty, he'd get a good look at her face, assuming she would even answer the door. Not answering would be a giveaway that she was involved. It would take an Oscar-worthy performance to not give away his real reason for being here if she was in on the operation, but he was confident of his abilities.

He touched the doorbell with a gloved finger, took in a breath and prepared to play Mel the concerned county worker.

From the moment she'd stepped into the Wilsons' house, something felt off to Isabel Connor. The hairs on the back of her neck stood at attention as her heart thudded faster. She couldn't let go of the feeling that she was being watched.

She shook her head, trying to free herself of her uneasiness. Maybe it was just because the Wilsons had chosen to show up three days earlier than expected. They'd texted her directly instead of getting in touch with her employer, Mary Helms at Sun and Ski Property Management. It was Isabel's job to get the houses ready for the clients. Stock the refrigerator, make sure the property was in working order, place fresh flowers in the vases, whatever it took to make clients feel comfortable in their vacation home.

Grabbing some books that had been left on an entryway table, she headed toward the upstairs library, stopping to turn the thermostat up a few degrees. She put the books on the shelf and then ran back downstairs to inspect the kitchen, where some papers and boxes had been left on the counter, probably by a cleaning crew. Since she still needed to unload flowers and groceries from her car, she'd left the alarm off so she could run in and out of the house quickly. She'd reset it when she left.

The doorbell rang.

Her breath caught in her throat as that gut feeling that something was off rose to the surface. Who on earth could that be? The Wilsons' house was miles from downtown Silver Strike and other homes. They hadn't been back here in months. News of the Wilsons' early arrival couldn't have gotten out that fast. Not even her boss knew the Wilsons had had a change of plans. She hurried from the kitchen but walked a little slower as she approached the front door.

Through the window by the door, she could see a

man with a clipboard. Her heart raced a little faster as she swung the door open.

The man offered her a warm smile. "Afternoon, ma'am. It seems there's been a gas leak at one of the homes under construction. We're advising all nearby homeowners to vacate their premises until we can be sure there is no danger."

Though she remained calm on the surface, a hurricane of suspicion raged through her. "What construction?" Isabel managed to hide her fear by squaring her shoulders and lifting her chin. A posture she had practiced in the mirror for hours. The way she dressed and how she carried herself were pieces of the professional image she'd taught herself to project so no one would ever guess her dark past.

"Up the road. I'm with the county. This is just a precaution." There was something genuine about that smile, but she wasn't about to be taken in. Charm was an inch deep. What if this man had come to rob this place, thinking it was going to be empty, and now he was trying to get rid of her? She had a responsibility to the Wilsons.

There might be construction up the road. She had no idea. Silver Strike was booming and people were willing to pay for building even in the winter. She knew there were other houses around here. The area was actually considered to be a subdivision, though each property was at least five acres. She angled her head to look past him. His van seemed somewhat official, though there was no logo on it.

He ran his hands through his dark hair and flashed blue eyes at her.

Trust your gut, Izzy.

She wasn't about to be dazzled by his good looks or his blue eyes. That always led to heartache. It had taken her seven long years to rebuild her life after falling for the charming petty criminal Nick Solomon when she was a teenager. Trusting a man on any level was never a good idea.

"You said it was just a precaution." She read his name tag, which was visible beneath his open coat and zip-front sweatshirt. "I'll take my chances, Mel." She lifted her hand toward the door to close it. "I have work to do."

"Work?" Now *his* voice sounded suspicious. He put his foot between the door and the frame.

The aggression of his move set off alarm bells for her. "Yes. I work for a property management company. I have to get the house ready for clients." She was pretty sure there was no gas leak. Her priority needed to be with her job. Mary Helms, the owner of Sun and Ski Property Management, had taken a chance on her in the first place. Though she'd turned her life around and over to God, Isabel had a criminal record that made employment tricky.

"Please, I think you need to leave the house…just for a short time. What is your name?"

"Isabel…" She stopped. It was none of his business who she was. She lifted her head to meet his gaze. The tone to his voice had been almost desperate. Though there was nothing plastic about his expression or the pleading look in his eyes, she was pretty sure he was up to something. He was probably just a very good actor— that was why she had doubts. Most men were good at pretending to care. "Thank you, sir, for the warning, and have a good day." She pushed the door into its frame so he had to step out of the way.

Hands shaking, heart racing, Isabel pressed against the wall by the door and took in a prayer-filled breath. What if that man meant to rob this place? She just didn't buy the gas-leak story.

I can do all things through Christ Jesus who strengthens me.

She peered through the window by the door, watching the man's van pull out of the driveway. She didn't like being here alone.

Tension coiled tight in her chest. What should she do? She hurried to the entryway table where she'd left her purse and phone. The Wilsons didn't have a landline. What if she was totally wrong? Other than her gut feeling, she really didn't have any evidence the man was up to something. It would not be good for Sun and Ski's reputation to have police swarming a client's property for no reason.

She clicked open her purse and felt for her phone. Maybe the smart thing to do would be to call her boss first.

She stepped back into the living room and stared at her phone, prepared to dial Mary's number. She hit the first number.

An arm wrapped around her waist and a knife pressed against her neck.

"So you and your partner are trying to horn in on my good fortune."

Her heart raged in her chest as her body stiffened against the prospect of having her throat slit.

The man pressed his cheek against her ear. The voice was not that of the man in the van.

Isabel jammed her elbow hard into the man's stomach. He grunted and loosened his grip on her. She twisted free of his hold and hurried toward the kitchen. She had only a few seconds' head start while the man recovered from the blow. Stepping into the large pantry of the kitchen, she slipped behind a shelf of canned goods, hoping the darkness would hide her from view. She knew the layout of the house well enough. This was probably the best hiding place on the main floor.

She'd lost her phone in the struggle. Closing her eyes, she listened to the raging of her own heartbeat, praying that the man with the knife only glanced into the dark pantry. If he left to search elsewhere, she could make a run for the door and get to her car. But she wondered if the man who had come to the door was in on this home invasion. Even if she made it to her car, she might have to deal with Mel. Her life now depended on all those what-ifs.

Isabel drew a prayer-filled breath and pressed deeper into the pantry.

Midway down the long driveway, Jason hit the brakes and listened to the engine hum. The smart thing would be to return to his hiding place and wait for the two thieves, the man and the woman who called herself Isabel, to emerge from the house, then do his job—get the photos the Bureau had hired him to take.

His job was to be invisible. If the smugglers knew they were being watched, the investigation would fall apart. In order to get to the mastermind, they had to let the petty criminals do the thefts and not involve local cops making low-level arrests.

No part of that plan made the tightness in his chest subside. He prided himself on being able to tell friend from foe. Discerning motives in people was part of what made him a good PI. Still, he was uncertain about the woman in the house. Yes, she'd given him the brush-off, but something about her had been so vulnerable, afraid even. Was she telling the truth about being the hired help or just trying to get rid of him so she and her partner could finish the job? Or maybe she'd been brought in on this against her will.

He had to know for sure.

He killed the engine and slipped out of the van, dashing toward the side of the house and pressing along the wall. The van would only be visible from upstairs north-facing windows, not from the downstairs. He crouched down beneath the window by the door and peered inside. Pieces of a shattered vase lay on the floor by the foyer table. A woman's purse was flung against the wall. Signs of a struggle?

He didn't want anyone to die here today.

Jason steeled himself and opened the door. He slipped into the dark house. Still determined not to blow this operation but to get the woman out of danger, he padded noiselessly through the foyer.

The silence on the main floor was eerie. The contents of a purse lay scattered across the ornate tile. Turning in a slow circle, he stepped over the shards from the broken vase. He scanned the main floor and then his gaze traveled up to the mezzanine and the second floor, where a creaking noise had come from.

He climbed stealthily up the stairs, his heart drumming in his ears. Once he made it to the second floor, the polished floorboards of the interior balcony didn't creak when he placed his foot on them. He hurried down the hallway, checking each room, bathroom, den, first bedroom. All empty.

Back at the mezzanine, Jason pressed against the wall and listened.

Down below, noise rose up from what was probably the kitchen. Isabel darted past his field of vision and disappeared through a door on the other side of the house. He sprinted to the top of the stairs.

A man burst out from where Isabel had come. The same tall thin man who had entered the house earlier—he glanced from side to side and then darted in the opposite direction of Isabel. He must not have seen where Isabel had gone. Jason caught the glint of a knife in the man's hand. Okay, so maybe she was in danger.

He rushed down the stairs, keeping his step light so as not to draw attention to himself. He ran across the black-and-white tile of the open entryway toward the door where Isabel had gone.

Even before he opened the door, he smelled chlorine. The humid air of the pool room assaulted him as he stepped across the threshold. As on a game show, there were four doors to choose from. Which one had she gone through?

He tiptoed on the tile and eased open the first door. Storage. When he opened the second door, he found a bedroom. Much more promising. He checked the closet and the bathroom first, then stood beside the bed. Before he could lean over to check underneath, a hard object slammed against his shin, sending a wave of pain through his calf muscle.

With pain shooting up his leg, he knelt to pull the culprit out from underneath the bed.

TWO

Isabel knew it was predictable to hide under the bed, but she'd been in a hurry. She'd grabbed a hairbrush from the vanity before slipping under the bed frame. If she was to save herself from the man with the knife, she knew she had to attack before he found her. She was no match for him physically, but she could outsmart him.

The man groaned in pain when she hit his shin with the brush. She crawled to the other side of the bed and rolled out. Just as she got to her feet, he grabbed her from behind.

She angled her body to get away and lifted her foot to kick his calf.

"Calm down, calm down. I'm not the bad guy here."

It was Mel's smooth voice. So he'd come back. She had no idea what Mr. Knife had meant by the partner comment. Mel and Mr. Knife were probably robbing the place together.

"Be quiet." He placed a hand over her mouth. "He'll find us."

Probably a trick to get her to stop resisting. She twisted her torso and dug her fingernails into his forearm.

Still he cupped her mouth, his other arm wrapped

around her waist, and held her tight against his chest. But he didn't hurt her or pull a weapon on her. She tried to twist free. He dragged her across the floor.

"Look, this place is not safe. I'll take you back to town." He guided her through the door and stepped into the pool room even as she continued to try to get away from him. He took his hand off her mouth.

"I have my own car." Like she wanted to go anywhere with this thief. She'd had enough of falling for the bad boy to last a lifetime.

She pulled free of him with so much force that she fell headlong into the pool. Cold water enveloped her. Strong arms grabbed the back of her collar and pulled her to the surface.

"Now for sure he's heard us," said Mel.

She gasped for air and reached for the edge of the pool. Mel let go of her and ran toward a door. He returned with a large towel, which he tossed toward her.

"You can't go outside like that. You'll freeze," he said. "Do these people have clothes here?"

The concern for her physical well-being gave her pause. But if he wasn't a thief, what was he doing here? She pulled herself to her feet as water dripped off her. "I can't wear a client's clothes." She picked up the towel.

He grabbed her at the elbow. "You're going to have to."

She was not keen on going anywhere with this man, but it felt like she was on a runaway train trying to stop it by dragging her feet.

Glancing around nervously, he led her through a door back out into the living room.

Her heart sank when she saw the broken vase and the mess in the entryway. Everything in this house was probably valuable. She spotted the contents of her purse on the floor, but not her phone. It must have been kicked out of view in the struggle with Mr. Knife.

"Where are the clothes?"

"Can't we just call the police?" She still didn't know what this guy's game was.

"That's a bad idea."

Her steps faltered. "Why?" What if this was a trap? He'd pretend to be helping her and then what? Kill her so he and Mr. Knife could finish the job they'd come to do?

"Trust me. We don't want the police here."

Isabel felt that familiar tightening in her stomach. Trust him? She didn't even know him, and so far almost everything he did made her suspicious.

He grabbed her elbow and led her up the stairs. "Which room?"

Noise rose up from a side room on the main floor. She hurried toward the master suite. Glancing over the balcony as they slipped behind the door, she caught a glimpse of movement down below. Mr. Knife was still looking for her on the main floor.

Mel searched the huge room. "That closet is the size of my apartment. Change in there. I'll keep watch."

She slipped into the closet and slid the door shut. How was she going to explain wearing a client's clothes to her boss? She grabbed the least expensive-looking shirt and pants she could find. As if that would make a difference. Even telling the truth about what had gone on would sound crazy, like she was trying to cover up her strange actions with a fantastic story. Because of her history with the law, she had a fear of not being believed.

Though her brain ached over what might happen, she knew she needed to focus on the now. Getting away from Mr. Knife and maybe even Mel. For sure, he wasn't some concerned official from the county. What was his game?

She buttoned up the shirt and then grabbed a sweater to put over it. Actually, this closet was bigger than her apartment. Her boss had been kind enough to rent her the studio apartment above the Sun and Ski office. She changed quickly and grabbed a pair of boots. Victoria Wilson was half a size bigger than she, but the boots would keep out the cold. Not sure what to do with her wet clothes, she put them on a hanger to dry. Another crazy action she'd have to explain. She looked around for a coat but couldn't find one.

Mel knocked on the door. "Hurry."

She slid the closet door open. Mel peered through the slightly ajar bedroom door out into the hallway.

He glanced in her direction, his expression tense. "He's upstairs. Is there another way out of here besides down the stairs and through the front door?"

She still didn't know what to think of this man. Friend or foe? "I suppose we could leave by way of the balcony." She pointed. Through the sliding glass doors, she saw that the snowfall had increased. The lazy flakes that had fallen out of the sky when she drove up here had turned into slashing swords.

Mel shut and locked the bedroom door. He stepped across the room and slid the balcony door open, signaling for her to follow. She hesitated.

The doorknob wiggled and then there was a thump against it.

Her heart seized up as she looked from Mel to the door.

"Come on, Isabel."

She had told him her name when she answered the door. But when he spoke it, something sparked inside her. Warm feelings aside, she still didn't know what Mel was up to. Why didn't he want to call the police?

A body thudded against the door again. And then she heard clicking noises. Mr. Knife was picking the lock.

Mel was the one without the knife. Maybe her odds were better with him. She darted through the open sliding glass door. Snow stung her skin. The cold hit her with full force, but the heavy wool sweater cut out much of it. Her wet hair seemed to freeze instantly, turning into hard straw-like strands.

"I'll lower you down. Hurry," he said.

She darted to the edge of the balcony and slipped through the wide railing. He grabbed her hands. His grip was like iron. He held on and eased her down.

The ground below her loomed closer. She looked up into Mel's blue eyes.

His expression was strained, face tight, teeth showing from the exertion. His body hung off the edge of the balcony at a dangerous angle. He strained. "I'm going to have to let you go."

She nodded. She fell through space, landing hard, her knees buckling. Mel slipped off the balcony and dropped to the ground with the grace of an Olympic gymnast. He grabbed her hand. They ran, feet pounding the fresh fallen snow.

She glanced over her shoulder just as she rounded the corner. Mr. Knife had come to the edge of the outdoor balcony. If he chose not to follow them and went back down the stairs and out the front door, it would buy them time.

As Mel pulled her around the house toward the drive-way where his van was parked, she had the gut-wrenching sensation that her life was about to switch into a retread of seven years ago. Here she was again, blindly following a man who might be a criminal.

Oh Lord, please protect me.

She'd been barely seventeen when Nick Solomon decided to rob a convenience store at gunpoint. He'd kissed her in the car and told her he was going inside for a bag of chips. When he slid into the passenger seat clearly agitated and commanded her to drive, she'd done what he asked. All because she'd loved and trusted him.

They hurried toward the van. Mel kicked the front tires. "Slashed." His forehead furled. "When did he find time to do that?"

She studied him for just a moment. Maybe Mel was telling the truth. Maybe he was the good guy. She wanted to believe that. She had a feeling she was staking her life on it.

"My car looks okay." She spoke between breaths and took off running toward her car. She jumped into the driver's seat and turned the key in the ignition. Because she'd thought she would be alone at the Wilsons', she had no reason to take her keys with her.

Mel got into the passenger seat.

She clicked into Reverse and hit the gas, then spun around and pointed the car toward the snowy road.

Mel gripped the armrest. "NASCAR, here we come. Who taught you to drive like that?"

A heaviness descended on her like a shroud, and she felt that stab to her heart. Nick had taught her to drive like that. Little had she realized he was grooming her to be his getaway driver.

She stared at the road ahead. Her car slipped to one side. She checked her rearview mirror. Mr. Knife stood in the driveway, arms crossed over his chest.

The car made a serpentine pattern and slid on the snow-covered road.

"Something is wrong here." She struggled to keep the car on the road. Even with the slick roads, steering was taking way more muscle power than usual. The car began to shake and vibrate.

"I think your tires are losing air." Mel's voice remained calm. "No way would he have time to do both cars." He studied the road and the surrounding trees as if he was trying to piece something together.

So her tires had been slashed too. Mr. Knife must have been in a hurry and not cut deep enough for the air to leak out fast.

She gripped the steering wheel as a tree loomed in front of her. The entire car seemed to be vibrating to pieces as the metallic clang of driving on her rims filled the front seat.

She scraped past the tree, but the car rammed into a smaller tree and came to an abrupt stop. Their bodies lurched forward then slammed back against the seat.

Mel craned his neck to stare out the back window.

Fear cut her to the bone. "Is he coming for us?"

"I can't see him."

Isabel tensed as she glanced over her shoulder. That didn't mean he wouldn't come after them.

"This car is not going to get us off this mountain. We're going to have to call…somebody." He pulled his phone out.

Somebody? What did that mean? Why not the police? Mr. Knife seemed to think they both were out to steal the fortune he'd come for. Whatever it was he was looking for in that house, it must be worth a great deal because Mr. Knife seemed determined that they not leave the house.

A chill ran up her spine. In fact, Mr. Knife seemed pretty bent on eliminating his perceived competition altogether. Why give him a chance at that?

Mel clicked open the door. "I can't get a signal. We can't stay out in this storm long. Maybe we can get a signal back at the house."

"Are you nuts?" she said.

"What other choice do we have here? It's five miles to the main road and another five into town. Who knows if any neighbors are home. Do you want to walk in a storm without a coat? You'll freeze to death."

She took in a breath. And it would be dark soon. He had a point. "Okay."

"You know the layout of the house, right? There must be someplace where we could make the call and hide out."

She clicked open her door, inviting the intense wind and cold in. "Mrs. Wilson has an art studio at the back of the property."

He hurried around the car and tugged on her elbow. "Let's get into the trees. More shelter and we won't be spotted off the bat if he does come after us. Maybe I'll be able to pick up a signal before we get to the house."

She doubted that, not with the storm brewing. She crossed her arms over her chest and put her head down. She had no choice but to go with Mel's plan. Even the short walk back to the house was going to leave her chilled to the bone at the very least.

The trees cut the wind and the snow by a little bit.

They'd tromped only a short distance before the cold settled into her bones. Mel slipped out of his coat and placed it on her shoulders. She could still feel the warmth of his body heat as she put her arms in the sleeves.

The gesture warmed her heart too. The front-zip sweatshirt he had over his uniform shirt couldn't provide much more warmth than her borrowed sweater.

"I'll be all right. I got my thermals on." He offered her a smile that brought a sparkle into his eyes. Beautiful blue eyes.

Don't be taken in, Izzy.

One small act of kindness did not reveal a man's whole character. "So you're not really with the county, are you?"

"No." He pressed his lips together and stared straight ahead, making it clear he wasn't going to tell her anything else. "The less you know, the better."

More secrecy.

As they forged through the quiet forest, Isabel felt a heaviness descend on her. What was God doing here? It felt like she was losing everything she'd fought for from the moment she'd given Him her heart in that jail cell. Her job was in jeopardy, her car had been sabotaged and she may be hooked up with another criminal.

Mel brushed the snow out of his hair. "We'll get this straightened out. Trust me."

She didn't fail to notice the flatness in his voice as if he was trying to convince himself that everything was going to be okay.

Trust me. Those were some famous last words. Wind gusted and swirled through the trees. Isabel zipped the borrowed coat up to her neck and prayed that Mel was right.

* * *

As he trudged through the snow, Jason's thoughts raced faster than a horse a mile from the barn. He glanced over at Isabel. Soft honey-colored curls covered her face as she bent forward to shield herself from the falling, blowing snow. She was pretty. He'd at least admit that.

She seemed innocent enough, but something about her just didn't ring true.

The thief hadn't found the bookmark yet or he would have left. Maybe the thief thought he or Isabel had it and that was why he was bent on taking them out. The guy was a fool to come after them. He wouldn't be utilized again by the mastermind. Whoever was orchestrating the smuggling had kept it very under the radar. These low-level guys were sometimes more brawn than brains.

The one thing he knew for certain was that he couldn't let this investigation fall apart. The agents at the Bureau had put in hundreds of labor hours to gather profiles of all the people involved. His job was just one small part of a bigger picture.

Once he got a signal, he'd call his contact at the Bureau to come and get them. He'd tell Isabel the guy was a friend. The less she knew, the safer she was.

A chill had settled on his skin and was making its way to his bones. He didn't regret giving his coat to Isabel, though. His father had taught him to be a gentleman. A lot of good it had done his dad. The man had endured a difficult marriage only to have his mom leave for another man. After the end of his own bad relationship, Jason had concluded that if women weren't cheaters, they were liars. Isabel might not be a thief, but she was still hiding something. He just wasn't sure what.

While they were working their way back to the house, he might as well try to figure out why she seemed to be acting a part.

"So how long have you worked for this property management place?" The trees thinned and he caught a glimpse of the obnoxiously big house with its central dome.

"What are you doing up here, anyway?" She turned, her expression filled with challenge.

If they were going to get out of this mess, he needed her to trust him. "I'm with the law. That's all you need to know."

She bent forward with arms folded over her chest. "He thinks we're partners."

"What?"

She stopped and stared at the sky. "When he held that knife to my throat—" She lifted her chin and squared her shoulders, but her quivering mouth revealed she was upset.

His emotions whiplashed from rage that a man would be so violent toward a woman to compassion for Isabel. "It's not right that happened to you."

As quickly as she had lost it, she regained her composure. "Anyway, he accused us of working together to steal his fortune."

Maybe he could still salvage this investigation. As long as the thief didn't think he was connected to law enforcement. "I'm sorry about the knife."

She shrugged. "It wasn't you that did it." She did a double take as though she were trying to ferret out some hidden motive in him or see beneath his skin.

She still didn't trust him.

The trees thinned.

Isabel stared up at the house, her voice filled with worry. "Perhaps he'll just go away."

He doubted that.

"He made a mess in the foyer," she said. "If we get out of here, I'll have to explain that to my clients and my boss."

Her priorities seemed a little out of order. "Let's just focus on getting out of here before he has a chance to come after us again." His phone still showed no signal.

Snow pelted them as they came out in the open and approached the circular driveway. "Hide behind my van. He might be watching."

He didn't want to worry Isabel. She seemed anxious enough, but another thought concerned him. How did the man with the knife have time to slash both sets of tires and come after them pretty much nonstop? He suspected there was not one but two thieves roaming around the estate. One of them had probably been waiting in the unseen car and been called in when things fell apart.

Isabel scurried up the driveway and crouched on the far side of the van. He slipped in beside her, leaning close to whisper in her ear. "Let's figure out where he is before we go to that studio. Is there a back way in?" Though he didn't want to alarm Isabel, he wanted to know if they were dealing with not one but two men.

She nodded. "Through the kitchen."

She led him around the house using the bushes for cover, then opened a door to a kitchen fit for a four-star restaurant. Stainless steel gleamed everywhere. An array of pots and pans hung above the island. The granite countertop displayed every gadget and more appliances than anyone could utilize in their lifetime.

The lights were out. Clouds covered the late-day sun, making the room dim.

Isabel rushed toward the swinging kitchen door. He peered through it at the open living room and expansive entryway with its black-and-white checked floor.

If the thief was watching any part of the house, it had to be the entryway. The second-story mezzanine provided a bird's-eye view of the main floor. The man with the knife could stand in the shadows and wait for them to cross the space. Jason studied each inch of the second floor as much as his limited view would allow. And if the thief had an accomplice, that only created more land mines.

Still no signal on his phone. The storm might be messing things up. He was going to need warmer clothes, or at least a coat, if they had to go back outside.

He cupped a hand on her shoulder. "You stay here. It'll be safer. I'm going to see if I can figure out exactly where those guys are."

"Guys?" she whispered.

He put his finger to his lips and signaled for her to stay.

He eased open the door. Keeping an eye on the second floor, he pressed his back against the textured wall. The whole house seemed darker. He wondered if the storm had taken out the electricity.

Jason's heart pounded wildly. He loved this part of his job. Most detective work involved sitting and watching the sordid lives of other people. As dangerous as the situation was, he couldn't help but relish the excitement.

He slipped into the living room, staying in the shadows and watching for movement. Gaze darting everywhere. Listening for the slightest out-of-place noise.

He waited for some time. No chance that these guys had just left. One of them might be searching the woods for them. The other looking for the bookmark they'd come here for.

Jason eased open the door and stepped back into the kitchen. His heart seized up.

Isabel wasn't there.

Heart racing, he opened the door to the pantry. When he tried the light switch, it didn't work. He whispered her name and circled through the pantry. No answer. He doubted she'd wandered off. Most likely, she'd been chased or…taken at knifepoint.

Either way, he needed to find her and fast.

THREE

Once again, Mr. Knife pressed the metal blade against Isabel's neck. He'd dragged her through the kitchen and into the media room on the far side of the house. Lighting strips marked the aisles between rows of chairs. A single light that must be battery operated blazed on the back wall, lighting the media equipment.

She could feel the cold blade against her skin. She cringed, envisioning that coppery smell and the warm seeping of her own blood.

Oh God, I don't want to die.

Mr. Knife leaned close and spoke in her ear, his voice raspy and filled with venom. "Where is it? What did you do with it?"

He let up the pressure of the knife so she could answer.

Her mind reeled. "I don't know what you're talking about."

"You don't know?" He pushed the knife against her neck again.

She shook her head. "I have no idea."

"Don't play coy with me. There are two of you. One of you will tell me where it is."

She dared not cry out, fearing that he might slice the knife across her throat and seek the information he needed from Mel. Mr. Knife had made it clear he wasn't opposed to killing her.

Still gripping her upper arm, he pulled the knife away from her throat, twisted her around and pushed her against the wall. He shoved an arm underneath her chin and pressed up. Her neck muscles strained, and she struggled for breath.

His eyes looked almost yellow. His breath stank like rotten eggs. Even in the dim light, she'd gotten a good look at him.

"That was our payday you took."

She shook her head. "No, I didn't take anything." He'd used the word *our*. Was there another killer stalking through this house? Mel had said as much.

"Liar." He took the pressure off her neck but pushed her to one side. Her chest slammed against a commercial popcorn machine.

She righted herself and prepared to fight back. The knife still glinted in his hand. Pushing the popcorn machine on its casters, she created a barrier between them and backed him into a corner. She took the opportunity to run from him past four rows of movie-theater chairs down toward a movie screen. The floor was raked just like in a theater.

There was no door by the screen. No way to escape. She hurried around it toward the door beyond the far aisle.

Mr. Knife raced after her, grabbing her shirt just as she reached for the doorknob. She turned and kicked him in the leg. He yelped in pain. Isabel flung the door open and found herself running down a long dark hallway. Straining to see clearly, she turned a corner and peered out a window. No footsteps came toward her. She must have shaken Mr. Knife or he'd taken a wrong turn.

She slid it open and climbed out into the cold. Snow swirled around her and the wind nearly knocked her over. With the pending darkness and blizzard, she could see maybe three or four feet in front of her. Grateful for Mel's coat, she shoved her hands in the warm pockets.

When she looked behind her, the wind was blowing enough to cover her tracks. Victoria Wilson's art studio was out here somewhere. Though she'd never had reason to go inside it, she'd seen it from the house.

The snow pelted her and she forged ahead until an A-frame structure came into view. Finding the door unlocked, she pushed inside and fell on the floor, out of breath.

Isabel shut the door and pushed a large metal sculpture against it.

In addition to the artist's supplies, the studio had a couch and a woodstove. She dared not start a fire. It might be spotted from the house. She gathered the blanket off the couch and wrapped it around her.

The sky was already growing dark. Was she going to die out here? Today was her day off and no one but Mel and the Wilsons knew she was up here. But she still wasn't sure she could trust Mel, and the Wilsons wouldn't know to worry about her until it was too late.

Isabel buried her face in her hands. What a mess.

She shook her head. "Izzy, you seem to have a gift for getting into messes."

Her mother had always said that she wouldn't amount to anything. Maybe Mom was right. Even when she was trying to do the right thing by being conscientious about her work, it seemed to end in disaster.

She wrapped the blanket tighter around her and the melody of a hymn came into her head. She hummed it and then sang the words. She calmed a little.

God was her refuge and she could rest beneath His wing. She closed her eyes tight. She had to believe that. Somehow this would all work out.

The door rattled and she jumped. A fist pounded on the thick wood.

"Isabel, it's me."

That was Mel's voice.

She hesitated. Did she really want to let him in? She still didn't know how he was connected to all this chaos. He seemed interested in keeping her safe, but his secrecy bothered her.

The pounding stopped. A moment later his face appeared at the window by the couch. He tapped on the glass.

She had a decision to make. Did she trust him or not?

Jason stamped his feet to stave off the cold. When he'd gone to search for Isabel in the house and couldn't find her, he remembered her talking about the art studio that was separate from the main house.

Was she really not going to let him in? He couldn't stay out here in the cold much longer. Though he'd grabbed a jacket he found hung on a hook, the chill had sunk down into his bones and his fingers were numbed.

He heard a scraping noise. She was moving something across the floor.

"Come inside." Isabel sounded out of breath.

He hurried around the little building and mounted

three steps to open the door. The room was full of metal, canvases and easels. Isabel had retreated to the far corner by a couch, a blanket wrapped around her shoulders.

"Are you cold?" She stepped across the room and pushed the heavy metal object back against the door.

He nodded. She'd hesitated but she'd let him in. Maybe she was starting to understand that he wasn't the bad guy.

She pointed toward the end of the couch. "There's a blanket over there."

He pulled back the curtain on the only window. Though the artist studio was only partially hidden by a grove of trees, he saw no sign that their pursuer had figured out where they'd gone.

He gathered the blanket around his shoulders. Silence descended and coiled around the room. With the blanket still wrapped around his shoulders, he rose from the couch and paced.

"I take it your phone still doesn't work?"

He shook his head. "The storm must be wreaking havoc with the signal." His eyes rested on a bowl full of wrapped mini candy bars. He picked it up and walked toward Isabel, who took several out of the bowl and whispered a thank-you. She gazed at him with big round doe eyes. Though most of the time she was so guarded, she had a softness to her that he felt drawn to.

"Mrs. Wilson must eat these while she's waiting to be inspired, huh?" He grabbed a few pieces for himself before setting the bowl back down.

The remark brought only a faint smile to Isabel's face. "I don't know that much about her personal habits." She rose to her feet. "She's got a sink over here to rinse her brushes out. Do you want some water?"

"Sure."

The faucet sputtered and spit while Isabel filled two paper cups, but at least it wasn't frozen. She handed him one of the cups and then sat back down.

The cool liquid soothed his dry throat.

Jason let the blanket fall to the floor while he paced. She really did act like she worked for a property management company just as she'd said when she'd first opened the door to him. It was clear to him now that she was an innocent in all this mess.

"That man who chased us. He wants something. He thinks I have it." She lifted her head and narrowed her eyes. "What's going on here?"

A debate raged in his head. How much should he tell her? So the thief was trying to find the bookmark. That meant it must have been moved. Only one person could have moved it.

They were trapped here until the storm broke. Taking the bookmark would reinforce the ruse that they wanted to be part of the smuggling ring. "Part of your job must be to tidy up before owners of the house come to stay."

"A little bit. Sometimes workers have left a mess in the owner's absence or things just look out of place." She shrugged. "That sort of thing."

Her eyes held a certain serenity, a total lack of guile. He wondered how much of his hand he should show. "Do you think you might have moved the thing the thief was looking for?"

She thought about it. "Nothing of value." She shook her head. "Besides, if he wants to steal things there is plenty of expensive stuff to take in that house."

"It sounds like he's looking for one thing in particular."

"It sounds like you know more than you're telling me, Mel." Her voice held a bit of an edge. "Like exactly what he's looking for."

His initial impression of her had been that she was soft and refined. But something in those eyes told him she had a spine of steel underneath. He admired that about her.

He let out a breath. "My name isn't Mel. It's Jason. I got that shirt at a thrift store. It's useful in my line of work."

"So, you lied about your name." She continued to study him, waiting for a deeper explanation. "What is your line of work?"

How much did he dare tell her? Chances were the bookmark was in some container that looked like junk but that the pickup man would recognize as his package. "So this thing that man is looking for. Do you think you may have been tidying up and moved it?"

"Why are you after the same thing they are, Jason?" Suspicion colored her words.

"He's not leaving until he gets what he came here for. Maybe we can find it." In order to keep the investigation under wraps, he needed to continue the fiction that he and Isabel were thieves who wanted in on the smuggling ring. Getting that bookmark might open the door to going undercover and infiltrating the smuggling ring, as long as he could get Isabel out of danger.

"And do what—give it to him? He disabled both our cars. I don't think he wants us to leave here alive. He thinks you and I are after the same thing he is." She looked right at him. "I don't like being accused of being a thief."

Her words filled with intensity. He didn't want her

involved in this. Once they were out of here—if they got out of here—maybe he could get her some protection. "I wish I could tell you more, but I can't."

"I don't even know what that man—or men, if there is another guy—came here for. But you do, don't you?"

He studied her for a long moment. Her stare made him feel like she could see beneath his skin. She was shrewd.

A hundred contradictory impulses charged through his head at once. The thieves thought he and Isabel were trying to horn in on their territory. Getting that bookmark would help the Bureau with their investigation and give him that much more cred with them, but he also had to find a way to get Isabel safely disentangled from this mess.

Private detective work could be feast or famine. The FBI throwing him a job from time to time would help keep the wolves from the door.

One thing was clear. Isabel was smart enough to play tit for tat. She wasn't going to give him any information until he gave her some. "I'm a private detective. Yesterday, a man dropped off a gold bookmark at this house. It's worth a great deal of money. The two men in the house were supposed to pick it up. You weren't supposed to be here. No one was." The less she knew, the better. Best not tell her about the FBI or the scope of the smuggling ring.

Her posture softened a little. Maybe she was warming up to him. "The people who own the house had a change of plans. They're coming earlier than expected. I'm the only one who knew that."

She rose to her feet and faced him, letting the blanket fall to the ground. "So what are we going to do?

We could wait the night out here. They probably don't know about this studio."

"They might start searching the property once they can't find us in the house," he said. "I'm thinking it's not just one guy either. He has a partner."

She pressed her lips together. "Yes, I think you're right about that." She started to pace. "I believe the one with the knife won't hesitate to use it." She shivered and wrapped her arms around herself. "We really need the police."

"It would be better if we didn't get the police involved. I can't say why. Besides, I'm pretty sure they wouldn't be able to get up that road until the storm stops and it's plowed." Making an arrest at this point in the investigation might tip the head of the smuggling ring off.

She flopped down on the couch and stared at a blank canvas across the room. Then she studied him again. Her cheeks were flushed with color and he liked the way her blond curls framed her face. He didn't like the suspicion he saw in her eyes, though.

Finally, she bent her head. She put her feet one on top of the other, then switched the bottom one to the top. "I've made a mess of everything. I'll probably lose my job. Trouble just seems to find me no matter how hard I try to do the right thing."

Picking up on the deep pain in her voice, he sat down on the opposite end of the couch. "None of this is your fault."

She laced her fingers together and then drew them apart over and over. "The Wilsons are expecting to come home to a cozy warm house."

It would be better for the operation if the homeowners didn't find the house in disarray. But they would probably just assume it was a run-of-the-mill break-in. He wasn't sure why she was fixated on doing her job considering a man with a knife was stalking them. "Look, the thieves are searching for that bookmark."

She lifted her head and stared at him as fear filled her voice. "Don't you think staying safe should be our priority?"

"We're not safe as long as they are here. Finding it could give us some leverage."

She wasn't totally buying his story. He had to hand it to her—she was pretty savvy at reading him.

"Chances are, it was in some kind of container. Did you throw things away? Did you move them around?"

"Of course I did. I hurried through the house and straightened up a bunch of stuff and then you knocked on the door. I don't remember every little item. I did throw some things away in the kitchen. I suppose we could check the garbage."

"That would be a start," he said. They still had to find a way out of here. "I didn't notice any cars other than yours or mine. Is there anything parked in that garage?"

She stood up and walked toward him shaking her head. "The Wilsons bring their own car."

Jason's thoughts raced as he tried to come up with a plan. "The thief must have parked his car a ways from the property." That meant even if the thieves wanted to leave, they probably couldn't until the storm let up. They wouldn't risk freezing in the blizzard. Jason and Isabel were trapped here and so were the two thieves.

What would be the best thing to do? To wait it out and hope they wouldn't be found here…or to go back to the house? One thing was certain: they needed to stay together.

He stood up and looked out the window.

Night would be falling soon. They'd have the cover of darkness. It wasn't that long a walk from the studio to the house, but in blizzard conditions, it would be easy enough to get disoriented.

As a boy, he remembered his father, a sheriff in another county, telling stories of men who froze to death walking from a barn to the house in whiteout conditions.

Isabel shifted a little closer to him. "We don't know anything about the other guy. What if he has a gun?"

Jason had thought of that too. "When are the Wilsons supposed to get here?"

"Tomorrow afternoon. I have other houses to deal with tomorrow, so I had to fit this one in today."

The door rattled and shook. Jason took a step back. It could have been the wind.

"It's really blowing out there." Isabel's voice held only a trace of fear. "I say we stay here."

He nodded and then looked around the studio space for anything that might be of use.

His search was interrupted by the glass in the window shattering.

FOUR

A scream caught in Isabel's throat. Glass flew everywhere as a gun was fired through the window. Both of them ducked to the floor. She lifted her head. Though she could only discern his silhouette, this was a different man than Mr. Knife, shorter and more muscular.

Jason grabbed her and led her toward the door, where he pushed away the heavy metal sculpture.

Mr. Gun must know they'd try the door.

Her gaze darted around the room. There was no other way to escape.

Jason yanked open the door and drew his own gun. They rushed out into the dark of night. The cold permeated her skin almost immediately. Wind pushed on her body. Swordlike snowflakes sliced across her face and neck.

Jason's hand slipped into hers. She bent her head to shield it from the assault of the storm.

Gunfire reverberated through the woods. Any doubt that Mr. Knife had an accomplice was removed. Mr. Gun was after them.

Jason's fingers gripped hers like iron. He pulled her

sideways until they entered a grove of trees that provided only a small amount of shelter.

Through the haze of snow, she saw a light bob past them. Jason aimed his gun toward the light but didn't pull the trigger. Once it was clear their pursuer hadn't seen them, he put the gun back in his waistband.

Mr. Gun was probably better dressed and equipped to deal with the snow, and he had a flashlight.

Isabel shivered. If she was cold, Jason must be close to hypothermia with thin layers of fabric to protect him.

He leaned close to her and whispered in her ear. "He's gone past us."

He took her hand again, which warmed hers despite the conditions. He wove through the trees.

"Do you know where you're going?"

"I'm hoping to see light from the house," he said.

The sheets of snow and darkness made it hard to see the landscape clearly. "There was no light on in the house earlier. I think the storm might have knocked out the electricity."

As they stumbled through the trees, she felt hope fading. One small light that pierced the reduced visibility of the storm was all they needed.

"He went ahead of us. Watch for his flashlight," Jason said. He had to lean close to her and shout to be heard above the shrill cry of the storm.

She could barely see three feet in front of her. They would have to be right on top of the thief before they saw him. It was a dangerous game they were playing.

Jason claimed he was not on the wrong side of the law. His story made sense…sort of. Why he needed the bookmark was a little perplexing. Even if he was a detective, maybe he saw the possibility of financial gain in finding it. It wouldn't be the first time a law-enforcement guy was on the take.

She leaned closer to him and trudged forward. Not because she totally trusted him, but because getting too far away from him increased her chances of ending up a Popsicle.

Up ahead, a light winked in and out of view. They veered toward where they'd last seen it.

Wind pressed on her from three sides like being inside a vacuum cleaner. Its howling and the creaking of trees surrounded her. She lifted her head slightly, hoping to see the light again.

Isabel squinted against the onslaught of icy snow and intense wind. The pinpricks of the flakes on her skin were like a thousand tiny needles.

Jason wrapped an arm around her waist and pulled her in a new direction. He must have seen something she'd missed. If they got too close to the thief, he would shoot them.

She lifted her head again, thinking the house should've come into view by now. Jason let go of her. She reached out for his hand as her heart squeezed tight with fear. He was her lifeline. She did not want to get lost in this storm.

He caught her hand again.

The house appeared suddenly in her field of vision. They were only feet away from it. Jason pulled her toward him. She reached out for the security of the outside wall.

When they got the door open, they both fell inside onto a tiled floor.

Before she even had time to take a deep breath— now that she wasn't fighting wind, snow and cold—she heard footsteps pounding, growing louder. The room was almost completely dark.

Jason tugged on her sleeve. He opened a small door, and they both crawled inside. The space was so small they sat facing each other, knees touching. They seemed to be in some sort of laundry chute.

Footsteps seemed to be pounding all around them. Had Mr. Knife figured out they were in the house or was his frantic search for something else? The footsteps grew closer. Maybe Mr. Gun was in the house by now.

Isabel could hear the sound of her own breathing in the tiny space.

The footsteps stopped.

Jason whispered only one word. "Down."

She angled her body and slid down the aluminum slide, landing on a pile of linens.

Jason's silhouette blotted out some of the bright light that shone from the top of the chute from the thieves' flashlight. Jason slid down beside her on the pile of dirty laundry.

She was grateful the cleaning crew hadn't tossed the sheets in the washing machine like they were supposed to.

Jason squeezed her elbow. "Come on. He's going to find this room soon enough."

She glanced back up the chute, which had gone dark. Apparently, Mr. Knife, or maybe it was Mr. Gun, had opted not to follow them down it, which meant he was using the stairs.

She leaped to her feet, falling in behind him and squinting to see in the dark room.

"There has to be a good place to hide," said Jason. Though she had been through the ten-thousand-

square-foot home many times, she hadn't been thinking about hiding places. Even as Jason started moving
toward the door, she racked her brain.

They hurried down a hallway.

She tugged on his arm. "He'll be coming down the
stairs. We can't go that way."

"I know, but he'll be looking for us on this floor."

She turned and ran in the other direction. There had
to be another way up to the main floor. They ran past
the laundry room. Footsteps sounded above them. She
sprinted toward a door and swung it open, finding a
narrow back stairway similar to servants' stairs in older
houses. These stairs led into the kitchen. Probably so
cooks had quick, discreet access to any food and wine
stored in the basement.

The stairs were not carpeted, which made the potential for noise that much greater. Stepping as softly
as possible, they hurried up and into the kitchen. There
was no place to hide in the kitchen that wouldn't be obvious. Isabel grabbed keys off a hook where they were
hanging. She filed through them, holding them close
to her face to see better.

She'd never been in the greenhouse but had noticed
the labeled key for it. Maybe they could lock it from the
inside. Jason leaned close to her, trying to see what she
was doing. She could feel his warm breath on her neck.

A pang of guilt shot through her. She wasn't supposed to go into the greenhouse. That wasn't part of her
job. She vowed that if she got a chance, she'd explain
and apologize to the Wilsons. If she got the chance...

Isabel felt along the wall for the door that led to the
greenhouse where it connected with the kitchen. She

leaned close to the keyhole in an effort to insert the key. Humid air floated around her when she opened the door.

They slipped inside. The room was filled with plants though she could not discern what kind in the dim light. The Wilsons must hire a gardener to care for the plants in their absence.

The door did not lock from the inside.

Through the clear glass, a shadow stalked past them.

Jason pulled Isabel to the floor. Her heart revved into high gear as they scurried around to the far side of a bench and slipped into a tight space between the tall potting benches. At least they were out of view. Once again, their knees were touching as they faced each other in a small space.

After a moment, Jason spoke in a hushed tone. "Can you remember what you straightened up and what you threw away?"

Isabel waited for her heart to slow down before responding. Of course he was thinking about the bookmark. She closed her eyes, trying to remember. "There were some things left in the kitchen by the cleaning crew, just packaging from cleaning products."

"No boxes or anything that something might be hidden in."

Her memory fogged. The whole thing felt like it had happened a lifetime ago. "I'm not sure. I just automatically straighten up as I do my first walk through the house."

"It's okay." He reached over and touched her knee. "I know this violence is probably not what you're used to."

He had no idea. She'd pulled off her impression of respectability enough that he probably would never guess that running from the law, sneaking around and hiding were what she was proficient in at one time in her life.

"Can you visualize the rooms you went into and what you did in each one?"

She understood what he was doing. They couldn't just randomly go banging through the house. They had to be stealthy about where they searched.

She closed her eyes and tried to remember. Her usual routine was to go to the kitchen first and throw out food in the cupboards that looked like it was past its expiration date and then walk through the main rooms in the house, but was that what she had done this time? "Mostly I just closed doors and straightened things."

She lifted her head in time to see a bright light flashing. "He's coming this way."

Both of them rolled underneath benches that held heavy foliage.

The door creaked open. Footsteps tapped on the concrete floor as the flashlight illuminated different sections of the room.

Isabel held her breath. Her stomach pressed against the cold concrete floor. The thief leaned over and shone the light beneath the benches, coming within a few inches of where she hid.

Oh God, don't let him find us.

The thief dropped the flashlight. It rolled across the floor, lighting up the area just in front of Jason's face.

The flashlight blinked on and off. The batteries must've been failing. The thief picked it up and tapped it on his palm. The light stabilized for a moment and then went out altogether.

The thief cursed.

She heard a second voice at the doorway. "Come on. We got to hurry."

"My flashlight went out, man." The voice was Mr. Knife's.

"Never mind. I have mine. Forget about those two for now. Let's keep looking. We got to get out of here as soon as there is a break in the storm."

"What if they have it already?"

After a long pause, Mr. Gun spoke up. "We'll find them soon enough and deal with them whether they have the merchandise or not."

Mr. Knife let out a heavy breath that sounded more like a groan. "Yeah, they'll get what's coming to them. No one horns in on our sweet deal."

The words chilled Isabel to the bone. She remained still until she could no longer hear their footsteps. Jason had already rolled out from underneath the bench.

Her eyes had adjusted more to the darkness, and she could see actual plants, vegetables and orchids instead of just shadows and outlines. Her eyes landed on a book placed on a waist-high bench, probably a book about gardening. Why else would it be in here?

A memory clicked in her head. Books...out of place. "I picked up some books that were by the entryway table and put them back in the library on the fourth floor." When she'd first arrived, she'd whirred through the house picking up, throwing away and straightening.

"That would be a good place to hide a bookmark," he said. "Lead the way."

They'd have to go through the house and take the main stairway to get to it.

As though he'd read her mind, Jason said, "Maybe I should lead the way."

"Good idea."

"Stay low and close to the wall," he said.

They slipped out of the greenhouse and into the shadows. Isabel pressed close to Jason and listened for the sound of approaching assassins.

Jason scanned the open area on the main floor and then searched the darker corners for movement. He hated putting Isabel at risk like this, but the last time he'd left her alone, the man with the knife had taken her. The safest place for her in a house with armed men bent on killing them was right by his side.

It made sense that the bookmark was in some books on the entryway table. Hiding things in plain sight was the strategy of the courier who dropped off the stolen treasure.

Jason had taken footage through a window of a painting stolen from a European art gallery. The drop-off man had hung it among the much more amateur efforts of the homeowner. This information helped the FBI understand the mind of the man or woman who was engineering the smuggling. There had to be easier ways to smuggle valuables into the country. There must be a reason why the mastermind chose vacation homes.

The whole investigation was quite involved. Several other private investigators had been hired to watch unoccupied houses for activity. Usually, the Bureau would get wind of items being stolen in different parts of the world from US Customs or foreign governments, and then within a week or so, activity would pick up in Silver Strike.

Jason and Isabel hurried toward the stairs with Isabel taking the lead since she knew the layout of the house.

Light flashed at the end of the hallway.

Jason pressed against the wall and held out a protective hand toward Isabel. She stood close enough for her soft hair to brush under his chin. Her hand cupped his arm just above the elbow. Her touch sent a charge of electricity through him.

She was afraid, but brave enough to keep her cool.

The light disappeared into a room.

Isabel tugged on Jason's sleeve and turned to take the stairs that led to the second floor.

The thieves had to know the bookmark was in a book. They must have found the library by now but clearly hadn't found the bookmark. He hoped they weren't walking into a trap.

He glanced over his shoulder. The light bobbed at the end of the hallway but didn't reach them.

They raced up to the second-story landing, which was almost completely dark. They had only a short stairway to get up to the dome.

The pounding of footfalls behind them reached Jason's ear. Then the cool metal of a knife blade pressed into his neck. He steeled himself against the attack, ready to fight back.

"Go," he said to the darkness, hoping that Isabel would understand.

He could handle this guy but he didn't want her hurt.

"Where is it?" said the thief. "We looked in the library."

Jason elbowed the man in the stomach. The man backed away. In the darkness, Jason had to rely on his other senses to figure out where his opponent was. He was grateful for the years he'd spent studying martial arts.

He swung at the air, colliding with flesh. A hand

gripped his wrist and yanked him around. His head rammed against a wall. Stunned, he whirled around and landed a blow that made the man groan. He hit the man's back with a karate chop. The thief fell to the floor, making a cracking sound followed by another thud.

Jason braced himself for the man to jump to his feet and lay into him again, but he didn't move. Jason kicked him. He must have hit his head against the banister. Jason leaned over. The man was still breathing but out cold.

He felt around for the knife but couldn't find it, and he couldn't waste any more time. The noise of the fight might have alerted the other man on the floor below and that guy had a flashlight and a gun.

Jason hurried down the hallway in the direction he'd heard Isabel's footsteps retreating. When he felt for his phone in his shirt pocket it was gone. It must have fallen out in the fight. There was no time to search for it now. He reached out a hand to the textured wall to orient himself. Up ahead he saw light.

The whiteness of the overcast sky provided some illumination through the glass dome of the library. It looked like the storm was letting up. Isabel was pulling books off the shelf and flipping through them. A stack already sat on the floor that she or the thieves had worked through.

She turned toward him. "Quick—lock the door."

He shut the door and turned the latch.

"You don't remember which book?"

"I know I put them away in this area here." She swept her hand across a section of shelves.

"Any sign that the thieves were here?"

She pointed across the room. The library was round

with books that ran from the floor to the edge of the glass dome. "Those books over there are arranged by size and color. Don't ask. It's a rich-people thing." She grabbed another book off the shelf and filed through it. "Anyway, they are out of place. Those guys must have gone through those books searching. I got to hand it to them. They are tidy."

Maybe the thieves wouldn't get as big a payday if there was any evidence of a break-in. During the other jobs, the thieves had used lock picks or had known the security codes and nothing had been disturbed.

With a backward glance at the door, Jason grabbed a book and riffled through it. "Is there another way out of here in case we have to make a speedy exit?"

She pointed to a door. "It leads to another balcony. This one has stairs. No way could we drop four floors and live."

He grabbed another book and leafed through it. If he lifted it toward the dome, he could see better. He put the volume back in place and grabbed another. At best, they had minutes before the thief on the floor below came to and headed toward them.

Isabel pulled books and flipped through them at a furious pace.

Someone banged on the door and wiggled the handle.

Jason worked even faster. "It's got to be here somewhere."

The pounding stopped. Jason moved closer to the door and listened. "He's picking the lock." He stalked back to the bookshelf and pulled another hardback.

Isabel slid a book back into place and grabbed another. She bent the spine of the hardback. A shiny object fell to the floor. She picked it up.

"Jason," she said. She had found it.

"Let's go," he said. She shoved the bookmark in the pocket of the coat he'd given her and zipped it.

The door burst open as they raced toward the balcony. The short muscular man raised his gun and fired off a shot. Isabel grabbed Jason's hand.

Jason pushed open the door that led to the balcony.

They descended with the armed man at their heels. Another shot blasted through the silent night but it went wide. Even with the flashlight, the man couldn't see much better than they could.

Jason could hear the footfalls behind him. They had to find a way to shake this guy and find a hiding place. Isabel held tight to his hand. She understood the importance of not getting separated.

He stayed close to the house, running the full length of it. They ended up in the driveway beside his useless van. He crouched low and Isabel slipped in beside him. Footsteps pounded past and then faded.

"He might come back," she whispered.

Jason hurried to the side of the van and eased the passenger door open. "Get in. I suspect he'll go in the house to get his accomplice first."

She complied.

"Crawl toward the back and stay low."

He got in behind her. His surveillance equipment was stacked in a corner though barely visible in the near darkness.

"How long do you think we should stay here?" Isabel kept her voice to a whisper.

"Not long." He rifled around in the dark, taking the time to lock each door. "I have another coat in here, extra hat and gloves." He slipped into the heavier coat and tossed the gloves and hat toward Isabel.

He dug through another pile of stuff to find a hat and pair of gloves for himself. It wasn't his first day at camp. He always had lots of cold-weather gear on hand.

He grabbed his keys out of the ignition. The key ring had a small flashlight on it that might be useful.

He pulled the gun out from his waistband and stared at it. Though he went to the range every week, he had never had to use the gun while working. It might come down to that tonight.

Jason could not see Isabel's expression in the darkness, but he sensed the tension that had invaded the tiny space.

"Detectives carry guns. That's just how it is." He held out his hand. "Can I see the bookmark?"

Suspicion clouded her voice. "Why?"

Jason's stomach coiled into a tight knot. Here they were, back at square one again. If she didn't trust him, they might not survive the night. They had to work together. Both their lives depended on it.

Why was it so hard to win her trust?

FIVE

Isabel looked at what appeared to be a computer screen and keyboard. "What is all this stuff? Surveillance equipment?" So far, Jason had done nothing to harm her and had risked his own safety to help her. Maybe he really was a detective. That didn't mean he was an honest detective. Past experience told her not to be too quick to trust. Jason was keeping secrets, and she didn't like that. What was he hiding? She touched the pocket where she'd placed the bookmark.

Jason let out a heavy breath and shook his head. "Hold on to the bookmark if you want."

Her chest squeezed tight with indecision. "I don't like liars." The intensity of her words surprised her. The pain of what she had been through with Nick was still very close to the surface despite how long it had been—she still had not let any man into her life or heart. But she had started to think Jason might be okay. That scared her. How had he managed find the chink in her armor in such a short time? So what if he was protective and kept her safe. He was still a man and men always let you down in the end.

"I don't like liars either, Isabel, but if I tell you what is going on, it puts you at greater risk."

Jason's voice had a soothing quality, not the anger or impatience she would have expected. She laced her fingers together and clenched her jaw.

Don't be taken in.

He turned from side to side, searching. "At least put some cardboard around it. If it gets damaged, it loses its value."

"Maybe you are a detective, but I think you are on the take." Her accusation lacked conviction. She could feel her resolve to not trust him weakening in the face of his gentle response.

He tore a section of cardboard off an empty box. "Give me the bookmark. I promise to give it back to you if that's what you want."

She unzipped the coat and slipped her hand into the inside pocket.

"I promise," he repeated.

How many times had she heard that?

She grasped the bookmark and handed it to him. Their fingers touched briefly. He placed it carefully in the folded cardboard. She tensed, waiting for the moment when he'd shove it in his pocket and pull the gun on her.

He held it out for her to take.

She let out a breath. "Keep it." So he'd kept one small promise. He still had a lot of explaining to do.

A light flashed outside.

"He's coming this way."

The light had shone through the windshield.

Jason touched her arm. "Out the back. Hurry."

He pushed open the van doors. They bolted toward

the house, pressing against the brick walls. The eaves of the roof provided even more darkness to hide in as footsteps pounded around the van and drew closer.

Jason pushed on Isabel's shoulder, indicating she should keep moving. The cold seeped into her face as she made her way along the outside wall. They needed to find a good hiding place.

Isabel thought about the layout of the house. The wine cellar in the basement had a stairway leading up to the outside. They wouldn't be trapped if they hid there and needed to make a run for it.

"This way." She tugged on the sleeve of his coat and led him around to a side entrance.

Isabel pressed her hand against the exposed brick and struggled to get her bearings in the dark house as they moved down a set of stairs. Footsteps pounded on the floor above them. They'd lost their pursuer for now.

Her heart raced as she felt along the wall, waiting for her eyes to adjust to the darkness. She pushed open a door. The shelves of wine were barely discernible.

Jason slipped in beside her. His shoulder pressed against hers. A tense silence fell around them, interrupted by footsteps above them that came in short bursts.

"They're still looking," she whispered.

"It's just a matter of time. We have to find a way to get out of here. They have a car parked somewhere close by."

"We could freeze trying to find it."

"We need a sure thing. Aren't there any neighbors close by?"

Isabel shook her head. "The nearest one might be miles away. They are up the road, not down. This is the first house in the subdivision." Though the storm had let up, it was still dark and cold out there. She squeezed her eyes shut, mulling over what Jason had said. A sure thing. There were no other vehicles on the property or houses close by, but… "There's a communal building. That is one of the perks of this subdivision."

"This is a subdivision?"

"Yes, but the houses are miles apart."

"What's in the building?"

"I've only seen it on a map. But it's like a clubhouse where you can have get-togethers, and there's a building with snowmobiles and ATVs. My boss explained to me what the building was used for."

"How far is it from here?"

"I'd estimate less than a mile. We can use the trees for cover but we'll get lost if we don't keep the road in sight." In these conditions, she'd be guessing at the location of the building.

His voice dropped half an octave. "That's a long way to go in the cold."

Footsteps pounded down the stairs. Both of them pressed deeper into the shadows. The footsteps drew closer. Doors opened and shut. The thief was searching all of the rooms in the basement, making his way down the hallway. Isabel's heart beat so loudly she feared it would give them away.

They had only seconds to make a decision. "We stay here, they will find and kill us." His hand slipped into hers as he led the way up the stairs to the door that took them back out into the cold night.

A blast of cold air hit her face, causing her cheeks to tingle. His gloved hand gripped hers.

"Which way?"

She pointed as the chill settled on her exposed skin. He ran toward the trees. She held on to his hand. When she glanced over her shoulder, she saw light glowing in the dome and a silhouetted figure.

By the door through which they'd just exited a light also bobbed. It loomed toward them for some time and then stopped. Would they give up the chase that easily? Somehow, she doubted it.

The trees grew thicker as the outline of the house disappeared. She focused on the sound of her feet padding on the soft snow. Her breath came out in vapory puffs as she struggled to keep pace with Jason.

Doubt plagued her every footstep. Would they be able to get into the clubhouse garage? She wasn't sure they'd even find the place in the dark.

She heard the sound of a motor, a car on the road.

The clang of an engine revving up landed on her ears. Headlights cut through the trees behind her. The thieves had gone back for their car. She quickened her pace. Jason grabbed her and pulled her into the trees as the thieves' car drew near.

Heart shifting into high gear, Jason climbed uphill through the trees to get off the road. Isabel remained close beside him.

The car motor grew louder, more menacing. The headlights flashed by them and then the motor settled into an idle. Voices were raised, commands shouted. A car door slammed and then the car eased down the road. One man must have gotten out to search on foot while the other moved past them.

Out of breath, Jason kept pushing uphill. He craned his neck, catching just a flash of light through the thick trees.

Isabel caught up to him. She spoke between deep breaths. They both kept climbing. "They must have seen us on the road."

Jason glanced around, not able to discern much of anything. They needed a hiding place, time to catch their breath. How were they going to find the clubhouse if they couldn't navigate by the road?

The car rolled by again on the road. This time headed in the direction of the house.

Jason sprinted faster, though his legs were screaming from the effort of moving uphill. The man on foot with the flashlight was still at the bottom of the hill, looking up in their direction.

Jason ran up to a large evergreen, gesturing toward Isabel and speaking in a whisper. "Scoot down toward the trunk. The boughs will hide us."

She complied with his order. He crawled in beside her. Both of them were out of breath. The tree sheltered them from the wind and snow.

"We need to get back down to the road," she leaned close and whispered. Her breath warmed his ear.

He nodded.

Branches creaked around them in the wind. Down below, the car continued to go back and forth on the road. He could not see the headlights anymore but heard the engine grow louder and then dim.

A distinctly human grunt emanated below them. A tree branch cracked, probably the searcher stepping on deadfall. Footsteps seemed to surround them. Isabel pressed closer to him. He could see nothing through the darkness and thick foliage.

The footsteps seemed to fade and then grow louder.

He couldn't hear the car engine any longer. Had the driver decided to search farther down the road?

His breathing slowed. They huddled in the darkness…waiting. He heard noises that were most likely human.

Isabel had pulled her knees up to her chest and wrapped her arms around them. Her head was tilted. After several minutes of silence in the forest, she spoke up. "Do you think he's gone?"

Five, maybe ten, minutes had passed since he'd heard any sound that might have come from their pursuers.

"Stay put." He crawled on all fours to get out from under the tree, then remained crouching, listening and watching. Though it was still snowing, the wind had died down.

He signaled for Isabel to come out. When she was close, he whispered, "We'll walk parallel to the road but use the trees for cover. Until we can find a safe spot to emerge."

She nodded as he rose and walked in a serpentine pattern through the trees. Always, his ears tuned for any out-of-place sound. Isabel stayed close to him.

The trees thinned, and he could see the road below. The thieves must have a pretty heavy-duty vehicle to be driving on the unplowed roads. At least five or six inches must have fallen since the start of the storm. Enough moonlight shone through to give the snow the appearance of being garnished with diamonds.

The quiet was deceptive. He knew he needed to stay on his guard. The two thieves were close, even if he couldn't hear or see them. Every step they took brought them closer to danger.

SIX

Isabel tried to ignore the tight knot in her stomach by focusing on the back of Jason's head. In the darkness, she could just make out the band of white on his knit hat. She took in an intense breath and looked side to side. They could be walking right into the thieves' path.

She heard a noise to the side of her. Jason kept walking. She reached for the hem of his coat. Then she saw the glint of light up the hill. He wrapped his arms around her and guided her behind one of the larger trees.

Her heart thudded in her ears. As they faced each other, she tilted her head and looked up at Jason, whose posture indicated he was still on high alert. He turned and angled around the tree, then looked back at her and lifted his chin, indicating they should keep moving.

He worked his way down toward more level ground and spurred himself into a jog. It would be hard to find the clubhouse, a place she'd never been to. What if they overshot it altogether? They could be wandering for hours. The cold was as much an enemy as the two thieves.

The trees thinned and the ground became more level.

Jason slowed so she could catch up. "We must be getting close."

The evergreens were so far apart they didn't provide any cover. They made their way toward the road. Tracks indicated that the thieves' car had come this far.

She stopped to scan the trees behind her, seeing nothing.

Jason picked up the pace. She sprinted beside him as a sense of urgency pressed in on her from all sides. Now they were out in the open, exposed. They needed to hurry. The tracks left by the car ended where the thief had turned around. A good sign that the men weren't waiting to ambush them at the clubhouse.

Up ahead she spotted a cluster of trees and the faint outline of what might be a building. Jason veered in that direction. She sprinted to keep up with him, scanning their surroundings.

Gradually two buildings came into view. Picnic tables outside were covered in snow. The clubhouse was about fifty yards from the road.

Isabel quickened her pace as she prayed they'd be able to access the snowmobiles. She ran ahead of Jason but slowed as she got close to the garage. There was a padlock on the door. She shook the doorknob out of frustration as her hope vaporized.

"Now what are we going to do?" Her eyes warmed with tears.

Jason peered into a window. "We made it this far. There has to be a solution."

She ran toward the clubhouse door. It too was locked. Even if there was a landline in there, it might not be working. She hung her head, squeezed her eyes tight to keep the tears from coming.

Come on, Izzy. You've been in worse situations. Be strong.

Jason squeezed her upper arm. His voice filled with compassion. "We'll figure something out. If I had something like a paper clip, I could pick the lock. Split up. Let's keep looking for a way in." He took off in one direction and she ran around the side of the clubhouse. The windows of the clubhouse were high and small, but maybe they could climb in.

"Isabel." Jason's voice came from behind the garage.

She ran along the garage wall to the back, where Jason was sweeping the snow off an ATV with a plow on it.

"Your chariot awaits." His voice was almost jovial.

"Someone must have left it out here because they knew they'd be plowing again."

"There's no key," he said as he dug into his pockets. He handed her a set of keys. "There's a tiny flashlight on there."

Isabel shone the light where Jason pointed.

On the road on the other side of the garage, a car rumbled. Isabel's heart squeezed tight. It had to be the thieves. No one else would be out on a night like tonight.

"Give me the light. I can kinda see if I put it on the seat." Jason's focus never wavered from the ATV. "Check to make sure it's them. It might be the guy coming back for his plow."

Jason's optimism didn't make much sense to her. All the same, she ran to the edge of the building and peered around the side of it. A car was parked on the road. A man had gotten out and was making his way in the deep snow toward the clubhouse. Though it was hard to see any detail, he was built like the short muscular man she'd encountered at the Wilsons' house.

She hurried back to where Jason was still pulling wires on the engine of the snowplow and then shining the light on what he'd done.

"I think it's one of them."

"Just a couple more seconds here." Jason's voice held no hint of the panic she felt. "Hold the light for me."

She shone the light toward his hands. While she appreciated Jason's cool head, she was having a hard time taking in a deep breath. She turned slightly but saw nothing. It would be just a matter of minutes before the thief found them even if he circled the clubhouse first.

Jason clicked something into place, and the engine sputtered to life. Now for sure the noise would send their pursuers toward them. He swung his leg over and got on. Isabel slipped in behind him before he had even settled in the seat. After he lifted the plow, the ATV lurched forward.

A gunshot echoed behind them. Isabel leaned close to Jason and held on tight. Jason steered around the building toward the road. But instead of taking the road, he cut across it down the hill. Smart. The car would only be able to traverse the road.

Another gunshot resounded behind them. Isabel held on to Jason even tighter. Her heart pounded wildly as adrenaline surged through her.

Behind her, the car engine started up. As Jason maneuvered the ATV straight downhill, the roar of the car seemed to press in on them from all sides. The snow grew deeper, slowing their progress. They might get stuck. They had no choice. Jason veered the snowmobile back onto the road.

The headlights from the car encapsulated them. Jason switched up a gear and increased his speed. They were risking an accident, but the ATV was able to progress on the unplowed road faster than the car. They slipped out of the grasp of the headlights as Jason put a little distance between them and their pursuer.

He cut off the road and headed straight downhill again. The ATV caught air and landed hard. Pain shot up Isabel's back but she held on. She peered over Jason's shoulder. Up ahead was a cluster of trees. Jason slowed as they drew close. He wove through the trees. As he lost speed, the noise of the ATV motor kicked down a notch. The hum of the car engine in the still night reached her ears. She could see the flash of headlights through the trees.

Fear squeezed her stomach into a tight knot. The car couldn't follow them into the trees, but they were going so slow, he could cut them off when they came back out on the road.

Jason steered sideways and continued to navigate through the labyrinth of the trees. The sound of the car faded into the distance. Gradually, the landscape became more open and flat. The ATV picked up speed once again.

When she looked to one side, the faint outline of the Wilsons' house was visible up the hill. They'd gone in a circle. Jason drove the ATV toward the road she'd come up hours earlier in her car. She took in a deep breath. It was only a couple of miles down the hill until the private road intersected with the two-lane that would take them back into town.

Jason didn't slow down when he got to the road. She caught the glimpse of headlights in her peripheral vision. They weren't home free yet. The car was still following them.

* * *

The exposed skin on Jason's face tingled from the wind and snow hitting it as he couched low. Though he couldn't hear the car, he knew it had made it to the road they were on and was still chasing them.

He revved the throttle. Isabel pressed close to him as he gained speed. He could feel the pressure of her arms around his waist though they both wore too many layers of clothing to feel her body heat. He liked having her so close. Maybe now she'd come to trust him.

With the motor humming, they descended the hill. The ATV seemed to almost hover over the snow, providing them with a smooth ride.

Isabel leaned close to his ear and shouted, "He's getting closer."

They must be within a half mile of the two-lane road. He turned the handlebars and directed the ATV toward the bumpier, more foreboding landscape where a car would not be able to follow.

He aimed toward a patch of trees, swerving expertly around them. The rough terrain didn't scare him. He'd grown up riding ATVs and dirt bikes with his father. The ATV headlights cut a swath of light in front of him so he could plan his next move.

Chances were the thief would patrol the two-lane and wait for them to emerge, but he could only go back and forth on a small section of road at a time. If he took the ATV far enough out they'd be able to get on the two-lane without being spotted.

A steep drop on the hillside caused them to catch air again. As they sailed through the air, he tried to maneuver the machine for a successful landing. The nose of the ATV pointed downward. Isabel screamed but held on tight.

They dived into a snowbank. The crash seemed to make all his bones vibrate.

He took in a breath and patted Isabel's gloved hand. "Are you okay?"

"I don't think anything is broken."

The motor of the snowmobile had died. "Can you get off? I've got to see if I can get this thing started and out of this snowbank." He was still a little shaky from the impact of the crash.

Isabel swung her leg over and stepped back. She pulled his keys out and shone the light for Jason.

"It looks pretty stuck." Her voice was monotone, devoid of any emotion.

Maybe she was just as exhausted as he was from all the running.

Fragments of light flashed below them, a car going by on the two-lane.

He lifted his head and met Isabel's gaze. Was she thinking the same thing he was? "This time of night there won't be many cars going by." Even fewer because of the storm.

"I still think it's our best shot." Her voice filled with resolve. "Maybe the snowplows are out by now. We can flag one down."

It was a huge risk. They'd have to dodge the thief in the big car and hope that another vehicle came along. "We can't stay here." The ATV was dead. Either the cold or the thief would be their demise.

Isabel held the flashlight in such a way that it illuminated her face. She nodded, but he saw the fear in her eyes.

"We'll stay in the trees as much as possible." He reached a gloved hand out for hers. She lifted her hand and he squeezed it, hoping the gesture would help quell her fear.

He turned. "Only use the flashlight when you absolutely need to. It makes us too easy to spot. The bright colors of my coat will draw attention too."

"I can turn it inside out." She slipped out of his coat and turned it to the dark lining.

He started walking. She trudged behind him. He breathed in a silent prayer that a car would come by sooner rather than later. Though the storm was no longer raging, staying out in the cold for any length of time would not be a good idea.

He was unable to see the ground clearly, so his footsteps were slow and measured. Isabel whispered something.

He kept walking but turned his head slightly. "What did you say?"

"Oh sorry. I didn't realize you could hear me. I was... praying."

"Yeah, we could use some of that." He felt closer to her, knowing that she'd thought to pray.

"Sometimes things have to be at their darkest before I think of it," she said.

He opened his mouth to answer but stopped when he spotted headlights through the trees. The car eased along the road. Most likely it was the thief searching for them. He crouched and Isabel slipped in beside him. The car stopped and the driver got out. Shining his flashlight, the man peered up into the trees where he and Isabel were hiding. It was clearly the thief. He must have seen their flashlight when they had it on. The thief continued to walk toward them in a zigzag pattern.

The car engine still hummed. The thief had left it running to keep the engine warm.

An idea sparked inside Jason's head. They could get to the thief's car and drive it to safety.

Jason squeezed Isabel's arm just above the elbow and tilted his head. She nodded in understanding. They'd be spotted if they went straight for the car. Still crouching, he moved from tree to tree, working his way down to the road in an arc. Isabel stayed close.

The thief's light bobbed through the forest maybe twenty yards from where they were. Jason scanned the landscape below. It was hard to discern much of anything. He chose his path and made a run for it, knowing that Isabel would be right behind him. He put his foot forward but found only air.

The hill dropped off abruptly. He lost his balance. He tumbled, rolling through the snow. He righted himself. The chill of the snow soaked through his skin. Isabel came to a stop beside him.

A gunshot reverberated through the silence as the light came toward them. The noise of the fall had been enough for the thief to find them. Cold and wet, he grabbed Isabel's hand and made a run for it, coming out on the road behind the running car.

Another gunshot stirred up snow in front of them. Isabel stumbled. He pulled her toward the car. The thief emerged from the trees, lifting his gun. Jason pulled Isabel to the ground as the third shot whizzed over them.

She bolted to her feet and raced toward the car. Jason pulled his gun from his waistband and fired a shot to deter the thief. He didn't want anybody to die here tonight.

The thief dodged back toward a tree. Isabel climbed into the driver's seat and slammed the door. Jason raced toward the car, grabbing the back-door handle as Isabel eased the car forward. He jumped in as another gunshot shattered the back window. Jason stayed low in the seat. Isabel hit the gas and sped down the road.

They'd have to turn around and go past the thief one more time if they were to get to town. The car rumbled down the road. Though it swerved on the unplowed pavement, Isabel kept it moving.

Jason glanced at the shattered back window.

Isabel stared straight ahead. "Just looking for a place to get turned around." Her calmness surprised him. She waited until she found a shoulder and performed a three-point turn with ease.

"Nice driving."

"Thanks. I've had a little experience."

He wondered what she meant by that. "He'll be waiting for us."

She focused on the road in front of her. "I know, but there is no other way off this mountain."

He liked that she was so cool under pressure. They rounded a curve. They weren't far from where they'd left the shooter. Jason pulled his gun out, rolled the window down and then crouched low in the back seat. Isabel did the same, though she had to stay high enough to see the road.

He listened to the rhythm of the car's tires rolling over the compressed snow where they'd driven before while he watched the trees for a flash of light or movement. He held his breath.

Isabel increased the speed of the car.

Tension threaded through his chest as he rested the barrel of the gun on the windowsill.

A single gunshot boomed through the air. Jason caught a flare of gunfire by the trees close to the road. He aimed his gun in that direction. The car fishtailed and swerved.

"I think he must have hit the radiator or something vital." Isabel sounded like she was speaking through gritted teeth. "I'm going to take this thing as far as it will go."

The car limped along down the dark road. The engine began to chug and then quit altogether.

Isabel sat behind the wheel, staring out at the darkness.

After a long moment, Jason said, "There must be a house between here and town."

"Not on the main road there isn't," she said.

"Maybe hidden back in the trees. We'd see the lights at this hour."

"Maybe." Isabel nodded. "There's that convenience store that sells fishing supplies in the summer. Maybe the owner lives there. Must be a couple of miles. Course, everything seems closer when you're driving."

A heaviness seemed to descend into the car. All of these ideas for getting to safety were long shots at best.

He pushed open his door, stepped out and reached for Isabel's door handle. Preparing to trek through the snow—again—he didn't need to see her face clearly to know that she was feeling the same despair as he was.

They hurried down the road, both of them looking over their shoulders from time to time. Maybe they had gotten enough of a head start on the thief to outrun him. Jason's feet padded on the fluffy snow. He scanned the area around them, peering through the trees for any sign of a dwelling. Isabel trudged beside him, her shoulders slumping forward.

"We're going to make it." Jason tried to sound upbeat. "We've made it this far."

She just kept lumbering ahead.

At one point, he had a view of the road below them with the switchbacks. No sign of any cars. The storm had dumped a ton of snow. Though no rational civilian would go out at this hour after such a downfall, he'd hoped to maybe see snowplows or the highway patrol.

Snow swirled out of the dark sky. Under different circumstances, the scene would have seemed almost serene.

Isabel stopped and turned toward the forest. "I thought I saw a light."

He followed the line of her gaze as a lump formed in his throat. Seconds ticked by and he saw only the shadowy outline of the trees. Was this just wishful thinking on her part?

"There." She grabbed his arm just above the elbow and pointed with her free hand.

He still didn't see anything. "Isabel, I—"

"I know what I saw." She planted her feet and continued to stare.

He glanced up the road, half expecting to see their pursuer. He caught the flash of illumination and turned to where Isabel was looking.

A light emerged from the trees and seemed to be gliding across the landscape. A cross-country skier with a headlamp and reflective clothing.

Isabel took off running. She shouted. The skier stopped, turned and came toward them.

Isabel spoke breathlessly. "Can you help us? Our car went off the road."

With her hat and gear on, it was hard to judge the skier's age. She wore a reflective vest that looked official. Her gaze moved from Isabel to Jason.

"Are you avalanche patrol?" Jason asked, hoping to allay the woman's suspicions.

"Yes. With all the snowfall, I thought I'd better get out and have a look. Plus, there's nothing in the world like skiing at night in the silence."

"Please, if we could just use your phone."

The desperation in Isabel's voice must have won the woman over. "My place is back through the trees. You can call, but I wouldn't recommend anyone come get you until the plows have been up this way. They get them out as soon as the storm lets up, so I would say another hour or so."

The woman led them back to a small trailer that had been skirted around the bottom to keep the plumbing from freezing. They followed her into the tiny space. The woman tore her hat off, revealing braids and a bright smile. She probably wasn't more than twenty.

She did a half turn in her trailer. "It's not much. But they pay me to ski, so I can't complain." She grabbed a phone off the counter and handed it to Jason. "You'll have to go outside to get a signal. I'll put a kettle on for tea."

Jason took the phone and stepped outside.

His contact at the Bureau would be the best choice. That way he could run the idea of going undercover past them. They'd been through a lot tonight, but maybe he could turn it around for the best.

The biggest concern was Isabel. She didn't need to be

caught up in the middle of this, but the thieves had seen her. Even now he felt himself drawn to her. She was a hard person to read. That kind of complexity intrigued him. More than anything, he wanted to protect her.

His contact picked up on the third ring. "Michael?"

"Hey, Jason, we were starting to worry about you."

Jason gave the edited version of what had happened and his approximate location. Michael agreed to send an agent to pick them up and decided on a location to meet them when they got to town. He and Isabel would probably have to hike out to the road to be seen. He'd have to make arrangements for his van to be towed from the location.

When he clicked off the phone, he was surprised to see Isabel standing in front of him. Her arms crossed over her chest.

"My friend will come and get us."

"You owe me an explanation for what happened here tonight. I could lose my job for the mess that house was left in."

Yes, things might work out for the best with the investigation. But then there was the problem of Isabel's safety and her demand to know more.

SEVEN

It was still dark when Jason's friend picked them up. The echo of the snowplows clearing the roads seemed to be everywhere. From the vantage point on the mountain where they stood waiting, Isabel could see three sets of headlights clearing different roads of the snow.

A truck approached them and slowed.

Jason waved and the truck came to a stop. He opened the door for her to get into the front seat and then climbed in beside her.

"Thanks for coming to get us, Larry," Jason said.

"No problem." Larry had graying temples and a beak-like nose. Though he wore a ski jacket, something about him seemed very formal or official in some way.

Back at the trailer, Jason had still not offered her an explanation that made sense. He'd been evasive.

She didn't think he was a criminal or up to no good anymore. He'd kept her alive at the risk of his own safety and stayed with her through everything. Why, then, was he keeping secrets from her?

They were squeezed like sardines in the cab of the truck.

She let out a heavy breath, relaxing for the first time

since she'd had a knife put to her throat at the Wilsons' house.

"I can't wait to go home, take a hot shower and get some sleep." A few hours, anyway. She had some explaining to do to her boss about the condition the Wilsons' home had been left in. The broken vase in the entryway, the shattered window in the studio... The groceries she was supposed to stock were still in her car, which was wedged against a tree. Her stomach clenched. Would she even have a job after all this? She couldn't tell Mary the truth. It sounded too outrageous. Always there was the fear that because she had a record, she would be suspected if any crime took place in her proximity. Mary had been nothing but supportive of her, but other people hadn't been so kind.

"Actually, Isabel, I need you to come with me." Jason's gaze darted to Larry. "Can you drop us off at Ralph's Café? I'll borrow your phone and have Michael meet us there."

Larry nodded and handed over his phone. Really, their interactions didn't seem like they were friends, more like coworkers. And who was this Michael person and what was Jason up to? Her stomach tightened. "Wait a minute. I need to get home. I have to be at work in four hours. And I don't have access to a car anymore."

Jason gripped her hand. "This is important for both our sakes."

Something in the force of his voice told her protest would be futile.

She pressed her back against the seat. "Just for the record, I need to keep this job and I need a car that runs."

They drove toward town in silence as a dozen anxious thoughts whirled through Isabel's head. She'd been so focused on staying alive, she hadn't had time to process what all that had happened meant for her future. By this afternoon, the Wilsons would be arriving to a home that was in disarray—or worse, where the thieves were hiding out. She needed to make sure the Wilsons weren't going into an unsafe situation.

"I'll go with you, but you have to let me call my boss in a little bit." Mary wouldn't be waking up for at least another hour, well before the Wilsons were set to arrive.

"We can do that." Jason nodded and then pressed the numbers on the phone and spoke to the man he called Michael.

Anxious thoughts pounded through her mind. What would she tell Mary? That thieves had been in the house, and she'd had to flee. The short version would be the best. Still nervous, she laced her gloved hands together.

They pulled up to an all-night café on the edge of town. Jason opened the passenger-side door, thanked Larry and held out a hand for Isabel to step down from the big truck.

He locked onto her with his blue eyes, watching her. "I'm sorry about all of this," he said.

The soft features of his face, the warmth of his voice. He seemed so sincere.

"Please, my job is very important to me."

He took her hand and led her toward the café. "I'm going to try to get this straightened out."

They went inside the café. Only a waitress and the cook were inside. Jason chose a corner booth.

"Are you hungry?"

"Starving." Her stomach rumbled on cue.

The waitress, who had orange hair, sauntered toward

them. She had to be at least in her seventies. "What can
I get you two?"

They both ordered burgers and milkshakes.

A car pulled into the parking lot. A moment later, a
tall man got out and stepped inside. He held a computer.
Jason rose to his feet. "I need to talk to Michael alone."

More secrets.

A weariness settled into Isabel's muscles. She needed
sleep. The two men took a booth at the other end of the
room with Michael facing her. The older man flipped
open his computer and started typing while Jason spoke
to him. Jason pulled out the bookmark wrapped in cardboard and handed it over to Michael. The conversation
went on for several minutes with Jason doing most of
the talking. Though she couldn't hear what they were
saying, she could read lips enough to know that Michael had said, "Sun and Ski Property Management."
He glanced in Isabel's direction and then proceeded to
type on his keypad.

Jason turned his head to look at her. Though she believed Jason could be trusted, suspicion and fear niggled
at the corners of her mind. She'd trusted Nick Solomon
too. She hadn't dated since Nick, fearing that she might
only be able to attract another bad boy. Jason and Michael caused that doubt to come back into her head.
Not that she saw him as dating material, but what if
she was wrong about Jason? Why was he insisting that
she stay close and not letting her go home? What if he
was up to no good?

While Michael pulled up files pertinent to the investigation, Jason tried to push past the tension knotting
the muscles in his neck. Would the Bureau be open to

the idea of his going undercover or would he be out of a job after tonight's fiasco?

After a moment, Michael spoke while still staring at the computer screen. "I thought the name Sun and Ski Property Management sounded familiar. It seems they manage a lot of the properties where the thefts have taken place." He glanced toward Isabel. "Are you sure your new friend can be trusted?"

He'd spent a harrowing night with her, both of them fighting for each other's lives. "I believe so, yes."

"Maybe she's clean, but that doesn't mean Sun and Ski isn't somehow involved." Michael scratched his chin. "They would certainly know when houses were vacant and have security codes."

"If we could just get her some protection. She saw the thieves more clearly than I did, and they can probably identify her."

"You said that the thieves think the two of you are partners."

"Yes, but it's too dangerous to ask her to become involved in the investigation," Jason said.

"Look, find out what her last name is. We'll run a check on her. Meanwhile hang close to her and see what you can find out about Sun and Ski. That will give her some protection. The couriers are pretty low-level thugs. Chances are their desire for revenge will blow over in twenty-four hours."

"I'm not so sure. They were pretty determined. And now they think we've horned in on their profit margin and can identify them," said Jason.

"Take her to the city police station and see if she can identify the two men she saw at the house. Maybe we can get them picked up for something else."

"Isabel deserves an explanation. All she knows is that I'm a PI."

"For now, we need to keep her in the dark," Michael said.

The waitress moved across the floor, holding two plates, but hesitated when she saw Jason at a different table.

"Why don't you go eat?" Michael closed his computer. "I'll make arrangements for a ride." He tossed a set of keys on the table. "You take her down to the police station."

Jason motioned for the waitress to take the plates over to where Isabel waited. He grabbed the keys and returned to where Isabel was already slathering ketchup on her burger.

He sat opposite her. The aroma of the burger made his mouth water and his stomach rumble.

"Is that guy a policeman?" She took a bite, closing her eyes while she chewed, savoring the taste.

There was something endearing about the way she enjoyed her food.

Jason shifted in his chair. "I still can't explain everything to you."

"Secrets make me nervous."

"It's for your protection. Please take my word for that."

She picked up a fry and popped it into her mouth while her gaze rested on him. She didn't speak until she finished chewing the fry. "Your word has been good so far."

He relaxed a little. At least she'd chosen to trust him. "We need to go down to the police station to identify the two guys you saw at the house. You got a better look at them than I did." He didn't want to worry her that she might still be a target.

"Fine, but I need to swing by work and talk to my boss first. She gets into the office bright and early. Plus, I've got to find a way to get my car back into town."

"Okay, we can do that." Driving her around gave him the excuse he needed to stay close until he was sure the thieves wouldn't come after her.

They finished their meal and got into the car Michael had loaned him. The sun was low on the horizon as they drove through Silver Strike, which featured lots of boutique-type shops. Isabel gave Jason directions that led them to the Sun and Ski headquarters, a Victorian house that had been converted to offices. The sign said that a real-estate company also had an office in the building.

As they pulled into the lot, she turned to face him. "I live upstairs. Mary, my boss, was nice enough to rent the one bedroom to me at a low rate." Despite her blond hair being a little disheveled, Isabel still had the demeanor of someone who had come from money. He wondered what her story was. Why she was so hard to get a clear read on.

"You like your job and your boss." Sun and Ski was under suspicion. That meant this Mary person wasn't off the hook yet.

"Yes." Her smile lit up her whole face.

"That's the first time I've seen you smile."

"It's the first time I've had a reason to smile since you met me." She let out a laugh that reminded him of songbirds.

"Indeed." For having known each other for such a short time, they'd been through a lot. The moment of connection between them seemed to make the car warmer and brighter. Guilt washed through him. He wished he could come clean with her. "Let's go inside."

She pushed open the door, taking in an intense breath. "I've got a lot of explaining to do to Mary for the condition of the house. The Wilsons will be there soon."

He followed her into an office that had three desks. A fortyish woman with coppery hair stood by one of the workstations, her purse slung over her shoulder.

"Isabel, I'm about to run out to a house but I'm glad I caught up with you." Her gaze rested on Jason.

Isabel glanced at Jason. "This is my friend. He gave me a ride."

Mary furrowed her eyebrows. "Yes, I was just on the phone to the Wilsons. They got into town earlier than expected. I guess they told you they wouldn't be here until the afternoon."

"But they are safe?" said Isabel.

"Safe?" Mary looked perplexed. "Why wouldn't they be? They said the house was in order. Only they wondered why your car was parked down the road and how the vase got broken. They found the shards in the garbage."

"The house was in order?" The Wilsons must not have seen the studio's broken window or found her clothes in Victoria's closet.

"You are a great employee and I am sure there is an explanation for all this. I'd love to hear it when I have more time." Mary tilted her head. "The problem I'm having, Isabel, is that they texted your personal phone to say they were coming early. All client calls need to go through Sun and Ski, regardless of what your relationship is with them. I need to know if one of our clients has had a change of plans."

"I understand. I'm sorry." Isabel hung her head. "I guess I was too focused on trying to keep the clients happy."

Someone must have picked the thieves up. Maybe they'd taken the time to remove all traces that they'd been in the house to protect the smuggling operation.

"I need to run. I'll catch up with you in a bit." Mary winked at Isabel and patted her shoulder. "I do appreciate your going up there on your day off." Mary hurried out the door. Her anger over Isabel not keeping her in the loop about the Wilsons' early arrival set off alarm bells for Jason.

Isabel shook her head. "I don't know what's going on here. Why the place was cleaned up. Mary didn't say anything about your van being there."

He suspected the Bureau had already been up there to have it towed. "It's just good that everything worked out."

"No, it's weird that everything worked out." She studied him for a long moment, as if expecting him to explain further. The phone rang. She picked up. "Sun and Ski Property Management. This is Isabel speaking. How may I help you?"

Isabel listened for a moment. Her face drained of color and she slammed the phone down.

He took a step toward her. "What is it?"

Fear permeated each word she uttered. "That was…a man. He said I have something he wants. And that I better give it back or pay with my life."

EIGHT

Jason had a hard time focusing on the road as they drove across town to the police station. Any hope he had about Isabel being safe had been removed. Maybe now she wouldn't be upset if he chose to keep close to her until he could get her some protection.

Had it been the thieves who phoned or someone higher up in the smuggling ring?

He glanced over at Isabel. She offered him a nervous smile and then stared out the window. The problem was someone in the ring had contacted Isabel first. Either because they hadn't figured out who he was or because she was the more vulnerable one. How was he going to get her out of this mess and make sure she wouldn't be harmed? Maybe the threat would be enough for Michael to be motivated to spring for some protection.

"How do you suppose they figured out who I was?"

"Is there anything in your car that would have helped them trace you back to Sun and Ski?"

"There's a logo on the back window. And my picture and name is on our website." Her voice filled with fear.

He hadn't noticed the logo.

He braked at a stoplight and studied her for a moment. Her fingers were laced together in her lap so tight that her knuckles had turned white.

"I'm sorry that you got dragged into all this."

"I can't live my life looking over my shoulder. A lot of the properties we manage are out in the middle of nowhere."

"Look, I don't have a lot going on. I'll stay with you through your workday if you don't mind my tagging along." He kind of liked the idea of being with her.

The light turned green. He rolled through the street checking his rearview mirror. A dark car that had been behind them before followed them as he clicked his blinker and turned up a side street. He didn't want to alarm Isabel. She was already scared enough.

She unlaced her fingers and rested her hands palm down in her lap. "You would do that for me?"

"Sure."

"Guess I was just in the wrong place at the wrong time. I thought what I was doing was giving a hundred and ten percent to my job. That totally backfired."

This was his chance to do a little probing. "Yes, your boss seemed more than a little miffed you didn't keep her in the loop."

"She's not usually like that. She's been very good to me."

"I just wonder why she was so upset, then."

She stared at him long enough to make him nervous. "I was in the wrong. I went against our standard practice. She's a good person."

Jason checked the rearview mirror. The car was still behind them.

"I see him too," Isabel said, her voice barely above a whisper.

He turned on the street that led to the police station. The car veered onto a side street. Once it was clear, Jason pulled into the police-station parking lot. No one was going to bother them when they were surrounded by a half dozen armed officers…he hoped, anyway.

Isabel appreciated the supportive hand Jason placed on her back as they entered the police station. She felt like she'd been trembling from terror ever since the phone call at Sun and Ski. Having him close at least helped her take a deep breath.

"Hey, Jason." One of the police officers waved at them as they entered the station. He stepped toward them. "What brings you here?"

"This is Isabel…?" He turned toward her raising an eyebrow.

"Connor. My last name is Connor."

"She needs to do an ID for me. You got your file of petty criminals loaded up?"

"Sure. Come this way." The officer held out a hand to her. "I'm Officer Nelson. Jason and I went to high school together about fifty miles down the road in a little town no one has heard of."

Isabel shook Officer Nelson's hand.

"Come right this way." Officer Nelson gestured.

She glanced over at Jason. "You're not coming with me?"

"I've got a call to make." He didn't quite make eye contact. "You'll be fine."

Officer Nelson led her to a desk where he opened up a laptop computer. "So you were a witness to a crime and Jason is helping you?" He clicked several keys until a police photo of a man came up on the screen.

"Something like that."

He bent to reach the keyboard. "Just click here to see the next photo." Officer Nelson squeezed her shoulder. "Holler if you have any trouble."

She filed through half a dozen photographs, studying each one. A picture of her old boyfriend Nick Solomon flashed on the screen. Her cheeks flushed as shame rose to the surface. She glanced around the police station, feeling as if everyone else would know she had once been connected with this petty thief.

Even in the police photo, Nick offered the camera his crooked smile and big brown eyes. She'd been so naive back then.

Her eyes came to rest on Jason, who was talking on an office phone. When he saw her staring, he turned away. The old quiver of suspicion and distrust returned. She wanted to believe he was a good guy. Everything he'd done and said so far backed that up. His kindness in offering to stay with her warmed her heart. But the look he gave her seemed filled with suspicion.

She stared at the photo of Nick again. What she didn't trust was her own judgment of character with men. She had such a lousy track record.

Officer Nelson walked by her, holding a stack of file folders. "Is everything going okay?"

"So far I haven't seen either of the men." She was still on edge from the phone call. Seeing Nick in all his criminal glory hadn't helped. "Actually, I need a minute to freshen up and clear my head. Where's your bathroom?"

"You'll have to use the one downstairs at the end of the hall. The one on this floor is part of a construction zone."

Isabel pushed her chair back. She stared through the window at Jason, who was still on the phone. He looked at her. Something in his expression had changed. He looked...pensive?

She hurried down the hallway past scaffolding, tool-boxes and cans of paint. But no workers. They must be on a break. The downstairs was quiet. The signs on the doors indicated the rooms were used mostly for storage of records and evidence.

She slipped into the bathroom and splashed water on her face, then stared at herself in the mirror. She looked frazzled, had dark circles under her eyes.

Come on, Izzy. Pull it together.

She bent her head and squeezed her eyes shut. "If God is for me, who can be against me?"

The door to the bathroom swung open. Before she had time to see who it was, a hand grabbed her hair and a knife was at her throat.

"You have something I want."

She shook her head, then tried to turn toward the mirror to see the man who held her captive. He pressed the knife deeper into her skin.

"Don't lie to me. You have twenty-four hours. We'll give you a drop-off point." He shoved her toward the wall and she fell. By the time she righted herself, she was alone in the bathroom.

She stood frozen and listening. Was the man with the knife waiting just outside the door? Her heart pounded wildly in her chest. She could manage only shallow breaths.

Isabel stepped toward the door and pushed it open. She peered up and down the empty hallway before stepping out.

Pounding footsteps made her turn to retreat back into the bathroom until she saw Jason at the bottom of the stairs.

She ran toward him. His expression registered that he saw how scared she was. He held out his arms to her.

"Hey, what happened?"

"They found me." Her voice was hoarse. Her words came out in broken fragments.

She rested against the soft flannel of Jason's shirt. His arms surrounded her, and she was able to take in a deep breath.

After a long moment of silence, he said. "I had a feeling when you didn't come right back. I hate that this is happening to you."

She pulled back and gazed into his blue eyes. "They want the bookmark. I have twenty-four hours. They are supposed to contact me with a location." Her chest felt like it was in a corset being pulled tighter and tighter.

"Could you tell if it was one of the men from the house?"

She shook her head. "I didn't see him. I don't have a good memory for voices and he didn't say much."

He took her hand and led her to a bench in the hallway. She sat down beside him. It still felt like someone was rattling her spine.

"I wish that they had gotten in touch with me. But it's you they want to deal with."

"What are you talking about?"

"I was on the phone to Michael." He studied her for a moment. His mouth twitched. There was something he was keeping from her.

"Who is he, anyway—your boss?"

"He's an FBI agent. Since you got the threat on the

phone, he gave me permission to share with you what is going on. I'm helping the FBI investigate a smuggling ring that often uses empty homes as a drop-off point. We're building profiles of all the people involved to try to get to whoever is behind it all."

She rose to her feet. "I don't want to be involved with any of this. I just want to go back to my job, back to my life."

He stood up and grabbed her hands. "I understand." He squeezed her fingers. "But I need to hang with you until they contact you...for your safety."

She knew he was right about that. She couldn't just go about her day as if nothing had happened. She needed his protection. "I don't like associating with criminals in any way, shape or form. Michael has the bookmark. The two of you can work this out."

"I will do everything I can to keep you out of harm's way and try to work it so they will deal with me."

His expression looked so sincere. "What are you going to do? Follow me around like a puppy?"

"Actually, I prefer the term *guard dog*." The corners of his mouth turned up.

His joke made her smile. "I guess this is the way it has to be. I need to head home to take a shower and get some sleep and then I have to go to work."

"I'll go with you to the houses when you set them up. You don't have a car anyway."

She pressed her hands against her mouth and stared at the ceiling. "I don't like any of this. I don't like being around...criminals."

"I think I understand." He locked eyes with her. "I know about your record. Even though it was sealed, the FBI has ways of finding these things out."

So that was why he'd looked at her that way. Her cheeks grew warm. "That was a long time ago. I was seventeen." She turned away from him as a sense of deep shame rose to the surface. "I'm not one of them anymore. And I don't want anything to do with thieves."

He touched the back of her arm. "I know you're not. I can see that you've made changes. Only someone who's turned her life over to God would have been praying while being chased. Michael had concerns, but I vouched for you."

She turned to face him, feeling tears rise up in the corners of her eyes. "You vouched for me?" Warmth pooled around her heart. Sometimes she felt like having been a juvenile delinquent in a small community where everybody knew your history flashed like a neon sign around her. So few people believed in her aside from Mary, her pastor, a few friends and now Jason. "Thank you."

He nodded. "Now let's drive you back to your place so you can get some sleep."

Snow twirled out of the sky as they drove back to Sun and Ski. The plows had worked through the morning creating walls of snow on either side of the city streets. They stopped at a store so she and Jason could buy new phones.

Jason parked the car outside the Sun and Ski office.

"You can come in and get some rest on the couch. You're probably tired too." The truth was she felt better knowing that he was close.

Isabel led him up the stairs to her place. She put her key in the lock and pushed open the door. The house was old and not well insulated. The top floor could get chilly but she'd done her best to make it cozy with lace curtains as well as a quilt thrown over the worn red velvet couch.

"Nice, very homey," said Jason turning a half circle.

It made her feel good that he liked her little apartment. His opinion was starting to matter to her.

"Make yourself at home. There's sandwich stuff and tea and coffee. I feel like I could sleep for a hundred years."

She took a quick shower and crawled in under her comforter. Heavy curtains blocked out the light. She closed her eyes, waiting for sleep to come. Her body was beyond tired, but restless, fearful thoughts made it hard for her to shut down her brain.

She'd worked so hard to cut ties with her past. Though Jason believed in her, any thought of associating with criminals brought up all the pain from her teenage years. She drew her comforter up to her neck. These men could be violent. Would they leave her alone once she delivered the bookmark or would she always be looking over her shoulder?

The only thing that eased her troubled mind was knowing that Jason was in the next room. She was safe…for now.

NINE

Jason collapsed on Isabel's couch. He pulled out his phone and dialed Michael's number to tell him about Isabel being attacked at the police station. The thieves were probably going after Isabel because she was the easier target...more vulnerable. That infuriated him.

He summarized for Michael what had happened and then said, "If there is any way we can get her clear of all this, we need to do it. She didn't sign up for this. I did."

Michael's response was measured. "Involving a civilian is never the best approach, but she's knee-deep in this already. I know you're willing to see her motives as pure. I have a wait-and-see policy. The Bureau has found that sometimes criminals can be a help in an investigation. Our end goal is finding out who's behind this operation."

Jason clenched his jaw. "She's not a criminal."

"In the meantime, we're going to put a tail on her boss and look into Mary Helms's connections. For now, you are Isabel Connor's protection. If you're seen together, it will further the cover that the two of you are thieves working together and maybe you can figure out Sun and Ski's level of involvement, if any."

"I'll let you know when they contact her about the bookmark." Feeling a little frustrated, Jason clicked off the phone. Michael could be really myopic when it came to the investigation. At least this way, Isabel would be safe. He'd see to that. He slumped down on the couch, closed his eyes and pulled his feet onto the couch, allowing the heaviness of sleep to overtake him.

He awoke to the smell of coffee and bacon sizzling in a pan. Isabel was dressed in a long skirt, boots and a sweater. Her honey-blond hair was pulled up into a loose bun. Soft tangles surrounded her face. She looked beautiful.

She offered him a smile. "Feel better?"

He rose to his feet. "Yes. I needed that."

"Coffee is on and I should have a late breakfast ready in just a minute."

He poured himself a cup and wandered around her small living room. Her walls were decorated with cross-stitched Bible verses and nature photos. He picked up one of the photos on the mantel. A boy of about ten smiled at him.

She plated the food. "That's my little brother, Zac."

Isabel must be about twenty-five. "Your mom had kids really far apart."

A shadow seemed to fall across her face. "He's a half brother. But as far as I'm concerned, he's just a precious little brother to me."

There were no other photos that could be family. Only a picture of Isabel with her boss at a picnic, both of them smiling for the camera, and one of Isabel with her arms around two women her age, a cabin in the background surrounded by forest. The women wore matching T-shirts that referenced a church retreat.

She handed him a plate of food. The aroma of bacon made his mouth water. Her brown-eyed gaze rested on him for a moment. "There's no room for a table. I usually eat on the couch."

They sat side by side. Her posture was ramrod straight, her chin slightly lifted. When she'd been afraid and tired, he'd seen a more vulnerable side to Isabel. Now she'd returned to that professional demeanor that had originally made him think she was from money. He thought he was pretty good at seeing past people's facades, but Isabel wore hers like armor. Now he knew why. Maybe she thought the more formal she seemed, the less likely people were to guess she had a record.

He helped her with the dishes and they headed downstairs to the office.

"Mary will have left me a message about which houses I need to get ready." She swung open the door to the office, which was empty.

"Is this door always unlocked?"

"We come and go all day. It's just easier. The real-estate people next door are hardly ever there."

He stared out at the street, wondering if they were being watched.

Tension threaded through Isabel's words. "Guess I should lock it from now on."

"Maybe this will all be over soon." His words held a note of doubt. Would thieves come after her because she could identify them even if they got the bookmark back? He had the feeling the demand for the return of the bookmark was being engineered by someone higher up in the pecking order. It took a level of criminal sophistication and moxie to come after someone in a police station. Maybe even someone with connections to the police or the financial means to bribe their way into what should be a secure building.

The office phone rang.

Jason swung around.

Isabel pressed her lips together. He read fear in her eyes. His heart beat a little faster, and he swallowed to produce some moisture in his mouth. "Go ahead. Answer it."

She remained as still as a statue.

He stepped toward her, his shoulder pressing against hers. "I'll be right here. And I won't leave until I know you're safe."

The stiffness in her body softened. She seemed to draw courage from what he said. She took in a breath and lifted the phone.

Isabel's heart pounded against her rib cage. She steadied her shaking hand. "Hello." It didn't even sound like her voice.

She could hear breathing on the other end of the line.

"Hello," she repeated, her voice growing stronger. She put the phone on speaker so Jason could hear too.

"The Clauson family home. You know it?" The man on the other end of the line had a husky voice.

"Yes." The Clausons were Sun and Ski clients.

"There's a big shindig there. An invite will be waiting for you at the front entrance of the Clauson house. At eight forty-five go to the library. *History of Rome*, volume seven, page twenty-five. Got it?"

Her hands were sweating. "Yes."

"Your friend is not invited."

The line went dead.

Isabel threw the phone down as though it was on

fire. The memory of everything that had happened at the Wilsons' bombarded her. These people played for keeps. "I can't do this."

From where he stood beside her, Jason brushed his fingers over her arm. "I'll find a way to be at that party. You won't be alone. I need to get a picture of the pickup man anyway. For them to believe that we really are thieves who want in on the action, we'll have to give them the real bookmark."

She shook her head. "He said you weren't invited."

"It's a party with lots of people around," Jason said. "I'll find a way to stay close and not be noticed."

The steadiness of his voice and his expression of unwavering resolve almost convinced her. "I guess if they wanted to hurt me, they would have chosen somewhere remote. Do you suppose they'll leave me alone if I give the bookmark back?"

His forehead wrinkled with concern. "I'm not sure. I'll stay with you until we know you're not a target."

"I want this to be over."

Before he could reply, the door burst open and Mary stepped inside.

"Glad to see you're ready to work." She turned toward Jason. "And you still have your driver, I see. I called the tow truck to get your car off the mountain." Mary leaned over and rummaged through a desk drawer until she pulled out a key ring with multiple keys on it. "The atmosphere is like a funeral in here. Isabel, is there something you want to tell me?"

"I'm… I'm just glad to be back at work." She gave Jason a nervous glance, wishing she could tell Mary the whole story.

"Good. We've got a couple of houses to get ready.

One of them is a new client. I texted you the instructions. I gotta run."

Mary was out the door. Isabel watched through the big bay window as Mary got into her car and drove off. A moment later, a car pulled away from the curb and fell in behind Mary.

Isabel's breath hitched. "Are you having my boss tailed?"

Jason didn't answer right away. "We have to rule her out. A lot of the houses where the drop-offs happened were managed by Sun and Ski. Mary would have the alarm codes."

"You don't know her. She's been good to me." That the FBI suspected Mary bothered Isabel even more than their suspicion of her.

"It wasn't my call. They just need to rule her out."

From the pit of her roiling stomach, Isabel could feel her resolve coming together. "I'll make this drop if it will help further the investigation and get Mary off the hook. She's innocent."

Jason's face brightened. His eyes held a twinkle. "Thank you for being so brave."

She wasn't so sure it was courage she felt so much as a desire to have all this be over. To get back to the life she'd built for herself, to not have a shadow of suspicion cast over a person she cared about very much.

"How are you going to get into the fund-raiser?"

"I have some connections. Big event like that is most likely catered. The Bureau will no doubt plant some people in there too. You're not alone in this, Isabel."

The words were like a soothing balm to her.

Jason gave her shoulder a supportive squeeze. "Well, come on. I'll take you to the houses you need to open up and then you have a ball gown to buy, Cinderella."

TEN

Jason felt itchy and uncomfortable in the waiter's uniform his friend had loaned him. Starched white shirt, tails and cummerbund were not his style. He was a jeans and flannel or wool shirt kind of guy. He tugged on his collar as he scanned the room and kept his eye on the door, looking for Isabel.

"Thank you." A tall woman in a sparkling gown grabbed a glass off his tray. Her dress was the same color as the champagne he served.

He spotted one other Bureau guy as he wove through the room. One of the older agents, a short man with a widow's peak, stood talking to a man in a cowboy hat.

Isabel had ten more minutes before she had to make the drop. She ought to have shown up by now. His heart squeezed a little tighter.

Jason had stayed with Isabel through the day and into evening.

After they'd found her a dress and picked up the bookmark from Michael, he'd dropped her off at her place to get ready with the understanding that she would text him when she left. He'd had to get to the party to be in place when she arrived. Her text had come through ten minutes ago. How long did it take to get across town? Had it been a mistake to leave her even for that short time? What if the fund-raiser party was just a ruse and they intended to grab her the first chance they got?

He checked his watch one more time. He needed to get into place in the library without being noticed. He had to assume the smuggler mastermind had planted people besides the pickup guy among the partygoers. Even if the smuggler had figured out who Jason was, the waiter's uniform would make him invisible.

Isabel appeared suddenly at the door, dressed in royal blue.

Jason breathed a sigh of relief.

Her cheeks were flushed with color. Her skin had something on it that sparkled when she stepped into the light and down the stairs. She looked stunning.

She spotted him but made only momentary eye contact. She wove through the crowd, stopping to shake hands and talk to people. A lot of these people were probably clients.

She whisked past him.

He spoke under his breath. "Everything go okay?"

"Yes, but I think I was followed. I had to take the long way."

Might have been the thieves they'd encountered at the Wilsons'. The higher-ups would have known she was headed to the fund-raiser.

The music stopped, and a woman picked up a microphone to make announcements about the money raised and silent-auction items still left to be bid on. While the attention of the crowd was on the woman, Jason set his tray down and headed toward the library. Isabel had explained the layout of the house to him earlier in the evening.

Knowing that a nervous glance might give him away, he kept his gaze on the stairs in front of him but listened to make sure he wasn't followed. The library was on the second story at the opposite end of the house, far away from any partygoers. Even someone who was lost or looking for a bathroom wouldn't be on that side of the house.

In order to make the drop, Isabel would be less than a minute or two behind him. They were cutting this pretty close. His heart kicked into high gear and adrenaline surged through his system.

The library was dark. He slipped behind a desk and waited for the sound of Isabel's footsteps. In this light, it would be nearly impossible to identify the pickup man. Jason would have to follow him back into the throng of partygoers and look for an opportunity to snap a photo. If that opportunity didn't arise, he'd have to get a good look at the guy and trust his memory.

All Isabel had to do was slip the bookmark into place and hurry back to the crowd. She'd be safe among the partygoers.

He heard the light tapping of footsteps on the wood floor outside. Isabel's dress made swishing sounds as she entered the room. She did a half turn in the middle of the floor, probably wondering where he was hiding.

His heart lurched. He wanted to say something to let her know he had her back. But it was too risky. She approached the bookshelf and clicked the light on her phone, bending close to the volumes. She held a gold clutch purse that contained the bookmark.

A shadow entered the room from a side door. The

man was so silent and quick, Jason heard only two footsteps before the dark figure grabbed Isabel and spun
her around, whispering something sinister-sounding
in her ear.

Jason jumped to his feet and hurried toward Isabel.
The shadow swung around so Isabel was between him
and Jason.

"I've got a gun on her. You come any closer, she
takes a bullet."

He couldn't see a gun, and though he was less than
four feet away, he couldn't make out the features on
Isabel's face.

"It's…true… Jason." Her voice, drenched in fear,
faltered.

"Back away…now," said the man covered in shadows. He was dressed in black, which made him even
harder to see.

Heart raging against his rib cage, sweat trickling
down his neck, Jason took a step back even as he tried to
come up with a way to overtake the man holding Isabel.

Isabel's frantic breathing seemed augmented in the
darkness and silence of the library. Dragging Isabel
with him, the man slipped toward a dark corner of the
room.

There was a brief burst of light as a door opened
and the man pulled Isabel through. The door shut and
he heard a clicking sound. Footsteps retreating downstairs. Jason raced toward it. Locked. This was an exit
the Bureau hadn't accounted for.

He ran to the window that was on the same side of
the room as the door. Down below, he saw Isabel being
dragged toward a black truck that was parked off away

from the other vehicles. From that side of the property, there was only one road out.

He hurried down the stairs toward his own car, praying that he would be able to get to Isabel in time. He sprinted through the back part of the main floor. The noise of the partygoers dimmed as he went through a part of the house where there weren't many people, only some of the hired help. There was no time to alert the agent on the premises. Isabel's life depended on his getting out to that road as fast as he could.

As he ran toward his car, the momentary image of Isabel's terrified expression when the light had come through the open door bombarded his thoughts.

Jumping into his loaner car, he shifted into gear. He could see the black truck winding its way up the road. He pressed the gas. His car swerved, but he straightened it out. Conditions were far from ideal.

Shadow man's truck disappeared around a corner. Jason prayed he would be able to get to Isabel before it was too late.

Isabel gripped the steering wheel as she struggled to take in air, to remain calm. She'd seen Jason's car behind them for just a moment on the straight part of the road. She slowed as they rounded the curve, hoping Jason would be able to keep up.

"Drive faster," said the man with the gun.

She glanced over at him.

He grinned, showing all his teeth. "Thought I'd never see you again, Isabel."

Nick Solomon. The last person on earth she wanted to see. "I heard you got out of prison." He must be connected with the smuggling ring. How else would he have known she was in the library?

"You've been following my exploits, have you?"

She had paid attention to his release date because she wanted to avoid him. "I thought I heard you went down to California."

"I did for a while, Blondie." He scooted closer, still holding the gun on her. "Let's just say a much more lucrative opportunity came up here in Silver Strike."

Nick instructed her to take several more turns. She wasn't familiar with this road. She checked the rearview mirror.

"I think we lost your little partner there. I don't know why you're with him, anyway. If you wanted to get back into the life, if the word on the street is true, you should have called me."

She pressed her teeth together. As much as she wanted to tell Nick she had changed and the last thing she wanted was a life of crime, she swallowed her words. The smuggling ring believed she wanted in on their action, and she had to continue that ruse. "I'm happy with my current partner."

"What's his name, anyway?"

So they hadn't been able to identify Jason. That was why they'd communicated with her.

"Decided to go all quiet on me, huh?" He sat back in the seat, staring at her in a way that put her even more on edge. They drove for at least twenty minutes. He waved the gun in the air. "Turn that way and park when you see the little cabins."

She turned onto a long unplowed driveway where there were several cabins and a larger lodge. This was probably a church camp that was only used in the summer.

"Stop before the truck gets stuck."

She pressed the brakes. Nick held out his hands for the keys. They were miles from anything or anyone. They had encountered no other traffic on the road or passed any houses.

She slammed the keys into his clammy palm.

Her clutch rested on the seat. Nick shoved it into her stomach. "I assume the item of interest is in there. Give it to me."

Her hands were shaking as she undid the clasp. "This is what you were supposed to get back for your boss, right? What good am I to you? Why complicate things?"

Again, the toothy smile. "I have plans for you, my dear."

His words were like mercury in her veins, spreading a deadly poison through her.

She pulled the bookmark from the purse, unfolded the protective case it was in and showed him.

"Very nice."

What had she ever seen in this man? She was sixteen when she met him. Her mother had had a string of boyfriends. She'd never known her father. Nick had paid attention to her at first, told her she was pretty, bought her gifts, given her the affection she'd craved.

He pointed the gun at her. "Get out of the truck and go over to the stone building."

She opened the truck door. Wind blew the snow around. Cold settled on her bare skin. Her ball gown had gotten ripped in the struggle. Her exposed arms were goose pimpled from the cold.

Nick trudged behind her, still holding the gun on her. "I have to say. You look so beautiful tonight. When I saw you, it made me think of old times. We could have been something for each other."

Isabel paused midstride briefly but didn't respond. Fear made it almost impossible for her to speak anyway. What was he planning?

The door to the large stone lodge had a lock and chain on it that had been cut.

"Go inside," Nick urged.

She pushed open the door. The main meeting area had a few benches and a large fireplace.

Without a coat, Isabel was shivering.

"Do you like it here? It's my home away from home. Why don't you build us a nice romantic fire?"

She pressed her lips together, fighting back the words she wanted to say. How he had ruined her life. How she wanted nothing to do with him or the people he associated with.

He pulled out a phone and stepped over to a corner of the room, still watching her and holding the gun.

Wood and kindling were stacked by the fire.

Nick blocked the door, so there was no way for her to escape. Besides, he had the truck keys. She wouldn't get far in the cold, not dressed the way she was.

She struck a match to the kindling she had stacked in the grate and tossed in more paper. Flames blackened and ate the paper and tiny pieces of wood.

Though Nick was speaking in a low tone, she gathered enough of the conversation to discern that he was talking to someone about the bookmark. At one point, he patted his chest where he'd placed it.

The fire increased in intensity, and she threw on a

small log. She held her hands out to the warmth and then rubbed her arms.

Nick finished his phone call and strode toward her. The look in his eyes turned her stomach.

She rubbed her palms over her arms. "I'm really cold. Can I see if I can find a sweater or something around here?"

"I could keep you warm." Again, that sick smile.

Repulsed, she took a step back. "I think I'll try to find a coat or blanket. Maybe some kid left something behind." She turned, looking for a door that might lead to storage or a closet.

She stepped across the room, swung a door open and found board games and outdoor equipment. A sweatshirt heaped in a box on the floor. She grabbed it, assessed it to be a few sizes too big and put it on. It hung down past her waist.

When she turned around, Nick was watching her. He'd put the gun away in his coat. "You sure looked beautiful tonight. You even look cute with that sweatshirt on. What do you say—join me? This isn't small-time. We could make a fortune."

She was struck by how pathetic and desperate he sounded. So that was why he'd dragged her here. He thought he could talk her into being with him.

She shook her head. "I just want to go home, please."

"Come on, Isabel. Don't you want to be rich? This isn't petty stuff for me. I'm connected all the way to the top."

Her senses went on high alert. Was he telling the truth? Did Nick know who was behind the smuggling, or was he just bragging to try to win her back?

He blocked the door so she couldn't step back out

into the main room. She had to play this thing to the end. "I'm happy with the arrangement I have."

Rage flared in his eyes and he reached out and grabbed her. "You were meant to be with me." His hands closed around her wrists.

"Nick, please, you're hurting me." She struggled to get away.

He pressed toward her trying to kiss her. She kicked him hard in the shins so he doubled over and got out of her way. She ran toward the door.

Nick was just recovering when she swung the door open and ran outside. She raced toward one of the far cabins hidden in the trees. The snow was of a soft enough texture that she hadn't left clear footprints. She was glad she'd chosen to wear boots with her dress. At least her feet were warm. He'd find her sooner or later, though. Though she'd gained access to the cabin, she needed to come up with an escape plan.

What could she do? Run to the truck and lock all the doors until he agreed to take her home? No, he would never do that. She could file kidnapping charges against him.

She took out her cell phone. She could tell Jason where she was.

She heard Nick moving through the camp, opening and shutting the cabin doors. No time to make the call.

She slipped out the back door of the cabin and hid behind a tree. His footsteps reached her ears.

"Come on out, Isabel." He sounded almost whiny. "It can be like old times. You and me."

She took in a breath, willing her heart to slow down. The only way off this mountain without blowing her cover was to play along. She'd make Nick think she was interested in getting back with him. Acid rose up from her stomach at the thought of having to pretend to like him.

She stepped out, prepared to call to Nick, when a hand went over her mouth.

ELEVEN

For the second time since they'd met, Jason had to subdue Isabel into silence by putting a hand over her mouth. This time, she must have sensed it was him because she stopped struggling right away.

"I've got the car down the road," Jason whispered.

Nick cried out. "Isabel. Blondie." He shone the flashlight in her direction. Both of them got caught in the light just as they turned to run.

Isabel scrambled down the snowy hill, slowed by her dress. When she looked over her shoulder, the flashlight was moving away from them. Nick was probably going to get his truck so he could chase them.

Jason jumped into the car and revved the engine. She swung the passenger-side door open and scooted in beside him, snapping her seat belt on.

"How did you find me?"

"I saw the smoke from the chimney." He pressed the accelerator and burst forward on the snow-covered road. "When I lost you, I called our friends at the Bureau. Couple agents are out looking for you." Affection and relief collided inside him. "I'm glad I'm the one who found you."

"Me too." Nuances of affection permeated her words. Isabel brushed a stray strand of hair off her face. When he thought he'd lost her at the party, he'd felt a chasm inside him he didn't understand.

"Nice outfit." Even after all she'd been through, she looked beautiful.

She stared down at the sweatshirt. "It's what all the divas are wearing these days."

He caught the levity in her voice, grateful that she could have a sense of humor even while they were still in danger. The guy who had taken her was bound to come after them.

"What's that guy's game, anyway? Why didn't he just take the bookmark?"

"Let's just say he's someone I would rather not associate with."

"But he knows you?"

"He's the reason I have a record." Her voice dropped half an octave and she turned slightly away from him.

Jason knew from what the Bureau had told him that Isabel's old boyfriend was named Nick Solomon. "The past is in the past." He hoped his words communicated that he still believed in her.

Headlights loomed behind them.

Jason stared in the rearview mirror. "Didn't take him long to catch up."

Nick closed the distance between the two vehicles.

Jason pressed the accelerator, feeling a surge of excitement in his veins. Danger did that for him. But he had Isabel to think of now. He needed to get her to a safe place.

Both vehicles slipped on the icy road.

Isabel braced an arm on the dashboard.

Jason righted the car and watched the speedometer nudge toward forty, a dangerous speed in these conditions. Nick was right on his bumper.

They entered a section of the road that was switchback curves. Jason stayed close to the inside as he maneuvered the car around the tight turns.

Nick tapped their bumper. Their car lurched. Jason gripped the wheel, bringing the car back under control.

Headlights filled the rearview mirror. "Hold on." Jason pressed the accelerator to the floor.

Nick's headlights got smaller.

"I think we're going too fast," Isabel said breathlessly as her hand clasped the armrest.

"We just need to put a little distance between us," Jason said.

Visibility was reduced in the darkness. A curve came up without warning. The car slid sideways. Jason turned the wheel in the direction of the skid, hoping to straighten the car.

They continued to slide. The car came to a stop. The engine had quit. Jason turned the key in the ignition.

Nick's truck barreled toward them, ramming them in the side by the back door. The whole car shook.

Jason tried to start the car again and the motor revved to life. Nick backed up, preparing to ram them again. Illumination from Nick's headlights filled the car, making it hard to see.

"He's trying to push us in the ditch." Isabel's voice filled with terror.

"Not if I can help it." Jason pressed the gas. The back wheels spun.

Nick's truck loomed toward them a second time. He rammed them hard enough that the car slid down the hillside and then tilted on its side. Metal creaked and groaned.

The driver's side of the car was closest to the ground. "Crawl out," Jason said as he unbuckled his seat belt.

He heard Isabel struggling in the darkness. "I can't get the door open. It's too heavy."

"Out the back, then." Nick was probably waiting for them. "Let me go first." He crawled through the car and pushed open the back hatch. His feet touched the snowy ground, and he reached a hand out for Isabel.

About fifteen feet above them, Nick's headlights glared down at them. He didn't see Nick anywhere.

Isabel wasn't dressed for running in the snow, but it was the only choice they had. If they could escape Nick's clutches, Jason could call for help. The other agents out looking for Isabel were in the area.

They took off running as gunshots exploded close to their feet.

Jason ran blindly, unable to make out what was in front of them. Isabel stumbled. He helped her to her feet. He heard footsteps behind them but saw no light.

They came to a cluster of evergreens. Jason and Isabel wove through them while Nick's footfalls seemed to surround them. If Jason could just get to a hiding place… Isabel's dress made swishing noises as they ran that could give them away.

He came to a spot where the trees were clustered close together and pulled her behind a tree with a thick trunk. Isabel's back was pressed against the tree and he stood facing her. Their breathing seemed augmented by the darkness and the silence.

Nick's footsteps drew near, slowed, stopped altogether.

Jason held his breath.

The footfalls were slower but very near. Nick seemed to be doing a circle around them, stopping every four or five steps.

As close as Jason was standing to Isabel, he could sense her body tensing.

Finally, the footfalls retreated and then faded in the distance. That didn't mean he wouldn't turn around and come back.

Jason pulled out his phone, praying he would get a signal. He stared at the screen. Nothing.

Isabel gripped his arm just above the elbow. "We can get back up the hill and take Nick's truck."

"Yes. Good." He took off running with Isabel right behind him. Had Nick doubled back or had he gone deeper into the trees? There was no way to know.

They scrambled up the hill. Her hand slipped into his as he pushed toward the top. Isabel had no gloves. Her hands were probably icicles by now. They ran past their overturned car.

Nick's headlights were no longer on. If Nick had taken the keys, Jason knew how to hot-wire a car, but it would cost them precious seconds.

Isabel hurried around to the passenger side of the truck. Jason reached for the handle of the driver's-side door. Cold metal pressed into his temple.

"I think someone here needs to die tonight." Nick's voice was menacing.

"No," Isabel shouted from the other side of the truck. She hurried around to face the two men. "You don't want to do that, Nick. You'll go back to prison."

"You should be with me, Isabel. You're my soul mate."

"You don't have to kill him." The silence surrounded them like a heavy blanket.

Nick pressed the gun barrel deeper into Jason's temple.

"Leave him out here in the cold. He'll freeze. Then you won't be charged with his death." Isabel took a step toward the two men.

"He deserves to die," Nick said.

"No, Nick. I'll go with you. You're right—we were meant to be together. But just leave him here. He won't make it back."

The pressure of the gun let up a little on Jason's skin.

"You'll go with me?"

"Yes."

What was she saying? This guy was a nutjob. How could she sacrifice her life like this? Or did she have something else in mind?

Nick pushed on Jason's back. "Get down the hill by your wrecked car. Don't try anything."

Jason took a step. Nick held the gun on him. Jason brushed by Isabel. In the darkness, she reached out, touching his fingers only briefly. Was that her way of saying she was going to be okay, she had a plan, or was it just a goodbye?

He turned, thinking he could grab her. They could run again.

She shook her head.

"Keep moving!" Nick shouted.

He had to fight for her. He wasn't about to give up so easily. He reached out for her arm, prepared to run.

"Jason, no."

A gunshot cracked the air around him. He felt a

stinging sensation on his upper arm. He'd been grazed by a bullet.

"The next one goes straight through your heart," Nick said.

"It will be okay, Jason. This is what I want. I want to be with Nick." Agitation colored every syllable she uttered.

His heart squeezed down to the size of a walnut as an invisible weight pressed on his chest. She was putting herself in so much danger…to save him, to help the investigation?

"Please," she said, her voice barely above a whisper.

Jason made his way down the hill and stood beside the overturned car.

"Now lie down on the ground on your stomach and don't move until we're gone."

Jason's hands curled into tight fists. He really hated this guy.

He lay down in the snow, a chill seeping through his layers of clothes. He squeezed his eyes shut, listening to truck doors slamming and an engine fading into the distance in the cold dark night.

What had he allowed to happen? He rose to his feet, vowing to rescue Isabel before it was too late.

Once again, Nick had forced Isabel to sit behind the wheel, pointing the gun at her.

"If we're going to be partners, don't you think you should quit pointing that thing at me?"

Nick leaned close and brushed a finger down her cheek. "You got to prove yourself to me. Show your loyalty, Blondie."

She steeled herself against his touch, not giving away how much he repulsed her.

For a moment, she listened to the sound of the car's tires rolling over packed snow. She stared out into the lonely dark night.

Nick would have killed Jason. She knew that much. Her life was only at risk if he figured out she was undercover or if his rage got out of control. She had to choose her moves carefully.

Jason had a cell phone. If he could get to a place where he had a signal, he'd be picked up. The other agents might even find him. She had to trust his survival skills. He'd be all right.

Somehow, she'd have to find a way to communicate with Jason. Nick had taken her phone. He'd hinted he knew who was behind the smuggling operation. This was the connection they needed to take this thing apart.

Saving Jason's life had been only part of the reason she'd made the choice she had. What she wanted even more than to help the investigation was to see to it that Nick Solomon went to prison for a long time.

Nick leaned so close to her she could feel his hot breath on her cheek.

"Show my loyalty? What do you want me to do, Nick?"

"There's a pickup tonight at a property Sun and Ski manages. The cabin on Old Fort Road."

"Yes, I know it." She took in a breath to steady her nerves as she stared out at the road ahead. "What time?"

"Midnight. We'll have time to go to your place so you can change into something that isn't so noisy."

Her neck muscles tensed. The ball had started at eight. Midnight had to be maybe an hour from now.

How was she going to get in touch with Jason before then? Nick would watch her like a hawk.

He leaned back in the seat and chuckled. "You play this right, and it could be the start of a great partnership." He kissed her cheek. "In so many ways."

"Yes, indeed."

He patted her hand. "You're looking forward to it, aren't you, Blondie?"

She cringed. She hated being called Blondie. "Of course I am, Nick. You and me, just like old times."

"You have an in with Sun and Ski, so no more having to fish out the entry codes."

At least now she knew her boss wasn't involved. "What do you mean fish out the entry codes?"

Any information she could garner would be helpful.

"What do you care?" Suspicion clouded his words, and she feared she'd overplayed her hand.

Nick kept the gun pointed at her as she came to the edge of town and made several turns to get to the Sun and Ski office.

As they approached the building, Nick sat up straighter. He looked from side to side, homing in on the dark cars parked on the street. He waved the gun in the air. "Go past. Keep driving."

The Bureau probably was watching the office and her home.

She checked the rearview mirror by raising her eyes but not moving her head. Just as she turned onto another street, headlights came on at the end of the street opposite the Sun and Ski office.

Nick instructed her where to turn until they came to a trailer park on the outskirts of town. They pulled up to one of the trailers where the lights were still on and a television glowed through the window. She'd been here before when she dated Nick.

"Go in and get a pair of black pants and a shirt from Aunt Phoebe's closet. Hurry." He lifted the gun slightly. "Don't try anything."

She met his gaze. "You know I wouldn't, Nick." Her voice had sounded a little too forceful. She remembered Aunt Phoebe from when she had dated Nick all those years ago. Chances were she was passed out on the couch with her two cats.

Isabel stepped inside the dimly lit trailer.

True to form, Aunt Phoebe snored away in an easy chair. There was only one cat resting on her lap, though.

Isabel saw no landline or cell anywhere in the living room. She hurried down the hallway to where the bedroom was. As she grabbed a black shirt and pants from a drawer, she glanced around, searching for a cell phone.

She spied it on the bureau beside Aunt Phoebe's bed. She slipped into the shirt and zipped up the pants. Phoebe was maybe a size bigger than Isabel. She'd stepped toward the bureau when Nick's voice pelted her back.

"You'll need a coat too." He held up a ratty-looking dark blue ski jacket, then stepped toward her and kissed her on the lips.

Everything in her wanted to push him away, but she planted her feet and let him kiss her as she went cold as a stone on the inside. She stepped back. "We better hurry, don't you think?"

Nick squeezed her upper arm. "Let's do this, baby."

He made her drive up to the cabin. She focused on the tiny bit of road illuminated by the headlights. Now was her opportunity to try to get as much information as she could.

"Why does the guy in charge pick these vacation homes for the drop-off and pickup? There has to be an easier way to do the smuggling."

Nick chuckled. "I think he likes the game of it. Breaking into rich people's fancy digs. He likes the idea of people coming into their homes and feeling like something is off but not being able to say why."

The guy behind this was a little twisted psychologically. She drove on in silence for a few more minutes. She had to choose her words carefully to not give herself away. She knew from experience that Nick could spin out of control if he felt betrayed. "He told you that?"

"Yeah. One night when we'd had too much to drink." Nick shook his head.

So Nick hadn't been bragging about being close to the top in this whole operation.

"I gotta hand it to you, Nick. I'm impressed. Word on the street is that millions in merchandise changes hands."

The flattery changed Nick's whole demeanor. He sat back in his seat, lowered the gun and tilted his head toward the ceiling. "I'm telling you, Isabel, this is the big time. I think I might be able to take over this whole operation."

Nick had always had an overblown view of his criminal skills.

She had a hundred other questions she wanted to ask him, but she needed to bide her time.

The road curved around several more times.

Nick sat up straight and peered out his window, suddenly alert.

Her heart squeezed tight. "What is it?"

She hadn't seen any headlights behind her since they'd left town. She couldn't assume Jason had made it to safety and been able to alert the agents, though she prayed that was the case.

Nick twisted from side to side, clearly nervous. Now she remembered how mercurial his moods could be. When she was with him as a teenager, it was like the ground was always shifting beneath her feet. "What's that helicopter doing out here?"

Was it possible the FBI had decided a helicopter was a better choice in tracking them on this remote road? "The resort does rides, remember?"

"Yeah, but at night?" He curled his hands into fists and pounded one against the other.

"Maybe. I don't know," she said.

Nick slammed the back of his head against the seat and stared at the ceiling.

"It's probably just a private citizen. Lots of people own helicopters around here." She struggled to keep her voice neutral. His volcanic personality affected her even now. "I think we should go forward with the plan. You don't want your boss upset with you, right?"

Tension invaded the car like a lead blanket.

Nick continued to stare at the ceiling. He let out a heavy breath. "Are you ordering me around, Is...a...bel?" He dragged out her name as his voice filled with accusation.

Sweat trickled down the back of her neck. To hide the fear in her voice, she enunciated each word with care. "I. Would. Never. Do. That."

The cabin came into view. The car rolled toward it as Isabel tried to calm her nerves with a deep breath.

Nick peered out the window again. "The chopper is off that way."

She stopped the car, turned off the ignition and waited for Nick to tell her what to do.

Unbuckling his seat belt, he turned to face her. He waited for a long moment before saying anything, probably because he knew the silence would make her even more afraid. "You sure ask a lot of questions, Isabel."

Whatever suspicion he'd had about the helicopter was now being transferred to her.

"I'm just curious about your life, Nick. We have a lot of catching up to do."

The answer seemed to satisfy him. "You know the code for this house?"

"Yes."

"You can get more codes, right?"

"Well, I—"

"It would really help me look good to the boss."

"Sure, Nick." She wasn't about to hurt Sun and Ski's reputation in that way, but for now, to keep Nick on an even keel, she would agree to anything he said.

"You'll be picking up five silver coins sitting in a dish on the entryway table. Don't turn on any lights. You know the layout of the place, right?"

"Yes."

He leaned toward her and kissed her on the cheek, then placed a leather pouch in her hand. "Put the coins in here." He let out a yelp. "This is the big time for you and me."

Her cheek felt slimy where he'd kissed it, but she didn't wipe it away. Nick Solomon was a bad man, and she would do whatever it took to see he went to jail.

"Okay, I'm ready to do this," she said. Her voice

didn't even sound like her own, all light and airy. Anything to not make Nick fly off the handle again.

"You do good tonight, and I'll let you do the meet-up with the buyer."

She pushed open the door, zipped up the old coat against the nighttime chill and hurried toward the house. Her heart pounded against her rib cage, and her fingers trembled as she touched the keypad and slipped into the dark house.

Maybe that helicopter had been the Bureau's. All she knew was that right now she was on her own. She'd be all right if she could keep Nick from erupting. He was paranoid. After this was all over, he'd probably stay close to her or demand that she check in with him every hour.

She felt around on the table until her fingers touched the bowl. She scooped up the coins and put them in the leather pouch Nick had given her. She'd unearthed some valuable information, and she prayed Jason had made it to safety so she could find a way to communicate with him.

TWELVE

Tension threaded through Jason's torso as he watched the glaring taillights of Nick Solomon's truck.

Through the use of a chopper, the Bureau had alerted him to their position. He'd slipped in to tail Nick's truck as soon as they were close to town. From the outside, it looked like Isabel had switched loyalties back to her old boyfriend. From the chatter on the radio, that was what the Bureau thought. He knew otherwise. Back on that remote road, Isabel had saved his life.

When she left him, it had taken him less than half an hour to get picked up by one of the agents. The Bureau had scrambled to put moving surveillance on Nick and Isabel.

Now it was his job to get to Isabel and have her explain herself to the agents in charge.

Nick's truck came to a stop outside the Sun and Ski office on the opposite side of the street.

Jason turned his own car up an alley and killed the lights. He slipped out onto the street.

Isabel and Nick got out of the car. She handed him something and he gave her a hug.

A twinge of doubt played at the corners of Jason's

mind. She sure hugged him like she cared about him.
Maybe Jason just didn't like the idea of her hugging
anyone. He was starting to have feelings for her.

Isabel crossed the street. Nick got back in the truck
but didn't drive away. So that was his game. He was
going to watch her all night.

Jason slipped around to the back of the building. The
offices were dark. Even if they didn't lock up during the
day, they must lock the place at night. The window of
Isabel's little apartment looked like the old-fashioned
kind that would swing open if it wasn't latched. He
climbed on top of a Dumpster that was just beneath the
window. He shimmied up a pipe and hooked his hands
onto the windowsill.

He hung there for a moment wondering if he'd made
a mistake. The rough texture of the brick wall provided
him with enough traction to push with his feet until his
hand touched the bottom of the window.

He pushed on the window. It didn't budge.

He heard footsteps in the alley.

Jason tried to pull himself up but felt his arms straining against his weight. He was going to fall on the hard
metal of the Dumpster, or worse—onto the concrete
below.

The footsteps grew louder. No one else would be up
at this hour. That had to be Nick doing some sort of patrol around the building.

He was about ready to let go and make a run for
it when the window swung open and hands wrapped
around his wrists. Isabel pulled him through the window. They sat on the floor in the dark.

"Stay low. He's out there."

"I know. I stayed on the couch so I could watch him

through the front window. I saw him leave his truck," she said.

The window above them was still open. Would that be a red flag to Nick?

He held his breath, tuning his ears to the sounds outside. The footsteps moved past and then faded.

Isabel's hand slipped over the top of his. "I'm glad you made it out. I was afraid I'd made the wrong decision."

Her hand felt warm and silky smooth on top of his.

He leaned close to her and whispered, "You saved my life. I'm pretty sure he would have killed me."

Warmth like a down comforter seemed to surround them as they sat very close together, their shoulders touching. It felt good to be this close to her, as if he'd known her all his life.

A long moment passed before Isabel spoke.

"I wasn't sure if it would work, but I thought I might find something out if I went with Nick."

"That was a risk. He's clearly unstable."

"I can handle him." Her voice wavered a little.

She'd been afraid, but she'd gone with Nick anyway. He admired her bravery. He turned to face her. "You've got some explaining to do to the agents in charge. They think you've gone rogue, but I never believed it for a minute."

Her face was very close to his, their noses almost touching. She reached up and brushed her finger over his cheek. Her touch sent a charge of electricity through him.

"Thank you for believing in me," she whispered.

Her voice reminded him of a mountain stream or a cool summer morning.

"What did you find out?"

"Nick knows who the kingpin is. He's in contact with him."

"That's huge."

"He's going to let me join in on the buyer pickup for the coins we took from the cabin."

"Isabel, there is risk involved with doing all this." The thought of her being in danger, of having to deal with the volatile Nick, made his chest tight.

"I know that. I'm willing to do it if Nick Solomon goes to jail for a long time."

He detected the resolve in her voice. Isabel had pushed the investigation further than anyone. Still, he didn't like her going into the line of fire again. "We need to talk to the Bureau. Tell them what you found out. See what they say."

"Nick will be watching me day and night. He's paranoid anyway, and I don't think he is totally convinced I'm on his side. I'm sure he'll come in and check on me first thing in the morning before I go to work. It was hard enough to convince him not to come into the apartment to guard me. Can I talk to them over the phone?"

"Michael will want to talk to you in person. They have this thing about reading body language and all that. I'll sneak you out tonight. You'll talk to Michael. We'll bring you back before first light so you can get some sleep."

"We can slip out the back. I have a rope ladder in case there is ever a fire." She burst to her feet and hurried down the hallway in the dark.

It would be a risk to even turn on lights.

Still crawling, Jason made his way into the living room. Light from the street shone in. Nick's car was now parked on this side of the street. He couldn't discern if Nick was in the car or not.

Isabel whispered from the corner of the living room. "I've got it."

He'd moved back toward the window when there was a knock on the door.

"Isabel, it's me. I need to see you." Nick's voice was filled with that nauseating whiny quality.

Isabel tossed the ladder toward Jason.

"Nick, I'm trying to get some sleep here." Her voice sounded groggy. "You'll see me in the morning just like I promised."

"Come on, Isabel. Just for a minute. Just give me a little hug. I need to see you, baby."

Jason scooted down the hallway and hung the ladder out the window, feeling his muscles knot up with tension. Why couldn't that creep leave her alone?

Come on, Isabel—don't open that door.

"Nick, I'm just really tired."

"Come on, baby. I'm out in that cold car." The intensity of his voice changed, becoming less pleading and darker. "Open the door, Isabel."

He heard the door handle rattling.

Jason craned his neck to see Isabel standing by the door. He wanted to run down the hallway, swing the door open and punch Nick in the face. The only thing that stopped him was that he knew it would put Isabel at risk in an even bigger way.

"Nick, I'm going back to bed. You should do the same." After placing a chair underneath the locked door, she stomped through the living room. "Good night." She opened and shut the bedroom door without going in.

Jason barely heard her footsteps as she scurried to join him in the hallway.

Nick continued to bang on the door and plead.

"We should go now before he gets back to his car," Isabel said.

"What if he breaks in and finds you're not here?" said Jason.

"That lock is pretty solid and I put the chair there."

The banging stopped and footfalls sounded on the stairs that led down to the street. Nick had given up.

Isabel burst to her feet, pushed the window open wider and swung her leg over the sill. Their plan was fraught with risk if Nick caught them. But the Bureau's coming here would be just as dangerous as long as Nick was watching and running patrols.

Heart pounding, Jason peered out the window. Isabel was halfway down. What if Nick decided to do another circle around the building?

Hearing her feet hit the concrete, he crawled out.

She shout-whispered up at him. "Make sure the window is closed."

After closing the window, he crawled down, struggled a little to disengage the ladder and then hid it in the Dumpster, so there would be no evidence of their escape. How they would get her back in unnoticed was a problem he'd solve later.

He led her around to the alley where he'd parked his car. Her hand found his in the darkness. He squeezed her fingers as warmth from her touch spread through him.

Here they were, inches from danger, slipping through the darkness, and the thought that was foremost in his mind was how much he liked being with her.

They got into the car. Jason started the engine but didn't turn on the lights. A truck blocked the alley up ahead. He'd have to back out onto the street where Nick was parked.

He clicked the lights on, reasoning that that would look less suspicious, then backed onto the street and rolled forward.

Isabel stayed low in the seat but craned her neck to watch Nick's truck. "He's not moving."

Jason phoned Michael, and they agreed to meet at an all-night coffee shop. He drove through the empty streets. Falling snow made the streetlights seem murky. They encountered only a little bit of traffic. A car slipped in behind them and followed them for several blocks but didn't pull into the coffee shop.

When they entered the coffee shop, there was a group of twentysomething people dressed in ski gear. Cars in the parking lot had been loaded down with snowboards and skis. They must have been gearing up for some early-morning skiing. The group of three women and four men joked and laughed as they drank their hot beverages.

A woman with a laptop in front of her was the only other patron besides Michael and the skiers. Michael's hair was disheveled and he had an overall droopy appearance despite the crisp white shirt and slacks he wore. A steaming mug sat on the table in front of him.

Jason and Isabel both ordered herbal tea. They took their warm mugs over to where Michael waited. Isabel scooted into the booth opposite Michael.

"Isabel has some important information." After squeezing her shoulder, Jason sat down in the booth beside her.

Isabel cleared her throat. "Nick Solomon knows the man behind all of this."

Michael sat up straighter. Light seemed to come into his eyes.

"He's invited me to go with him for the buyer pickup. I think he's testing my loyalty."

"I think it's too risky," Jason said.

Michael smiled at Isabel. "You've pushed this investigation over the top. We might be able to wrap things up." Michael couldn't hide the excitement in his voice.

Maybe the investigation had been the most important thing to Jason at one point, but now he just wanted Isabel to be safe and away from that nutjob Nick.

"There's something else," said Isabel. "Nick says that the reason the guy does the pickups in empty vacation homes is to stick it to rich people to make them feel uneasy in their own homes."

Michael nodded slowly. "That might be something our profiler could use." He looked directly at Isabel. "We could provide you with protection for the buyer pickup."

Jason opened his mouth to protest.

"I'll do it if you promise me Nick Solomon goes to jail when this investigation is all over."

"We can manage that," Michael said.

That was a promise they might not be able to keep. What if Nick ran off or slipped through their clutches in some other way? Michael was so fixated on catching the kingpin, he wasn't being realistic with Isabel.

"I'll do it, then, and keep up my cover until you catch the guy and charge Nick."

Jason leaned forward. "I want to be there as part of

the protection team." If he couldn't stop Isabel, at least he could see to it she was safe.

Michael nodded. "When is the buyer exchange?"

"Tomorrow night. Nick will let me know when and where, probably at the last minute."

"He's watching her pretty closely. I need to get her back to her place before first light," said Jason.

"Once Nick tells me the when and where of the buyer meet-up, I might not be able to let you know."

"Leave that to us. We'll stay close to you, Isabel. You might not see us, but know that we are watching," Michael said.

Isabel nodded. "I'm ready to do this."

Underneath the soft lights of the coffee shop, her skin appeared smooth as porcelain and her cheeks had a rosy glow. Maybe she was afraid, but the intensity of her features, the determination he saw in her eyes, did not give that fear away. What courage.

"We'll get a man to tail you within a few hours. And we'll have someone watching Nick." Michael looked at Jason. "You stay close until we can get that in place."

Jason nodded.

They said their goodbyes, and Jason and Isabel returned to his car. They drove across town, not seeing a single car.

"Are you sure you want to do this?"

"Yes. Don't try to talk me out of it," she said.

That was that. He drove on in silence. When they were a block away from Isabel's place, he saw that Nick's car was no longer parked on the street. He circled the block and drove up the alley to make sure Nick hadn't parked somewhere else.

"He must have given up and gone home for some sleep," Isabel said.

They couldn't get in through the door because of the chair Isabel had put in place. He helped her through the window by standing on the Dumpster and boosting her up.

When she'd pulled herself through the window, she turned around and looked down at him. "Thank you, Jason, for everything." The moonlight brought out the softness of her features. He felt a surge of deep affection for her that went beyond admiration for her bravery.

Several times he drove the car around the block to see if Nick had returned before settling in his car in the back parking lot. He slept in short spurts through the night. Toward morning, he stared up at the window where he'd last seen Isabel and prayed they weren't making a mistake letting her go through with this.

THIRTEEN

Isabel awoke feeling like her heart was in a vise. She squeezed her eyes shut, touched her palm to her beating heart and prayed that God would give her the strength and courage to face this day and what she had to do.

When she looked out her back window, Jason's car was not in the parking lot. Of course, he needed to go home and get some sleep. She stepped into the living room. A sense of dread filled her when she saw Nick's car parked out front again. She stared at it and took in a deep breath to clear her head. One of the other cars on the street must be the FBI guy.

Once she checked in with Mary and got her marching orders for the day, she stepped outside, where Nick waited for her.

He offered her a crooked grin with lots of teeth in it. "Thought I'd tag along while you did your work."

Nick drove her while she picked up groceries and flowers and got two houses ready. All day long, she sensed that they were being followed and watched. Though when she glanced around or checked her rear-view mirror, she could never spot the tail. She just had to trust what Michael had promised. Toward evening,

Nick suggested they have dinner together. He hadn't said anything about the buyer pickup all day.

The restaurant was one of the more expensive in town with soft lighting and a hushed atmosphere.

"Go ahead—order the most expensive thing on the menu," Nick said.

Her stomach was so tied in knots she doubted she could swallow a pea. "Think I'll just get a salad."

He gritted his teeth and narrowed his eyes at her. "I said order the most expensive thing on the menu."

She wasn't sure how much more of his controlling behavior she could take. She glanced around the restaurant, wondering which of the patrons was her protection. She noticed Larry, the man with the graying temples who had picked Jason and her up after they got away from the Wilson house.

A man two tables over lowered his menu. Jason winked at her and put the menu back up to cover his face. The exchange sent a spark of light through her.

She turned her attention back toward Nick. "Okay, I'll get something besides salad."

"Now, that's my Isabel. Thank you for dropping the bad attitude," Nick said. His phone rang. He checked the number and a shadow seemed to fall over his face. "I have to take this." He got up and stepped toward the men's restroom, speaking in low tones.

Jason dropped his menu again and made a face at Isabel.

She wanted to laugh out loud.

The waiter was approaching their table just as Nick burst into the dining room, clearly agitated. "Come on—we're going."

She looked at the waiter. Jason covered his face with the menu again. "But we haven't ordered yet."

Nick squeezed her arm so tight it hurt. "I said we're going."

She got up as Nick pulled her through the restaurant. Jason was no longer at the table where he'd been watching.

A light snow twirled out of the sky as Nick dragged her through the parking lot, yanked the door open and pushed her toward his truck.

"What's going on?" Her heart was beating a mile a minute.

"We're going to the buyer pickup." Nick glanced from side to side, surveying the parking lot. "Get in the truck."

She climbed in. Nick got behind the wheel and sped out of the parking lot. She didn't dare look around to see if her protection was there and give herself away. She had to trust that they would be. Seeing Jason, knowing that he was close, eased her fear.

The streets of Silver Strike were bustling with activity. The winter music festival had brought additional tourists and weekenders.

A light turned red before Nick could get through. He cursed at the traffic and slammed his hand on the steering wheel.

His agitation made her stomach churn. Maybe a buyer pickup made him nervous, but this felt over the top. His mood had changed after the phone call. Traffic remained heavy even once they got out on the highway.

She glanced up at the rearview mirror without moving her head. Several cars were behind them. She struggled to take a deep breath.

He took the exit that led to the venue for the music festival.

"Why here?"

The parking lot for the festival was filled with people.

"Public places are best." He adjusted his hands on the wheel and stared straight ahead.

Nick found a parking space after cursing out several other drivers. He was out of the truck and on Isabel's side of the truck just as she pushed the door open. He grabbed her sleeve and pulled her toward the venue, which was at the base of the ski hill. Inside, a band was just taking the stage. The venue had a large open floor with high-top tables around the edges and a bar and grill at the far end of the concert hall.

Nick manacled his hand around her wrist and pulled her through the thick crowd. How was he going to find a buyer among all these people? She glanced around at the concertgoers. For a moment, she thought she had spotted Jason, but then the face disappeared in the crowd.

The band struck up an intense blues number that pummeled her ears. People pressed on her from all sides as they squeezed through the bodies. Nick held her wrist so tight it hurt. She wanted to pull free and run.

But she needed to stick with the plan, play her part and meet this buyer. He got to a wall and led her up some stairs into a private box for viewing the concert. The room had several leather couches.

Nick closed the window, muffling the noise of the concert.

"This is where we're meeting the buyer?"

"Yeah." He shoved his hands in his pockets and didn't make eye contact. "You ask too many questions. Stop."

He paced the floor, stopping to stare out a window that looked out on the ski hill. He checked his phone.

She stared down at the clusters of people. Her heart leaped when she saw Jason. He was turning in a half circle, searching the crowd.

Look this way.

A moment later, he glanced up. She pressed her hand on the glass. Could he see her?

"Get away from there."

She stepped back. Jason was eaten up by the crowd again. There had to be agents out there too. Michael said there would be.

Again, Nick checked the window that offered a view to the outside. She walked over to where he was staring. The window looked out on the base of the ski hill. A car rolled into place in an area where there was no road or parking space. A man got out and walked toward the concert hall.

"Now we can go."

"What? I thought we were meeting the guy up here." Something felt really wrong. Why the constant changing of plans? Clearly, Nick had been waiting for the man with the car to show up.

"Don't argue with me, Isabel. This is how it works." He leaned close to her, his eyes like piercing daggers. "Are you all in or not?"

Sweat trickled down the back of her neck. She struggled to keep the tone of her voice even. "Course I am."

Something about the look in his eyes was darker and more threatening than she had ever seen before with him.

He led her back down the stairs and out to where

the car was parked. She hesitated in her step. "Where's the buyer?"

He yanked her along. "We'll meet him."

She planted her feet, unable to move, yet knowing that she needed to go through with this to win Nick's loyalty.

He turned to face her. "Having second thoughts?"

"This just seems a little crazy." Maybe he was testing her.

"Get in the car." He grinned at her and alarm bells went off in her head. The look on his face told her everything she needed to know.

Nick knew. He knew that she was undercover. Somehow he'd figured it out. He'd been upset after the phone call. Maybe that was it. She turned to run, but he grabbed her and tackled her.

He sat on her stomach, held her hands down and put his face very close to hers. "Do you think I'm dumb? Is that it, Isabel?"

She shook her head. "Please… I…" What could she say? How could she get out of this?

"I was going to let you in on this. It could have been like old times." He put his face so close to hers their noses almost touched. "Traitor. No one betrays Nick Solomon and lives to tell about it."

His words were a knife in her chest.

"You are dumb," he said. "I took you through that concert hall so we could lose your tail." He got off her. "Yeah, that's what the phone call was about. One of my guys spotted the tail on me."

She flipped over, intending to get to her feet and run. But he grabbed her by the back of her collar and swung her around. "Do you see how important I am?

I arranged for this car to be dropped off by the organization I work for. No one crosses me."

Her fear ramped up a notch. "I'm so sorry." The words fell flat. Nothing she could say at this point would stop the volcano from erupting.

"Get over to the car." His rage was out of control. He pulled out his gun.

"We're driving somewhere secluded. Now move."

Isabel stepped toward the car, knowing that it was just a matter of time before she was dead.

When he'd seen a car park off by itself and a man walk away from it, Jason had grown suspicious. He'd decided to circle the building after losing Isabel in the concert hall. Sure enough, the car was unlocked and the keys were in the ignition. Hiding in the back seat, he'd slipped inside to wait and observe. A moment later, Nick and Isabel came out of the back of the concert hall. He'd watched as Nick pulled a gun on Isabel. They'd struggled. Rage rose up in him, but he remained still. He couldn't hear their conversation. If he showed himself, their cover would be blown.

Isabel got into the driver's side of the car. Still pointing the gun at her, Nick slipped into the front passenger seat. Jason pressed even lower in the back seat.

"Nick, you don't want to do this." Isabel's voice vibrated with intense terror.

"Start the car."

She turned the key in the ignition and shifted into gear.

"To think that I pledged my undying love to you." Nick's voice filled with rage.

Jason tried to assess what was going on. Nick seemed

especially agitated. Were they still going to meet the buyer or had something changed?

She pressed the gas pedal and eased toward the road, driving slow. "This is rough going. It'll take a minute to get to the road."

"Quit making excuses, Isabel." Nick's voice dripped with sarcasm when he said Isabel's name. "You're going to die. No one betrays me."

So their cover was blown. Jason leaped up from behind the seat and reached to get the gun from Nick.

"Jump out."

While the car was still rolling, Isabel pushed the door open. She disappeared. He prayed she'd been able to roll clear of the tires.

Nick and Jason continued to struggle. The gun went off, and Nick held on to it.

The car hit something and shuddered to a stop. Both Jason and Nick were jolted by the crash. Jason pushed the door open and crawled out. He was still wobbly on his feet from the impact. Up ahead, he saw the dark figure of Isabel lying on the ground.

Nick stepped out and leaped on Jason. The two men wrestled. Nick must have dropped the gun when the car hit the curb.

Nick got on top of Jason and landed a blow to his face that sent stinging pain all through his skull. Jason's vision blurred. He struggled to get some leverage.

"Get off him." Isabel's voice sliced through the darkness as she wrapped her arm around Nick's neck and tried to pull him off.

Nick turned on her, trying to take her to the ground. Jason scrambled to his feet, grabbed Nick, spun him around and hit him once in the face and once in the stomach. Nick doubled over.

Jason grabbed Isabel's hand, but Nick blocked their way back to the concert hall. They'd have to double back to get to where people and help were. He'd lost his cell phone in the struggle with Nick.

They took off running. Nick sprinted back toward the car, probably to look for the gun.

They ran up the empty ski hill.

A gunshot sounded behind them, spurring them to run faster. Another gunshot, even closer. The ski hill was frozen and slick. Nick was gaining on them.

They neared the chairlift. Jason flipped the switch to turn it on. The lift eased to life as he and Isabel got on.

Jason looked over his shoulder. Nick had gotten on four or five chairs behind them. Far enough away that it would not be an easy shot to make with a pistol.

Jason wiggled in his chair, then lifted and dropped his legs like he was on a swing.

"What are you doing?"

"A moving target is harder to hit."

Several more shots were fired. One pinged off the metal of the chair.

"We're going to have to jump before we get to the exit platform." He stared down. The lift had elevated them a good thirty feet above the ground. He could wait until the distance was closer to ten or fifteen feet. The snow down at the base of the hill had been hard packed and icy. Maybe they could hope for some powder and a softer landing toward the top of the mountain.

"Now?" said Isabel.

She pointed at the landing platform up ahead.

Jason glanced over his shoulder. He could make out

the outline of Nick's body four seats behind them. "Let's do this."

He flipped around, slipped off the chair and hung on to it before letting go. He sailed through the air. His knees buckled from his collision with the ground, and he rolled a few feet. Isabel still hung from the chair. She let go and fell to the ground below. Hearing her moan as she landed, he prayed nothing had been broken.

The concert hall was just a set of distant glowing lights barely discernible through the trees clustered on the mountain. Nick had dropped from the lift, as well.

Jason sprinted over to Isabel and grabbed her hand to help her to her feet. "You all right?"

"Just a little shaky."

Nick was setting an intense pace as he ran toward them.

This was a remote black-diamond part of the ski hill.

Jason led Isabel toward the shelter of the trees. The canopy blocked much of the snowfall from gathering on the forest floor, allowing them to move faster and not leave many tracks.

They ran until they were both out of breath. The forest thinned, and they were out in the open again. A light winked on and off as if moving over hills, appearing and disappearing.

"Snowmobile," said Jason. "Maybe ski patrol."

"Or Nick called in reinforcements. He was able to arrange for that car to be dropped off." Isabel came up beside him.

She might be right. The snowmobile rounded another hill. He heard the hum of a motor as it drew closer. Maybe they should hide until they were sure the snowmobiler was one of the good guys.

He couldn't see Nick anywhere.

As Isabel pointed toward a sign that showed a map of the trails on the mountains, the headlight of the snowmobile pointed directly at them.

They hurried over to the sign and crouched behind it. The snowmobile worked its way up and down the mountain. Jason peered around the sign. It was too dark to see anything but the outline of the snowmobile and its rider.

The snowmobile was set to idle. A shadowy figure emerged from the tree on the other side of the black-diamond run. The figure walked toward the idling snowmobiler, shouted above the hum of the engine and then got on the back behind the driver. The voice had been loud enough so they could tell that it was Nick. He had called in reinforcements.

The snowmobile worked its way back up the mountain.

Now was their chance to run. Without a word, they both took off.

The snowmobiler stopped at the top of the trail run on a ledge. A moment later, a powerful searchlight illuminated sections of the mountain piece by piece.

Jason led Isabel toward an overhang of snow that was used for jumps. They hid underneath it, the shadows covering them as the searchlight swept past.

After the last time they were forced to brave the cold for survival, he'd prayed it wouldn't happen again. But here they were, Isabel pressed close to him, shivering. Though she was dressed for winter, they had been out in the elements for at least half an hour.

He wrapped an arm around her and whispered in her ear. "It won't be long now. They'll give up."

They'd be warmer if they could stay on the move.

The hum of the snowmobile still pressed on his ears. They couldn't run...not yet.

He drew Isabel even closer.

Ten minutes passed before the snowmobile noise faded.

"Let's get back over to the chairlift."

"What if they are waiting there for us?"

They could both get hypothermia by the time they made it down the mountain on foot.

The wind blew, chilling his skin. Isabel wrapped her arms around her body. He'd skied these hills all through high school. "There are warming huts around here. At least there used to be." That would give them time to come up with a plan.

He ran down the hill back toward the map. Isabel stood beside him as he leaned close to the map to see better. "There used to be a warming hut by the Crystal run. If memory serves."

"I'll take your word for it. I never skied."

He started walking in the general direction he thought the hut might be. "Really? I thought everyone in Silver Strike skied. I lived fifty miles up the road and made it almost every weekend."

She hurried to keep up with him as they cut across the ski run. "Mom said it was a rich person's sport." A note of sadness filled her voice.

There were all sorts of programs for kids who couldn't afford to ski to get help. His father had signed him up for everything he could. Isabel's mother just hadn't wanted to make the effort. "Maybe I'll have to take you sometime."

"Once it's okay for us to go back out in the open, right?"

Both of them had targets on their backs. Now that the

smugglers knew they were being watched, the whole investigation was tainted. "Maybe we should just focus on getting down the mountain."

"I appreciate the offer." He detected warmth in her voice.

They trudged ahead. He tuned in to his surroundings, listening for the sound of the snowmobile.

The warming hut was right where he remembered it. They slipped inside out of the wind. It had benches on three sides and a fire pit in the center that was usually lit on cold days when the ski hill was operating. They sat down on one of the benches.

"If we could just build a small fire." Isabel sounded like her teeth were chattering.

"We'd be spotted, Isabel."

He took his down coat off. She was wearing a wool dress coat. "Here, come closer. We can wrap up in this, use our body heat to get warm."

She slipped out of her wool coat, wrapped her arms around his waist and pressed close to him while he formed an insulating shell with the two coats.

"Better?"

She nodded. "I'm only doing this because I'm freezing."

"Oh, come on. You like me a little bit." He hoped she picked up on his joking tone.

"I like you more than a little bit."

"Really?" She had given a forthright response to his half-joking comment. He felt like he was glowing all over. Isabel liked him.

"It's just that after Nick, I decided maybe dating wasn't my thing. Something inside me died after him. I don't know how to explain it."

"Yeah, I watched my dad get burned real bad by my mom. He never dated after that." Watching his father in so much pain had made him conclude that maybe love was not all it was chalked up to be. The little bit he'd dated had only confirmed that. It seemed he attracted women who only knew how to take and to hurt.

He drew her closer until she stopped shivering. Even if there couldn't be anything between them and despite these trying circumstances, there was something really wonderful about holding Isabel.

"You warmed up?"

She nodded. "Maybe we should try to get to that chairlift. It would be faster."

Riskier too. Since Nick and his friend weren't chasing them down, they were probably watching the lift. "I don't know. Once that lift started to move, it would be like a red flag if they're anywhere close by."

"Jason, I know I was against it before, but I don't know if I can make it hiking down." She held up her hands covered by the leather gloves. "I can't feel my fingertips."

He weighed their options. It would take twice as long to walk down and that was if they weren't chased. They'd have to move from one cluster of trees to another, and even then they'd be out in the open some of the time.

"Let's get over to the lift. We can figure out if it's being watched." They both rose to their feet, facing each other. He reached out and squeezed her hands. "Try to keep your hands in your pockets."

She nodded. "I really messed up. Nick had his suspicions about me from the start. Otherwise, why would he have asked someone to figure out if he was being tailed?"

He pulled his glove off and touched her cold cheek. "Don't blame yourself. The Bureau could have been more careful about their tails."

"The investigation is going to fall apart because of me." Her voice faltered. "And Nick won't go to prison."

He gathered her into his arms, holding her close. "We don't know what is going to happen."

The best-case scenario was that the FBI would have to lie low with the investigation and hope the smuggling would resume once the thieves thought the heat was off. They'd been so close too, one person away from identifying the mastermind behind the whole thing.

He drew Isabel even closer. All he could think about right now was comforting Isabel and giving her some hope.

He spoke into her ear. "We'll get off this mountain and we'll get it figured out."

"We. I like the sound of that." She stepped back, swiped at her eyes and tilted her head. "Thank you, Jason."

"No problem." He pressed his hand against her cheek, wishing they could stay in the warmth of this moment forever…but that wasn't possible.

The wind gusted and swirled around them when they stepped outside. They ran in the general direction of the chairlift, using the trees for cover and shelter whenever possible.

The silhouette of the chairlift came into view. They crouched low by the trees. A moment later, the lights of the snowmobile appeared at the top of the hill and traveled in a circle. The motor hummed as it whizzed past them. They pressed back even deeper into the trees.

Once the snowmobile was some distance from them and headed back up on the other side of the lift, Isabel spoke up. "I guess that's it, then. We go on foot." He detected the fear in her voice.

"Let's do this."

They sprinted around the trees and wove through the forest until there were no more trees to hide them. Jason glanced up the hill where he could see the headlights of the snowmobile. He and Isabel were some distance from the top of the run, but it would be just a matter of minutes before they'd be spotted. They were dark figures on a field of white—easy targets.

He prayed they had enough distance between them to get to the next cluster of trees before they were caught and killed.

FOURTEEN

Isabel's heart pounded. She willed her feet to pump faster. The buzz of the snowmobile grew louder as her boots pressed down the crunchy snow. They came to a steep part of the run.

Jason plopped onto his behind. She stared down at the incline below, which dropped off at a steep angle. It would be easier to slide than walk. She sat down beside him and pushed off with her hands.

The snowmobile would have to loop around the steep terrain. Still, the sound of its engine seemed to surround them, persistent in its pursuit.

They slid, gaining speed. She held her hands out to slow down. The searchlight swept over them as the incline leveled off. They burst to their feet and ran until they came to another steep drop-off. She slid, trying to brake with her hands. As she felt herself propelled head-first, she tucked, falling forward into a half somersault. She stopped, landing on her behind but disoriented.

Jason appeared beside her. He grabbed her arm to help her to her feet and pointed up the hill. "He's doing this the hard way."

The snowmobile, with only one rider on it, was about

to make the first jump. The rider revved the motor and sailed through the air.

Both of them sprinted, half sliding and half running on the treacherous terrain. The noise of the snowmobile told her he was making the jumps and getting closer. The machine sounded like a groaning angry monster.

Then the noise stopped.

As they ran, Isabel glanced over her shoulder. The snowmobile was on its side. The rider had gotten to his feet and was lifting off his helmet, probably preparing to pursue them on foot.

Isabel dug her heels in to keep from sliding. Jason sprinted six or so feet ahead of her. She watched the back of his head in the moonlight. The reflective material on his jacket made him look like a bouncing set of stripes moving down the mountain.

The rhythm of her own rapid footsteps surrounded her. She filled her lungs with air and pumped her legs even faster, drawing close to the tree line. Her feet slid out from underneath her and she fell.

A set of hands yanked at her from the side. Before she could scream, a hand went over her mouth and she was dragged sideways. She watched the stripes of Jason's jacket disappear over a hill as Nick swung her around. He dragged her toward a cluster of evergreens. His hand slipped from her mouth.

She called Jason's name, her voice barely above a whisper and filled with desperation.

"Oh sure, call for your boyfriend." Nick loomed toward her, pulling off his gloves.

"I lost my gun somewhere." He flexed his hands. "Guess I have to do this the old-fashioned way." His words dripped with menace and an intense rage she had never seen from him before.

The blood froze in her veins.

In the distance, the sputter of a coughing engine reached her ears. The snowmobiler must have decided to try to get the machine unstuck.

She crab-walked backward to get away from Nick, knowing that nothing she could say would change his mind. He meant to kill her.

She flipped over and scrambled on all fours. Nick pounced on her, grabbing her by her collar and jerking her to her feet.

He pressed his lips close to her face, his breath like lava on her ear. "Get up. Let's get deeper into the trees so lover boy can't find us."

She tried to twist free of his grasp, which only seemed to feed his rage. Once they were hidden by trees, he swung her around and clamped his hands on her neck. As she twisted her body and struggled for breath, she kicked him in the shin. He groaned but squeezed tighter around her neck.

Her eyes watered and white dots surrounded her field of vision. She drew her hands up to his, clawing his fingers and trying to break free. She pried his fingers off enough to speak each word delivered between gasping breaths. "You. Don't. Want. To. Go. To. Prison."

His grip loosened. "What?"

Her throat felt like it had been scraped with a utility knife. "Make it look like an accident. Like I fell off one of those steep jumps." The move would buy her time and a chance at escape.

His fingers still pressed against her windpipe. "You

think I'm that dumb. You're just trying to find a way to escape."

He pressed harder. She screamed, but it seemed to fade before it was out of her mouth. By now Jason would have glanced over his shoulder and come looking for her. But he'd have no way of knowing where they'd slipped into the trees.

She managed to pull his fingers away from her throat for just a moment.

"Please, Nick. Don't do this."

"Beg all you want." His hands gripped her neck even tighter, shutting off all the air.

She scratched at his fingers and tried to turn her body to break free. Her vision became a single dot of light as all the breath left her lungs. Her knees buckled. Nick pushed her so she fell on her back. She took in one sharp breath before his hands were on her neck again.

Darkness surrounded her. Her last thought was that the snow felt cold on the back of her head.

As he sprinted back up the hill, Jason mentally kicked himself. It had only been a matter of a minute that he'd run without checking over his shoulder for Isabel. Nick must have been stalking them as they moved down the hill. Jason rounded the hill. The snowmobiler had righted his machine and was revving the motor, preparing for takeoff.

Jason darted into trees to avoid being spotted. He ran. Did he dare call Isabel's name? He zigzagged around trees, pushing past the rising panic. The snowmobiler whizzed by along the tree line, his engine sputtering and humming. The headlights reached some feet into the forest. Jason ran deeper into the trees, seeing nothing. He was out of options. He'd do anything to find her.

"Isabel." He spoke her name rather than shouted it.

To the side, a rustling of tree branches caught his attention. He darted in the direction the noises had come from. Weight landed on him. He fell on his back. A fist landed a hard blow to his head while something pressed on his chest.

"She's gone, lover boy. If I can't have her, nobody can."

The thought of anything bad happening to Isabel ignited a fire inside Jason. He slammed Nick's back with his knee. The blow was enough to surprise Nick and knock him off balance. Jason landed another blow to Nick's stomach. Nick groaned and doubled over. Jason pushed him off, jumped to his feet and kicked Nick in the head just before Nick tried to pull Jason's feet out from under him. Jason hit Nick with leg jabs, one to his side and one to his head. Nick fell over and remained motionless. When Jason checked for a pulse, Nick was still alive but unconscious. Though Nick would probably only be out for a few minutes, Jason had no time or rope to restrain Nick with. His priority was finding Isabel.

Some strange energy flowed through Jason. He refused to believe Isabel was dead. Nick must have been bluffing to weaken Jason's resolve. He ran in the direction Nick had come from, pushing tree branches out of the way. His heart beat intensely as he searched the ground made darker by the tree canopy.

He said her name not once but three times.

The snowmobile continued to patrol the perimeter of the cluster of trees. Light flashed through the trees and Jason spotted something of a light color, maybe yellow, lying on the ground. It was the knit scarf Isabel had worn with her wool dress coat.

She could have lost it in a struggle. He picked it up, held it close, picking up the scent of her floral perfume. Racing deeper into the trees, he spotted her dark form in a clearing. The porcelain skin of her face the only discernible part of her.

He dived to the ground and touched her cold cheek. Fear flooded through him at the thought of losing her. He cared deeply for her.

"Isabel."

His finger trailed down to her neck, where he felt a pulse. She was alive.

He patted her cheeks.

"I'm here." Her voice was scratchy, hoarse-sounding.

"Hey." He cradled her head.

"I must have passed out."

Nick probably heard Jason calling her name and decided to get rid of Jason before he had the chance to check to see if Isabel was still breathing.

"We don't have much time. Can you stand?"

"I think so."

He held out a hand for her and helped her up. He handed her the scarf, which she wrapped around her neck. The snowmobiler was still patrolling the tree line and Nick would be hounding them in minutes. They had no choice but to head down the mountain.

"Jason, I'm really cold." Her voice was weak. It was clear from the inflection of her words that she was giving up.

Lying on the frozen ground for at least five minutes had only brought her that much closer to hypothermia.

"We're halfway down the mountain already. If you

stay with me there is a hot bath and a steaming cup of tea waiting for you at the end." He pressed his hands on either side of her cheeks. "Can you do that for me, Isabel?"

"I'm sorry I messed up the investigation. But I can't keep running like this." Her voice cracked.

He gathered her into his arms. "I know. They'll put you in protective custody. Don't give up."

Protective custody for her seemed like the only option now. Whoever was behind all this was clearly powerful, connected and relentless.

Jason held Isabel close. Her hat felt soft against his chin.

"Let's go." Her words seemed to be undergirded with new strength. "We don't have much time."

"That's my strong lady." He kissed her on the forehead. Their eyes met momentarily. He touched her lips with his gloved hand, feeling a magnetic pull toward her as an intense warmth washed through him. He wanted to kiss her on the mouth.

He pulled back. "This time I won't lose you," he said. "Not even for a second."

As they ran through the trees, he could hear the snowmobile growing closer and then farther away as it searched for them. They moved out into the open, sliding down the steep parts of the hill.

A lamp outside the dark ski lodge came into view, a tiny light in the distance. He breathed a sigh of relief when he saw the first sign of civilization. Glancing over his shoulder at where they had emerged from the forest, he could discern moving shadows among the trees. It could be Nick.

They made their way toward the ski lodge. There

would be a phone there. He quickened his pace, making sure that Isabel stayed with him.

They neared the lodge. When he'd skied here, he and his buddies had found a window with a loose latch. Maybe it hadn't been repaired even after all these years. He glanced up the hill at the sound of a motor. The snowmobile was headed their way, close enough that the men could see he and Isabel standing outside the lodge. He led Isabel around to the far side of the lodge.

The window latch was still loose. They crawled into what was the boys' locker room.

"There's probably a phone in the office," he said, taking her hand and leading her upstairs.

The door to the ski-lodge office was locked. His hope deflated. They had only minutes before the snowmobiler would be outside.

"Now what?" Her words were saturated with fear.

His mind raced. "Lost and found. People might leave cell phones."

He located the lost-and-found bins by the cafeteria just where they had been ten years ago when he'd skied here as a teen. There were bins filled with hats, orphan gloves, scarves and ski goggles and one bin filled with electronics. The first cell phone he tried was dead.

"Here, this one still has some battery left." Isabel handed it to him.

The bright lights of the snowmobile shone through the window. Both of them ducked down as he pressed in the numbers for his contact.

While he dialed, Isabel scurried across the floor and peered through the window. The main door shook. It would take Nick and his accomplice a few minutes to break in.

"Two of them got off the snowmobile and are at the door." Isabel's voice was flat, devoid of emotion. "We have to hide."

Jason held the phone to his ear. One ring. Two rings. *Come on, Michael—pick up.* The agents had to be out looking for them and waiting for a call.

Glass shattered. The men were breaking in.

Jason hurried to the far end of the cafeteria back into the boys' locker room with the phone still pressed against his ear.

Finally, Michael picked up. "Yes, who is this?"

"Help us."

"Jason, where are you?"

"We're at the ski lodge and on the run."

"I'll get a man to you as soon as I can."

"We'll be headed toward the concert venue." He doubted the concert was still going on, but maybe there would be a cleanup crew or someone still around.

The footsteps of Nick and his accomplice seemed to echo through the empty building, growing ever closer. He set the phone down. Isabel was already crawling through the window when Nick appeared in the doorway.

She glanced at Nick and then at Jason.

"Go," said Jason. "I'll catch up with you."

Nick dived for Jason. Jason hit him hard twice against the jaw. The blow caused Nick to take a step back.

Jason jumped up to the open window. Nick charged toward him again, and Jason flipped around, kicking him hard enough to make him stumble backward and fall.

The move gave Jason enough time to get out of the window. He sprinted downhill, praying that Isabel had not been captured by Nick's accomplice.

FIFTEEN

Isabel ran in the direction she thought the concert venue might be. Much of the forest in Silver Strike had been preserved, even in town, so she darted from one clump of trees to the next looking for the building. She found a snow-packed road that led downward. Sooner or later she'd run into something, but being on the road made her too easy a target. She couldn't stay on it for long.

She wondered too if Jason had made it out. Her heart ached to know that he was safe. She should have stayed behind to help him. That was what he would have done for her.

The hum of a snowmobile engine told her she needed to get off the road. She veered back into the trees. The snowmobile putted past her, clearly searching. She tore off the yellow scarf and threw it on the ground, knowing that it would make her more visible through the trees. Why hadn't she thought of that ages ago? She darted from one tree to the next, taking the time to catch her breath and peer around the trunk of a tree. As the snowmobile eased by her, she saw only one rider.

A hand squeezed her shoulder and she nearly jumped out of her skin. She swung around, ready to fight. Jason stood only inches from her. He placed a finger up to his lips, indicating to be quiet. The snowmobile faded in the distance. She looked up into Jason's eyes, blue even in the shadows of nighttime. The memory of him kissing her forehead and then touching her lips rose to the surface. His eyes had grown wide as he leaned close. She had thought he would kiss her. In that moment, she realized she wanted to feel his lips on hers. He brought to life feelings that she had long thought were dead.

He tilted his head and raised his eyebrows up toward the lodge. A gesture that indicated Nick was in the forest searching for them.

As the noise of the snowmobile died out altogether, she heard faint sounds, the crackle of a branch, a padding noise that could be footfalls on snow.

Jason wrapped his arm around her waist and eased her around to the other side of the tree. His lips brushed her forehead as they faced each other. The rhythm of his breathing surrounded her. Nick's footsteps became more distinct and louder.

The seconds ticked by. The sounds stopped as though Nick were looking around.

Her breath caught in her throat.

Judging from the volume of the footsteps, Nick was maybe ten feet away from them.

She tilted her head and looked into Jason's eyes, drawing strength from his proximity and the calm of his expression.

The footsteps resumed, this time making almost a squeaking sound on crunchy dry snow.

It seemed to take forever for the footsteps to get far away. Finally, the quiet of the night forest fell around them like a soft blanket.

Jason and Isabel stood very close together. Moonlight sneaked through the trees and washed over them. He bent his head and brushed his cheek over hers. Fire ignited, covering her skin and traveling through her muscles as his lips found hers. He brushed lightly over her mouth and then deepened the kiss as his hand touched her cheek.

She remained suspended in the moment, relishing a sensation like warm honey being poured over her head and dripping down her skin. He held her close for a second longer before whispering in her ear. "We're almost home free, Isabel."

The kiss had made her dizzy, light-headed. "Yes, I suppose we should make a run for it."

He kissed her one more time, took her hand and led her through the thick of the trees until they were able to run. There were no lights on at the concert venue, but the silhouette of the huge building was plain enough. There were only two snow-covered cars in the parking lot as they approached. Snowmobile tracks indicated the other pursuer had circled the building at least twice.

She looked over her shoulder. Nick emerged from the trees, running straight for them. The snowmobile came around the side of the building.

Jason pivoted and she followed. An SUV turned off the road into the lot. Michael's car.

The snowmobile made a beeline for them, the clanging of the motor pressing on her ears as she sprinted toward Michael's car. Jason got there first, swinging open the back door. She piled in and Jason got in behind her.

Michael revved the motor and sped forward, swerving and fishtailing through the icy lot. The snowmobile blocked their exit. Michael hit the accelerator and drove over a snow-covered lawn back up to the road.

The snowmobile followed them until they turned onto a plowed road. Nick stood at the edge of the parking lot. The stiffness of his posture suggested rage.

"Good timing, Michael," said Jason.

"We aim to please," said Michael. "We've got a temporary safe house set up for you. You'll both need to be debriefed, but I imagine you'd like to get a good night's sleep first."

"I'm looking forward to a hot bath and a steaming cup of tea." She smiled at Jason. The softness in his expression, that look of affection in his eyes, made her heart skip a beat.

"As promised." He placed his gloved hand over hers and squeezed.

She pressed her shoulder against his, still caught up in the exhilaration of their kiss.

Jason leaned forward to talk to Michael. "So is the investigation blown?"

"We'll have to lie low for a while until they think we've backed off. Once things cool down, we've got quite a few people to keep an eye on, especially Nick Solomon, thanks to Isabel."

She was glad Michael saw it that way.

Michael said, "The profiler thinks the kingpin is working class or came from humble roots because of what Isabel told us about getting a thrill out of making the wealthy uncomfortable in their own homes."

They drove on in silence. Jason put an arm around Isabel and she rested her head against his chest, listening to his heart beat. The heaviness of fatigue invaded her body and she closed her eyes.

She was safe…for now.

Nick was still out there. Still set on her demise.

Jason rolled over on the bed as sunlight streamed through the blinds of the safe house. He'd had only a few hours' sleep before morning came. He intended to get a few more. The safe house was a three-story affair in a subdivision outside of town that had gone belly-up. They'd driven past half-finished homes, some just framed, others nearly complete. The outside walls of the house they were in were done, but he could look across the floor to where Isabel slept on a mattress inside a room that had only two-by-fours for walls. In order for this to be a functional safe house, the Bureau had gotten the plumbing in the bathroom and kitchen done. Electrical wires were exposed in the kitchen where the drywall had not been put up before the stove and refrigerator were put in place.

Isabel had had to settle for a hot shower instead of a bath, but he had been able to give her a steaming cup of tea.

Only one agent, playing solitaire at the kitchen table, watched over them, his gun belt slung over a chair.

Jason tossed and turned several times before he realized it was an act of futility to try to sleep. He sat up on his bed.

Isabel looked peaceful covered in a soft pink blanket drawn up over her shoulders. Her cheeks had a rosy glow. The kiss they'd shared had been wonderful, but it had probably been brought on by the terror they were in the midst of at the time. He doubted the attraction would survive once this was all over, if it was ever over. He intended to return to his work as a PI even if the Bureau didn't need him anymore. He could take care of himself. But Isabel might need to go into witness protection as long as Nick Solomon was at large. She'd have to move and change her name, cut all her connections. No, as much as he cared for her, he couldn't see a future with her where she would be safe unless they caught Nick.

Jason rose to his feet and ambled into the kitchen. He was still dressed in his clothes from the night before. The agent gave him a nod. He swung the refrigerator door open. It was fully stocked.

"I'm going to get some air," said the agent. He rose to his feet, shrugged into his ski jacket and stepped out the back door.

The subdivision was miles from town, surrounded by forest. Jason didn't relish the confinement. Hopefully, he'd be back to work in a day or so. First, he needed to make sure the Bureau took care of Isabel.

Jason broke some eggs into a bowl and stirred them with a fork. The bacon sizzled when he placed it on the griddle. He melted butter in a frying pan and poured the egg mixture in.

The aroma of bacon filled the air.

"One of my favorite smells in the world." In her room, Isabel sat up on her mattress. She gathered the blanket around her and strode into the kitchen.

"I made enough for two. I don't think the agent is hungry. Saw some orange juice in the fridge if you want to pour some."

She retrieved some glasses and the juice and then settled on one of the stools at the island where Jason was cooking. Bruises on her neck from where Nick had tried to strangle her were still visible. The thought of that man touching her enraged him. He served up their food and pushed the plate toward her.

Isabel made sounds of approval as she ate. She looked up at him with her doe eyes, and he was struck by how beautiful she was. Affection glowed on her face. "My compliments to the chef."

He could pretend this was some sort of scene of domestic bliss, even imagine that they might have something like this waiting in their future. But he had to be realistic. They both did.

"How long are they going to make us stay in this house? I want to get back to work and I need to call my boss."

"Isabel, I don't know if you can just go back to that."

Her forehead creased. "I want my life back, Jason."

"Whoever is behind this has a lot of power and isn't opposed to violent solutions," Jason said. "You've seen that for yourself."

Her mouth formed a flat line as she pressed her lips together. "But this will end soon, won't it?"

"Not while Nick is still out there. Be realistic. You might need to think about witness protection."

"I'm not giving up the life I've built here." She stared at the ceiling for a moment. "Can't you stay with me until they catch him?"

"I don't know," Jason said. "I think you need more protection than I can provide." Guilt washed through him. If he had been paying attention, Nick wouldn't have been able to strangle Isabel.

Her eyes became glassy with tears. "What are you saying?"

"I'm saying I don't want you to die. I'm saying the

best thing is for you to move to another town with a new name."

She shook her head. "I thought… I don't know. That something was happening between us."

He took her empty plate. More than anything, he wanted to hold her. To tell her everything would be okay and that they could be together, but that might get her killed. He made his voice sound cold and distant on purpose. "I'm only thinking of your safety."

"My safety?" A single tear rolled down her cheek. "I need to go brush my teeth." She jumped off the stool and disappeared around the corner. The bathroom at least was Sheetrocked and had a door.

Jason put the plates in the sink and stared out the window. There were boot tracks outside, but he didn't see the agent anywhere.

He could hear Isabel running the water in the bathroom.

Feeling uneasy, he put on his boots and slipped into his coat. He stepped outside onto the threshold, visually following the tracks that went some distance from the house. He took a few more steps away from the house. The footprints ended and were replaced by drag marks leading to another half-finished house.

Heart racing, he turned and sprinted back into the house. The agent could take care of himself. It was Isabel he was worried about.

Isabel splashed water on her face and stared at herself in the bathroom mirror. She pulled a strand of blond hair behind her ear. So that was it. She'd opened her heart to Jason, let herself feel something for him and he was pushing her away.

Of course, it wasn't realistic that they go into witness protection together. They'd known each other less than a week, but he acted like he didn't want to be with her at all. He'd kept her safe so far. Maybe he was just looking for an excuse to push her away. He could be scared of his feelings for her or he might have just been caught up in the moment when he kissed her. It didn't matter. The point was she wasn't going to open herself up to this kind of stinging pain. Not ever again.

She reached for a towel. The back door opened. Jason must have been coming back inside. She'd heard him step out earlier.

She patted her face dry, covering her eyes. Footsteps echoed down the hallway.

She wasn't about to call out to Jason. The last thing she wanted to do was talk to him.

She replaced the towel on the bar, then realized she hadn't heard the back door close. The bathroom door swung open. Before she could turn, a gun pressed into the middle of her back.

"Thought you'd get away from me, huh? You scream, I'll shoot." Nick wrapped his arm around her waist and pointed the gun at her head. "Lover boy is distracted right now. Don't expect him to come rescue you."

He pulled her through the door. Nick had her in such a tight hold, she couldn't move.

He half lifted, half dragged her through the snow into one of the other incomplete houses. He pushed her onto the plywood floor and pulled a bandanna out of his pocket. Diving to the floor, he grabbed hold of her hair. "Hold still."

Her head stung where he'd yanked on her ponytail.

In the distance, she heard Jason call her name. He sounded so very far away.

Nick must have heard the cry, as well. Panic filled his words. He pointed the gun at her. "Cry out and you're dead." The tone of his voice told her he wasn't lying. "Give me your hands."

She flipped over and tried to crawl away, knowing he would overpower her, but at least it bought her some time.

Jason and the agent would most likely go through the front door of the safe house and search there first. In the minutes it took them to find the tracks and drag marks at the back of the house, Nick would be able to escape with her if he had a vehicle nearby.

Nick pounced on her again, flipping her around and tying the bandanna around her wrists. He pulled her to her feet and pushed her through the empty house, their footsteps echoing on the plywood subfloor. He pushed her out the back of the house.

She heard the sound of a diesel truck before she saw it. Nick had left it running for a quick escape. He led her around to the side of the house and shoved her in the driver's seat. "Scoot over." And then he jumped behind the wheel.

The truck eased through the deep snow.

Isabel lifted her head to look out the back window. The truck bed was covered with a tarp.

"Stay down," Nick barked.

She reached for the door handle, seeking to escape before the truck was going too fast. Though her hands were bound, she was able to wrap fingers around the door handle. Nick grabbed the collar of her robe and pulled her back.

"Don't even." He pulled a gun from his waist and pointed it at her. "Just in case you want to try that again." Nick pressed the accelerator, trying to go faster, which only made the wheels of the truck spin. He cursed.

The truck gained some traction and he sped toward the road.

The Bureau had taken great pains to make sure they weren't followed to the safe house. "How did you find me?"

"You pay someone enough money and they will tell you anything."

So one of the agents had turned on them. The investigation was even more tainted.

"Everyone has a price, Blondie." Nick sped up a winding country road. "Once we figured out the Feds were following us, it just took a little research to figure out who would turn because of debt and a gambling problem."

"Which agent?"

Nick shook his head. "I'm not telling you." He grinned. "After I deal with you, it won't take much to get rid of lover boy too."

Ice replaced the blood in her veins. Nick was going to kill Jason, as well, and she had no way to warn him that one of the agents was dirty. "Where are you taking me?"

"Someplace where they won't find you until spring, if ever. And it will look like an accident. Just like you suggested on the ski hill." Nick stared at the road ahead as a sinister smile spread across his face. "Got to hand it to you, Blondie—you have some good ideas. We could have been such a great team. Living large." He turned to look at her as the road straightened out and his eyes were as cold as stone. "Now you won't live at all."

Terror crushed her lungs, making it hard to take in even a shallow breath.

SIXTEEN

Jason wrapped his arms around himself and drew his knees up to his chest. Even with his ski jacket on, it was chilly underneath the tarp of Nick's truck, where he'd hidden.

The truck had been rolling away as he'd jumped in the back, too fast for him to get to the cab and pull Isabel free. If the passenger-side door was locked, he would have lost his chance altogether. Nick had been distracted by Isabel trying to escape when Jason climbed in the back.

The bed of the truck vibrated as it rumbled up a hill and slipped into a curve. Once Nick stopped, Jason would have a chance to get to Isabel. It had been at least twenty minutes and Nick hadn't even slowed down.

Jason eased toward the side of the truck and peeked out at the winter landscape. Nick must be taking Isabel deep into the hills far from witnesses. He checked his pocket. Though he'd been issued another phone, he'd left it on the kitchen counter of the safe house.

He rolled back to the middle of the truck bed. His hand wrapped around a tire iron. That might come in handy.

He focused on the rhythm of the wheels turning for what must have been another twenty minutes.

Finally, the truck lurched to a stop. He heard the driver's-side door open and slam shut. Then the passenger door eased open. He waited for at least three minutes before lifting the tarp and peering above the rim of the truck bed.

He didn't see Nick or Isabel, but their tracks were easy enough to follow. They'd gone toward a cluster of trees. He grabbed the tire iron and jumped to the ground, pressing close to the truck to avoid being seen if they came back out.

He ran toward the forest, then dashed from tree to tree. Nick shouted something at Isabel, disturbing the quiet forest. Fearing for her life, Jason sprinted through the evergreens. An old log cabin leaning to one side stood in a clearing. Nick stomped past a glassless window. Jason lifted his head but couldn't see Isabel anywhere.

Jason edged closer as fear was embedded in every muscle of his body. What if he was too late? He dashed toward another tree and then crouched as he approached the house. At least he hadn't heard a gunshot.

Nick's voice rose above the sound of scuffling. "If they ever find you, it will look like you froze to death. My hands will be clean. We are miles from everything. No one comes up this road this time of year."

Jason raised his head above the rim of the window. Isabel lay on the floor with Nick kneeling beside her, removing the bandanna that bound her hands.

Isabel was still in pajamas and a robe. Her feet must be icicles by now in the slippers she wore.

His tire iron was no match for the gun he saw in

Nick's waistband. Because he'd just gotten up less than an hour ago, he hadn't had time to grab his own gun.

If he could surprise Nick, Jason might be able to overtake him. Nick stepped through the door on the opposite wall from where Jason was hidden.

Isabel rose to her feet.

Jason made a hissing noise to try to get her attention. She saw him just as Nick, standing in the doorway, turned in the direction of the sound. Jason ducked down behind the cabin wall.

"Did you say something, Isabel?" Nick's voice dripped with suspicion.

"Sorry I made that noise. I just wish you'd reconsider what you're doing here," Isabel said.

Nick stomped back into the doorway. "No one betrays me and gets away with it. You stay in this cabin while I drive away." He lifted the gun and pointed it at her. "Don't try to follow me."

Jason pressed against the cabin wall, waiting for the sound of Nick's retreating footsteps. A long heavy silence followed. Nick halted.

"You win," said Isabel.

The answer must have satisfied Nick because he stomped away. Jason hurried around the side of the cabin. Nick was still in view with his back to the cabin. Isabel's footsteps pounded inside the cabin.

Nick spun around. Jason shrank back along the side wall, hoping he hadn't been spotted.

"I said stay in there. Go sit in a corner," Nick said. His voice filled with rage.

Nick must be able to see Isabel through the glass-less windows.

Isabel's light footfall padded on the wood floor of the cabin.

Jason pressed against the wall, unable to gauge where Nick was at. The guy had almost a sixth sense for when he was under threat. Jason needed to wait, but if they waited too long, they would miss their ride out of here.

He peered out from the side of the cabin. Nick was nowhere in sight. The trees hid the view of the truck.

He dashed to the front of the cabin and stuck his head in the door. "Hurry."

She ran toward him. He reached a hand out for her.

Through the trees, the sound of the diesel truck starting up reached them. Isabel seemed to understand the plan without his having to explain. If they couldn't get under that tarp without being spotted, they would both freeze out here.

He slipped behind a tree.

Nick would take a few minutes to let the engine warm up before taking off down the road. They'd have to jump in once the truck was rolling and Nick's focus was on his driving.

The grind of gears shifting reached Jason's ears. He ran out toward the tailgate. The truck couldn't be going faster than five miles an hour. Still, it was a challenge to climb over the tailgate quietly. He reached out a hand for Isabel, who struggled to run in her sheepskin slippers. She leaped and got a foothold on the bumper, then piled in. Glancing over his shoulder to a view of the back of Nick's head, Jason lifted the tarp and they rolled under it. He drew her close so they were completely covered.

She was shivering. He unzipped his coat, drew her to his chest and wrapped the coat around her.

He listened to the rumbling of the truck motor. Her soft hair brushed his chin as her shivering subsided.

"Are your feet cold?"

"Some. The sheepskin lining is pretty warm," she whispered.

He prayed Nick would stop at a gas station soon. Somewhere public so they could slip out before Nick noticed the extra lumps beside his toolbox underneath the tarp.

"Jason, one of the agents is dirty. That's how Nick found the safe house."

"Really?" Not Michael, surely not Michael. Yet they couldn't take a chance until they knew for sure. They were on their own for now.

The truck continued to rumble on, though the change in pitch of the rolling tires told him the road had gone from snow packed to paved. They must be getting close to something.

The truck slowed and the road changed again. Judging from the sound the tires made, they might be on dirt. Finally, Nick braked and turned off the engine. The truck door eased open and slammed shut. Jason didn't hear any retreating footsteps.

Jason tensed, fearing they'd been spotted beneath the tarp.

Isabel gasped. She pressed closer to him.

Tension covered them like a shroud as they lay still, clinging to each other and praying.

The vague padding of footsteps in snow pressed on his ears. He remained still, not even daring to breathe yet.

When he could hear no more noise, he rolled free of Isabel, turned over and lifted the tarp just enough to see above the edge of the truck. Isabel scooted beside him to watch, as well. They were parked in what was in the summertime a recreation area with picnic tables, playground equipment and a lake. But this time of year, it was completely abandoned.

Nick had walked less than twelve feet away from the truck, too close for them to risk climbing out. The closest hiding place was a cluster of bare bushes by the lake.

Nick's back was to them. He checked something on his phone and peered toward the road as if waiting for someone. A car appeared around the curve leading into the parking lot. It stopped, and Nick walked toward it as a woman in a uniform, maybe a maid's, got out. She handed Nick an envelope.

Now was their chance, while Nick was distracted. Isabel followed as Jason crawled under the tarp to the far side of the truck away from Nick.

Jason slipped out from beneath the tarp. He was exposed for only a second as he swung his leg over the side of the truck and crouched down. As Isabel did the same, Jason could hear the car starting up and speeding out of the snowy parking lot.

Nick got into his truck and started it up. The motor ran for several minutes warming up while both of them crouched close to the passenger side. Isabel rested her hand on Jason's back. They'd be seen if they made a run for it now.

If Nick pulled out and didn't look back, they'd have a chance.

Jason's gaze darted from the picnic table to the bushes a little farther away.

The truck eased forward. Heart racing, Jason glued

his gaze to the back of Nick's head. Even the slightest movement meant they were dead.

Isabel dashed toward the picnic table. Nick's head tilted as though he were checking his rearview mirror. His truck continued to roll forward.

Jason froze. He was exposed, but movement might alarm Nick, as well. The truck reached the edge of the parking lot.

Isabel crouched on the far side of the picnic table, which didn't entirely conceal her. She was probably cold again. It wasn't that far back to the edge of town, but it would be an arduous journey for her dressed the way she was.

Nick's truck rumbled as it pulled out onto the road.

Jason raced toward the picnic table. The truck disappeared around the curve.

He reached Isabel. "There's a hiking trail on the other side of the lake. Houses at the end of it."

They sprinted through the snow. He was grateful it was only a few inches deep.

They both heard the rumble of the diesel truck at the same time.

Nick had turned around and was headed straight for them. His big truck lumbered over the barriers in the parking lot and bore down on them.

They edged toward the frozen lake, running along the bank. Nick's truck turned around. The driver's-side window rolled down.

Jason caught the glint of metal just before the first shot was fired. He stepped out onto the frozen lake. The ice looked thick and solid. Across was the fastest way to get to the trailhead and the shelter of the trees there. He knew the lake was solid. Kids played hockey on it.

Nick got out of his truck and fired several more shots.

Isabel reached for Jason's hand. The ice cracked around her where a shot was fired.

"Hurry." He could see the trailhead not more than twenty yards away. Nick fired another shot.

An eerie quiet descended around them, their feet tapping on the ice the only noise. He looked over his shoulder. Nick was headed back up the bank toward his truck. Probably to swing around to the road to try to catch them on the trailhead before they could get to a house.

They came to the edge of the lake. "We'll have to cut through the trees. He'll be waiting for us at the end of the trailhead."

The trees were more like tall bare bushes. Within minutes, the menacing sound of the diesel truck reached Jason's ears. Would Nick come in after them or just wait for them to emerge?

The brush became thick and hard to navigate through.

"We can't go back." Isabel's whisper filled with panic.

The bright colors of Jason's coat would be easy enough to see if Nick chose to come in after them.

"Get low," Jason whispered as he squeezed between two bushes. They worked their way through the labyrinth of bare branches and brush.

When he lifted his head, he saw smoke rising up through the air. Someone's woodstove.

The brush ended at the edge of a property. A small cottage-like house with a barn beside it was a welcome sight.

Isabel let out a breath. "We made it." She rushed toward the door and knocked.

Jason stood beside her. "We'll get warmed up and I'll call a friend to come get us. I don't think we should go back to my place or yours."

She cast her gaze downward. "I'm sure Nick or whoever he works for will have people watching."

A woman of about forty opened the door. She was short and round with granny glasses. She held a coffee cup in her hand. Her expression changed from confused to fearful as her eyes grew wide. "Can I help you?"

"Please," Isabel said. "I know this looks crazy." She touched her robe. "It's a long story. We just need to get warmed up and use your phone."

"I can have a friend here to pick us up in ten minutes," Jason said, hoping to allay the woman's understandable wariness.

The woman's gaze traveled from Isabel to Jason and then back to Isabel. "Okay, come in and sit by the fire."

Jason glanced from side to side, not seeing any sign of Nick or his truck. That didn't mean they were in the clear. Nick knew they were both alive. Sooner or later he'd come for them.

Though the woman at the house had grabbed a blanket for Isabel to wrap around herself, it felt like the cold had sunk down into her bones, and she would never be warm again.

Pulling the curtains to one side, Jason watched out the window. He stepped back and paced the floor. "The man I called is not connected to the Bureau in any way. He's a family friend."

If she wasn't so exhausted from running and being cold, she might be just as agitated. She drew the blanket around her shoulders.

Despair sank even deeper into her bones than the cold, down to the marrow. She was tired, hungry and scared. They couldn't count on help from the Bureau until the turncoat was outed. She couldn't go back to her cozy apartment.

The woman brought Isabel a steaming cup of coffee. "Here you go, dear."

"Thank you so much for your kindness," Isabel said.

"We'll be out of your hair in a few minutes," Jason said. "My friend doesn't live too far from here."

The woman nodded and disappeared into the kitchen.

Jason peered out the window again. He whirled around, swinging his hand up and down. "Get out of view."

Isabel jumped up. Her coffee splashed in the cup as she moved away from the window and stood beside Jason.

"His truck went by. Going real slow."

So Nick was trolling the neighborhood looking for them. "We can go to the police and tell them we're being stalked. They'll pick Nick up."

"That's a short-term solution. They'll hold him for a few hours and then someone from the organization will bail him out," Jason said. "I can't tell the police anything about the investigation."

She leaned close to Jason, touching his upper arm. The desperation of their situation sank in. They really were in this alone together.

Outside in the driveway, a car pulled up and flashed its lights three times.

Jason took Isabel's hand. "That's the signal. Let's go."

Isabel put her nearly full cup of coffee on a side table

and yelled a hasty thank-you to the kind woman in the kitchen. They hurried outside into the overcast gray of late afternoon. This time of year it got dark around five o'clock. They had been on the run all day.

The friend turned out to be an older man, balding and broad through the shoulders. Jason got into the front seat and Isabel slipped into the back, but not before a quick glance around. She saw no other vehicles.

As the driver backed up, Jason turned sideways. "Isabel, this is Fred. He used to be a cop and a friend of my father's."

"Pleased to meet you." The formality felt odd considering the threat they were under. *There's always time for manners.* The thought was almost sarcastic.

Fred nodded.

"Can you set us up with a place to sleep and food and maybe a car after we are rested?"

Jason seemed to have come up with some kind of plan. Right now, all she could think about was food, rest and getting warmed up.

"Can do," said Fred.

Isabel glanced over her shoulder, expecting to spot the black truck. She saw only the dark road. This part of town didn't have streetlamps.

Fred took them to a tiny apartment on the second floor of an apartment building. The living room and kitchen were tidy but very impersonal. No photographs or pictures. There was a display case with antique hand-guns in it and a rack on the wall that held several fishing poles.

"You should be able to find something to eat." Fred kept his boots and coat on while Isabel and Jason took off theirs. "I'll run some errands. Get her some clothes.

Sleep where you're comfortable. I'll wake you in a bit."
He looked at Isabel. "What size do you wear?"

"Eight."

After Fred left, Isabel opened the refrigerator and
several cupboards, looking for inspiration. "Guess it's
my turn to cook since you did breakfast."

Their time at the safe house felt like eons ago. For a
brief moment, she had caught her breath, felt safe. But
she hadn't been safe, and neither was her heart. The
sting of Jason's rejection still felt raw.

Jason stood beside her, staring at the contents of the
cupboard. "Lots of bachelor food."

"So tomato soup it is. There's a loaf of bread here.
If there's cheese in the refrigerator, we can have some
grilled cheese sandwiches too."

They worked together to make the meal. Jason but-
tered bread and sliced cheese while she heated the grill
and stirred the soup. Again, she was struck by the con-
tradiction of what they were doing. If anyone were to
observe the scene, it would be a picture of domestic
bliss, just a couple working together to make a meal.

But the whole thing was a lie. They weren't safe,
and they weren't going to be together when this was
all over...if it was ever over.

Metal scraped against metal when she stirred the
soup. The sound set her teeth on edge. She put the spoon
down on a paper towel by the stove. Maybe it wasn't the
noise that bothered her but that reality that was rapidly
sinking in. They were together for now only because
they had to be. The Bureau couldn't protect them.

Jason flipped over the sandwiches as an uncomfortable silence settled between them.

She had to say the words that were on the tip of her

tongue since their car ride over here. "So it sounds like you have a plan. You want to use one of Fred's cars for some reason."

Jason lifted the sandwiches off the grill. "Nick is in contact with the guy who set this whole thing up. We can't depend on the Bureau for help. What if we follow Nick and he leads us to the kingpin? Since someone in this field office would leak information that could cost us our lives, we can get the information to a different field office."

"If Nick was behind bars, if the mastermind was caught, then I wouldn't have to go into witness protection. I could have my life back." Would it still be a life without Jason?

Jason's blue-eyed gaze rested on her. He nodded slowly as if thinking about what she had said. "Yes, that might be the case."

His features softened and she wondered if he was thinking about the kiss. Did it mean anything to him at all?

She found some bowls and poured the soup into them. He carried over the sandwiches on a single plate and sat down at the table opposite her.

"Do you know where Nick lives?"

"I'm not sure. He might stay with his aunt Phoebe. I know where she lives. She's the only relative who has anything to do with him."

He took a bite of sandwich. "Then we start the surveillance there."

"Do you think the Bureau is still watching Nick?"

Jason shrugged. "Michael said they would have to lie low with the investigation for a while. Plus, that's how Nick figured out we were onto him. So I would guess not."

"The agents must be looking for us, wondering about us?"

"Unless the mole told them some lie about us, that we were dead or that we were the turncoats."

Isabel dipped her spoon into the soup. The meal had always been good comfort food when she was a kid. A neighbor lady who felt sorry for her made it, but right now she could barely taste the soup.

The plan was risky. What if Nick figured out he was being followed? Their future was filled with so much uncertainty. The potential to end up dead was huge.

She took in a breath and shifted in her chair. "I guess that's what we have to do."

Jason placed his hand over hers. "I wish it could be some other way."

His touch brought back the memory of the kiss. She pulled her hand away as a barb shot straight through her heart. Did he feel anything at all for her?

"I know it's really dangerous. I wish there was a way for you to be safe and to have your life back."

"I'm afraid. Can we pray?" Whatever happened to them, God would always be with her.

He nodded. "We should have done that a long time ago."

Jason bowed his head and she folded her hands and closed her eyes, as well.

She started. "Lord, we need Your guidance and protection. Please help us to bring Nick and this other man to justice."

After a second of silence, Jason said, "We are both

really afraid. Would You show us the right course of action?"

She lifted her head and looked across the table at Jason.

"Amen," said Jason.

There seemed to be a warmth in his expression, but maybe she was seeing what she wanted to see.

"Let's get some sleep. I'll take the couch. You can have the bed."

Isabel snuggled under the comforter and was asleep within minutes. She was awakened by Jason shaking her shoulder. "Time to get up. Time to go."

He clicked on the light beside her bed. She winced, still trying to clear her brain of the fog of sleep. "How long was I out?"

"Three hours. It'll be enough to keep us going." He held up two shopping bags. "Fred got you some warm clothes. And a phone for me."

Isabel dressed quickly.

When they stepped outside, it was pitch dark. She could see her breath as she exhaled. Though her cheeks chilled from the cold, she felt snug and warm in the ski jacket Fred had gotten for her.

"The car is in the underground parking lot."

Jason led her into the dimly lit garage where the car was stored along with ten others that must belong to the people in the apartment complex.

Isabel got into the passenger seat. She breathed in one final prayer and then her gaze rested on Jason as he buckled himself in behind the wheel.

"Let's do this," she said even as the fear squeezed tight around her chest.

SEVENTEEN

"Surveillance is actually very boring," said Jason. They'd stopped for coffee at an all-night kiosk before parking outside the trailer court where Nick's aunt lived. "A lot of sitting and waiting."

Isabel took a sip of her steaming beverage and tilted her head toward the ceiling. "I just hope this works." She tugged on the collar of her shirt.

Her voice was tempered with anxiety. He didn't blame her. If there was some place he thought he could hide her where she would be safe from all this, he would have taken her there in a heartbeat.

There was only one entrance to the court and they'd spotted Nick's truck outside the trailer when they'd circled through. If Nick left, it would be easy enough to tail him.

"Sometimes the waiting can be more nerve-racking than the tailing," Jason said.

"Did you always want to be a detective?"

"I kind of fell into it. My father was in law enforcement. I made it through the academy but hated all the paperwork once they put me on the force." He took a sip of his coffee. "How about you? You can't tell me you played property manager with your dolls when you were little."

She laughed. "No, I did what every little girl did. Put a wedding dress on the doll and pretended she married the boy doll, moved into their town house with the cool plastic furniture and lived happily ever after."

"I know some people find happily-ever-after. I've seen it at church. Looking at them from the outside, anyway."

"You're a pessimist about true love?"

"It's just I saw my father torn to pieces by his belief in happily-ever-after. I saw the way a woman could destroy a good man."

"It works both ways, Jason. Men shred women too." Her words were drenched in pain.

"Sorry. I'm sure Nick was no picnic."

She shook her head. "I was very young and very naive. I thought when a man said he loved you, he didn't have ulterior motives." She turned her head and stared out the window and then glanced in his direction.

It felt as though a wall had gone up between them. Like there was something going unsaid. The kiss had meant so much to him, but he wouldn't risk her life so they could be together. He didn't want to send her any more mixed messages.

She took another sip of coffee. "I had this big hole in my heart because of my childhood that really only God could fill. But when I was a teenager, I thought having a boyfriend would make it better."

"You've overcome so much, Isabel." He couldn't help but admire the woman sitting beside him. The only thing that meant more to him than the kiss was their prayer together.

A soft smile graced her face. Then she turned to watch through the windshield. "I've been thinking. That woman who met Nick at the recreation area. I recognize the uniform shirt she wore. It's for Happy Homes, a maid service. Sun and Ski uses them for cleaning jobs sometimes."

"Interesting. What do you suppose she was giving him?" Jason said.

"Well, I don't think it was a sentimental card or a grocery list. They were meeting in an out-of-the-way place." Isabel continued to stare straight ahead.

"It would have to be something you couldn't send in a text or you didn't want a record of. Maybe cash or instructions," he said. Something about the clandestine meeting place suggested the maid might be connected to Nick's illegal activities.

They'd been sitting and waiting for over an hour. What if this didn't work? They could hide out at Fred's for a few days. But Jason didn't want to put his friend at risk after he'd been so kind.

Isabel sat up a little straighter. "Headlights."

He leaned to see better through the glass. The lights were high enough to be a truck. It had to be close to midnight. Whoever was leaving at this time was up to no good.

They were parked off to the side of the trailer-court entrance behind the sign that gave its name. Their headlights were off.

The truck rumbled by without stopping.

"It's him, all right." Jason placed his fingers on the key but didn't turn it.

Nick's taillights were still visible. The turn signal

on the truck blinked. Jason started the car and turned onto the road.

With little to no traffic, and as hypervigilant as Nick was, tailing was going to be tricky.

Jason rolled down the road and turned where Nick had turned. Nick was headed back toward town. That was good. A greater possibility of other cars. Late-night revelers on their way home.

Jason stayed back, grateful that the road into town was straight. One other car got between them before they entered the city limits. Once in town, he was able to take some side streets and still track Nick. The truck stayed on the main street of Silver Strike, went all the way through town and then exited on the other side. They passed a car dealership with dark windows and drove a little way out to the country.

Jason pulled off the road onto a shoulder.

"What are you doing? We'll lose him."

"We're the only car out here. I don't want him to get suspicious. There are only three or four places he could turn off out this way. Some businesses, a few homes, I think."

They waited in silence. The snowfall had intensified since they'd left the trailer park. After a few minutes, Jason pulled back out onto the road. They passed a home set back from the road. No black truck was parked by it. They drove by a meat-processing business where no cars were parked.

Isabel wiggled in her seat. "What if we lost him?"

"We'll go a little farther." Jason checked his rear-view mirror. His real fear was that Nick was onto them and had pulled off the road, waiting to come up behind them.

Isabel lifted off her seat a little and pointed. "There."

Up the hill was a large warehouse-looking building teeming with activity. Nick's truck was parked outside, as were several others illuminated by the outdoor lamps. Light glowed in the windows of the building.

Jason turned off the main road. There was a car in front of him headed in the same direction as well as one behind him. Something was going on.

He pulled into the parking lot. Nick was not in his truck or anywhere around the building.

"What is this place?"

Jason shook his head. "We've come this far. Let's have a look around...together."

She reached over, wrapping her fingers around his forearm. "I feel safe staying close to you."

He nodded. Her touch warmed him to the bone.

The two other cars parked and the drivers got out and headed around the side of the building without a backward glance at Jason's vehicle—which probably indicated that a lot of cars coming into the lot was expected. Something was going on inside that building.

"Okay." Jason pushed open his door as his heart skipped a beat. "Follow me."

Snow came down even harder as they hurried through the parking lot, ducking from car to car. Jason pressed against the side of the building with Isabel leaning against his back. They couldn't just walk in. They had no idea what they were facing.

The door popped open. Jason dived for the trees surrounding the property as a man dressed in a snowsuit headed in the other direction.

He signaled for Isabel to follow him, then skirted through the trees and bushes close to the building. If

they could find a window, they might be able to peer inside and figure out what was going on in there. It didn't
seem like the smuggling operation would be so above-
board as to be operating out of a building.

They ran around to the far side of the building, still
not finding any windows.

"Are you up to sneaking inside with me?"

She nodded. The door on the east side of the building was the only one no one had gone into or out of.

He reached for the handle and eased it open. He
stared at metal shelving that ran from floor to ceiling
containing boxes and what looked like auto parts. "I
don't see anyone. Come on."

As Isabel placed her hand in his, he prayed he hadn't
made a mistake in letting her come with him.

Isabel's heart pounded as they stepped inside what
looked like a storage area for an auto-parts store. She
could hear voices faint and indiscernible.

Jason held her hand as they rushed around the
shelves of parts toward an open doorway. He signaled
for her to crouch by the door while he got on the other
side and peered out.

The three-story warehouse-like structure was built
into the side of the hill, and they had actually stepped
into the middle floor. One floor up was a glass wall
that looked to be some sort of office. Two people, a
man and a woman, were talking. The woman, dressed
in a fur coat, threw back her head and laughed. Something about her seemed familiar. The man reached out
and gathered the woman into his arms and kissed her.
He was a broad-shouldered man with a belly. Judging

from the gray hair, he was substantially older than the woman.

Isabel scooted over to where Jason was so she could look down below. If they had gone around to the final wall of the structure, it would have been obvious what they were dealing with. Down below on the ground floor were four huge garage doors and four snowplows. Men, including Nick, were standing around talking. Suited up and ready to get on the snowplows. One of the garage doors opened, and a man headed toward a plow, leaving Nick and two other guys. The rest of the ground floor looked like a repair shop with a scattering of tools and machines and one plow blade.

Jason whispered in her ear. "He's just going to work?"

"He takes odd jobs. Nothing permanent," she said. "So I guess this is a dead end." Disappointment colored her words. She wished she could place the woman in the glass office. Why did she look so familiar?

Nick glanced up in their direction. Her heart skipped a beat. She shrank back against the wall.

"We'd better get out of here." Jason hurried toward the door and Isabel was right behind him.

Jason pressed along the wall, preparing to ease around the corner if the coast was clear. He put a protective arm on her, letting her know it wasn't safe to go yet.

Several inches of snow had fallen in the short time they'd been up here. It was coming down fast and heavy.

Jason peered out again, then pressed his back against the metal wall. "They're starting to get busy. They didn't seem alarmed by our car. But I don't want to take a chance that they would know we didn't work here. I think this is a legit snowplow business but something still feels off to me. We should circle through the trees and then down into the parking lot."

That would take an extra ten minutes at least. Jason dived behind the bare brush that was part of the landscaping close to the building. Isabel followed as a man came around the corner from the parking lot.

He shone a light in her direction just as she dipped behind the bush. "So it's you. What are you doing here?" the man shouted.

Her heart beat faster. She'd glimpsed the man's face. "That's the guy with the gun from the Wilsons' house."

They both sprinted deeper into the trees, knowing that Mr. Gun would probably come after them.

It took only a moment before Isabel heard the footfalls behind her. Following the path Jason chose, staying close on his heels, she glanced over her shoulder at the dark figure pursuing them. The terrain became rockier as they ran past some large boulders. She could see her breath in the cold night air. Her legs pumped hard as they worked their way uphill.

Jason grabbed her and pulled her into a crevice between two boulders. She was so out of breath she was afraid the man would hear her inhaling and exhaling. The rock was hard and cold against her back as she faced Jason.

Were their tracks visible in the snow?

The crunch of footsteps landed on her ears. She took in only a shallow breath, fearing that the pursuer might see her breath.

The man turned a half circle, searching. Both of them slipped deeper into the crevice. She willed herself to be smaller.

Fear settled in around her, heavier than the snow

falling from the sky. If Mr. Gun was at that warehouse too, there was something going on with that place other than snowplowing.

Mr. Gun spotted them and lunged in their direction. They slipped through the other side of the crevice and kept running. They were getting farther away from the warehouse. Would it even be safe to go back down to the parking lot? What choice did they have? They had to get out of here.

They ran for several more minutes before Jason glanced over his shoulder and then stopped, surveying the snowy hill below. They'd just come through an open area. "I think he gave up."

"I doubt it. He probably went back for reinforcements," she said.

"You're probably right. The fact that two people connected to a smuggling ring are working there can't be a coincidence," he said. "We need to get this information to someone we can trust."

That was a tall order. The men in the warehouse would probably be watching the parking lot by now. "How far away was that house we passed on the drive here?"

"It didn't seem that far when we were driving, but on foot—" Jason shook his head "—it could be an hour or more of walking."

"It's closer to get back to the parking lot. Maybe we can catch them with their guard down."

Her heart raced at the thought of plunging into the danger that awaited them. If the kingpin was one of the men in that building, he would be combing the mountain for them soon enough. The man in the glass office

kissing the younger woman must be the owner or manager of the place. Was he the kingpin?

They ran along the ridgeline and then dived back
down the mountain, passing another rock outcropping
and coming out on an unplowed road. Isabel mulled
over all they had seen. She slowed her steps. "I know
who that woman was."

"The woman in the office?"

"Yes. I couldn't place her because she wasn't wearing the uniform, but it just clicked in my head. She
was the maid who handed Nick that envelope. Whatever was in the envelope, he needed it before he got to
the warehouse."

Jason nodded as though he were making sense of the
information. "The guy with her was probably in charge
of the snowplow business, maybe even the owner."
Jason trudged along the unplowed road.

"They were clearly romantically involved. I don't
know what it all means—maybe he has nothing to do
with anything, but she does."

"Would maids have access to security codes?" Jason
said.

"Yes, they would. And snowplow operators would
know when a house was empty."

Before she could process all the conclusions they had
come to, a mechanical roar filled the forest. A snowplow rounded a curve in the road. In the cab of the
plow, Isabel could see Nick behind the wheel, barrel-
ing toward them.

EIGHTEEN

Jason turned and ran in the opposite direction as the snowplow loomed toward him. With Isabel right beside him, he searched the woods for a place to escape off the road.

The road had been cut into the side of a mountain. One side was sheer cliff and the other a steep rocky drop-off.

The rumble of the plow's motor was menacing. Isabel skirted toward the edge of the road and then jumped down the incline. Jason followed her down the steep slope.

Above them, the plow stopped. When he glanced up, Nick had gotten out of the cab and was stalking toward the edge of the road, holding a rifle. Jason grabbed Isabel and pulled her behind a boulder. The first shot glanced off the rock just above their heads.

He surveyed the area around them. Nick would probably chase them down the mountain on foot. The incline was steep and treacherous. He pointed to the next rock they needed to make it to for cover. Half crouching and half running, they dived toward the boulder.

He caught a flash of movement in his peripheral vision, the reflective material on Nick's snowsuit. Nick had not left the road yet. The rifle had substantial range, hundreds of yards.

Jason huddled down behind the rock. Isabel pressed close to him. He couldn't see anything below him that would shield them. They'd have to move sideways, which meant they were still within rifle range.

"He can't shoot at both of us at the same time. I'll go first. Then you run and get behind that outcropping as fast as you can." He pointed. "I'll get to you as soon as I can."

She tore off her glove and pressed a hand to his cheek. Her round brown eyes filled with warmth. "You're making yourself a target...for me."

"It'll be okay." Her touch, the softness in her expression, drew him in and warmed him to the marrow of his bones.

"You could die. I don't want you to die."

He kissed her forehead and then her lips. He loved her. In that moment, he knew that he loved her. Even if they couldn't be together, he loved her. "I don't want to die either but this is the best way for us to get a safe distance from him. We have to work our way down the mountain and get out of rifle range." The plan was not foolproof. Nick still might choose to follow them.

Another rifle shot reverberated through the forest, stirring up snow close to the rock. They both crouched lower.

"After I go, count to three and then run as fast as you can."

She nodded.

Jason burst up from the rock and ran in a zigzag pattern, jumping around the smaller rocks. Two rifle shots zinged past him, one so close that the displaced air pummeled his eardrum. He dived to the ground.

He caught a flash of color below him. Isabel had chosen to go toward a cluster of trees instead of the outcropping. Another shot shattered the silence of the wild. It was aimed at her. From where he lay on the ground, he prayed that the shot had missed her.

She disappeared into the cluster of trees.

Using the moment it would take Nick to reorient himself, Jason burst up from the ground and darted toward the shelter of the trees. He glanced to his side. Nick had worked his way down the mountain by maybe ten yards. He'd have to stop to line up another shot.

Jason could see the trees up ahead and spotted Isabel's jacket again. His foot hooked on a rock and he stumbled and fell facedown into the snow. The fall shocked and disoriented him. His brain told him he needed to stand up and to keep running, but his body remained unresponsive.

Isabel emerged from the trees, reaching out to pull him to his feet. Another shot sounded. So close. They hurried toward the shelter of the trees five yards away.

Another shot echoed down the mountain, breaking a branch above them. Birds fluttered into the sky. Jason grabbed Isabel and held her close.

"Don't do that ever again. You could have died."

She nestled against his chest. "I didn't want to lose you, Jason."

More than anything, he wished they could remain suspended in the moment. He wanted to hold her forever. He kissed the top of her head. "Not if I can help it."

A groaning noise reached his ears, followed by a

thud: Nick's feet as he jumped off a large rock, making his way down toward them.

"We have to keep moving." Jason peered through the trees, searching for their next point of cover. It was dark enough that most objects were only shadows.

"What if we worked our way back up to the road and got to that plow?" she said.

"It's worth a try. Move parallel to the road for a while, so he doesn't figure out what we're doing," whispered Jason.

Through the trees, he could see Nick turning from side to side, searching the landscape for them. The glint of the rifle caught in the moonlight.

They sprinted from one rock outcropping to another, from brush to clusters of trees. Twice, rifle shots zinged over their heads, forcing them to drop to the ground and crawl.

Jason gasped for breath as they ran toward a boulder closer to the road. He could see the edge of the road just above him. Isabel kept pace with him as they half ran, half climbed up to the road.

Once they were on the level footing of the road, he leaned over, resting his hands on his knees to catch his breath. It had been at least ten minutes since a shot was fired. He didn't see Nick anywhere down below.

Isabel patted her heart and took in a quick breath. She glanced nervously down the steep incline, shaking her head. "He doesn't give up easily."

As crazy as Nick was, he seemed to have the stalking instincts of a lion.

Once his breath slowed, Jason pivoted and jogged down the road with Isabel beside him. His leg muscles strained from all the running and climbing they'd done.

They rounded one curve and then another. Still no sign of the plow. They must be getting close.

Jason slowed down enough to talk. "He may be waiting for us at the plow, suspecting that we would try to get to it."

Most of the landscape was repetitive. It was hard to know how close they were.

Isabel shot ahead of him. "I see snowplow tracks down there."

He saw them now too, but no snowplow. When they got to the tracks, it was clear that Nick had backed the plow up until he came to a place where he could turn around and head back down the road.

"So much for that plan." Isabel slumped down onto a tree stump beside the road.

The plow probably had a radio in it. Had he been told to get back to work? Or maybe he'd just decided to leave them to the elements for now. How far were they from shelter?

"This road has to lead somewhere."

"Can I rest for a minute?" she said.

He could tell from her tone of voice she was giving up hope.

"Sure." He paced down the road, looking for smoke rising in the air from a woodstove or lights, any sign of civilization. He didn't see anything but trees and rock.

It was a sure bet that whoever was behind all the smuggling wouldn't risk their getting back to civilization. Sooner or later, someone would come looking for them to kill them.

From the tree stump where she sat, Isabel tilted her head. Clouds slipped over the moon, making it darker. The snowfall had stopped at least.

Sitting still made her feel the cold more intensely. She rose to her feet and rubbed her arms, pushing the despair that plagued her to the back of her mind. No matter what, she needed to not give up hope. They couldn't be that far from a place where they could find help and shelter.

Jason returned and held out a gloved hand for her to take. "Let's head down the road. We're bound to run into something or someone."

"I suppose that's what we should do." She couldn't hide the weariness in her voice.

Jason scanned the area above them as though he were looking for potential threats. Then he looked at her. His eyes filled with compassion. "It's the best plan I have for now."

They were both exhausted and cold, but being with Jason somehow made it bearable.

They ran for what felt like miles. The ground leveled out. They passed an area that was fenced off with barbed wire, but there were no cows or ranchers, no sign of life anywhere.

They drank from a mountain stream, the water icy cold as she cupped it in her hands. Isabel stood up from the creek and put her hands on her hips. With the terrain so flat, she could see for miles and still there was no sign of people.

"I guess we were pushed farther back into the hills than I realized."

They heard the sound of a vehicle on the road before they saw the headlights. Any noise echoed in the quiet. Both of them moved toward some brush and crouched. If it was someone who could help them, they'd have a hard time catching up to him, but they couldn't risk being spotted if Nick or one of his cohorts came looking for them.

The battered old truck came around the bend and stopped. A man got out and peered down the road, shining a flashlight. Their tracks where they'd made their way down to the mountain stream were clearly visible.

"It's not Nick. Not his build." The truck hadn't been one of the ones in the parking lot at the snowplow facility.

Isabel jumped to her feet and waved. "Hey." She ran across the field as the man took notice of her.

Jason followed her.

She hollered as the man came to the edge of the road. "Boy, are we glad to see you."

The man was maybe thirty years old. Fringes of red hair peeked out from beneath a knit cap. He pointed across the field. "Saw your tracks. Not many people come up Copper Junction Road. You folks break down or something?"

"You could say that. Could you give us a ride back into town or at least some place where we can phone for someone to come pick us up?"

The man pulled his hat off and rubbed his hair. He wasn't wearing gloves. "Sure. I can do that."

They made their way up the hill. Isabel got into the cab first. Jason squeezed in by the passenger-side door of the old truck as he and the man made small talk about fishing and hunting.

The truck lumbered down the road until they came to a crossroads and took a right turn.

Isabel tensed. Maybe she'd gotten all turned around when they were running away, but it seemed like town was in the other direction.

"There's a little gas station up the road where you folks will be able to make your phone call," said the man as though he had read her mind.

Maybe because they'd been running for so long and seen the dark side of humanity, her trust in the goodness of people had been dismantled. She couldn't let go of the feeling that something wasn't right.

The man continued to drive down a two-lane that didn't connect with a main road.

Isabel squeezed Jason's leg just above the knee to get his attention. She raised her eyebrows, hoping he would indicate that he felt the same uneasiness.

Jason kept talking about where the best fishing holes were, but he pressed his shoulder a little harder against hers.

The bleak unsettled landscape rolled by.

"How far did you say it was to that gas station?" She hoped her voice didn't give away the fear that had taken up residence in her body.

"Oh, just up the road a piece." The man shifted gears.

They came up over a hill.

Terror crashed through Isabel.

Down below was the warehouse with the snowplows. The man reached into the side compartment of the door and pulled out a pistol, which he aimed at Isabel. His voice grew sinister and dark. "Don't think about jumping out or fighting back. I'll shoot her faster than you can blink."

The truck rolled down the hill so fast, it would have been dangerous to try to escape. The parking lot was empty except for one car. Theirs was nowhere in sight and Nick's black truck was gone.

Isabel's heart pounded against her rib cage. The man

parked the truck, still pointing the gun at her. "Now
we're going to go inside. No funny business. Got that?"

They both nodded.

"I'll get out of the cab first, understand," the redheaded man said.

She stared at the barrel of the gun and nodded. Her
hands were trembling, and her mouth had gone completely dry.

The man pulled the keys out of the ignition. He
smiled. This time she saw the darkness behind his eyes.
"Just in case you were going to try something."

Snow swirled lightly out of the sky as the man
marched them into the warehouse. Isabel glanced at
Jason, trying to read his expression. It was two against
one, even if one had a gun.

Jason lifted his head in a nod, indicating that they
should try to take the man with the gun.

Isabel stopped.

"Keep moving." The redheaded man aimed the gun
at her.

Jason used the moment of distraction to whirl around
and kick the gun out of the man's hand. It flew, landing in deep snow. While she ran to find the gun, Isabel
heard the slap of skin against skin as the men exchanged
blows.

Heart racing, she scanned the snow for the gun while
the men continued to fight.

Then she heard it. The click of a shotgun shell being
ratcheted into the chamber. "Put your hands in the air."

She turned, staring into the cold eyes of the short
muscular man who had come after her at the Wilsons'
house. Mr. Gun.

"You too." The short man aimed the gun at Jason.

The redheaded man scrambled in the snow to retrieve his handgun and then pointed it at Isabel.

"I told you not to try anything funny," he said between gasps for air.

Jason and Isabel marched side by side. She wasn't about to give up. There had to be a way to get free. The man with the handgun ran ahead and opened the door. Just outside the glass-walled office, they stepped out onto a mezzanine that provided a view of the entire facility.

All the plows were back in place. There was no one behind the glass of the office or down below by the plows.

The men led them down to the room where the snowplow parts were stored and commanded them to sit on the floor with their backs to each other. The redhead bound their hands and gagged their mouths with duct tape and tied the two of them together with rope back to back.

"Now, you just sit tight until the boss gets back. He can decide what to do with you." The man traced a finger down Isabel's cheek. "At which time, I get to collect a bonus for finding you."

He winked at Isabel, rose to his feet and slipped out the door. Mr. Gun followed. The door closed. As far as she could see, there were only two men in the facility right now. If they could get out of this room, they might be able to escape.

Jason wriggled, struggling to break free. Isabel twisted her hands, hoping to loosen the duct tape that bound them. Her wrists hurt from the effort.

After a moment of stillness, his head brushed against the back of hers as he studied his surroundings. He scooted across the floor toward the metal shelves that held the motor parts. Isabel pushed with her feet to move with him. He must have seen something on the shelf that might help them escape.

She had no idea what his plan was or when "the boss" would return and decide how to kill them. She had no doubt their death was imminent if they didn't find a way to escape their captors and get to one of those vehicles.

NINETEEN

Jason had spotted a piece of metal protruding from one of the lower shelves. He might be able to cut himself free and then remove the duct tape from Isabel, as well. He lifted his hands, which were tied in front of him, and scraped the tape along the metal.

Even though he had no idea if they had ten minutes to escape or ten hours, a sense of urgency made it feel like there was a weight on his chest. He sawed back and forth as the layers of duct tape were cut away. He was nearly free when he heard footsteps outside the room.

They both scooted back across the floor to where they had been put. Jason pressed the cut tape back around his wrists and held his hands as though they were still bound. The door burst open and the redheaded man stepped in.

He crossed his arms over his chest. "Boss is back. Just a few minutes and we'll get this mess wrapped up." The man punched his fist against his palm and narrowed his eyes. His expression chilled Jason to the bone.

The man grinned. "Don't go anywhere now." He laughed, shaking his head. "I crack myself up." He closed the door.

Jason listened to the man's boots pounding on the concrete floor before twisting free of the rope that bound him to Isabel. He tore the gag off his mouth, and then, still crouching, he came to help Isabel. She stared up at him. He touched the corner of the duct tape on her mouth. "This will hurt."

She nodded, her eyes filled with trust. He ripped it off in one quick motion. A tiny gasp escaped her lips.

He tried to peel the tape off her hands. He pulled, winding the layers of tape off her wrists until she was free.

He ran to the outside door they had used when they first entered the building. Locked.

"Let's see if we can find another way out." They wove through the shelves that reached up to the high ceiling until they found a back door. The door opened to a landing and a stairwell leading upward.

It was too much to hope that it would lead them straight outside.

He pressed against the wall and stepped lightly up the stairs. Isabel touched his arm as she stood one step below him. At the top of the stairs, he eased the door open slowly.

Raised voices drifted down a hallway. He slipped through the door, not daring to open it all the way, and then he crouched on the carpet. They must be in the hallway behind the glass-walled office.

Three men were arguing. The only voice he recognized was Nick's.

He couldn't pick up all the conversation. It sounded like an argument over money for a job they'd just done. Thundering footsteps came up the hallway into the office as the voice of the man who had tied them up blasted through the room. "They've escaped."

Jason angled around the corner just in time to see three men running out of the office. Nick, the man who had been kissing the maid and a third man—Larry, the FBI agent who had picked them up when they'd escaped from the Wilsons' house. Now they knew who the turncoat was.

All the men ran in the opposite direction of where Isabel and he were hiding. The fourth man, the redhead, trailed behind. He waited until he heard the sound of the slamming door and moved toward the office. Isabel grabbed his arm. "What are you doing?"

"There's probably a phone in there." He stepped into the empty office and she entered behind him. "We can call Michael now. He's not the turncoat."

"I don't think we have time to wait for help. We should get out of here."

Her thinking was clearer than his.

"I'm sure they will send a man out to the parking lot to make sure we can't get to those cars."

Light came into Isabel's eyes. "The snowplows. They won't be expecting us to use one of the snowplows."

He peered through the glass wall of the office. Down below, a man ran by. Jason and Isabel crouched out of view but where they were still able to watch the activity. The man looked from side to side and then took a door that led to the parking lot.

They heard the thunder of footsteps up metal stairs.

They needed to get out of here and fast. The door they'd come through led back to the parts storage room. Jason ran down the hallway and tried another door that had stairs leading down. Just as he closed the door he heard voices in the hallway headed back toward the office.

There were at least five men in all. The three who had been in the office and two who had tied them up. He had to assume that at least one of those men would remain in the glass office watching the snowplow area. This plan was fraught with risk, but it was the best they had. The stairs opened up on the floor where the plows were. Jason pressed against a wall by the door so shadows covered him.

Sure enough, the man who must be the boss or owner, and was probably the mastermind behind all the smuggling, stared down from his office. Even if they stayed close to the wall, there was a ten-foot stretch where they'd be spotted before they could hide behind one of the plows.

Isabel remained at the base of the stairs, door slightly ajar, waiting for the signal from him. He could just make out her face in the little slit where the door was open.

Jason tilted his head and watched the man above them, waiting for a second of distraction when he and Isabel could traverse the area where they'd be visible.

The seconds ticked by. The man continued to survey the area below. Jason became aware of the hardness of the wall against his back, of his own breathing and of Isabel perched behind the partly open door, her gaze fixed on him.

Finally the short muscular man, Mr. Gun, came into the office and the owner turned his back to Jason.

Jason bolted toward the first snowplow. The soft padding of Isabel's footsteps behind him pressed on his ears. He crouched in front of the machine in between the plow blade and the garage door. Easing around to the side, he glanced up. The owner was staring out the office window again. Jason shrank back into the shadows as his heart pounded out an erratic beat. No way could he climb into the cab and not be spotted. That meant they would have only seconds to get out of the warehouse before someone would be on their tail.

He slipped back around to the front of the plow by the blade where Isabel still hid.

She leaned close and whispered in his ear. "The plow on the end doesn't have any lights shining on it."

He peered down the line of plow blades before nodding that her idea was the most viable one. They scurried from one plow to the next. He eased open the cab door of the last plow. Isabel got in after him on the other side.

He stared down at the control panel, trying to get his bearings, grateful to see that the key was in the ignition.

"The garage door. There's a switch." Before he could say anything, she had jumped out of the cab and headed toward the wall.

He started the vehicle as the door eased open and Isabel raced to get back in the cab. Now for sure they'd be noticed. He eased the plow forward even before the door was all the way open.

Isabel grabbed hold of the door and tried to climb into the cab as the tracks of the plow rolled forward. He reached out a hand and pulled her in.

Two men were behind them. One jumped onto the cab of the plow.

Jason hit the accelerator as the plow eased forward onto the flat area outside the garage doors. Another garage door opened, and the lights of a second plow glared out at them.

Jason gained speed, climbing the hill toward the road. He chose the steeper terrain, hoping that would get rid of the unwanted guest clinging to the outside of the cab.

The man jumped off. Jason caught a glimpse of movement as the man raised a gun.

"Get down." He threw a protective hand over Isabel. Gunfire shattered the glass of the cab and rained down on them. His skin stung where the glass cut him. A chilly breeze blew in around them.

The plow lumbered up to the road that led back into town. Top speed looked to be about thirty miles an hour.

The other plow slipped in behind them.

Isabel sat back up, craning her neck. "Nick is in the other plow."

Jason pressed the gas pedal to the floor, wishing they could go faster. He turned out onto the main road. One of the cars from the warehouse passed him and then slowed to a crawl. Nick was still bearing down on them in the plow.

"They're trying to box us in." Jason stared at the road ahead, where a car was coming toward them. He couldn't risk the life of an innocent person.

He eased off the gas.

The car going in the opposite direction whizzed by.

Metal scraped against metal as Nick rammed into the back of them. Both of them jostled around in their seats.

Jason pressed the gas, turned the wheel and prepared to ease around the slow car in front of him. The car edged onto the wrong side of the road.

"Fine—that's how you're gonna play it?" Jason jerked the wheel in the other direction. The blade collided with the car as Jason pushed him toward a ditch.

The car was no match for the power of the plow. With one final push, the car slid into a snowbank. But Nick still rolled toward them.

Nick rammed against the side of them with the blade raised.

Jason pressed the accelerator and cranked the wheel as the other plow pushed them down the road sideways. He disentangled his plow from Nick's.

Jason rolled forward off the road to get away from Nick. The tracks of the plow bit through the snow as they lumbered up a hill and down the other side. Nick was right behind them.

The hill grew steeper. The plow listed to one side.

"We're going to tip over." Isabel's fear-filled words seemed to come from far away as he struggled to get the machine onto stable ground.

The plow rolled over on its side, and Isabel fell on top of him.

The motor was still running. Tiny gasps escaped Isabel's lips as she struggled to right herself. She climbed out the back of the cab's broken window.

Jason pushed himself up. His hands were bleeding from the broken glass. He pulled himself through the same opening Isabel had used. Isabel jumped down into the snow.

Nick was maybe twenty feet from them, still behind the wheel of the other plow. The headlights glared at them.

Isabel took off running before Jason had jumped down off the plow. Drops of blood in the snow revealed that she was cut up, as well. He raced after her as the plow drew closer, the engine noise surrounding them.

* * *

Isabel felt the warm seep of blood on her forehead as she struggled to navigate through the deep snow.

The clanging of the plow's motor stopped. She looked over her shoulder. Not wanting to risk the same outcome as their plow, Nick had turned the motor off and was crawling out of the cab. He held a gun in his hand.

Jason was at least twenty yards behind her and struggling even more than she was. She lifted her feet one after the other as she slogged up the snowy hillside. When this was over—if they survived—she never wanted to trudge through snow again.

A gunshot echoed across the terrain. She winced but kept moving, trusting that Jason would catch up with her.

She was nearly to the tree line when she looked over her shoulder. Jason was lying facedown on the ground.

Her heart stopped. She was out of pistol range, but if she ran back to help him, she would be a target too.

She turned and hurried back down the hill toward Jason. If they both died out here today, fine. She wasn't about to abandon a good man to the forces of evil. Before she could get to him, Jason rose to his feet. His hands were bloody and he'd left stains in the snow.

He signaled for her to keep running. Nick was having as much trouble navigating the deep snow as they were. The only way he could aim a shot was to stop moving.

She heard another bullet whiz through the air just as she reached the tree line. She slowed, looking behind her for Jason.

Finding a large tree with long branches, she hid underneath it, peering out and hoping to see Jason's boots. She caught her breath as the minutes ticked by. She heard a rustling off to the side and a moment later saw Nick's dark boots moving past.

What was going on here? Where was Jason?

She rolled out from underneath the tree and headed back toward the tree line. Down below, Jason had crawled into the cab of the working plow. He must have doubled back once Nick entered the trees and had no view of the plow. He signaled for her to come back down.

Her feet sank three feet down as she struggled to get to Jason. A pistol shot zinged past, close enough to send shock waves through her. She heard groaning behind her. Nick had fallen in the deep snow.

Jason got out of the cab and waved his arm, indicating she should get down the hill. The pistol rested on the surface of the snow.

Once and for all, she would see to it that Nick Solomon wouldn't escape justice ever again. She hurried toward the gun and picked it up.

"Get on your feet." Her voice held unexpected strength.

Nick pushed himself up. He was covered in snow. "Oh, come on. You're not going to shoot, Blondie."

"Try me." She aimed the pistol close to Nick's feet and squeezed the trigger.

"Whoa." Shock spread across Nick's face as he did a jig with his feet and held his hands up in surrender.

She could never shoot anyone. Nick just needed to know who was in control now. "My name is not Blondie. It's Isabel."

Jason came up behind her. "Turn around and put your hands behind your back." Jason held a scarf that he must have found in the cab of the plow.

Nick sneered. Isabel raised the pistol and pointed it at him. Nick glared but turned his back to them and put his hands together behind him.

They led Nick down the hill with his hands bound. Isabel held the gun while Jason drove. Once they were out on the road, he checked the rearview mirror several times.

Both of them knew there was a good possibility that the others from the warehouse were after them.

Isabel felt a sense of satisfaction as Nick hung his head and closed his eyes. "I'm telling you, baby, you and me would have made a great team."

"I don't want to be on that kind of team." She glanced at Jason, feeling warmth spread over her as he gazed at her before focusing on the road.

She cared deeply for him. They had been through so much together. He had shown over and over that he would give up his life for her. What was going to happen now that all of this was close to being over?

TWENTY

Jason and Isabel sat in the FBI field office waiting to be debriefed after a trip to the emergency room to deal with their cuts. The head of the smuggling ring had opted not to chase them. Knowing that he'd been found out, he had booked a ticket to Argentina along with his girl-friend, the maid. Agents had caught him at the airport.

Michael came out of his office. "We'll need to inter-view each of you separately."

Isabel's hand grasped his. "I'll go first." She squeezed his fingers.

He saw an affection in her eyes that made his heart race. Still, was the attraction just because they had needed each other so desperately to stay alive or was there something deeper there that could survive their return to ordinary life?

He had opened his heart to her but old fears returned. He didn't want to end up like his father, a broken man. Women left, they betrayed—that was what they did. He picked up a magazine and flipped through it. Maybe Isabel was different…maybe.

Ten minutes later, Isabel emerged from the office. Her round doe eyes rested on him. "Your turn. I've got to get over to the office and explain things to Mary." She reached out and squeezed his hand. "I guess this is it."

He took in a breath. Should he say something about how he felt but how the doubts plagued him? "Yes, maybe I'll see you around."

A shadow seemed to fall across her face. "Sure. That would be nice." Was that disappointment that tainted her words?

Michael came out of his office and stood in the doorway watching them.

Jason stepped toward Michael's office as the door to the outside opened and closed—Isabel was gone.

"You two have been through quite an ordeal together," said Michael, turning to position himself behind his desk.

"Yes. Yes, we have." Jason nodded.

He stepped inside Michael's office and closed the door.

Michael clicked the keyboard of his laptop. "It seems our rogue agent has decided to run too, but I suspect it will just be a matter of hours before we have him in custody."

"And the other men we saw at the warehouse?"

"Isabel was able to identify them. Petty criminals. The locals can pick them up and bring them in."

Jason turned sideways and stared at the door, thinking about Isabel stepping outside. "So they're not in custody yet. What if they come after her for revenge?"

"They don't have the economic resources to flee. It's just a matter of hours before we pick them up. You can stay with her for a little longer, can't you?"

"Give me a minute." Jason jumped up from his chair

and bolted for the door. He took the stairs two at a time and raced out to the street.

Isabel was already two blocks away, walking into a headwind with her head down and her arms crossed. He ran to catch up with her, calling out her name when he was a block away.

She turned to face him.

"Jason, what is it?"

"You know the two men that came after you at the Wilsons' are still at large and the redheaded guy."

"Michael mentioned it. They don't want to get caught. I'm sure they're hiding," she said.

He shifted his weight from one foot to the other. "Why take a chance? What's another day or two together, watching each other's backs?"

"Jason, is that really why you ran all the way up the street?"

"Yes. I'm worried about your safety."

Her expression drooped. Her brown eyes glazed. "Oh, is that all?"

He reached his hand out to her. "Isabel, I didn't mean to make you cry."

"When I saw you coming up the street I thought that maybe… I don't know… That it wasn't about this whole smuggling thing. That you were coming after me to be with me, just to be with me."

The vulnerability in her voice floored him. He let out a breath and shook his head.

"What?" A faint smile graced her face as she leaned closer to him.

"Guess I was telling myself a lie. I was looking for an excuse to be with you. Isabel?" He knew he loved her. Why was it so hard for him to admit that?

"Yes?" she said.

He pulled his gloves off and tossed them on the ground. Then he inched her gloves off, as well, so he could hold her hands in his. "Isabel Connor. I do want to be with you. Not just for another day until those men are picked up but for the rest of my life."

She bounced from toe to heel. Her face brightening. "Yes. I want that too. I want to be your wife."

"Well then, there you have it. I love you, Isabel."

"I love you, Jason."

He leaned in and kissed her with the snow swirling around them and the early-morning sun shining on them.

* * * * *

WE HOPE YOU ENJOYED
THIS BOOK FROM

LOVE INSPIRED SUSPENSE
INSPIRATIONAL ROMANCE

Courage. Danger. Faith.

Find strength and determination in stories
of faith and love in the face of danger.

6 NEW BOOKS AVAILABLE EVERY MONTH!

LISHALO2021

SPECIAL EXCERPT FROM

LOVE INSPIRED SUSPENSE
INSPIRATIONAL ROMANCE

*A wedding party is attacked in the Alaskan wilderness.
Can a K-9 trooper and his dog keep the bridesmaid
safe from the lurking danger?*

Read on for a sneak preview of
Alaskan Rescue *by Terri Reed in the new*
Alaska K-9 Unit series from Love Inspired Suspense.

A groan echoed in Ariel Potter's ears. Was someone
hurt? She needed to help them.

She heard another moan and decided she was the
source of the noise. The world seemed to spin. What was
happening?

Somewhere in her mind, she realized she was being
turned over onto a hard surface. Dull pain pounded the
back of her head.

"Miss? Miss?"

A hand on her shoulder brought Ariel out of the foggy
state engulfing her. Opening her eyelids proved to be a
struggle. Snow fell from the sky. Then a hand shielded
her face from the elements.

Her gaze passed across broad shoulders to a very
handsome face beneath a helmet. Dark hair peeked out
from the edge of the helmet and a pair of goggles hung
from his neck. Who was this man?

The pull of sleep was hard to resist. She closed her eyes.

"Stay with me," the man murmured.

His voice coaxed her to do as he instructed, and she forced her eyes open.

Where was she?

Awareness of aches and pains screamed throughout her body, bringing the world into sharp focus. She was flat on her back and her head throbbed.

Ariel started to raise a hand to touch her head, but something was holding her arm down. She tried to sit up, and when she discovered she couldn't, she lifted her head to see why. Straps had been placed across her shoulders, her torso, hips and knees to keep her in place on a rescue basket.

"Hey, now, I need you to concentrate on staying awake."

That deep, rich voice brought her focus back to the moment. Memory flooded her on a wave of terror. The horror of rolling down the side of the cliff, hitting her head, landing in a bramble bush and the fear of moving that would take her plummeting to the bottom of the mountain. She must have gone in and out of consciousness before being rescued. She gasped with realization. "Someone pushed me!"

Don't miss
Alaskan Rescue *by Terri Reed,*
available wherever Love Inspired Suspense
books and ebooks are sold.

LoveInspired.com

Copyright © 2021 by Harlequin Books, S.A.

LISEXP0321

LOVE INSPIRED
INSPIRATIONAL ROMANCE

UPLIFTING STORIES OF FAITH, FORGIVENESS AND HOPE.

Join our social communities to connect with other readers who share your love!

Sign up for the Love Inspired newsletter at **LoveInspired.com** to be the first to find out about upcoming titles, special promotions and exclusive content.

CONNECT WITH US AT:

Facebook.com/LoveInspiredBooks

Twitter.com/LoveInspiredBks

Facebook.com/groups/HarlequinConnection

LISOCIAL2020

Get 4 FREE REWARDS!

We'll send you 2 FREE Books plus 2 FREE Mystery Gifts.

Love Inspired Suspense books showcase how courage and optimism unite in stories of faith and love in the face of danger.

FREE Value Over $20

YES! Please send me 2 FREE Love Inspired Suspense novels and my 2 FREE mystery gifts (gifts are worth about $10 retail). After receiving them, if I don't wish to receive any more books, I can return the shipping statement marked "cancel." If I don't cancel, I will receive 6 brand-new novels every month and be billed just $5.24 each for the regular-print edition or $5.99 each for the larger-print edition in the U.S., or $5.74 each for the regular-print edition or $6.24 each for the larger-print edition in Canada. That's a savings of at least 13% off the cover price. It's quite a bargain! Shipping and handling is just 50¢ per book in the U.S. and $1.25 per book in Canada.* I understand that accepting the 2 free books and gifts places me under no obligation to buy anything. I can always return a shipment and cancel at any time. The free books and gifts are mine to keep no matter what I decide.

Choose one: ☐ **Love Inspired Suspense Regular-Print** (153/353 IDN GNWN)   ☐ **Love Inspired Suspense Larger-Print** (107/307 IDN GNWN)

Name (please print)

Address   Apt. #

City   State/Province   Zip/Postal Code

Email: Please check this box ☐ if you would like to receive newsletters and promotional emails from Harlequin Enterprises ULC and its affiliates. You can unsubscribe anytime.

Mail to the Harlequin Reader Service:
IN U.S.A.: P.O. Box 1341, Buffalo, NY 14240-8531
IN CANADA: P.O. Box 603, Fort Erie, Ontario L2A 5X3

Want to try 2 free books from another series! Call 1-800-873-8635 or visit www.ReaderService.com.

*Terms and prices subject to change without notice. Prices do not include sales taxes, which will be charged (if applicable) based on your state or country of residence. Canadian residents will be charged applicable taxes. Offer not valid in Quebec. This offer is limited to one order per household. Books received may not be as shown. Not valid for current subscribers to Love Inspired Suspense books. All orders subject to approval. Credit or debit balances in a customer's account(s) may be offset by any other outstanding balance owed by or to the customer. Please allow 4 to 6 weeks for delivery. Offer available while quantities last.

Your Privacy—Your information is being collected by Harlequin Enterprises ULC, operating as Harlequin Reader Service. For a complete summary of the information we collect, how we use this information and to whom it is disclosed, please visit our privacy notice located at corporate.harlequin.com/privacy-notice. From time to time we may also exchange your personal information with reputable third parties. If you wish to opt out of this sharing of your personal information, please visit readerservice.com/consumerschoice or call 1-800-873-8635. **Notice to California Residents**—Under California law, you have specific rights to control and access your data. For more information on these rights and how to exercise them, visit corporate.harlequin.com/california-privacy.

LIS21R